HIS EYES WERE ABLAZE WITH PASSION

Stryker drew her to him abruptly and pulled her head back. Lorinda gasped as his mouth fastened on hers in a caress that was full and heavy, far different from any she had ever known. Her lips took fire from his. She twisted her head to escape him and pushed against his chest with both hands. "Please . . . Please, don't, don't . . . I—" But then his firm lips were in possession of hers again, and her resistance collapsed.

He pulled her closer; her body molded itself to his while her hands moved to his arms and clutched at them convulsively. He tugged at the neckline of her dress until her breasts were bared completely. Then his mouth swept like a prairie fire down her throat and onto her breasts.

Suddenly, as his lips closed on a pointed nipple, her soul seemed in danger of being drawn right out of her body. "Oh, no! My God! Stop . . . please stop!"

**She moaned and swayed against him,
face buried in his shoulder,
her whole body aquiver ...**

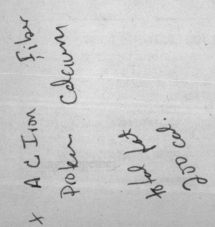

LOVE'S WICKED WAYS

DIANA SUMMERS

PLAYBOY PRESS
PAPERBACKS

LOVE'S WICKED WAYS

Published simultaneously in the United States and Canada by Playboy Press, Chicago, Illinois. Printed in the United States of America. Library of Congress Catalog Card Number: 78-61742. First edition.

This book is available at quantity discounts for promotional and industrial use. For further information, write our sales-promotion agency: Ventura Associates, 40 East 49 Street, New York, New York 10017.

ISBN: 0-872-16502-7

CHAPTER 1

Raven hair streaming out behind her, Lorinda de Farbin spurred her blooded stallion Firedrake as they sped between the brooding, moss-hung oaks on either side of the drive. She had been riding with her usual reckless abandon along the banks of Bayou Carlisle, which bordered Solitaire, her father's Claiborne County cotton plantation.

At the big house Lorinda reined in Firedrake at the bottom of the steps leading up to the columned gallery, leaped from the saddle and tossed the reins to a waiting groom.

"Jes' look at you, chile!" scolded a large, dark mountain of a woman in a spotless gingham gown. "You gonna be the death of old Chatti yet! We got guests here already and a houseful more comin' for dinner, and look at you, all sweaty and streaked with dirt!"

The girl mounted the steps to the veranda, her lithe, high-breasted figure stunning in its perfection under the soiled riding habit. She smiled at the old black woman and patted her cheek. "I'll be fresh as a daisy in ten minutes if Sissy has my bath ready," she promised. "I'll be clean and sweet and so charmin' we'll have to beat the boys off with a stick."

"Pretty soon you gonna have to stop fightin'

young gentlemen off and pick one for settlin' down and havin' babies.''

Lorinda arched an eyebrow at her old nurse. "Lawdy me, why? Papa hasn't settled down yet, what with all his mistresses and fancy girls in N'Orleans, so why should I?" Lorinda asked as she stepped through the door into the main hallway. She was halfway to the stairs when her father called to her from his study.

"Please come in for a moment, my dear," Jules de Farbin said in his cultured voice. "There's a . . . gentleman . . . here I'd like you to meet."

The slight hesitation isolating the word *gentleman* made Lorinda wonder if their visitor was perhaps not of their class. Pushing her windblown hair back from her forehead, she walked slowly to the doorway of the study.

Jules de Farbin was a tall, handsome man in his middle forties, with just a hint of gray in his black sideburns and Van Dyke beard. Tall as he was, the man standing beside him, planter's punch in hand, was even taller.

Lorinda's eyes flicked briefly over the stranger. He was good-looking in a rugged, outdoors way. His face was tanned almost to the color of fine leather, and his whipcord-lean body, clad now in fashionable clothing, looked like it might be more used to buckskin. His level gray eyes held the look of approval she was used to from young men, but there was a twist to his lips that seemed to indicate he was less impressed with her beauty than most men who beheld her for the first time. Perhaps he found her appearance, the dusty riding habit and hair in disarray, a trifle hoydenish. Well, if he stayed to dinner, he would be surprised at how ladylike and elegant a true daughter of the South could look.

"My dear, I'd like you to meet Kirk Stryker, Captain Kirk Stryker, late of the Second Texas Volunteer Rifles," de Farbin said. "Captain, my daughter Lorinda."

"A pleasure, ma'am," Stryker said, bowing. His voice had a definite Western twang to it. "A real pleasure."

"Thank you, sir," Lorinda murmured.

"Captain Stryker introduced himself to me at the Hotel St. Louis when I was in New Orleans last week," Jules told her. "It seems he knew your late cousin, Jerold Corbett, in Mexico."

A stab of pain at the mention of Jerry's name erased Lorinda's polite smile. She still could hardly believe he had fallen at Buena Vista in the recent war with Mexico.

"He was as brave a youth as any in General Taylor's army," Stryker said, his tone one of condolence but his eyes lingering on her breasts.

What an ungentlemanly thing to do, Lorinda thought. But obviously he wasn't a gentleman, in spite of the "Captain." What kind of an outfit was the Second Texas Rifle Volunteers? Certainly not an elite troop of men like the Claiborne Hussars, with whom dear, laughing Jerry had ridden off to die in the dust of Buena Vista.

She gave back Stryker stare for stare and could

have sworn his lips twisted again in that knowing half smile. She decided she didn't like Captain Stryker at all and hoped he wasn't staying to dinner. It was bad enough to have to endure the weasellike presence of the Wenzels—other cousins, not nearly as nice as Jerry—without having to put up with the sneering of this big lean man.

"I must go," she said, turning toward the door. "Our guests will be arriving shortly, and I have to dress."

In two long strides Stryker was at the door ahead of her, his arm brushing her shoulder as he reached to hold the polished oak portal wide.

"Your guests?" he said with a rumbling chuckle. "I am already here."

"Yes, you are, aren't you?" Lorinda said coolly to cover how strangely shaken the brief physical contact had left her. "I had forgotten that fact."

Stryker's grin showed a row of even white teeth. He pretended to shiver. "I think I just felt a chill wind from the South."

"Perhaps it will disperse in the hot air from the West," she said and walked past him with her chin up and her back very straight.

Jules de Farbin cleared his throat. "Ahem. Shall we continue with our business, Captain Stryker?"

Lorinda heard her father's voice clearly. She stopped at the bottom of the stairs to listen.

"I have a check ready for you drawn on my New Orleans banker. It is for five thousand seven hundred and fifty dollars. Is that correct?"

"Exactly correct, sir," Stryker replied, "although I must say I am embarrassed by the amount. After all, in a friendly game of——''

"Debts of honor are debts of honor," Jules interrupted, "even between—ahem—acquaintances."

Lorinda started up the stairs, whispering to herself. "So that's it! Stryker is a gambler! A common riverboat gambler! I'll bet he never knew poor Jerry at all! That was probably just a ploy to ingratiate himself with Papa. But good Lord, almost six thousand dollars! Papa of mine, won't you ever learn not to draw to a pair of tens?"

She took the rest of the stairs two at a time, with the clean tomboyish grace that was the despair of Chatti. Chatti had been trying to make her into a "real proper lady" ever since her mother had died when Lorinda was two.

"I'll never be a 'real proper lady,' " Lorinda thought as she reached her room, "but there's no reason I can't dress and look like one tonight. I'll make Kirk Stryker's eyes fall out and roll around on the drawing room floor—*where I can step on them!*"

Sissy, a round-faced, light-skinned slave girl Chatti was trying to turn into a proper lady's maid, was waiting with a steaming tub of water. She had already laid out clean underclothes and a dress suitable for the occasion.

Lorinda picked up the dress and tossed it aside. "Put that back in the closet. I'll wear the gold brocade with the low-cut neckline tonight."

Sissy blinked and stared. "What you want to show all that bosom for? That Mista Gideon nevah takes his snake eyes off you anyhow, and Rev'rend Mista Morgan will only turn red when he sees you."

"I'm not wearing it for Gideon Wenzel," Lorinda said, tossing her jacket and skirt to the black girl. "Nor for Isaac Morgan. I'm wearing it to please myself."

That wasn't quite true and she knew it, but she shrugged and skinned out of her chemise and pantaloons and walked toward the tub Sissy had prepared for her.

"I swar, Miss Lori, if you don't look more fit and pretty every time I sees you bare."

Lorinda laughed as she tested the water. "That comes from riding two hours a day and dancing away half the night."

"Well, you gonna be a mighty fine surprise for some gent'man when he sees you on your wedding night. Yes, ma'am, you sho is."

"Sissy, you shouldn't say such things," she said reprovingly, feeling herself blush. She realized she wasn't at all sure just what young ladies did on their wedding nights. Did they strip naked and let their husbands ogle them like slave girls up on the vendue table? Or did they just let their husbands discreetly lift their skirts and do all those things she had heard men did to their wives? This subject was frequently discussed against a background of girlish giggles at Miss Gardner's school for young ladies.

The temperature of the water was exactly right, as she had known it would be. Sissy always saw to it that her bath was kept hot no matter how late she was. There was nothing unusual about her doing it;

the people of Solitaire always saw that everything was just right for Jules de Farbin and his daughter.

She raised one slender, shapely leg and scrubbed vigorously at the trim ankle, wishing that it was just a bit slimmer and that the calf and thigh were not quite so firmly muscled but a trifle more femininely plump.

Of course, Dick Nevis, who swore he loved her more than life itself, always said she had the most beautiful ankles in the South. But he probably was just joshing. How could he know what her ankles, or any other girl's, looked like—lest he'd been looking when he hadn't ought to be, and she wouldn't put that past him, not for one minute!

Dick was only one of several young men from good families who had expressed more than casual interest in the hand of Jules de Farbin's raven-haired daughter. Her father, indulgent as always, had never urged her to give marriage serious thought, and she kept telling herself that eighteen was a mite early to think of settling down. There were always handsome young men with whom to dance, to ride and to share an occasional kiss. Her life seemed very good, and she could think of no reason to change it before she had to.

"That Cap'n Stryker is mighty handsome, ain't he, missy?" Sissy said, shaking fragrant bath salts into the steaming tub. "I expect he'll have an eye for you like all the rest of 'em."

"I expect he'd better not!" Lorinda said, " 'Cause I can't stand him even a little bit!"

Sissy giggled and rolled her eyes. "Jest the same, he'll be starin' pop-eyed at you in that new dress. The Rev'rend Morgan will be lookin', too. Bein' a man of the cloth don't mean he ain't got an eye for the pretties even iffen it do make him turn red when he sees 'em.''

''I don't know why papa has to invite Morgan and Harriet, that long-faced sister of his,'' Lorinda said, although she didn't really dislike the earnest young clergyman who had come down from New England to serve as the pastor of Vicksburg's small Episcopalian community. He at least was sincere in his opposition to slavery and didn't rant about it as some abolitionists did. He seemed to understand that there was some right on both sides, an understanding his sister Harriet certainly didn't share.

Lorinda was not looking forward to dinner. In addition to Stryker and the Morgans, there would be her mother's cousins, August and Charlotte Wenzel, their two sons, Jacob and Gideon, and their awful pudgy-faced daughter, Elsie. No, she would not enjoy this gathering at all. Still, she couldn't entirely repress the tingle of excitement she felt at the prospect of wearing the daring new dress.

That brought her back to the question of just who she was wearing it for. Not for Isaac Morgan, certainly. He'd probably be so shocked he'd deliver a sermon when he got her alone. And it surely wasn't for the Wenzel brothers. She shuddered slightly at the thought of their blond, fuzzy hair, pale blue eyes and tightly pursed lips. She found them repulsive and would have worn a nun's habit rather than stir whatever passed for passion in their frozen hearts.

''I said before I'm wearing it to please myself,''

she declared. "I'll do whatever I want to do."

"Yes'm, I reckon you will 'cause yo' pa nevah says you no," Sissy said. "Most easygoin' man I evah did see."

"Papa is a dear," Lorinda agreed as the girl helped her into a dressing gown and started to fuss with her hair. "I'm ever so lucky to have him."

CHAPTER 2

Lorinda's eyes were open, but her mind was closed as she tried to shut out the dreary political talk the men were engaged in over dinner. The subject was the same one the entire country had been discussing since the end of the war with Mexico—slavery and the South's rights to its peculiar institution. Lorinda had her own feelings on the subject but didn't think the endless repetition of arguments at every social function contributed much to the solution of the problem. And she hated the sound of Harriet's tight voice as much as she did the nasal twang of the Wenzels opposing her abolitionist views with their rabid proslavery sentiments.

"I would not put myself in the position of defending the institution of slavery in the abstract," Jules was saying, "nor do I say it is the only, or even the best, state of things in our country, but I do think it is highly important that we should look at this perhaps evil institution as it actually exists and consider its results as fairly as possible. That way I think we may discover what is possible—not what might be desirable in some utopian society."

Harriet Morgan cleared her throat loudly and began to reiterate her belief that kindly, concerned slave owners such as Jules de Farbin were the real culprits, because by treating their charges with de-

14

cency they lent moral support to the vile institution of slavery. "I'd rather see every slave groaning in chains than a few thousand contented ones being offered as examples of how the evils of the institution can supposedly be mitigated by kindness."

Urbane as ever, Jules sipped the sparkly white wine that was one of the specialties of Solitaire and smiled. "But my dear Miss Morgan, would you have me mistreat my people simply to give you a talking point?"

"I would have an end to slavery once and for all," the woman said harshly.

"Anarchy! Absolute anarchy would be the result," August Wenzel said. "What slave in the South is not better off in his condition than the ordinary working man of the North?"

"That is true," his eldest son, Jacob, said. "Since we've been in Mississippi, I've had many occasions to note the relative well-being of our slaves as compared to, say, the Irish immigrants of our Northern cities. All those I have seen are coarsely but comfortably clad and wear the cheerful, good-humored expression of countenance that seems to be the compensation granted by a paternal Providence for their loss of freedom. Why, measured by mere physical enjoyment and absence of care or worry about tomorrow, the slave is doubtless far happier than his master. His wants are few, he is easily satisfied, and his toil is not excessive."

Harriet Morgan made a most unladylike sound. Her brother looked at her, his handsome face showing his concern at the rancor that was beginning to surface in the argument.

"I think a lot of their placidity comes from their sheer lack of intelligence," Gideon, the younger Wenzel son, said. He was as blond and as square of face as his brother but had, Lorinda thought, an even meaner streak. "I've heard it said they are almost incapable of learning. One planter told me, 'Let a hundred men show him how to hoe or drive a wheelbarrow, he'll still take the one by the bottom and the other by the wheel.'"

The Wenzels all snickered at the tired old saw.

It was Kirk Stryker who spoke up in answer to the Wenzel argument. "May I ask what you would do given the same situation? It may be a trifle presumptuous for a person who has never been a slave to pretend to know how slaves feel, but it seems to me that they smile and bow and say, 'Yes, master, kind master,' because they understand their masters expect it of them. A soft answer turneth away blows, and an inability to distinguish one end of a hoe from the other turneth away work in which the slave has no stake. Sometimes I wonder if the slaves aren't duping their masters more than the masters dupe the slaves."

"Really, *Captain* Stryker." Lorinda let her slight emphasis cast doubt on the authenticity of the title. "Do you honestly think your profession qualifies you to judge the thoughts of these people among whom we live?"

Stryker grinned. "My profession, as you call it, certainly gives me an insight into what other folks are thinking. If I couldn't tell when a fella was holding a pair of deuces and betting like he had a full house, I'd be the poorest gambling man on the river."

"Perhaps, but you don't understand the relationship we de Farbins have with our people here at Solitaire. It is not that of master and slave, it is rather that of the head of a family and his children. It is their welfare we think of first and last. Why only this afternoon my maid Sissy said to me, 'Whatever would we all do without you and master? We is family, you and us.' "

Harriet Morgan snorted. "Are you in the habit, Miss de Farbin, of selling members of your family?" the minister's sister asked.

"No," Lorinda said with more sharpness than she intended, "and neither have we ever sold one of our people here at Solitaire. They all have a home for life and they know it."

Harriet Morgan was about to reply when Jules quickly suggested that it was time for the gentlemen to have their cigars and brandy while the ladies retired to the drawing room for coffee.

Playing hostess to Charlotte and Elsie Wenzel as well as the hostile spinster Harriet Morgan was an ordeal for Lorinda. She longed to be up on Firedrake's back, glorying in the excitement of a moonlight ride while his strong legs ate up the miles and the wind blew fresh on her face. Instead she had to sit primly and listen to the catty gossip of the Wenzel women interspersed with an occasional sour comment from the waspish Harriet. She breathed a sigh of relief when her father and the other men rejoined the ladies. After a few minutes she was able to slip out onto the gallery.

Leaning against one of the columns, she stood looking out across the broad lawn toward the slave quarters. The candlelit cabins were already slightly blurred by the mist that was starting to drift up from Bayou Carlisle. The peacefulness of the familiar scene slowly calmed and restored her good humor. Soon she heard a step behind her.

"Ahem. Excuse me, Miss Lorinda, I didn't mean to interrupt your—" Isaac Morgan hesitated, looking as bashful and unsure of himself as always but with an intensity in his dark eyes that made them glisten in the moonlight. "I just had to speak to you about—about a matter of some importance."

"But of course, Reverend Morgan," Lorinda said graciously. "You know how much father and I value your spiritual counsel and how pleased we are to have such a godly young man visit us, even though you are not of our faith."

The minister's big hands were twisting together as though he couldn't control them and his face reflected his inner turmoil. "It—it isn't a matter of faith I wish to talk to you about, Miss Lorinda. In fact, I'm afraid my thoughts of late have not been those of a totally godly man. They have been, so to speak, more of the flesh than the spirit."

"Why, Reverend Morgan, you do surprise me. Is it a young woman who is troubling you—a girl in Vicksburg perhaps?"

"No—no, there is no one in Vicksburg, but it is a girl. I can't get her out of my thoughts. I try to fix my thoughts on spiritual things, but all I can see is her face and her bod—her form before me. I don't seem to be able to think straight at all anymore. I have trouble sleeping and my appetite has quite evaporated."

Lorinda's eyes moved over Morgan's big, square

frame. Since he lived a quiet, contemplative life and exercised very little, she thought it might be just as well if his appetite did fail him for a while. She was sure she detected the beginnings of a slight bulge around his middle.

"I thought perhaps if—if this lady who is always on my mind at least knew of my—my delicate passion for her—although I do not expect her to reciprocate in any way—it might relieve me of some of the torment—of the burning I feel at the very thought of her."

"I think you should tell her," Lorinda said teasingly. "You really owe it to the young lady."

"I—no, I had better not." Isaac shuddered suddenly as though caught in a wintry blast. "I couldn't stand it if she knew and were repelled by my feelings."

He started to turn away, and Lorinda, moved to pity now and regretting her half-mocking air, reached out to place a hand on his arm. "Wait, Isaac. I think you should say what you came to say, and I'm sure no one would be repelled by your feelings."

"Oh, God, if only I dared believe that!" he said, staring down at her slender white hand as though it were a chain of steel that held him in place. "If only I could think that she might tolerate my feelings even though she couldn't return them."

Lorinda moved closer to the young minister. "Why don't you say what you came to say, Isaac, and find out?"

For a moment she thought the New Englander was going to faint. Then he sucked in a deep breath and words tumbled over one another in his haste to get them said. "Miss Lorinda—Lorinda, I love you. I want you. I can't seem to get you off my mind. When I saw you tonight in that somewhat brazen but altogether lovely dress, I could hardly stay in my chair. I wanted to—oh, God, no, I can't tell you what I wanted to do. It is too earthy for a man of the cloth to think such things and—"

"Really, Isaac? I've heard there is at least one man of the cloth, the Reverend Henry Ward Beecher, who not only thinks about such things but does them quite often."

Isaac Morgan looked deeply embarrassed. "Yes. Henry, despite his godliness in many areas and his strong stand on slavery, is a man of the flesh who has been much troubled in spirit and—"

"And in the courts," Lorinda put in.

"Yes. Ahem—his problems with the wives of some of his flock have indeed landed him in court. Very troubling to all who admire him."

"You, however, are not a married man like he is," Lorinda said flirtatiously, "and I am not the wife of one of your parishioners."

"No, of course not," he agreed hastily.

"So I think it would be perfectly all right if you were to kiss me." She smiled seductively. "If you want to, of course."

"Want to? Of course I want to, but I never dreamed you might be willing to—"

"Well, I am," she said, rising on tiptoes and closing her eyes.

With a convulsive movement, the young man

threw his arms around her and gathered her close in a fair imitation of a bear hug.

"Kiss me, Isaac; don't squeeze me to death," she gasped as air was forced from her lungs and her feet left the floor.

"Oh, I'm sorry, very sorry, Miss Lorinda. It's just that I've dreamed of this so often that—"

She reached up, put her arms around his neck and pulled his head down to hers as his grip loosened a little on her waist. The kiss was hard and enthusiastic, but the man's inexperience was obvious.

Isaac was trembling all over as he set her down. Lorinda stepped back, breathless and impressed by the minister's ardor but not exactly thrilled by the brief, smothering caress.

"I've been so obsessed by thoughts of you that I haven't been able to keep my mind on my work," Isaac confessed. "I've been remiss in some of my pastoral duties. Harriet has noticed it, but of course she doesn't know why I've been so upset. I haven't told her about my feelings for you."

"Why haven't you told her?" Lorinda asked. "That would seem like a natural thing to confide to your sister."

"No, not to Harriet. I'm afraid she wouldn't approve."

"Wouldn't approve?" Lorinda said with a note of irritation in her voice. "And may I ask why not? Is it my appearance she finds distasteful, or perhaps it's my morals she objects to?"

"Miss Lorinda, please," the minister said, making placating gestures with his hands. "It isn't personal. Actually, Harriet said just the other day that considering your background and your upbringing you were really quite decent.''

"Did she indeed? Quite decent? Well, she does have a knack for phrasing, doesn't she?''

"Miss Lorinda, please don't misunderstand what Harriet meant,'' the big man said, wringing his hands in distress.

Lorinda's laugh was brittle. "Oh, no, I understand very well what she meant, and I'd be ever so grateful if you thanked her for her appraisal of me. I'm flattered, thrilled, in fact, that a whey-faced New England spinster with more gall than good manners thinks I'm 'quite decent'!'' She whirled and stalked off down the gallery, leaving Morgan staring after her in perplexity.

He walked back to the drawing room, shaking his head disconsolately. As he entered, he found himself the recipient of one of his sister's penetrating stares. Obviously she knew he'd been up to something, and he'd hear about it all the way home. He turned away from her and walked over to join the men.

"Well, Reverend,'' Kirk Stryker greeted him as he accepted a cigar Jules de Farbin offered. "You look like a man who just saw a ghost. Do you have such unpleasant haunts at Solitaire, Mr. de Farbin?''

"None that I've ever seen,'' Jules said.

"Some of us carry our unpleasant haunts with us,'' Isaac said with a cryptic smile.

Stryker rolled the cigar between thumb and forefinger. "I believe I'll go outside to smoke this and enjoy the balmy Mississippi evening I've heard so much about.''

"I think you'll find it's turned somewhat chilly," Morgan said, moving wearily toward his sister.

Kirk Stryker stepped out onto the gallery that encircled the house. His alert gray eyes swept the length of the moonlit veranda and came to rest on a female figure. She was standing with hands on the railing and gazing off into the advancing river mist, which cast strange, swirling shadows in the intense October moonlight.

"Well, well," he murmured to himself, "the young preacher hurries in with a bewildered look on his face, and the beautiful mistress of Solitaire stands staring off into the mist. What do you suppose that means, Stryker?"

Lorinda heard his footsteps as soon as he stepped onto the uncarpeted gallery and turned to watch him approach.

"Well, Miss de Farbin, I was just told it was rather chilly out here, but you seem warm enough even in your light attire," he said, staring at the deep cleavage.

"Yes, the temperature can be quite changeable this time of year here so close to the river," Lorinda said, wishing he weren't always so direct. She wasn't at all sure she wanted to be alone with him

"Perhaps I could get you a wrap," he said, "although it would be a shame to—well, to obscure the beauty of the evening."

His gray eyes gleamed silver in the moonlight as he gazed at the honey-colored slopes of her partially bared breasts.

Suddenly Lorinda felt trapped as the tall, lean man moved closer to her. For a moment she thought of darting past him and racing for the drawing room, where she could surround herself with people and wouldn't feel so vulnerable under the arrogant stare.

"It's such a lovely evening," Stryker said, sliding the cigar into a pocket, "that I don't think I'll blot out the smell of jasmine with smoke, even from one of your father's fine cigars."

His words surprised her. She had been expecting something more in keeping with his intense preoccupation with her breasts. "Yes, it would be a shame to spoil the scent of the night-blooming vines," she said nervously, knowing that if he came any closer her knees would begin to knock. Why on earth did this man have such a disturbing effect on her? With most young men she was perfectly at ease and never at a loss as to how to handle them or turn aside their most audacious advances. But this big, quiet Westerner seemed to reduce her to a state bordering on panic.

"That preacher fellow came in looking as though he'd seen a haunt," he remarked, "but your father says there aren't any hereabouts."

"I think Isaac has his own private haunt," Lorinda said, thinking of Harriet. "And if she's not careful, *I'll* be haunting *her*."

Stryker chuckled. "I suspected you were a lady of spirit when I saw the way you ride."

He took another step toward her, and Lorinda debated whether she should flee or stand her ground. But what was she afraid of? What, actually, could he do to her? She didn't know, but she was gripping the rail behind her so hard her fingers ached.

"I was interested in the various views expressed on the subject of slavery at dinner," he said. "It isn't a subject that is of paramount interest in Texas, so I've been surprised at how much attention it attracts in the rest of the states."

"Yes, no one talks about anything else," Lorinda said. "For several years now we've argued and reargued the Missouri Compromise, nullification, the Wilmot proviso and squatter sovereignty. After a while it becomes very boring and will be, I should allow, the end of polite society in much of the country. Of course, we here in Mississippi are all of one mind. We devote our lives to these black people. What would happen to them if we should desert them? Where would they go? Who would take care of them?"

"Perhaps they might prefer to take care of themselves," he suggested lightly.

"I swear, Captain Stryker, I begin to suspect you of being a member of Mr. Garrison's Anti-Slavery Society. Are you perhaps a captain in the Underground Railroad rather than the Texas Volunteer Rifles?"

He laughed. "I plead innocent to both accusations. I'm a rather unpolitical person without firmly held convictions on slavery or any other subject, save the virtue of holding a good hand." While he spoke, he had reached out and taken Lorinda's hand in one of his hard but smooth-skinned ones. "Hmmmm. Yes, this is a good hand, too, although a little cold at the moment."

"Captain Stryker, I—"

He drew her to him abruptly, tilted her head back and moved his lips toward hers. "This is something I've been wanting to do ever since we met. It's something I figure I owe myself before moving on."

She gasped as his mouth fastened on hers in a caress far different from the ineffectual kiss of Isaac Morgan. Her own lips took fire from his in a way that frightened her.

She twisted her head to escape him and pushed against his chest with both hands. "Please—please, don't—I—"

But then his firm lips were in possession of hers again, and her resistance collapsed. He pulled her closer. Her body molded itself to his while her hands moved to his arms and clutched at them convulsively.

Lorinda didn't know how long the kiss lasted; the whole fabric of her universe seemed to be dissolving under its impact, the night turning to fire.

One of his hands began stroking her bare back. The other moved up her side, edging between their tightly pressed bodies and closing over a breast. She sucked in her breath at the contact, quivering under the exciting touch. No one had ever been so bold before, and the feel of those strong fingers curving around the resilient flesh was almost as devastating as the kiss itself.

She knew she should be indignant. After all, she barely knew the man. And he was a gambler hardly fit to sit across the table from her, much less treat her like a common street girl. She should tell him those things. She should push him away and order him to leave, but she seemed to have no strength and no voice.

His lips left hers, worked their way down the side of her throat, and still she couldn't move or speak. Her knees threatened to give way as she felt his fingers slip into the low-cut neckline of her dress and find the peaked nipple. Flashes of indescribable sensation radiated from the sensitive tip he was manipulating to further render her helpless.

Now his tongue was snaking into her mouth, a fiery serpent that teased and tormented, flickering over her teeth, touching the roof of her mouth, sliding over and around her own. Trapped by this expert stimulation of her senses, she was unable to keep from surging against him. When her belly was glued to his, she felt for the first time in her life the flaring hardness of a man's phallus.

Her head spun with the knowledge of his excitement. Having been raised around animals, she knew the basic facts of reproduction, but as a virgin she had no personal comprehension of how large and rigid a man's organ could become. Through the layers of cloth that separated them, she felt it rubbing against the soft mound of her womanhood, and she went weak with surrender. Lorinda knew that she would do anything he asked her to. If he should suggest that she go someplace with him where they could appease their wildly surging passion, she would go.

But now Kirk Stryker released her as suddenly as he had seized her. She almost staggered and had to cling to the railing to keep from falling. Speechless, she stared at him as he stood looking at her with a mocking half smile.

"My, my, you are a little wildcat, aren't you?" he said.

"You—you—how dare you!" she choked, but her voice held no conviction. She knew that if he reached for her again, she would surrender as completely as she had seconds before.

"I knew I was playing with fire, but I didn't realize how hot it could get," he said. His cool, emotionless tone enraged her even more than the fact that she was still shaking and unsure of herself.

"That must never happen again! If you ever dare put your hands on me that way again, I'll—"

He looked at her with raised eyebrows. "Are you telling me you didn't like it? Surely you're not going to try to deny that you were as excited as I was."

"Why you arrogant swine! I ought to tell my father and have you horsewhipped!"

"I wouldn't do that if I were you," Stryker said. "In the first place, if you did, I might not kiss you anymore, and in the second, your gallant father might feel compelled to challenge me. And I assure you I am a deadly shot, an excellent swordsman with saber or épée and no mean hand with a Bowie knife."

Lorinda doubled up her fists and stamped her

foot. "You—you filthy swine! If I were a man, I'd kill you myself!"

Stryker threw back his head and laughed. "I've known a woman or two who tried it, but I don't think you will."

"Damn you, I'll—" She flew at him, fingers curled into claws intended for his eyes.

He grabbed both her wrists in one hand, yanked her close and again captured her lips with his. Pushing her farther into the shadows so anyone who happened to move to the French doors couldn't see them, he tugged at the neckline of her dress until her breasts were completely bared. Then his mouth swept like a prairie fire down her throat and onto her breasts.

Suddenly, as his lips closed on a pointed nipple, her soul seemed in danger of being drawn right out of her body.

"Oh, no! My God! Stop—please stop!" She moaned and swayed against him, face buried in his shoulder, her whole body aquiver with an excitement even more intense than before. "Please, you mustn't! I've never been with a man. If you have any decency at all, you won't do this to me. You'll give me time to think, to catch my breath, to—"

He laughed huskily, and the sound told her he wasn't totally unaffected by the same passion that was raging in her.

"Give me your hand," he said, taking it in his. "I want you to feel something so you'll know what you've done to me."

His trousers were open and he thrust her trembling hand inside to touch the swollen hotness of his penis. Fascinated, she felt the length and thickness of it and found her fingers curling around it of their own accord, caressing it.

"Easy. Take it easy, little lady, or you'll have a handful of something you won't be able to explain," he whispered, removing her clinging fingers. "That's what you've done to me and it hurts. It hurts like hell because it wants to be buried in that warm little nest between your thighs. But since you say you're a virgin—and I tend to believe you, although a fellow would never know it from the way a few kisses set you on fire—I'm not going to carry you off into the bushes. I'm going to let you go. I'll give you until tomorrow to think it over. Then you're going for a carriage ride with me and we'll talk it over some more. Do you understand?"

"Y—yes," she said in a shaken voice as he released her. "I understand."

"Good. Then you be ready bright and early and we'll go for a ride at ten," he said. "Right now, you'd better fix your dress."

Lorinda didn't know how she got through the rest of the evening, but once in bed she lay awake for hours whispering hate for Kirk Stryker.

What had happened to her? She had always been flirtatious, but in a cool, controlled way so that no situation ever got out of hand. She had been kissed often, sometimes quite passionately, but had never experienced more than a mild excitement or feeling of warmth. Now she found herself tormented by visions of herself naked on a lush bed of pillows while Stryker, also nude, spread her limbs wide to receive his huge erection and then sank deep into her, deeper and deeper until she was pinned like a butterfly, forever his.

"Oh, God, I've got to escape him. I've got to! If I see him again, I'm lost!" she sobbed. "I've got to get away and never see him again!"

CHAPTER 3

The next morning, as she sat across the breakfast table from her father, she hoped he wouldn't notice the circles under her eyes. It had been almost dawn before she had fallen into an exhausted, troubled sleep. She also hoped he couldn't see the bruised condition of her lips, which she had tried to hide with just a hint of rouge.

She sighed without meaning to, and Jules looked up from buttering one of Chatti's light-as-a-feather biscuits.

"Aren't you feeling well, my dear?" he asked.

"I'm fine, papa," she said, "It's just that I didn't sleep too well."

"Oh? Any particular reason?"

"Well, first it was a loud mockingbird and—"

"Odd that I didn't hear it," Jules said. "I sleep very lightly, you know."

"And then there was the moonlight," she hurried on. "It was so bright and intense."

Jules stopped with the biscuit halfway to his mouth. "That's strange. I thought the mist had entirely obscured the moon by the time we retired."

"Oh. Well, maybe it wasn't the moon. I—I guess I'm just restless, papa. Do you suppose I could go to New Orleans for a couple of days?"

Jules took a bite of biscuit and a sip of coffee,

considering her over the rim of the cup. "I thought you were busy making plans to attend the Johnsons' ball."

"I am," she said quickly. "That's the reason I want to go to New Orleans, to get a new dress for it."

"A new dress? I was under the impression you'd already bought one, the one you wore last night. It's a little daring, but it certainly becomes you."

"Thank you, papa, but I don't want to wear it. I want a new one."

Her father sighed and looked at his watch. "Well, the *Cotton King* will probably pass the landing around nine-thirty, but that doesn't give you much time to get ready."

"I'll be ready," she said. "I'm already partly packed."

"What about the house in town? It's closed and—"

"The servants are there," she argued, "and I'll take Sissy with me. Only one bedroom and sitting room need be opened because I won't have time entertaining."

Jules glanced at his watch again. "Lawyer Kelandes is riding out from Vicksburg at nine. There's an important matter I have to discuss with him, so I won't be able to drive you to the landing."

"Old Simon can take me in the gig," Lorinda said. "If you'll just send one of the boys down now to hoist the signal for the boat to stop, I'll go get my things together."

* * *

Less than an hour later Lorinda came downstairs dressed in traveling cloak and bonnet, pulling on her gloves.

Chatti came puffing after her. "Lawdy, chile, I don' know why you has to go rushin' off to New Orleans all by yo'self."

"She ain't gonna be by herself," Sissy said crossly, " 'cause I gotta go 'long."

Chatti gave her a disapproving stare. "Well, I worries 'bout Miss Lori in that big, wicked ole city without Chatti to look out for her."

"I might be safer in New Orleans than I am here," Lorinda said without thinking.

"What you mean by that, chile?" Chatti's round brown face was filled with puzzlement and alarm.

"Nothing, nothing," Lorinda said, forcing a teasing smile. "I was just funnin'." She paused at the door of her father's study. "You go on out and wait in the carriage, Sissy, and Chatti, will you see to my things while I say good-bye to papa?"

"That ole lawyer in theah wit him," Chatti said. "Cain't stand thet man—'minds me of a snake."

Lorinda was not overly fond of Henry Kelandes, either, but she shushed Chatti and hurried her on her way. Turning the knob, she opened the door a crack and then paused as she heard her father's voice saying, "Now see here, Kelandes, I've been after you for months to draw up those papers. I want it settled *now* and with no more delays."

Kelandes answered in a low rumble, but she caught "these things take time," and "no hurry to do something that maybe shouldn't be done at all."

For one of the few times in her life, Lorinda heard anger in her father's voice. "I want that manumission completed before the end of the week," he said. "If you won't do it, I'll get another lawyer."

So papa was freeing one of the slaves. No wonder Kelandes was dragging his heels. He hated the very idea of free blacks. Lorinda wondered briefly which of their people it was and why she hadn't been told about it. But there wasn't time to go into it now.

Tapping lightly on the door, she pushed it wide and stepped into the room. Jules looked up in surprise; a strange look she couldn't interpret crossed his face. Kelandes nodded to her, his liverish lips turning upward in the barest excuse of a smile.

"All ready to go, my dear?" Jules said. "I didn't think you could possibly make it in time."

Lorinda laughed. "So I have put to rest once and for all the myth about women taking hours to dress. I just came in to say good-bye."

"I had better be on my way," Kelandes said, heaving himself to his feet and wiping at his bald head with a red bandanna.

"No, it is I who must be going," Lorinda said. "Stay and finish your business with papa."

"I am quite finished," the lawyer said, picking up his white straw hat and lumbering toward the door.

"You remember what I said, Kelandes," de Farbin said in a sharp voice. "I want those papers before the week is out."

"I remember what you said," Kelandes replied, but to Lorinda it didn't seem that he was really agreeing.

As soon as the man was gone, Lorinda put her arms around her father and kissed him.

He returned the embrace warmly. "So you are really going. I shall miss you."

"It's only for a few days, papa. I'll be back in plenty of time for the ball. I wouldn't miss that for anything."

"Nevertheless, I shall miss you. I wonder—I wonder if I have ever told you how much I love my little girl."

Lorinda giggled. "A pretty big girl now, papa. Big enough to take care of herself in wicked old New Orleans."

"I never have any doubt of you, my love," Jules said. "No matter how wicked the city, I know my daughter is good. Now, you'd better be on your way or you'll miss the *King*."

She kissed him again. "Good-bye, dear, dear papa."

An hour later Lorinda stood on the deck of the *Cotton King*, listening to the churning of its paddles as it nosed its way out into the Mississippi, located the central channel of the river and started south.

Just about now, back in Claiborne County, she knew, Kirk Stryker was hearing that his rude invitation to a morning's drive had been just as rudely declined. He'll be furious, absolutely furious, she thought as she made her way to the lady's section of the salon for coffee. "It serves him right for being so high-handed! It's time he learned that there's at least one woman in the world who won't pull up her skirts just because he says to. He'll be in a rage, and I'm glad!''

It was only later, when she remembered the feel of the man's arms around her and the fiery assault of his lips on hers, that her sense of triumph faded. Tonight or tomorrow night some other woman would probably be locked in his strong embrace, responding to his passionate kisses, and Lorinda was surprised to discover that she hated that unknown woman.

The first couple of days in New Orleans were spent in shopping for just the right material to make her dream dress, and the next two were devoted to fittings with Madame Mortain to make sure that the gown was molded to her figure.

"Mademoiselle de Farbin, you will be the scandal of Claiborne County but also its envy," Madame Mortain said as the final fitting came to an end.

"And you, madame, will be the richest dressmaker in New Orleans as soon as my poor father pays your bill."

The woman laughed, showing large white teeth. "Ah, but even he will have to say it is worth every penny when he sees all the handsome young men in Mississippi at his daughter's feet and the proposals start pouring in."

"I think we can do without those for a little while longer," Lorinda said, standing before a mirror to tidy her mussed hair and pin her hat in place.

"Most girls in your class are married before their eighteenth birthday," Madame Mortain said, "especially the beautiful ones."

"But I'm not most girls, madame. I am myself and I make my own rules."

"Ah, you headstrong ones! You either make some man deliriously happy or drive him mad."

Lorinda arranged to have the gown picked up the next day and left the shop. She found Sissy waiting for her on the banquette, shamelessly flirting with a mulatto footman who belonged to another of Madame Mortain's exclusive clientele.

The black girl hastened to join her mistress in the carriage. "Is the dress most done now, Miss Lori?"

"Yes, and the cost is scandalous," Lorinda told her. "I feel positively wicked."

"Maybe you shoulda boughten something down to Rampart Street," Sissy said. "Prices theah allus half what they is othah places."

"They should be! That stuff is smuggled in by what's left of Jean Lafitte's pirates at Barataria," Lorinda said as the horses clop-clopped over the cobblestone streets.

When they pulled up in front of the de Farbin town house, Peter, the butler and majordomo, was waiting on the veranda. He hurried down the steps with such a look of concern on his face that Lorinda was immediately alarmed.

"What is it, Peter?" she asked as he helped her from the carriage.

"One of the boys from Solitaire is here, miss. He rode all night and half the day to bring the news."

"What news?" she asked, fear gripping her heart.

"Boy say your papa fall from a horse and get hurt. He say Chatti say you should come quick."

"Oh, no! Is papa going to be all right?"

"Don't know, miss. Boy say they send for Dr. Townsend and the doctor work on him for hours. Masta must be right sick, I reckon, for Chatti to say you come quick."

"Sissy, start packing at once," Lorinda ordered. "Peter, send someone to the docks to find out when the next packet leaves for Vicksburg. If there isn't one leaving this afternoon, hire a coach. I've got to leave at once."

"Yes, miss. Right away, miss," Peter said and hurried off, forgetting his usual dignified strut.

"Oh, Lord, Sissy, why did I have to be away when this happened? Why was I such a coward?" Lorinda moaned as they rushed into the house.

"Now, don' you take on so, Miss Lori," the black girl said. "Youah papa will be awright. Ole Chatti de best nurse I ever seed. She brung Sam the carpenter back from death's door, she did, jest with goose grease and ludlum."

"Pack my small bag," Lorinda said when they reached the bedroom. "I won't take anything but that."

"How 'bout yo' new dress? You wants me to send a boy to fetch it from—"

"Damn the dress! I don't give a hang about it now!"

* * *

The trip upriver seemed endless. It was nearly noon the next day when it docked at Port Gibson on the tributary Bayou Carlisle.

It took Lorinda almost an hour to hire a rig to drive her to Solitaire, and the drive home over the rutted, sometimes muddy roads seemed as interminable as the trip upriver. Lorinda sat on the edge of the seat, praying silently and hoping that she had somehow built up a little credit in heaven.

Chatti was standing on the gallery of the house when the rig turned up the driveway. As soon as Lorinda saw her face, she knew the news was bad.

"Oh, Miss Lori, honey, Ah is so sorry, so sorry," Chatti said when Lorinda dismounted from the carriage. The big black woman put her arms around the girl and pulled her close. "You is too late. The neemonia jes' took him so fast. He couldn't wait, jes' couldn't wait, though he seemed to have somethin' he wanted to tell you."

"Oh, no, papa, papa, not papa." She had never known her mother and now the wonderful loving father who had cherished her and filled her life was gone, too.

"Where is he, Chatti?" she asked through the flood of grief that engulfed her. "I want to go to him."

" 'Course you do, chile. Dr. Townsend is still heah. He spent the whole night with your papa, but this mawnin' theah warn't nothin' moah he could do."

Townsend, a tall, spare man in his mid-forties, was just coming out of the washroom, his sleeves still rolled up and his coat off. He took off his spectacles and folded them as he came toward Lorinda.

"I'm sorry, Miss Lorinda. Sorry as I've ever been. Don't know who I had more respect for than Jules de Farbin, and I hated to see him go, but there just wasn't anything else I could do. One of his lungs was pierced by a broken rib, and as soon as the pneumonia set in, he started sinking fast. Did everything I could to save him, but it wasn't enough. I did my very best."

"I know you did, Doctor," she said through her tears. "Can I see him now?"

"Of course. You go right on in. Some of the neighbors will be coming by to help with things and we should notify those cousins of yours in Vicksburg. What's their name?"

"Wenzel, but there's no hurry about telling them. I'd rather not have them here now—just his old friends and neighbors."

"Sure, honey. You go on in and see your papa now. He sure did love you a lot. Talked about you all the time these last couple of days—seemed to be troubled about something but never would say what it was."

Lorinda turned and went into her father's room. She stood beside the bed for a moment, looking down. He was lying under a sheet, but his face had been left uncovered; so it appeared he was just taking a nap until one noticed the pallor of his skin and that there was no rising and falling of his chest.

"Papa, oh, papa, I loved you so," she cried and threw herself on her knees beside the bed, picking up his cold hand and kissing it. "If I hadn't gone off and left you, this might not have happened. Oh, papa, dear papa.''

She couldn't help blaming herself. If she had stayed at Solitaire instead of running off to New Orleans like a frightened schoolgirl just because a man put his hands on her. Damn him! Damn Kirk Stryker! Part of this was his fault. If he hadn't treated her like a whore, hadn't stirred such wild uncontrollable feelings in her . . .

But would it have made any difference? Jules de Farbin was a consummate but somewhat reckless horseman, and it was entirely possible that he would have been riding alone even if she had been at Solitaire and would have fallen, anyway. And what made her think her nursing would have been any better than Chatti's?

No, there was no use blaming what had happened on Kirk Stryker or on herself. If she had been fated to lose her father in her eighteenth year, it would have come about no matter what.

Slowly she got to her feet, filled with a numb despair, and went out into the hall just as the first carriage full of mourners pulled up outside.

The next few days were like a dream, a sad, sad dream from which she prayed every night to awake. But every morning she rose to face still another day without her father. Finally the owner of Solitaire was laid to rest in the family cemetery, overlooking Bayou Carlisle. His grave was next to that of his wife, the mother Lorinda had never known.

Most of those who attended the funeral were from nearby plantations, with a sprinkling of friends and business acquaintances from Port Gibson and Vicksburg. Her father had not been a particularly religious man, but he had clung to his father's Catholic faith. So Lorinda had asked old Father Turgot from Natchez to preside and had suggested that Isaac Morgan might like to say a few words.

When it was all over and the neighbors had left, Isaac approached her, the sincerity of his sympathy so obvious that she warmed to him.

"I just wanted to say Lorinda—dear Lorinda— that my heart goes out to you in your time of grief," he said, taking her hand in both of his. "My sister and I liked and respected your father in spite of the differences in our beliefs on the subject of slavery, and we know how bereft you must feel."

Lorinda leaned against the young minister's shoulder briefly but then straightened as she caught the eye of Harriet, who waited several feet away with a look on her face that could only be interpreted as antagonistic.

"I also want you to know," Isaac was saying, "that if there is anything we can do, any way we can assist you, you have only to call on us. My sister and I are your friends and want to help you in any way we can."

"Thank you, Isaac. I appreciate your concern and know that you mean what you say," Lorinda said, but she was thinking, *Your sister hates me and wouldn't lift a finger to help me.*

"And Lorinda," Isaac's voice dropped lower and took on a more intimate tone. "I—I want you to know that my feelings for you are much deeper than mere friendship. They—they are of a nature that this occasion precludes discussion of, but they are sincere and, I believe, of an enduring nature, so that when you have recovered from your immediate grief, I hope you will permit me to speak of this again.''

Harriet's slate-gray eyes were unblinking as she stared at Lorinda. The younger girl shivered inwardly, feeling a twinge of fear. Why did the woman hate her so? Was it because she was beautiful and Harriet was plain in spite of regular features and a slim figure? Her dark brown hair was wound into a prim knot at the back of her head; her breasts were tightly bound and her lips thin and colorless. In fact, she lacked any appeal that might have won her a husband.

Was that the reason for her inexplicable hatred? Harriet would probably never marry, and her brother was all she had. She obviously knew of Isaac's love for Lorinda and so considered her a threat. Dependent on her brother for financial and emotional support, she probably feared that Lorinda would marry him, leaving her alone and perhaps destitute. Lorinda wondered if there were some way she could assure Harriet that nothing was further from her intentions. Later, she decided, when her grief for her father had diminished somewhat. For the moment she could only smile faintly at Isaac and receive another shaft of hate from his sister's eyes.

Then the Morgans were gone, driving back toward Vicksburg in their buckboard, and Lorinda turned to find her chief overseer waiting to consult her.

Nelson was a tall, husky man in his early forties. After he had paid his respects, he asked, "Will you be wantin' any change in the work on the crops, Miss de Farbin?"

"No," she said. "I don't think so. Papa knew the way things should be done, so just go ahead the same as always. Please also keep in effect his orders against the use of the whip. Be sure to send someone to the New Orleans house to report to me from time to time."

"Yes, ma'am," the man said, putting on his hat and heading for his house in a grove of trees a short distance from the main house.

When the overseer was out of sight, Chatti came forward out of the shadows. "You gwine back to New Orleans? Why for you do that, chile?"

"I—I just can't stand it here without him, Chatti, not right away at least. There are too many memories. I see him everywhere."

"Ah know, honey, but a chile like you hadn't ought to be alone in that bad old city."

"I won't be alone, Chatti," Lorinda said, "because you'll be there with me just like you always have been."

"Sho nuff? Sho nuff I will, and Chatti look out foah her baby," the woman said, tears running down her round cheeks.

"I know you will," Lorinda said. Bursting into tears, she threw herself into Chatti's arms as she had done so often as a child. "Oh, Chatti, I'm going to miss him so much."

"Theah, theah, honey. You jes go ahead and cry it out, an' when you is feelin' bettah, Chatti and Sissy will pack youah things an' we all go down to de othah house till we gets ourselves back togethah again.''

"Oh, Chatti, I'm so lucky to have you. You're the only mother I've ever had.''

" 'Course I is. Loves you jes like you my own chile. Loves you moah I 'xpect.''

"We'll have to meet with lawyer Kelandes later, I suppose, and the will will have to be read. I'm sure the Wenzels will be here for that. Since poor Jerry died at Buena Vista, they're my only living relatives. I'm afraid we de Farbins are not a very numerous clan.''

"Don' fret 'bout that, honey. Pretty soon you be findin' de right man and gettin' married and havin' babies yo'self.''

"I don't know if I'll ever marry, Chatti. It's so terrible to love someone and then lose them. I don't know if I could face it with a husband and children I loved.''

"Lovin' someone and losin' 'em is a sight bettah, chile, than goin' all life through wit'out love.''

"Is it, Chatti? Is it really?'' Lorinda asked.

"You know it is, honey,'' the black woman said. " 'Sides, iffen you don' marry up and have lots of chillun, them old Wenzels is gonna get they hands on Solitaire like they been schemin' to evah since they come South. And what would happen to all us folks iffen they did?''

Lorinda raised her head and sighed heavily. "Yes, that's so. It would be a tragedy if they ever came into possession of Solitaire, wouldn't it?''

"Yes, ma'am! An' I spect yoah papa would turn ovah in his grave iffen they took ovah his plantation like they plan.''

"Well then, I guess it's my duty to get married and have children one of these days, isn't it?" Lorinda said with a weak smile.

"It sho is, honey, and jes as soon as we gits you settled in the city and feelin' bettah, ole Chatti is goin' to put her mind to it fust thing."

"*You're* going to put *your* mind to it?"

Chatti nodded her bandannaed head emphatically. "Yes'm. I is gonna look ovah all the 'vailable young gentlemen and pick one out wit de right kind of breedin', lotsa money to keep you right and lotsa love to warm your heart as well as your bed."

"Chatti, oh, Chatti, you are impossible!" Lorinda said, laughing through her tears.

CHAPTER 4

Several months later, on the day her father's last will and testament was to be probated, Lorinda rose early and stood for a few minutes looking out her bedroom window into the garden, where there were a few flowers still blooming under a wintry New Orleans sun.

Chatti tapped on the door and brought in a tray with a cup of hot chocolate and a brioche—Lorinda's early, or French, breakfast. In an hour or so she would have her regular breakfast with Clement Jennings, the young New Orleans attorney she had hired to represent her. She no longer trusted her father's lawyer, Henry Kelandes.

"You goin' have a tryin' day, honey, and you needs something warm inside to start you off; so drink it all," Chatti urged.

"Yes, I will," Lorinda said obediently, but her mind was elsewhere. She was troubled by the way the Wenzels and Henry Kelandes had been behaving since her father's death. Although she knew for a fact that Solitaire, the New Orleans house, fifty slaves and everything else had been left to her, the Wenzels had decided to contest Jules de Farbin's will, and friends in Claiborne County had written Lorinda that August Wenzel had been constantly closeted with Kelandes.

LOVE'S WICKED WAYS 49

Sissy came in while her mistress was still sipping hot chocolate and started fussing over the outfit Lorinda intended to wear to the hearing.

"Them Wenzels ain't gonna git hold of us, is they, Miss Lori?" Sissy asked anxiously.

"Of course not, Sissy," Lorinda said. "Whatever gave you an idea like that?"

"Well, when you let me go up home to see my man, theah was a lot of talk. Them Wenzel boys been braggin' 'round how they goin' own Solitaire and make big lot of changes."

Lorinda removed her negligee and nightdress and stepped into her pantalettes. "Sissy, that's just gossip and rumors you heard, so just rest your mind easy."

Sissy helped her into chemise and corset, shaking her head and looking worried. "Some folks don't think it's jes gossip or rumors. Them Wenzels is gettin' credit on what they call they 'future expectations,' Miss Lori."

Frowning, Lorinda let the girl shake her two underpetticoats into place, one of which was flannel. "I don't understand that. I know the Wenzels are sharp at business, but why would any honest merchant extend them credit based on a ridiculous claim to my property?"

"Don' know, Miss Lori," Sissy said, adjusting the principal stiff petticoat and following it by still another of embroidered muslin. "But them yaller-haired boys been sayin' it gonna be different foah us when they takes ovah."

"That's ridiculous," Lorinda said as the black skirt and white ruffled bodice were dropped over her head and buttoned up the back.

Sissy shrugged and held a little zouave jacket that matched the skirt for her to slip into. "Ise jes sayin' what they say. We'uns has it too soft and easy and is spoiled, they say, and needs the whip to make us work right."

"Sissy, you mustn't allow talk like that to trouble you," Lorinda said. "Solitaire is mine and things are going to be done just like they were when papa was alive. No one is going to be treated any differently. Do you understand?"

"Yes'm, I unnerstan, but I hopes that young whippersnapper lawyer you got is as smart as ole Kelandes. That one is de slickest lawyer in the state, and he up to somethin' wit them Wenzels."

"Slick or not, he can't go against the law," Lorinda said, dabbing a touch of perfume behind her ears before donning a black velvet bonnet, the wide brim lined with white satin and lace. "You just remember that, Sissy. We got the law on our side and August Wenzel and Henry Kelandes will find that out from the judge today."

A trifle annoyed by Sissy's seeming lack of faith, Lorinda went down to the morning room, where Clement Jennings awaited her, a sheaf of papers in his hand and a smile on his face.

"Ah, there you are, Miss de Farbin," he greeted her. "How lovely you look. I've never seen mourning clothes so becoming. Are you all ready to claim your not inconsiderable inheritance?"

"I would rather have my father alive and enjoying it with me," she said gravely. "Mr. Jennings, is there any possibility that any claim against the estate by distant relatives would be valid?"

The young man took off his rimless spectacles and peered at her nearsightedly. "None at all. I've never seen a more simply drawn nor more ironclad will. There is nothing that can go wrong, ma'am, believe me."

But a few hours later everything had gone wrong. Lawyers were shouting legal jargon at each other which she could not understand. The judge was sounding his gavel, and Lorinda was sitting at the front of the courtroom staring in shock and disbelief as her whole world crumbled around her.

"And I have here," Henry Kelandes was saying, "indisputable proof in the form of birth records from the county seat of Claiborne County that the person known as Lorinda Elizabeth de Farbin was born to a woman named Felice Provost, the mistress of Jules Nicolas de Farbin. Also here in my hand is proof that Felice Provost, a woman of color, was the slave of Mr. Riley Rinehard of Warren County, Mississippi, and was sold at the vendue in Jackson on March 10, 1826, to the aforementioned Jules Nicolas de Farbin, who installed her on his plantation Solitaire as his mistress. Here is the bill of sale, Your Honor, and—"

Jennings had leaped to his feet and was protesting, "What is the meaning of all this? What bearing has this on the probate hearing? These things happened a great many years ago and can have nothing to do with the simple probating of a will."

"On the contrary, Your Honor," Kelandes's heavy voice intoned triumphantly. "These records have everything to do with the probating of this will since they prove that the person named as sole heir cannot inherit under Louisiana, Mississippi or United States law.''

"I object to this whole proceeding," Jennings said.

"Your objection is overruled," the judge said. "Mr. Kelandes, why do you claim the person named in the will cannot inherit?"

A smile of outright pleasure crossed Kelandes's bejowled face, and a short, barking laugh came from August Wenzel.

"The person sometimes called Lorinda de Farbin cannot inherit under the law because she was the slave of Jules de Farbin and one-sixteenth black,'' Kelandes said and paused dramatically to pick up another paper from the table in front of him. "In proof of that I have here manumission papers drawn up by me on the orders of Jules de Farbin a few days before his death. These papers were meant to free his illegitimate daughter by his octoroon mistress Felice Provost.

"Unfortunately, from the viewpoint of Jules de Farbin and this—'' He made a gesture of contemptuous disdain in Lorinda's direction. "—this wench, but fortunately from the point of view of society, de Farbin died before he could carry out his plan, before he could sign these papers, which never should have been drawn up in the first place.''

Lorinda was on her feet, shouting, "That was your doing! I heard you that morning and you were trying to talk him out of drawing up the papers! You'd been doing that for months and he was angry with you and threatened to get another lawyer! You were hoping something would happen to him so you could rob me!''

Kelandes sneered. "Your Honor, would you be good enough to instruct this slave to keep silent?''

"Be quiet, girl,'' the judge said, not unkindly. "I hope, Mr. Kelandes, that you have indisputable proof of all you've been saying because this is a most unusual and serious affair.''

"Yes, Your Honor, I have proof that Jules de Farbin and Felice Provost were not married. I have proof that she was sold to de Farbin as a slave. I have proof that she, and not de Farbin's wife, gave birth to the child who posed as Lorinda de Farbin.'' His yellowish teeth showed in a savage grin. "I even have proof, although it does not affect this case, that Felice Provost was a practitioner of voodoo and that she had borne a child called Ajona earlier to a troublemaking black from Haiti. After de Farbin pensioned her off by giving her a house in New Orleans—the deed to which remained in his name—she took as a lover one Caliano Valera. Two years ago the Provost wench was convicted of stabbing Valera to death and in this very parish was subsequently hanged by the neck until she was dead.''

Lorinda stared at the man in shock. This was like some horrible dream, the kind of dream she had heard opium eaters in the Far East had. It couldn't be true; she knew it couldn't. She knew who her mother was, had seen her grave, had placed flowers on it and prayed beside it. She had seen her father buried next to her mother. Why was Kelandes saying some woman named Felice Provost—a *black* woman—was her mother? This had to be some insane plot dreamed up by Kelandes and the Wenzels. In just a moment her lawyers or the judge would see through it and everything would be all right.

"This is why, Your Honor, I said it was fortunate that the manumission papers were never signed," Kelandes was saying. "If they had been, there might have been lengthy litigation aimed at depriving August Wenzel and his family of their proper inheritance from their cousin. However, since it is positive that Lorinda de Farbin is neither a white woman nor a free woman of color but a slave belonging to August Wenzel, such litigation can be avoided. Instead you will be requested to approve probate in the name of August Wenzel. In addition I request that for the welfare of society you issue an order requiring that the slave wench heretofore known under false pretenses as Lorinda de Farbin be handed over into the custody of her rightful owner, August Wenzel."

Slave! Slave! Slave! Lorinda de Farbin the slave of August Wenzel! The words echoed through Lorinda's mind like an insane chant. It was all so wrong, so terribly wrong!

"Mr. Jennings, you've got to do something!" she said, putting a hand on his arm. "None of this can be true! You've got to prove it's all lies!"

"Really, miss." Jennings paused on the word *miss*, drew his arm out of her grasp and gave her a look of slight distaste. "I'll—I'll look at the documents presented by Mr. Kelandes, but frankly I was not prepared for any such thing as a slave posing as a free person and—"

"Posing? I was not posing! I was raised as Lorinda de Farbin! I *am* Lorinda de Farbin!"

"I'll look at the documents," Jennings repeated primly, "but unless there is rank forgery, which I don't expect from a man of Mr. Kelandes's standing and reputation, there is nothing I can do."

He thinks I'm a slave! He drew away from my touch as though I had defiled him!

Lorinda wanted to scream, to tell everyone that she was being cheated, that none of this was true, but she could only sit and watch with her heart beating fast while the judge, Kelandes and Jennings mulled over the documents that would determine her fate.

"Yes, yes, I see what you mean," the judge was saying. "Let me see that other one. Hmmmm. What is the date on this? Yes, that is the seal of the state of Mississippi, and here is the notary's signature. Hmmmm."

"I think you will find everything in order and just as I have said it is, Your Honor. And you, Mr. Jennings, will see that your—ahem—client has no standing in this court. I'm afraid you'll even be out your fee since she is only a penniless slave."

"Perhaps I will be amply paid by the lesson you have taught me in choosing my clients in the future, Mr. Kelandes." Jennings was all smiles at the heavy-handed jest.

The judge was clucking to himself as he read the documents one after the other, nodding his head sagely at the conclusion of each.

"Yes, Mr. Kelandes, these all seem to be perfectly in order, and I see no reason why I can't hand down an immediate order granting the property to your clients." He looked up and directed a stern gaze at Lorinda. "They may have immediate access to all of their property, including the slave who formerly posed as Lorinda de Farbin."

"No, no! Please, Your Honor, there is something wrong, something terribly wrong," Lorinda protested, moving toward the bench. "This is all a mistake!"

"Place that wench under restraint, bailiff," the judge ordered, "and see that she is delivered into the keeping of her rightful master."

Instantly a man's hand gripped her wrists and she was dragged out of the courtroom into a corridor. A pair of manacles was produced and she felt them being fastened around her wrists.

"You behave yerself, gal, till yer masta picks you up, or we'll put leg chains on you, too," the bailiff growled.

The last thing she saw through the swinging doors into the courtroom was Kelandes, August, Jacob and Gideon Wenzel shaking hands with her attorney.

Lorinda began to sob, quietly and helplessly. They were a gang of conniving thieves who were stealing her home, her money and her people. Her people—oh, poor Sissy! And Chatti—oh, God, Chatti! She cried harder for her father's slaves than she did for herself, still unable to think of herself as black and the property of the hated Wenzels.

A few minutes later August and his two yellow-haired, freckled-faced sons came into the anteroom, where Lorinda stood manacled and weeping.

"Yer property is ready to be delivered ovah, Mistah Wenzel," the bailiff said, "soon as you sign this heah receipt for one slave wench."

"Be glad to," August said, his usual scowl replaced by a jovial smile.

He scrawled his signature on the form and handed it back with a flourish. "Here you are, my good man, my receipt for one light-colored Negro gal in good condition—untouched and intact, I trust."

Twenty-three-year-old Jacob and his nineteen-year-old brother nudged each other and snickered at their father's reference to the possible condition of Lorinda's maidenhead.

"Won't take long to remedy that, will it, Jacob?" Gideon said. "She's too likely a looking wench for that state to last."

August's expression became more severe. "Once we get up to the plantation I don't care what you boys do, but until then you keep your peckers in your pants. I don't want no scandal in New Orleans. We got too much business at stake here."

"Sure, pa, sure," Jacob said. "We won't do nuthin' here in town. We'll wait until we get the uppity bitch off by ourselves, but that's prime meat and I mean to have my share of it."

The bailiff withdrew, looking slightly disgusted. August returned to his jovial mood while he surveyed Lorinda with his cold, glittering eyes. "If you boys ever repeat this to your mother or your sister, I'll break your necks; but I might have a try at that fluff myself."

Lorinda felt as though she were going to vomit.

The prospect of being raped by Jacob or Gideon was horrifying enough, but to have the old man with his bad teeth and revolting appearance leering at her lustfully was too much. She wouldn't let it happen. She would rather die than be used by such swine.

"Did you get your gear on board the *Mississippi Belle* like I told you to?" August asked as the three of them hustled Lorinda out into the street.

"Yeah, pa, but what's the big rush?"

"I want this female out of New Orleans as quick as possible," his father said. "I want her up at Solitaire before any of de Farbin's fancy friends can start asking questions. There ain't nuthin' wrong with our claim, but influential people can still cause trouble. That's why I made arrangements for you to take her upriver while Jacob and I go to the town house, take it over and get the other slaves. The sooner we get her to Solitaire and break her in as a breeding slave, the better it'll be for all of us."

Gideon's eyes lit up. "So you're gonna do it, pa. You decided to breed slaves for selling."

"Course I am," August said. "There's a law against importing slaves, but none that says you can't breed 'em like cattle. These uppity plantations owners thinks they're too good to do it, but we ain't. We're going to be rich, boys, real rich, and you can have all the fun you want bustin' the wenches."

Lorinda wished she could drop dead right on the spot. Being a slave was a terrible fate, but being one in the hands of vicious creatures like these was beyond bearing.

"You take the hack, Gideon," his father ordered. "It's closed, so no one'll see what you got in back."

"Yeah, pa, me and my little girl here will be nice and private," Gideon said, jerking Lorinda away from his brother and pushing her toward the waiting rig.

"You be careful, boy," August warned. "If anything goes wrong, I'll break your head."

"And I'll break worse than that for you if I get to Solitaire and find the wench ain't still cherry," Jacob said.

As soon as the hackman pulled away from the curb, Gideon reached for the manacled Lorinda and hauled her over close to him.

"Please, Gideon, don't—"

"Mister Gideon, you bitch!" His open palm stung her cheek. "You treated me like dirt when you thought you were my cousin, but from now on you show respect, or you're gonna get your pretty hide cut up."

"Oh no, no," she sobbed as the thin line of his lips closed over hers and he forced her head against the back of the seat.

"Now we're gonna have some fun, now and for two whole nights on the river. Course I won't be able to bust you 'cause I promised pa and Jacob, but there's other things I learnt from them whores in Natchez that we can do to make things lively."

His wet, sloppy kisses were all over her mouth and face, his hands all over her body, and there was nothing she could do to prevent it. His fingers sank into the tender mound of her breast, the other hand roughly feeling her thigh.

Lorinda tried to keep from retching. The taste of his saliva in her mouth was sickening. She wished she could faint so that anything he did would be blocked out of her consciousness. Unfortunately she wasn't the fainting type, so she could only try to avoid as much contact as possible under the circumstances. Any woman with her hands manacled was helpless; a slave was doubly so because she couldn't even scream and expect help.

"Onct you come down off your high horse, you'll like what's gonna happen to you from now on," Gideon whispered. "You been so busy bein' uppity you wasn't having any fun. Now you won't have time to be uppity, but you'll have lots and lots of fun with me and Jacob and maybe pa, and of course with the breeding studs pa is gonna buy down Biloxi way. You are gonna be the most pestered gal in this here country. You'll be busted and rebusted, you'll get knocked up and have a bunch of little bastards to take care of when you ain't wiggling your ass off in bed."

The life he was describing was like a vision of hell to Lorinda. And she knew that if she didn't waken from this nightmare, from the horror that had turned her world topsy-turvy in the last few hours, she would kill herself. Even manacled she would somehow find a way.

Gideon rucked her skirt and petticoats up, bunching them in her lap so her slender, perfectly curved thighs and calves were exposed in their pure silk stockings and flower-embroidered pantalettes. He fumbled under her jacket and squeezed her breasts with deliberate cruelty, his eyes still on her legs.

"Please don't. You're hurting me," she whimpered, but he paid no attention.

"Let's see if we can't get those damn drawers off so we can fool around a little," he said and reached for the waistband of the pantalettes.

"No! No, you have no right!" she gasped and tried to scramble across the seat toward the far side.

"No right? What do you mean I got no right? Your body and soul belong to me and I can use you any way I please."

Lorinda shut her eyes against the vileness. The closeness in the cab and the rank odor of the youth's lust were making her dizzy. She prayed again that she would faint. Shame and humiliation flooded through her and she sat rigid with clenched teeth while his fingers slithered up the inside of her thighs till at last she passed out in horror and disgust.

CHAPTER 5

The trip to the wharf where the *Mississippi Belle* was loading cargo and passengers for the trip up-river finally ended. It was a shaken, despairing Lorinda who was hurried on board, wondering how much worse the next two nights could be.

Gideon Wenzel's cabin off the main salon had two bunks, but he laughed as he shoved Lorinda inside and shut the door. "We won't be needing but one bunk, will we, honeypot? You and me can do fine with just a single bed to snuggle on."

Lorinda cringed away from him. The mauling she had endured in the hack would be as nothing compared to what was possible in the intimacy of a private cabin. Her only protection, and a small one it was, was his father's and brother's admonitions and threats as to what would happen to him if she didn't arrive at Solitaire with her virginity intact.

But virginity, she thought bitterly, was a relative thing. Even though she was still technically chaste, she had been subjected to indignities that shamed her.

"Just to show you I'm not as bad as you think I am," Gideon said as though reading her mind, "I'm going to unlock you as soon as the boat gets under way. Then I'll go get a couple of drinks and something to eat. Maybe later I'll let you out to get some vittles. Slaves ain't usually allowed, but you ain't an ordinary kind of slave and no one would know.''

Suddenly a small frame of hope sprang to life inside Lorinda. Given the freedom of the ship, she might have a chance to leap overboard and drown herself before this buck-toothed lout could abuse her further.

Yes, she was ready to face death. There was nothing left in her life but horror. If one could not live with honor, one was better off not living at all.

True to his word, as soon as the *Belle* was out into midstream, Gideon removed the manacles and tossed them onto the second bunk. ''There. Now just sit yourself down and wait, wench. Try not to get too lonesome for me. I'll be back before you know it.''

I hope you never come back! I hope you get drunk and fall overboard! she prayed silently as she heard him lock the door from the outside and go off whistling happily.

But a short respite was better than none. At least it gave her time to sit quietly and think. She had to plan her moves carefully and do nothing to make Gideon suspicious when he let her go out into the salon to eat. That would be her one and only chance to escape from his clutches. She would go with him meekly, manage to drop behind a pace or two, and when they passed the door to the outer deck she would bolt through it, scramble up on the rail and throw herself into the river. The swiftly moving current would carry her away before anyone could possibly launch a boat or otherwise try to save her.

Yes, that was what she must do. Gideon Wenzel would never again shame her with his vile lust, nor would his brother and father use her as they planned.

The cabin was warm, and Lorinda began to grow drowsy. Despite the fact that if her scheme were successful this would be the last day of her life, she drifted off into a troubled, dreaming state.

She was back at Solitaire, dressing for the ball at the Johnsons. Her father was still alive and looking very handsome in elegant evening clothes with ruffled shirt and dramatically draped cape as he waited for her at the foot of the stairs. But there was also another man waiting there, a tall, hawk-faced man with an arrogant twist to his lips and eyes that seemed to burn into her very soul—Kirk Stryker. She had almost forgotten him in her grief over her father's death and the sea of troubles into which she had been plunged. The way she had fled from him seemed ridiculous now. Being seduced by one man seemed a minor problem compared to the future the Wenzels had planned for her.

It had grown dark in the cabin by the time she awoke, the portholes seeming only slightly lighter against the deeper blackness of the small compartment. She could hear piano music and an occasional burst of laughter beyond the locked door and knew it must be late. She stretched and was about to get up when she heard the key turning in the lock.

Gideon came stumbling in, swore as he fumbled to light the lantern and then leaned over her. He was half drunk and disheveled looking, and she realized it must be later than she had imagined.

"Come on, wench, up on your feet! I got use for you."

"What do you mean?" Lorinda asked, pretending to be still half asleep. "What use?"

"Don't ask questions, bitch!" he snarled, grabbing her arm and yanking her to her feet. He groped around on the other bunk until he located the manacles and fastened her wrists again.

Sick with disappointment, she let him hustle her out of the cabin, knowing that her chances of making a break for it now were very slim. They were even slimmer than she thought because instead of taking her on deck or into the salon Gideon hurried her along toward the door of another cabin.

He was muttering to himself in his whiskey-slurred voice, "Gotta git that money back. Pa'll skin me alive. Damn cards can't keep goin' against me forever. Gotta get cotton money back."

"What is it?" Lorinda asked. "Where are we going?"

"Gambler's cabin. Game goin' on," Gideon mumbled and shoved open a door into a large smoke-filled room. Three men were sitting at a table drinking and playing cards. A large open window overlooked the river, and a waiter in red livery tended bar.

"You can deal me in again," Gideon said. "I got something here to use for a stake just like I said I would. This wench is worth at least fifteen thousand dollars."

Numb with shock, Lorinda felt herself being pushed into the circle of light created by a lamp suspended directly over the table.

A beefy man in shirt sleeves and a checkered vest surveyed her with hard black eyes. "Well, she's a handsome enough wench."

"Yeah, looks good," said a thin, balding, tight-lipped man whose cravat was undone and collar open, "but how do we know what she looks like under all them clothes?"

" 'Cause I tell you," Gideon said. "She's something special, and she ain't been busted yet."

Appalled at hearing herself discussed as though she were a prime head of beef or at most a blooded horse, Lorinda could only stand there and listen while she cringed inside.

"Shucks, boy, you're bound to tell us how great your stake is," the beefy man said, "but I'm not the sort of jasper who takes things on faith. That just ain't Lou Lang's way."

"It's not Kirk Stryker's, either." The third man at the table had been turned away taking some bills from a money belt, but now he swung into the light and placed cash in front of him. "I say before we allow you fifteen thousand for table stakes, we should see her papers and have a look at what we're playing for."

With a feeling of utter unreality, Lorinda stared into the cool gray eyes of the man whose kisses had so excited and terrified her that she fled to New Orleans.

"Yeah, let's have a look at them papers," the balding man said. "I want to make sure if I win her I really get her."

"You've hit the target straight on, Mr. Partridge," Lou Lang said. "We want to be sure who owns this little piece of fluff and who doesn't.''

"Here they are," Gideon said eagerly and handed them over. "All signed and sealed legal-like by the judge and the parish clerk."

"You say this Negro was posin' as a white lady?" Partridge asked, looking through the papers.

"I can testify to that, gentlemen," Kirk Stryker said. "I met her on her father's plantation a few months back, and she fooled me completely. I thought she was as white as I am."

I am as white as you are, Lorinda wanted to shout. *Look at me!*

"It's shameful what some of these Negroes get away with," Lou Lang was saying. "If I win this one, she'll get a taste of the whip every time she don't toe the mark."

"I got something here she'll get more than a taste of," Partridge said, touching the front of his trousers. "These octoroon gals are real animals in bed."

"I suspect, gentlemen, that this one isn't an octoroon, but a genuine mustee, at least ninety-nine percent white," Stryker said. "It's a shame she has to be polluted by that other one percent."

He certainly was talking differently than he did that night at Solitaire, Lorinda thought. She supposed his moderate views then were just intended to impress people. He was no better than the rest of these swine.

"Well, these papers seem to be in order, gentlemen," Lang said after a few minutes. "Shall we take a look at the merchandise before we put up five thousand dollars apiece as we agreed?"

"You bet," Partridge said, looking at Lorinda

and licking his lips. "I want to see what this looks like without the wrappings. Come on, boy, tell her to shuck down so's we can see what we're gettin'."

Lorinda stood frozen to the spot. The idea of stripping before four men, two of them complete strangers, was horrifying. Her eyes darted from one of her tormentors to another, searching for some understanding or pity; but she saw only anticipation and lust on three faces and cool indifference on Stryker's.

"Shuck down, wench," Gideon ordered, "and do it fast!"

"I—I can't," Lorinda moaned.

"She'll do it fast enough if we send for a whip," Lang said, his voice thick with excitement. "I like to see these high and mighty ones cut a little, anyway."

"Please—please, Mr. Partridge, Mr. Lang. I've never done anything like this before. I'd die of shame to strip naked in front of a group of men."

"Quit stallin' and get those clothes off!" Lang said.

"Do it!" Gideon growled, drawing back his fist, and for a second Lorinda thought she saw a flicker of something more than cold unconcern in Stryker's eyes.

"I can't," she said as desperation gave her a wild idea. The cabin door hadn't been locked behind her. If she could just get out and get to the rail.

She lifted her manacled hands. "I can't because of these."

"Oh, is that all," Gideon grinned drunkenly and fished the key out of his waistcoat pocket. "Didn't think you was all that backward. Sure didn't seem that way when I was pesterin' you in the hack.''

Kirk Stryker's eyebrow lifted slightly, and, re-membering how she had responded to his caresses, Lorinda wondered if he was thinking she was easy prey for any man. Then she shook off the specula-tion. What difference did it make what Stryker thought of her? With any luck she'd be dead in a few minutes and the only effect it would have on any of these men was that Gideon would be out fifteen thousand dollars and the others would lose their chance for some pleasure at the expense of a helpless girl.

''There,'' Gideon said, removing the manacles and stepping back unsteadily. ''Now get on with it! Show 'em what you're worth.''

''In just a second,'' she said, rubbing her wrists and taking a step backward as though to position herself better under the light.

Stryker was on the opposite side of the table from her, watching closely. As she lowered her hands and shifted her weight to take another step, he swore and yelled, ''Look out, boys, she's going to make a break for it!''

She darted to the door, threw it open and ran for the stairs leading up to the main salon, which opened onto the upper deck of the ship. She reached the passageway, made it to the stairs and leaped up them two at a time, holding her skirts high with both hands.

The sight of a beautiful young girl, hair in disar-ray and skirts held high, startled the passengers in the salon. Women looked up from coffee cups and men stared, mouths agape. One or two leaped to their feet and at least one chair crashed over backward as Lorinda sped through the room and out onto the deck.

"Stop her! Stop her!" someone shouted. "She's going to jump overboard!"

She was at the rail then, hearing heavy footsteps behind her but knowing no one could reach her fast enough. She put a foot on the lower rail, conscious of the rush of water beneath her and of the great paddle wheel churning up white fountains at the stern of the ship.

Maybe it would be even quicker than she thought. Maybe the paddle wheel would hit her and crack her skull. That would be quick—quick and final.

She breathed a quick prayer and flung herself from the rail, hearing behind her the sound of men cursing and women screaming.

She hit the water feet first, and her dress and petticoats billowed out around her. As she started to sink, instead of being plunged into the churning water around the paddle wheel, she was pushed away from the ship by the wake. Then the water was closing over her head and a sense of regret filled her. But even now death was infinitely preferable to what the Wenzels had planned for her.

The river was muddy, and she felt something slimy slithering across her arm. In a moment of horror, she recalled stories of bodies having been fished out of the river, eaten by shrimp and other river life. But even that was better than. . .

Suddenly her head broke through the surface.

She could have screamed in frustration. She had hoped to sink right to the bottom, but her voluminous petticoats and dress had trapped air under them and were lifting her head clear of the water. It would take long minutes before they were soaked sufficiently for her to sink again. By then she would be well away from the *Belle* in the pitch darkness and no one could possibly reach her.

She could hear the sound of the ship's paddle wheel being reversed, the ringing of bells and the blowing of a whistle on board, and then her ear caught another sound, one that startled and dismayed her.

It was the sound of someone swimming not far from her. Someone must have jumped in and come after her. Why, oh, why couldn't they just let her die! Stryker had been the closest behind her, and she had heard him cursing as he reached the rail a moment or so after she had jumped. Without pausing to consider the danger, he had probably leaped to retrieve a valuable piece of property in which he had a financial interest.

If she kept very quiet, maybe he wouldn't see her in the darkness. But what if he did and searched and searched until he became lost himself. Suppose he drowned? Could she bear to know it was her fault? How would she stand it? She wouldn't have to stand it, she reminded herself, because she'd be dead, too.

"Lorinda, where are you?" Stryker's voice was close at hand. "Say something, you little idiot, so I can find you."

Be quiet, don't even breathe, she told herself as

she drifted on downstream, her dress and petticoats rapidly losing their buoyancy.

"Lorinda, please, nothing is worth this. Say something," Stryker pleaded. "I want to get you out of here."

Stay very quiet. You are sinking. In a few minutes you will be beyond anything he can do.

"Damn it, where is she? Why doesn't she make some kind of sound?" The voice seemed to be going away from her now. It would be all over very soon.

Suddenly something long and slimy slithered across the back of Lorinda's knee and an involuntary squeal escaped her lips.

In an instant there was splashing coming nearer and out of the darkness a hand reached to grasp the back of her dress. "There you are. Thank God," Stryker said fervently and pulled her into his arms. "What's the matter with you, little fool? Why are you trying to kill yourself?"

"Let me go. Please let me go. If you have any decency or pity, you'll let me drown," she sobbed.

"What kind of nonsense is that?" he demanded, swimming on his side, towing her. "Why do you want to die?"

"My God, do you have to ask? Don't you know what's going to happen to me?"

"They say there are fates worse than death," he said, "but I've never encountered any of them."

"Of course not," she said bitterly. "You're a man and men can't be turned into sex slaves."

"Oh, come on, it can't be that bad. Maybe you'll end up with a man you like to sleep with."

"You've seen Gideon Wenzel. You've seen his brother and father. And that will only be the beginning."

"I don't think the Wenzels will own you after tonight," he said. "That yellow-headed youngster has supreme faith in his ability to fill inside straights, but by tomorrow morning he'll be minus his fifteen thousand dollars and his slave girl."

"Maybe, but that Partridge and Lou Lang aren't any better. I almost think I'd prefer the Wenzels."

"Well, there's one other alternative," he said. "There's me."

"I know I'd prefer the Wenzels to you!" she choked.

"Why, you little vixen! I ought to leave you—" He was laboring for breath as he struggled toward the lights of the steamer, dragging her after him.

"Let me go," she begged. "The weight of my clothes is pulling me under and you'll go down, too."

He stopped swimming and began treading water. "We'll soon fix that," he said, and one strong hand took hold of the neckline of her dress and ripped it down the front, shoving two of her petticoats off along with it. The rest of the petticoats and her chemise followed, leaving her in pantalettes and corset. "That'll make it easier. Now you're dressed for a swim."

But she wouldn't swim. She just let herself go limp, hoping to become such a burden that he'd let her go.

Stryker got an arm around her just under her almost bare breasts and began swimming strongly, making better progress now that the hindering skirts were eliminated. She could feel the firm flesh of his biceps pressing into the softness of her tender mounds, and the tingle of desire the contact caused somehow made her despair deeper.

"Damn them, where's that boat?" Stryker panted. "Surely they must have a boat over by now."

"Please, God, don't let there be a boat," Lorinda whimpered. "Let no one come. Let me set myself free."

Stryker was treading water again and cupping a hand to his mouth to yell. "Hey! Hey, on the *Belle!*"

There was an answering shout and the sound of oars moving in oarlocks. A man standing in the bow of a boat, holding a torch high, finally located them. A few minutes later three sailors were dragging them into the skiff.

"You folks sure are lucky," the sailor in charge said. "We were just about ready to give you up for dead and get up steam again when we heard you yelling."

Stryker dropped down on a seat with Lorinda on his lap, her head lying on his shoulder and his arm still tight around her waist. She seemed to be in a half faint, and he was becoming increasingly conscious of her near nudity and the way the sailors were staring at her high young breasts.

The boat was pulling back toward the steamer. There were cheers from the passengers lining the deck. But under the sounds of joy at their rescue, Stryker could hear the exhausted sobs of the girl he held and feel the warm wetness of her tears against his shoulder. For one of the few times in his life, he wondered if he had done the right thing. He had once said that it was pretentious of anyone who had never been a slave to comment on how slaves felt about their condition of servitude. Yet tonight he had told Lorinda that slavery was preferable to death, had denied her the oblivion she sought and had brought her back to become the sex toy of any man who owned her.

It was a situation to give any man pause, and yet the feel of her body lying across his changed the direction of his thoughts again. He had found her wholly desirable when he believed her to be a white woman. Was she any less so now that he knew she was black—if the minute amount of blackness she had inherited could be said to make her black. No, she was actually a white woman who through the strange mechanics of the black code was considered not only black but also a slave. It was almost as unfair as the institution of slavery itself. Unfair, yes, but as his body responded to the light pressure of her gently rounded thighs, the flare of hips and buttocks, he knew that no matter how unfair it was that she should be a slave he intended to take advantage of her status.

Yes, it would be very nice indeed to have a tender, loving little bundle like this in his bunk every night on the *Mississippi Belle* or some other boat as he followed his profession of gambling up and down the river. He had taken up gambling to raise a stake with which to buy acreage in the soon to be opened Kansas territory. There he intended to build his dream house and take as his bride Alice Randolph, the daughter of a prosperous Cincinnati merchant.

Fair or unfair, he mused while a rope ladder was being lowered from the deck of the steamer, the Alices of the world were the ladies you married, and the Lorindas were the ones you warmed your bed with until the wedding day.

CHAPTER 6

On deck they were immediately surrounded by chattering passengers. As Stryker stood the dazed Lorinda on her feet, several ladies moved quickly to take her in charge.

"The poor dear looks half dead from her terrible ordeal," said a plump, motherly woman. "How did she happen to fall in?"

"I'm not rightly sure she did fall in," Stryker said laconically.

"Bring her along to my cabin," invited a gray-haired, patrician woman. "I think my daughter has a dress that will just about fit her."

Stryker decided he had better set the matter straight before things got out of hand. "I don't think she ought to be wearing a lady's clothes or spending the night in a lady's cabin," he said, "seeing as how she's a slave."

"A slave? Oh, surely not!" the gray-haired woman said. "She's as white as I am."

"Nevertheless, there's a gentleman on board who has papers to prove she's his slave," Stryker said. "So if one of you ladies has a slave girl who can spare a dress, this little gal will be grateful for something warm and dry to put on."

Most of the crowd faded away. Those who had been so concerned about the fate of a young white girl cared little for that of a black one. The plump, matronly woman did remain behind long enough to say her maid was about Lorinda's size and she would send her around with a suitable change of clothing.

"My cabin is B-1," Stryker told her. He picked Lorinda up under one arm and carried her down the companionway, followed by the curious glances and whispered comments of the other passengers.

Lorinda didn't say a word until he had unlocked the door of his cabin and tossed her on the bunk. "Why didn't you let me die?" she cried. "It would have been so much better."

"Don't take on so," he said, producing a coarse towel and tossing it to her. "As soon as you get dried off and get a couple of shots of good whiskey inside you, you'll feel better. You might even discover things aren't as bad as you think."

"They're probably worse," she muttered, shivering.

"Get out of those wet things and dry yourself off before you catch pneumonia!" he ordered.

She stared at him and then at the towel, but he made no move to leave or even turn his back. "I—I can't get undressed in front of you."

"Listen, gal, you're going to have to get over your Nice Nellie scruples. Observing the proprieties was all right when you were pretending to be white but is pretty silly for a slave."

"I wasn't pretending to be white. I—I thought I was."

Stryker grinned at her. "Sure you did, honey, sure you did. And you sure fooled me."

Lorinda's shoulders sagged. It was hopeless. No one believed she hadn't known about her ancestry. No one knew or cared what she was going through. Overnight she had ceased being a pampered, protected member of the ruling race and become a piece of property, entitled to nothing but food and a place to sleep. She shivered again.

Stryker reached for his carpetbag and took out a bottle. "Take those wet clothes off! You want to die of the flux?" He poured whiskey into two small glasses. "If you do, our fifteen-thousand-dollar investment in young Wenzel's education won't be worth a damn. Don't think Lang and Partridge would care for that."

"Can't you at least turn your head?"

"And have you make another try at the river? I'm not that stupid."

"Oh, God, I can't stand it!" she wailed and started to cry again.

He crossed the cabin and held out the glass to her. "Here, drink this and I'll pour you another. It might help ease the pain as well as the cold."

She looked at the glass of amber liquid through the mist of her tears. Could it really help lessen the hurt and shame she felt?

"Come on, gal, drink up and cheer up. After all, you must have known it would all come out someday, and you had a lot of good years posing as the lady of the plantation with all the young beaus buzzing around."

"No, no, I didn't! I tell you—"

"Drink!" he said, forcing the glass into her hand.

Choking back a sob, she lifted the glass and drained it. For a moment she felt as though she had swallowed liquid flame. The whiskey burned her tongue, the inside of her mouth, her throat and all the way down to her stomach, where it exploded like a ball of fire. "Oh my—oh my," she gasped.

Stryker laughed and poured more liquor into her glass. "This will fix you up. It'll take away the taste of the river and wash away your silly prudishness as well."

Lorinda didn't know what to say, so she took another sip and felt the warmth begin to spread all through her.

"Now get those wet things off like I said." When she still hesitated, he reached out and hooked his fingers in the waistband of the pantalettes and stripped them off. Then he started untying the laces of her corset and loosening the stays, ignoring her protests. When she stood before him stark naked, he stepped back and stared at her as though he were seeing a nude woman for the first time in his life.

"Well, well. I'll be double damned and blown to hell," he murmured, eyes moving from the perky, pink-tipped breasts down over the creamy perfection of thigh and knee and ankle, then back up to the taut belly with the luxurious tuft of curly brown hair at its base.

"Fantastic," he said, putting a hand on her shoulder to turn her around so he could look at the straight back and the sweetly dimpled buttocks. "Yes, indeed, you're worth fifteen thousand dollars of any man's money."

Lorinda was blushing so furiously that she was

sure the rosiness must have spread all over her body. Her sense of shame was tinged with a strange kind of pride as she felt his appraising eye examining every curve and indentation on her naked trembling form.

"You'll do," he said, and the hands on her shoulders tightened their grip. "You'll do just fine."

Fear replaced her other emotions. She was shaking as much from that as from the chill of her damp flesh. "Wh—what are you going to do—" she began but couldn't finish the question and gulped at the whiskey instead.

"I know what I'd like to do with you," he said, and one hand dropped to her breast and began stroking the peaked nipple.

"No—no," she said, but her whole body was burning from the effects of the liquor, or perhaps from the sensations his fingers were stirring in her. She felt dizzy and the walls seemed to be tilting slightly.

His mouth was against the side of her neck, his breath warm in her ear. She felt herself sway toward him and knew once her body touched his she would be powerless to resist him.

Then suddenly he released her. "No, I guess I'd better not. Not yet, anyway. Wouldn't do to mess with another fellow's property."

There was a knock at the door. Stryker picked up the towel and draped it around Lorinda. Then he answered the knock and found a light-skinned Negro girl standing there holding a dress out to him.

"Miz Marker sez I should bring this foah youah

woman but not to take money foah it.''

Stryker laughed, reached in his pocket and took out a cartwheel. ''This isn't for the dress, it's for a kiss,'' he said, lifting the girl's chin and kissing her lightly on the lips.

The girl giggled, handed over the dress with a wide-eyed stare at Lorinda and retreated.

Stryker closed the door and tossed the dress to Lorinda. ''Here, put this on. You're putting indecent ideas in my head standing around like that.''

Indignation flared up in Lorinda. It hadn't been her idea to take off her clothes! But she held her tongue, shaking the folds out of the dress to look at it. It was coarse, cheap cotton material. Mrs. Marker's maid obviously hadn't put herself out by giving away one of the better slave dresses.

''Don't stand there staring at it. Put it on. We've got to get back to the business of the night, which is deciding who you're going to belong to tomorrow.''

Despair filled Lorinda again. It hadn't even been a day since she had belonged to herself, she thought bleakly, or at least believed she did. The dress was just one more symbol of her new lowly position, and she loathed it already.

''Put it on!'' Stryker snapped. ''If I take you in there without it, those three vultures will try to settle the matter with pistols and knives instead of cards.''

Lorinda shot him a look of pure hatred but raised the dress over her head and began to struggle into it. The rough material was harsh against her delicate skin. Stryker's avid stare at the way her breasts flared upward when she raised her arms only made her more miserable.

To make matters worse, the garment was too small. Mrs. Marker's maid must have been a bit less voluptuous than Lorinda. The dress was uncomfortably tight across breasts, hips and thighs.

Stryker whistled as he surveyed her. "Now I know why they keep women like you dressed in full skirts and ruffled blouses. It wouldn't do to have you walking around looking like that. There would be no controlling the male half of the population."

I'm the way God made me, Lorinda raged silently. *I didn't plan it to make you or any other man feel lustful!*

She had another half glass of whiskey before they left his cabin. As they walked toward the cabin where the three men were waiting, she swayed a little.

"You're tipsy, aren't you?" Stryker said. "Well, that's good. It might make things easier for you."

"So you got her back, huh?" Partridge said as they entered. He and Lang were playing two-handed poker for small stakes, while Gideon sat on the sidelines, palms pressing down on his knees and his face showing the strain of his desire to get on with the game.

"I told you he did," Gideon said. "I was up on deck when the skiff brought 'em in."

Partridge gave the youth a look that said that neither his word nor his judgement was worth much.

"Of course I got her back," Stryker said smoothly, "and as soon as you gents finish your hand we can start the real game."

Lang looked up from his cards. The flashy ruby and diamond rings on his fingers were reflected in his beady eyes.

"You've been gone quite a while," he said. "Is the merchandise still in its original condition, or has it been tampered with a little bit?"

Stryker stared at him coolly. "Except for a good dunking and the loss of a couple hundred dollars worth of fancy clothes, it's still in the same condition. What wasn't busted then isn't busted now."

"I figure maybe that's something we got the right to find out for ourselves," Partridge said and started to reach for Lorinda.

"And I figure that's something one gentleman ought to take another gentleman's word for," Stryker said, pushing his waistcoat aside so they could see the Navy Colt that was stuck in his belt.

For a tense moment it seemed as though Partridge was going to challenge Stryker. Instead he shrugged, tossed his hand in and leaned back in his chair. "Oh, I believe you, Stryker, you and your friend there under your coat, but if I'm gonna be bettin' fifteen thousand dollars, I figure I'm entitled to see more of what I stand to win."

"Yeah," Lang agreed. "Shuck down, gal, and let's see the prize in this race."

"Do like he sez, wench!" Wenzel said, trying to reassert his position as her owner. "Show 'em what's under that dress."

"I propose, gentlemen," Stryker interceded,

"that since this is a tasty bit of untouched female flesh we're dealing with, the man who wins it might want to reserve the privilege of seeing it stripped to himself and himself alone."

Now that he'd seen his fill, Lorinda thought cynically, he was trying to keep the others from looking. Then suddenly she realized he was doing her a favor, saving her the shame and humiliation of standing naked in front of all of them at once.

"Seems you're settin' the rules here to suit yourself," Lang said, his voice lazy with menace. "Maybe you brought your own deck of cards, too."

Stryker didn't answer, but he took off his money belt and tossed it on the table. "The original deal was for each of us to put up five thousand to stake Wenzel. There's twenty-five thousand in that belt, fifteen goes to Wenzel and the rest is my stake. You gentlemen don't have to put up anything but your own stakes and you get as good a chance to win the girl as I do."

Lorinda sucked in her breath. Through the haze of alcohol she was jolted into an awareness of just how much Stryker wanted her. So he wasn't quite as careless and unconcerned about her fate as he had seemed. Apparently he was willing to risk everything he had to win her. She felt a strange, warm glow of pride, which took the edge off her misery.

"You're mighty sure of yourself, Stryker," Lang said, tapping his fingers on the table. "Mighty sure."

"Seems like yer willin' to go a long way just to keep us from takin' a look," Partridge said.

"What's it matter? Lots of men'll be seein' her from now on."

"Lots of men have probably seen her already," Lang said, "but I just don't like buyin' no pig in a poke."

Stryker reached over and picked up the deck of cards the pair had discarded and examined them closely. "That isn't any pig in a poke, gentlemen. It's something you would never believe unless you saw it. It's worth fifteen thousand, or twice fifteen thousand for that matter, and I intend to win it. And since it's going to be mine, I'm willing to pay to keep it for my eyes only."

Lang laughed and sank back in his chair. "It's your money, mister, but you ain't won her yet. If I win her and she's half what you say she is, I'm gonna bust her myself and then peddle her ass up and down the river and retire on the profits."

"*That* profession might suit you better than gambling, Lang," Stryker said. "Shall we cut for deal? The night isn't getting any younger."

Wenzel insisted on putting the manacles back on Lorinda first and he whispered to her, "Don't you fret none, gal. I ain't gonna lose you. I feel lucky tonight, real lucky."

With the door locked and her manacles fastened to the head of the bunk, Lorinda had no hope of escaping. All she could do was watch with eyes that wouldn't quite focus as the four men began to gamble for her body.

Lang won the deal and began flicking the cards to the other three after each had contributed a thousand-dollar ante. "There you go, gents. Five cards all around. Anyone want to bet?"

"Yeah," Gideon said in a happy, excited voice, "I'll bet a thousand."

"That's a thousand to you, Stryker," Lang said.

"I'll see it," the tall Westerner said.

"I'll just bump you another thousand," Partridge said to Gideon.

"I'll fold for this round," Lang said, tossing down his hand and picking up the deck. "You seein' Partridge or raising, Wenzel?"

"I—I'll see him."

"I'll stay with you," Stryker said.

"Anybody want any cards?" Lang asked.

The voices faded away as Lorinda's head fell back on the pillow. Although her immediate fate, and perhaps the rest of her life, was being decided by the fall of the cards, she couldn't keep her eyes open any longer.

An exclamation of joy from Gideon roused her briefly and she realized he must have won the first hand. But somehow that didn't worry her. She had the feeling that Gideon was a sheep in the midst of a pack of wolves and that his chances of winning were nonexistent. That left only the question of which of the professional gamblers would bed her tonight. In her half-drunken state it hardly seemed to matter.

She had no way of knowing how long she had been sleeping when there was a shout and the noise of a chair tipping over. Sitting bolt upright, she saw Gideon on his feet, reaching across the table toward a handful of cards lying in front of Kirk Stryker.

"Let me see those, damn it! Let me see if you bluffed me out of that pot!"

"You didn't call me, sonny," Stryker said. "You have to pay to see my cards."

"You can't pull that on me!" Gideon raged. "I want to know if I'm being cheated or not!"

"Don't be a total ass, Wenzel" Partridge said. "Nobody shows his hand unless you pay to see it."

"Look, I've lost thirty thousand dollars here tonight and I want to know how!"

"*Mister* Wenzel, are you suggesting that you have not had a square deal from anyone at this table?" Stryker's voice was low and so loaded with silken menace that Lorinda shivered.

"I—I—I'm just saying that I lost a lot of money and the papers to a valuable slave and—"

"And I think that if you pick up that chair and walk out of here quietly, I might be able to restrain myself from throwing you overboard," Stryker said.

"I could challenge you to a duel," Gideon said.

Stryker laughed. "If you do, I'll insist on Colts at twenty paces and as many shots as it takes to kill."

"G—gentlemen don't f—fight with Colt revolvers." Gideon's voice was shaking now and remembering what a beastly bully he had been with her, Lorinda wanted to laugh.

"Whoever said I was a gentleman?" Stryker said. "But I'll give you a choice between that or Bowie knives."

"Bowie knives?" Gideon started backing away from the table. "I—I haven't challenged you yet."

"Then get your ass out of here like a good little boy and leave us men to the game," Stryker told him.

"Please give me a break," Gideon whined. "Let me write you an IOU for another ten thousand and—"

"You'd better *git* before I—" Stryker half rose from his chair, and Gideon went scrambling to the door and out of it as fast as his feet could carry him.

As soon as the youth was gone, Stryker turned out the lantern and opened the curtains on the portholes so the morning sun could stream in, then sat back down and picked up the cards.

"Well, gentlemen, shall we start the real game now? Now you play *me* for the wench. But perhaps we should eat first."

There was a break in the game as a waiter brought coffee and eggs for the men and a bowl of porridge for Lorinda. She had awakened with a headache and a vile taste in her mouth. The porridge, reserved for the slaves on the steamer, was terrible but she hadn't eaten in almost twenty-four hours; so she forced it down as the men settled back and continued their game.

From the occasional curses and low-voiced words it seemed that the game was beginning to go against Partridge and that Lang and Stryker were about equally lucky.

"I'm about tapped out," Partridge said after a while. "If I don't win this hand, I'm through."

"You can win it if you can beat a full house," Lang said.

"Damn! Damn it to hell!" Partridge threw his

hand down and stomped out onto the deck.

Lang pulled in the money. "So now it's just you and me butting heads," Stryker said, reaching for the cards.

"Deal 'em fast," Lang said, licking his lips as he looked toward Lorinda. "I'm in a hurry to get the wench into my bunk."

Lorinda's head was splitting and her stomach churning so badly that even the man's words couldn't make her feel any worse. What difference did it make who won her? She was going to die, anyway. The prize would be nothing but cold, dead flesh by the time they decided who had won it.

"I'll take two cards," Stryker said, tossing down his discards.

"I'll play with these," Lang said, and Partridge stared in fascination at the pot of almost eight thousand dollars.

"You got a pat hand, have you?" Stryker said, carefully arranging the new cards in his closely held hand. "Well, I'll check to the man with the cards."

"It'll cost you to see these, Stryker, cost you plenty," Lang said, shoving a stack of gold pieces into the middle of the table. "Another five thousand for a fact."

Stryker stroked his chin. "Hmmm. That makes it thirteen thousand, doesn't it?"

"That's the way I figure it, unless you want to let the eight thousand go and try again next time."

Stryker leaned back and looked up at the angle of the sun. "Getting on pretty late. We must be almost to Vicksburg. Why don't we finish it all on this hand and get some shut-eye?"

"Finish it all?" Lang said and Lorinda saw his Adam's apple move as he gulped nervously.

Stryker was busy counting the money stacked in front of him. "You bumped me five thousand, right? Well, I'll see that and raise you fifteen thousand."

"Jesus!" Partridge breathed. "Twenty-eight thousand!"

"Twenty-eight thousand dollars and the papers to one female slave," Stryker said, his voice as cool as though he were discussing the weather.

"Yeah, one octoroon wench," Lang said, eyes narrowing as he considered the situation. "What could you have? You drew to three of a kind, or maybe you didn't. Maybe you just had a pair and kept something for a kicker. Or maybe you're bluffing like you bluffed young Wenzel right out of the game."

"Those are three possibilities," Stryker said, "And there's only one way to find out."

"Yeah, and there's another possibility, isn't there? That you got a full house."

"To match yours maybe?" Stryker said.

Lang looked at his cards again as though to reassure himself that they were as good as he had thought. "I ain't never been bluffed out of a pot in my life, and a lot of men have tried."

"My money's in there," Stryker said. "Let's see yours."

Lang tipped his hat farther back on his head and took a cigar from his pocket. He made an elaborate little ceremony of clipping off the end of it with a gold clipper. "Nope, ain't never been sandbagged out of a pot in my life, but then I never seen a pot that big, either.''

Stryker didn't say anything. He just sat smiling, his hands perfectly still and his cards covered by his palm.

Lang lit the cigar and puffed on it hard a couple of times. ''I think you're bluffing, Mr. Kirk Stryker, and you're gonna have to beat a full house, jacks over tens.'' He was pushing all the gold pieces stacked in front of him into the pot. ''Yeah, beat jacks over tens, my friend.''

Stryker spread his cards out on the table. Lorinda heard a gasp from Partridge and a grunt from Lang.

''I'll be damned if he didn't do it,'' Partridge said. ''Four threes. Four goddamn threes!''

''I drew to three threes and got another one,'' Stryker said. ''Guess my luck was just in tonight, gentlemen.''

He was pulling the money over to his side of the table as the other two men got up, stretched and started to leave. Pushing one stack toward each of them, he said, ''A thousand each, to stake you to your next game.''

''Thanks,'' Partridge said, picking up the gold pieces. ''Maybe I'll see you next trip. Your luck ought to be running out by then.''

''Thanks, Stryker,'' Lang said. ''Remind me never to butt heads with you again in a two-handed game. A man could lose his ass that way and not even know it was gone.''

''The cards have a funny way of falling,'' Stryker said, raking his winnings into a canvas bag as the other two moved toward the door.

Lang paused before he went out to look at Lorinda crouched on the bunk. "Too bad. I had plans for you, missy. I think you'd have made the best whore on the river, and I always did have a hankering to be some money-making strumpet's fancy man."

Lorinda didn't say anything. She was too numb for it to matter.

Then Stryker was standing over her. "Come on, gal, you're mine now," he said, stuffing her papers into his pocket.

CHAPTER 7

He unlocked the manacles from the head of the bunk, and Lorinda got to her feet and followed him meekly out into the corridor. Although she had watched her fate being decided by the flip of a few cards, she still couldn't feel that it was actually happening to her. After all, Lorinda de Farbin wasn't a slave to be gambled for; she was the daughter of a Southern gentleman, the belle of Claiborne County. Men didn't fondle her at will or gamble thousands of dollars to win her body and then command her to follow them to their bed.

"Guess I'd better hang on to you until we reach my cabin," Stryker said. "I don't feel like taking another swim."

"Don't worry," she heard herself saying. "I won't kill myself now."

"Glad to hear it," Stryker said.

"I'll wait until afterward," she muttered.

"After what?"

"After you get your money's worth," she said. "I wouldn't want you to think you'd been cheated."

He gave her an amused glance. "You're a strange girl."

When they reached his cabin, he removed the manacles from her wrists and tossed them into a corner. Sunlight was filtering through his cabin portal and in the distance were the banks of Ole Miss. "Don't imagine we'll be needing those anymore. You seem tame enough."

"Of course," she said. "I'm very tame. I come when I'm called and I sit up and beg when I'm hungry."

He eyed her with one eyebrow cocked. "I guess you're feeling kind of bitter, but like I said earlier, you couldn't expect to get away with your masquerade forever. Sooner or later someone was bound to find out you weren't white."

She sighed. No one, not one human being in the world would believe she hadn't known who her mother was, that she hadn't deliberately posed as white.

Stryker had taken off his coat and cravat and was unbuttoning his collar. "Come here, gal," he said, flopping down in a chair.

She went to stand in front of him. She couldn't keep from flushing as he looked her up and down, the cool gray eyes noting the flare of breasts, the faint roundness of belly and the smooth curve of thigh emphasized by the tight calico dress.

"Are you satisfied?" she asked with a touch of sarcasm. "Is the merchandise worth what you paid for it?"

He shrugged. "Since all you cost me was a night's work with a deck of cards, I guess—"

"Perhaps it would have been better if Lang had won," she broke in angrily. "He at least seemed to know what he wanted."

Stryker laughed at her. "Yeah, to put you to

whoring so he could laze around as your fancy man.
Do you think you'd make a good whore, gal?''

"I'd rather be anything but your woman!''

"Well, maybe I've changed my mind. Maybe I
don't want you to warm my bed. Maybe I'll just use
you like an ordinary slave. You know, someone to
wash my clothes and clean up after me.''

That jolted her. "You—you want me to wait on
you—wash clothes and—''

"And take my boots off,'' he said, sticking out a
foot. "Here, these need cleaning. Take them off
and polish them.''

She stared at him in disbelief. This was outra-
geous! She was not a common drudge. She knew
she was beautiful and many men had wanted her.
Stryker had wanted her when he thought she was
white and even when he knew she wasn't, just a few
hours ago, after he had fished her from the river.
Why had he changed his mind?

"You'd better do what I tell you, gal. I don't
want to have to buy a whip.''

"Buy one!'' she said, tossing her head defiantly.
"Buy the biggest, blackest bullwhip you can find
because that's what you'll need! You'll have to beat
me to death before I'll clean your boots!''

He grinned at her without humor. "You mean
you're willing to let me bed you?''

"A slave doesn't have any choice, does she? If
her master orders her to shuck down and get into his
bed, she has to do it.''

"A slave doesn't have any choice about cleaning
boots, either,'' he said. "She does it, or she gets
her hide tanned.''

"Then you'd better buy that whip," she said. "You're going to need it."

"I don't think so," he said, standing up. "My hand will do well enough."

"Your hand? Her eyes widened as she watched him roll up his sleeve.

"Yes. Apparently you were raised like a fancy lady instead of the little slave gal you are. I'll bet no one ever tanned your bottom in your whole life."

She drew herself up proudly. "No one would have dared! My father was a gentleman and would have killed anyone who had suggested such a thing."

"Well, it's about time you were introduced to the good old custom of spanking, the applying of the palm of the hand to a bare bottom until owner of same would rather stand than sit down for supper."

"No—no, don't you dare," she said, taking a step backward as he came toward her. "I'm—I'm not a child."

"No, you're not a child," he said, "but you are a slave. I gave you an order and you refused to obey it, so now I'm going to teach you to obey all my orders."

She screamed as he grabbed her arm, pulled her to him and dropped down on the bunk to bend her over his knees.

"Stop that! Stop, you brute! Don't you dare hit me!" She struggled and kicked out wildly as she felt her skirt being raised to expose her buttocks.

Then his hand connected stingingly with her bare flesh, and she let out a yelp and twisted desperately to escape his grasp. But the arm that held her down was like steel and the hand pinning her wrists was as confining as the manacles.

She was almost helpless, but there was still one thing she could do. The thought had no more than crossed her mind when her teeth sank into the firm flesh of his forearm.

It was Stryker's turn to yelp, but he didn't let go. "Damn you, you little devil! I was only going to give you a couple of light whacks, but now you're going to get it good!"

His big hand came down on her rounded bottom again and again.

"Stop it! Oh, please stop it!" she howled.

"What about the boots? Are you going to do the boots?" he demanded.

"Yes, yes, I'll do them!" she gasped tearfully. She could have endured a lashing with a whip, she told herself. She would have defied him and let him cut her to shreds, but to be treated like a naughty child, to be paddled in such a humiliating fashion was worse than real punishment. Anything was better than being handled in such a debasing manner.

He released his grip on her. "All right, now get down on your knees and take off my boots like a proper slave."

Sobbing from hurt pride as much as the smarting of her flesh, Lorinda dropped to her knees in front of him and began to unlace his boots.

"That's a good girl. That's a nice, submissive little wench," he said as she drew the first boot off. "If she keeps behaving, she might even get a reward."

Lorinda's tears fell faster, and when the second

boot came off, she burst into hysterical sobbing.

"Oh, come now," Stryker said. "I couldn't possibly have hurt you that much. I barely touched you."

His words failed to stem the flow, so he took her by the shoulders and pulled her up to face him. "Damn it, you're not hurt! What the devil are you crying about?"

"Because I'm a slave! Because I'll have to spend the rest of my life washing dirty clothes and cleaning muddy boots! I'd rather be dead or—or what Lang intended me to be!"

Stryker threw back his head and roared. "So you think you would have been better at that, do you? Well, let's see. Let's see how good you are, and maybe I'll turn you out on the turf myself."

He lifted her up onto the bunk with him, ripped at the buttons on the cheap cotton dress and stripped it off. Then his big hands closed on her still tender bottom and pulled her to him.

His lips were against the side of her neck, burning kisses down to the pulse that was beating so wildly in the hollow of her throat. Her tears had stopped and her whole body was quivering with excitement as he rolled her on top of him and his hands began to move over her flesh, caressing, exploring, possessing.

"So you don't like to clean boots, little witch? You think you'd prefer to let any man who comes along pester you for six bits? Well, I'll show you what that profession is like. I'll show you how a man treats a whore."

She wasn't really listening to his words. She was

too athrob with the sensations his hands were causing. His fingers stroked the sides of her breasts,
teased the nipples until they peaked and then relin-
quished them to his lips and tongue. The hands
glided down her sides, one veering from the indentation of her waist toward her back to fondle the
rounded half moons it had paddled so vigorously
such a short while before, and the other snaking
across her belly to search through the silken muff
that hid her womanhood. She sucked in her breath
as she felt his fingertips touch the soft, pouty lips.
She became intensely aware of the massive pole of
his maleness.

She wouldn't be doing his washing or cleaning
his boots. She knew that now as clearly as she knew
anything. No woman who was wanted as much as
the throbbing of his flesh said he wanted her would
have to do anything except pleasure the man with
her body. And she was ready to do that, she
realized, wanted to do it, in fact. What difference
did it make that she would do it as a slave? Could he
want her any more if she were the free white woman
she had thought herself to be? No. The feel of his
tormented flesh told her that, and it gave her a sense
of power she hadn't known even when she was free.

She was lying on her back then with her legs
spread wide apart and his lips running over her. The
words he was murmuring against her flesh didn't
sound like Stryker at all.

"You beautiful sweet thing. Your skin is like
rich cream. Your body like a marble temple. Your
thighs like alabaster pillars with an altar between
them where a man must worship."

His kisses were making her dizzy with passion. She wanted him to take her, to use her for his pleasure and her own. The fires he was setting inside her were becoming a conflagration. Her hand fumbled for his belt buckle and then the buttons of his fly. Slipping her fingers through the opening, she found the bare, hard rod she had touched once before. In renewed amazement at its overheated size, she explored it and heavy spheroids from which it seemed to rise like a stately tower.

"Oh, my God, Lorinda, dear little Lori," he sighed as she caressed him.

He freed himself from her embrace long enough to skin out of his pants and shirt and then was back pressing down on top of her. Eyes gazed with desire, she opened for him with a wriggle of anticipation. Then, for the first time in her life, she felt the firm push of man flesh between the tight softness of her womanhood.

He groaned, caught her bottom in his strong hands and drove deep, obviously freed of any qualms he might have had for her present comfort or future regrets.

It was like being struck by lightning between the thighs. Lorinda gasped in pain and tried to push him away, but he was too strong and too highly aroused to pay any attention to her efforts to escape. He made husky sounds deep in his throat and pounded into her relentlessly, making her feel like a butterfly wriggling on the head of a pin.

There was no use struggling. She was helpless in his grip, and he seemed turned into a madman whose only intent was to hurt her to give himself pleasure. Her movements only served to incite him further.

She could feel the stickiness of blood on the inside of her thighs as the stabbing pain gradually gave way to a mild sensation of discomfort. Then that began to give way to something else, a warmth and building excitement that lubricated her tight passageway and made it more receptive to his plunging maleness. But just when she thought she might be about to find out what it was all leading up to, she felt his body go suddenly rigid.

"Oh, damn—damn! You're so beautiful, you little bitch, I can't wait."

She felt him jerk inside her and then it was over, leaving her tired and disappointed.

After a few moments he rolled away from her and lay looking at her with his familiar sardonic grin. "So now you know how beastly a man can be. Do you still think you'd want to be a whore?"

"Do you intend to make me one?" she asked, slowly sitting up and wondering what would have happened if another man had been waiting to use her. Would the second one have lasted long enough to have enabled her to experience the ecstasy she sensed it was possible for a woman to feel?

"You're all bloody," he said abruptly. "Go wash yourself off and then come back and wash me off."

She swung her feet to the floor and walked over to the stand holding a basin and a pitcher of water. With her back toward the bunk, she dipped one end of a towel into the water and cleaned the sticky mess off the inside of her thighs.

Stryker had turned on his side to watch her as she came back across the room, head held high, shoulders back and buttocks tucked in.

"You look better naked than you do dressed," he said. "A lot of women don't, you know. Some of them look like real beauties all dolled up in expensive clothes, but when the clothes come off, you see that their breasts sag, their legs are like toothpicks or their bellies are fat and ugly."

"I suppose you've seen a lot of women naked."

"That's none of your business," he said. "Wash me off."

She knelt between his thighs, secretly hoping that the touch of her fingers would inflame him again so he would take her a second time and finish what he had left half undone.

Instead, he let out a yelp at the first touch of the wet towel.

"That water's cold, you little idiot! What do you think you're doing?

She gaped at him in astonishment. "But you told me to use it. It was cold for me, too."

"Yes, but what's good enough for a slave wench isn't good enough for her master, is it?" He took the towel from her, warmed it in his palms and gingerly finished the washing himself and pulled on his underdrawers. "Put something on so I can order lunch. I'm starved, but I don't want the waiters seeing what a shameless hussy you are."

She made a helpless gesture toward the torn dress on the floor. "Somehow my clothes seem to keep getting ripped off my back. Master is so masterful," she said sarcastically.

"And you're a bitch with a smart mouth."

Her mockery seemed to have more effect than pleading or anger. It seemed to make him unsure of himself, perhaps made him wonder if she were really inferior to him because of her ancestry.

"There's a couple of dresses and other things in a package in my trunk," he said. "I picked them up in New Orleans."

"That sounds kind of fancy," she said, wondering who he had bought women's clothes for. A wife? A sister? A mistress? "You said I was to wear slave's clothes."

"Get them and put them on!" he ordered, exasperated at her defiance. "And here, you forgot to clean these," he added, reaching for his boots.

He tossed them to her and she caught them automatically. Then she stood looking down at them, all her brash confidence gone as suddenly as air from a ruptured balloon. Her shoulders drooped, her mouth twisted and tears spilled down her cheeks.

"Oh, all right. All right, damn it!" he said. "Leave them! Hurry and get some clothes on so we can eat."

He opened the trunk and handed her the package. Inside were two expensive outfits, one an exquisite gray traveling dress and the other a silver-blue lamé ball gown. Each had its own petticoats and the proper underthings.

"These are beautiful," Lorinda breathed, wiping away her tears. "Were they for your sister?"

"It's none of your damn business who they were for," he said. "Right now they're yours. I hope they fit, or I'll have to lock you in the cabin to keep the crew and half the passengers from chasing you around the promenade deck.''

She giggled as she started to get into the gray traveling dress. ''But think of the nice fat fees you could charge for your whoring slave girl, master.''

''Don't tempt me, gal, or I'll turn you out first chance I get,'' he said severely. ''And if you aggravate me too much, I'll sell you to a breeding farm.''

Lorinda shivered at the threat. That was the same fate the Wenzels had intended for her and one that she couldn't bear to even think about.

While she finished dressing, Stryker pulled a cord to summon a waiter, shrugged into a shirt and then turned to inspect her.

''Damn if you don't look just like a lady,'' he said. ''I swear you could pass for white at the governor's ball.''

''I did pass for white at the governor's ball,'' she reminded him. ''Half a dozen times, in fact.''

''My, my,'' he said, shaking his head, ''the things that go on in this part of the country amaze me.''

She realized then that he was turning her own use of mockery against her. She'd have to think of some other way of annoying him. On second thought maybe she'd better not. He probably hadn't meant what he said about selling her to a breeding farm, but it was just as well not to take any chances.

There was a tap on the door. Stryker opened it to let in a tall, dignified black waiter, whose bald head was circled by a fringe of kinky white hair. The man showed no surprise at Lorinda's presence in the gambler's cabin, and she was sure word had spread all over the *Mississippi Belle* that a slave girl had been part of the stakes in a high-roller poker game the night before. The only thing that could possibly have surprised the waiter was that the slave was dressed so elegantly and gave the appearance of being as white as any woman aboard the steamer.

"Bring me a pair of lamb chops, a dish of oysters, some fruit and a bottle of champagne," Stryker said.

The waiter nodded. His eyes strayed toward Lorinda, asking a silent question.

"Oh, don't concern yourself about her," Stryker said. "I'll feed my wench off my tray. She's got to get used to eating scraps."

CHAPTER 8

When the food arrived, Stryker perched Lorinda on his knee and fed her raw oysters as though she were a pet poodle.

"Speak, girl, speak!" he said, holding an oyster over her head.

When she remained mute, he dropped the oyster down the front of her bodice and pretended to search for it while he fondled her breasts.

"Stop that. Stop!"

"Stop that, who?" he demanded.

"Stop it—master."

"Say please," he laughed, running his fingers back and forth across a nipple. "Say, 'Please stop it, master, sir.' "

"Please stop it, master, sir," she repeated.

"That's a good girl." He popped another oyster into her mouth and insisted she drink half a glass of champagne.

The wine tickled her nose and she sneezed, spraying a few droplets on the gray silk dress.

"Oh, my dress! Look, I've ruined it!" she wailed.

"I'll buy you half a dozen more," he promised. "I won nearly thirty thousand dollars playing for you, my girl, so I guess you deserve something from it."

"What will you do with so much money?" she asked. "Gamble it away again?"

"Ten thousand of it will be my next stake," he said, "but the rest will go into a bank in St. Louis."

She gave him a surprised look. "I've never heard of a gambler putting money away for his old age."

"Not for my old age, for my dream," he told her. "I'm putting it away for the dream that kept me going all the time I was campaigning with Zack Taylor and herding cows in Texas."

"You mean you want to own a gambling club on Rampart Street in New Orleans or a riverboat all your own with card tables and roulette wheels in every cabin?"

"No, no, nothing like that," he said. "My dream has nothing to do with cards or wheels, not that kind of wheel, anyway."

He got up, set her down in the chair and placed one of the lamb chops and the rest of the oysters in front of her. "Here, be sure to eat all the oysters. They say they make a woman passionate, and you're going to have need of that."

Lorinda felt herself blushing, but she finished the bowl of oysters, washing them down with sips of champagne.

Stryker was standing at the porthole watching the banks of the river as the steamer chugged slowly upriver. "No, my dream has to do with land, lots and lots of land. When I was in Texas, I saw spreads where a man didn't have a neighbor within twenty miles, where he had elbow room and then some. I liked that. I aim to buy me a place where a loud shout won't disturb anybody else and a fellow can ride for miles without setting foot off his own land.''

''Are you going back to Texas to find such a place?''

''No. I thought about it, but it's too hot down there in the summer and too cold in winter. I hear they're going to open up the Kansas territory as soon as they decide if it's to be slave or free. I want to be there sitting on my ten thousand acres with my crops already planted when the crowds start pouring in.''

''*Decide* if it's to be slave or free? Wasn't that decided when they wrote the Constitution? That guarantees the right for a citizen to be secure in his property, and slaves are property.''

Kirk turned from the porthole and lifted an eyebrow at her. ''You mean you haven't changed your mind about slavery?''

''No, of course not. Why should I——'' She stopped in midsentence, a little choked laugh escaping her lips. ''Oh, I see what you mean. Yes, I see what you mean.''

''You were slave-holding, and your opinions were somewhat colored by your position in life,'' he said. ''Now, however—''

''Now, however, I am a slave,'' she finished for him. Saying the words was difficult, but it was even harder to adjust her mind to them. ''I recall that you said something about it being presumptuous of anyone who had never been a slave to discuss how a slave feels about slavery.''

"Yes," Stryker nodded. "Of course, when I said that, I had never been a slave owner, and now I am."

"So all of a sudden the institution of slavery begins to look much more pleasant to you."

"On the contrary," he said, walking over to the bunk and sitting down with his long legs stretched out. "I still feel that the institution of slavery is the curse of the South and may, indeed, be the curse of the nation itself. In fact, I can see that it may someday destroy our country as we know it."

"But when presented with a chance to own a—a valuable slave, you forfeit your belief."

He laughed but looked a little embarrassed. "I'm afraid that most men would under such circumstances. Not the Gerrit Smiths or the William Lloyd Garrisons, of course, but most ordinary men like me, given the chance to have total power over a beautiful woman, would jump at it."

Lorinda felt a glow of pleasure at his admission of her beauty. He must mean it to say it so calmly in the middle of such a discussion. She was pleased, but her voice was tart as she asked, "You admire Garrison?"

"No, I think he's a madman who is as likely to destroy the Union as some of the madmen on the other side of the controversy."

"You seem to know a lot about the problem," she said. "I didn't know gamblers were students of social and political affairs."

He grinned lazily. "When you're living under canvas in army camps or herding cows or sheep along the Brazos, you have a lot of time to read and think. I had a sidekick in Texas, fellow named Gus Lasley, who used to be a schoolteacher until he got in a mess with one of his girl pupils and turned up 'gone to Texas' like so many others who get in trouble. He used to get Garrison's paper, *The Liberator*. I didn't have to read very many issues of that to be convinced there were fanatics on both sides who would like nothing better than to plunge the whole country into a bloody civil war.''

"But now you're on the side of the slaveholders,'' she said.

"Just about as much as you're on the side of the slaves,'' he countered. "You haven't found out yet, little lady, what it's like to be a slave, and if you stick with me, maybe you never will.''

Lorinda got up and crossed to the washstand to soap and rinse her hands. "Some people might think that being forced to submit to your sexual urges was a particularly vile form of slavery.''

He shrugged. "It's no worse than what many wives have to endure when a husband insists on exercising his connubial rights.''

"Then aren't all women slaves in a way?'' she asked. "And shouldn't the abolitionists be crying, 'Free the women!' as well as 'Free the slaves!'?''

"Some of them are,'' he told her with a chuckle. "I believe Miss Amelia Bloomer, in addition to inventing the article of clothing that bears her name, is a firm advocate of the emancipation of women.''

"Yes, I think I could support her in that,'' Lorinda said, passing in front of him, "although I can't say I care much for her bloomers.''

Stryker reached out to lift her skirt and examine her legs in the lacy pantalettes with an appraising eye. "I agree. Covering up those underpinnings with baggy trousers would be a crime against nature.''

Blushing but flattered, Lorinda pulled loose from his grasp and shook the dress back into place. "You have no right to do that. A girl ought to be entitled to some privacy.''

He took a folded document out of his pocket and waved it at her. "This gives me the right, my lady. These papers that your dear cousin so recklessly gambled away are the right to your life, limb and certain other notable parts of your carcass.''

Lorinda flinched as though he had struck her. "Yes, I guess you do own me, don't you?'' she said with a catch in her voice.

"Just as surely as ever you owned the black folks on your plantation,'' he said firmly.

"You say that as though you think I'm not black, but a while ago you were calling me a little slave gal.''

"Oh, that was just my way of joshing you,'' he said, "and maybe bringing you down a peg or two. All you have to do is look in a mirror to know you're as white as I am.''

"And yet I'm the slave and you're the master.''

"Yes, because it happens to be known that you have a drop or two of black blood in your veins. You were just unlucky enough to get caught.''

"Unlucky enough to have relatives like the Wenzels who wanted my father's money," she said bitterly. "I might have gone on like I was if August and his family hadn't been such greedy weasels boring from within. They won my father's confidence just so they could poke around in old records to discover something in his past that could ruin my future. I'll bet they even had a hand in what happened to my mother—my real mother."

"What do you mean?" Kirk asked. "What about your mother?"

"She was a slave my father bought from another plantation owner," Lorinda said, trying to remember exactly what Kelandes had said in the probate court. "She was supposed to have practiced voodoo, and they say she killed a man a couple of years ago and was hanged for it. But the Wenzels were here in Mississippi then and must have been already scheming to get Solitaire. Yes, the more I think about it, the more I feel that they could have plotted to have her executed just to get her out of the way."

"But why would they do that? She was already out of the picture as far as the estate was concerned. I don't see where they'd have anything to gain," Stryker said.

Lorinda thought for a minute. "Maybe because of the little house she lived in on Rampart Street. Kelandes said the deed was still in my father's name, and the Wenzels are so greedy they wouldn't want me to get even that." She sighed deeply. "That's where I should have been raised, there in that house with my real mother. Instead, my father took me to Solitaire and passed me off as the daughter of his white wife. I don't understand what made him do it.''

"Perhaps he loved you too much to give you up,'' Stryker suggested quietly.

"Well, he did me no favor,'' Lorinda said angrily. "If I had been raised as I should have been, as the daughter of a Rampart Street woman, I would have known my place and gotten used to what my fate would be. But no, I was raised to think I was white, free and an heiress, only to find out at this late date that I am black, a slave and without hope.''

"Everyone has hope of some kind,'' Stryker said. "That's what keeps us going in life, and if you believe the preachers, there is the hope of heaven after death.''

Lorinda turned away, the picture of utter despair. "There is no hope for me in this world.''

"Well,'' he said, "you could always run away. The Underground Railroad could slip you across the border into Canada.''

She looked at him questioningly. "You sound as though you're encouraging me to run away.''

He shook his head, "No, and frankly I doubt the opportunity would ever present itself. But to get back to the Wenzels and your mother, how could they have implicated her in a murder? Who was the man she supposedly killed?''

"Her lover, old pasty-faced Kelandes said, and I'm sure he had something to do with it, too,'' Lorinda said. "He's worked hand in glove with the Wenzels all along. He hates me for some reason.''

"While I was in Claiborne County, I did some business with lawyer Kelandes; so I can tell you that if he hates you, it isn't personal but just part of his racist attitude."

"Yes, I suppose that could be true," she conceded. "He is a candidate of the Know-Nothing Party for Congress from the district."

Stryker scowled at mention of the Know-Nothings, the group of anti-Catholic, antiblack and antiforeigner bigots who called themselves the Native American Party but had been given the nickname because they answered all questions concerning their party with the words, "I know nothing in the Party's doctrine that is contrary to the Constitution."

"He could be elected, you know," Stryker said. "The Know-Nothings have done well even in largely Catholic cities like New Orleans. Hate is an easy commodity to sell."

"And Kelandes and the Wenzels have a lot of it to sell," she said. "I still think my mother was innocent and they had her hanged to hide something."

"Forget it, little love," he said, tipping her head back against his shoulder and turning her lips up to his. "There's nothing you can do about what happened to your mother, and there's no way you can change what has happened to you."

"You wouldn't want it changed if it could be," she said after a dizzying kiss. "You are very happy with what has happened to me, aren't you?"

His hand slid over her knee and up along the inside of her thigh. She sucked in her breath as his fingers parted the portals leading to her most secret flesh and stroked along it gently.

"Yes, I'm glad," he said before his tongue slid inside her mouth even as his fingers did between those other lips. "I wanted you so much the first time I saw you that I couldn't control myself. I wanted you and knew I could never have you. I never would have if your luck hadn't turned bad and mine good."

"I hate you," she whispered against his lips.

"You won't in a little while," he said and caught her tongue with his and pinned it against the roof of her mouth while he licked at it tantalizingly.

A warm feeling of surrender engulfed Lorinda just as it had the other times when she had been in his arms. The weakness and the anger at that weakness struggled inside her, but this time the struggle was lost before it even began. She felt her legs part of their own accord to welcome the invasion of his fingers in the warm dampness of her womanhood.

"No, you won't hate me, little love. Not even the tiniest bit because this time it is going to be for you. Now you will learn what it's all about and there will be nothing but pleasure."

He sat up suddenly and flipped her onto her back. Quickly and expertly, he removed the gray dress and the petticoats under it, tossing them along with his own clothes onto the deck. Then she was lying naked under him, his lean, hard body pressing down on her while he held her thighs wide to permit his entry. She moaned with anticipation as he pushed into her soft folds with a steady, unrelenting pressure.

There was none of the pain she had known the first time, but he was big, and a sense of stretching fullness swelled inside her. She gave a little cry of fierce delight, and her arms went around him, her fingers caressing his shoulders and strong back. Just as slowly as he had entered, he withdrew. She moaned in protest and raised her body with his, not wanting to let him go.

He held still for a long moment. Then, while she rolled her hips in aching need, he pushed back with a thrust that took her breath away. She wriggled, not quite knowing what to do, and he slid his hands under her, cupping her buttocks and guiding her into a rhythm to match his. She was beyond speech, beyond teasing, beyond mocking. All she was aware of was the heat of her desire, the thrill of his body moving against hers and the joy of their being together. She was light-headed with the wonder of it.

She felt his lips against her face and turned her head to meet his kiss. Everywhere he touched her she started to tingle, and it flashed through her mind that it had been that way from the very beginning. They seemed to kindle fires in each other that neither felt with anyone else. She didn't understand it, but she couldn't deny the existence of the strong attraction between them. It was almost as though she needed him to make her complete.

"Oh, Kirk, Kirk," she breathed, using his name for the first time.

"Lori, sweet, beautiful Lori," he answered. "You're a girl in experience but a woman in your ability to love."

Emotion swirled through her as her body seemed to melt into his and become part of it. Suddenly she trembled and cried out and then was drifting off on a cloud of ecstasy, carried beyond herself into an unearthly paradise, where Kirk joined her and they clung together as though they would never let go.

"Was it better this time?" he asked lazily when he finally found the strength to move and lie beside her.

"Oh, yes, yes," she sighed, still caught up in the warm vibrations of love, of having become a woman at last. Then she giggled as the thought came to her that if this was what slavery was going to be like, she wanted to be a slave all her life.

CHAPTER 9

The next few weeks were exciting but also troubling at times for Lorinda. Kirk Stryker was one of approximately six to eight hundred gamblers who worked the big riverboats that plied the Mississippi from New Orleans to St. Louis. Lorinda shared his cabin aboard these fabulous floating palaces. She became acquainted with many of the other gamblers and found them interesting, although somewhat flamboyant.

Most of them wore black broadcloth coats and trousers, soft black hats and black high-heeled boots, but that was where the soberness of their dress ended. Their white shirts were cut low in the neck with loose collars, the ruffled, frilly fronts partly concealed by gaudy vests fastened with pearl, gold or diamond buttons. Unlike Stryker, many of them wore at least three diamond rings and another diamond called "the headlight" on their shirts. In the pocket of the loud checked, plaid or embroidered vest was usually a large gold repeater watch set with gems and attached to a long gold chain draped across the front.

Many ship captains on the river considered it bad luck to leave a dock without a gambler on board, and there was never any attempt to hinder their operations. They would set up shop in the main salon, the bar or the barbershop. Occasionally it might be in the texas, a structure on the hurricane deck containing the officers' cabins with the pilothouse on top.

After the first few days, Lorinda found her relationship with Kirk changing. Gradually both of them began to forget that she was his slave and came to think of her as his mistress. That was the way she was regarded by everyone else as well. At first she had remained in their cabin at night when Stryker was at work, but one day as the *Star of the West* was preparing to cast off from the wharf at Natchez, Kirk presented her with a red silk dress, high-heeled slippers, black silk stockings and a handful of rings and beads.

"We're going to add a little class to my act," he said. "Out West when a gambler is working he often takes his fancy lady with him. There they are usually dance-hall girls, so we're going to dress you like one."

Lorinda inspected the gaudy dress with a critical eye. "It's awfully short, isn't it?"

"That's the point, love," he grinned. "We want to show off those fabulous legs of yours. Encased in those black stockings, they'll turn even the coolest head from his cards."

"You mean you want me to display myself so you can have an advantage at cards?"

He shrugged. "You have to admit it's better than dealing from the bottom of the deck."

"I can't do it," she said, throwing the low-necked, ruffled dress over the back of a chair with a gesture of distaste. "I'd feel so cheap and common wearing it."

"Come on, honey," he said, putting an arm around her. "There's nothing common or cheap about you, just the opposite, in fact. You should be proud of the way you look, and in that outfit you'll be sensational."

So, of course, she did it. She dressed in the clothes she thought made her look like a hussy, and she sat on the arm of Stryker's chair with the skirt carefully arranged to reveal a rounded knee and just a hint of silk-covered thigh. It embarrassed her, but she did it. After all, she told herself, she was no longer a lady, she was a gambler's wench and she might as well act like one.

The effect of her presence was every bit as devastating as Stryker had expected. No matter who he was playing, the minute she took her place every eye at the table would wander from the cards they held to the tantalizing view she offered.

"That's a mighty pretty little lady you got there, Stryker," John Powell observed one day. He was a tall, handsome Missourian and one of the most famous gamblers on the river. "Mighty pretty and mighty distracting. Kind of wish she could wear a slightly longer dress."

"She's my good piece of luck, John," Stryker said, "and her legs are part of my luck."

"Hmmm." Powell was a well-educated man, always richly dressed but without the vulgar flashiness of many of his colleagues. He admitted, however, to having an eye for a pretty face and even more so for a pretty pair of legs. "I guess we can't ask a man to leave his luck in his cabin, but as for myself, I'll not play any more until we reach the next town and I can buy a pair of horse blinders to keep that dazzling spectacle from distracting me."

He cashed in his chips and with a courtly bow left the salon.

"Never knew Powell to show the white feather before," mused Colonel Charles Starr, a dignified, amiable man in his late fifties.

Lorinda kept a smile on her face as she waited for whatever the colonel was going to say next. Kirk had told her that the man was considered the biggest liar on the river, constantly bragging about his mythical plantation holdings. His oft-repeated story was that he was a gambler only for pleasure and to relieve the boredom of his life as a lord of vast acres. To back up this contention, he had been known to hire blacks to meet whatever steamboat he was traveling on, to hail him as Massa Starr and report on the activities of his local holdings. It was also rumored that he had hired white men to represent themselves as overseers and come asking for instructions on the management of his plantations. He always obliged, telling them in great detail and in a loud voice what he wanted done so that no one on the riverboat could possibly miss hearing.

But all that seemed far from his mind now as he shifted his gold-mounted toothpick to one side of his mouth and grinned at Lorinda. "No, sir, never did think Powell would let a little gal with pretty legs scare him out of a good pot."

He shuffled and reshuffled the cards, his gaze

never leaving the entrancing vision across from him.

"See here, Colonel, we're not a couple of jakes," the third man at the table said, his mild blue eyes intent on the shuffling fingers. "You can't get away with laying the bottom stock on us, you know."

The colonel laughed good-humoredly and the others joined in. They had all heard the tale of the colonel "laying the bottom stock," ringing in a cold deck, four times in the same hand during a friendly game with four other gamblers. Dealing each of his opponents four aces, he had then sat back and watched the fun. One by one the others had stared poker-faced at their hands and then started betting everything they had. Finally, when the betting was over and it came time to show the cards, the colonel had owned up to his joke and listened to his friends cursing as they redivided the money they'd tossed into the pot.

"I was just thinking, little lady," the colonel was saying, "that I'd like to make a side bet with you."

Lorinda shrugged. "I don't have any money, Colonel."

"I wasn't rightly thinking about your betting money, my pretty," he said.

"Colonel! You ought to be ashamed of yourself at your age!"

"Age may have something to do with performance, my dear," the colonel said, "but it seldom affects ambition."

"Well, you'd better take your ambition elsewhere," Lorinda said. "I'm not only Kirk Stryker's luck, I'm his woman, and his alone."

"Wasn't rightly going to ask you to surrender your virtue, Miss Lorinda," the colonel said. "Rather, I was only interested in preserving my nerves."

"How do you mean, sir?"

"I'll put up a five-dollar gold piece as a side bet with you on each pot."

"And what am I supposed to put up?"

"Actually it's more in the line of putting down," the colonel said. "If you'll lower your skirt an inch each time you lose, I'll pay you a five-dollar gold piece each time you win. Hopefully your skirt will soon be down far enough to prevent an old man from having a heart attack."

Stryker threw back his head and roared with laughter as he reached to pull Lorinda's dress down over her knees. "Who did you say was a coward, Colonel? There. That's a special concession to the elderly and fainthearted."

"Praise the Lord!" the colonel said, raising his eyes piously heavenward. "I'm saved!"

With less experienced players, the effect of Lorinda's display was even more startling. A handsome young gentleman from Natchez managed to lose five thousand dollars on a pair of threes because he was so busy ogling he threw away the third three he was betting on. A fat, red-faced banker from Cairo became so enthralled with the view that he threw in a stand pat hand and lost three thousand dollars.

"You are my luck," Stryker said one night as they lay side by side in their bed on the *River Queen,* bound for St. Louis. "The first time I saw those lovely legs of yours I knew they were going to be my good luck charm. Not only did I win twenty thousand dollars trying to get them, but they've been helping to bring in the money ever since.''

''I thought you were known on the river as a square player, one who never ran a brace like the sure thing players do.''

''No one has ever seen me so much as palm a card,'' he said, sipping contentedly at the wine they'd brought from the salon after the nightly game had ended.

''What's the difference between running a brace or using your paramour to rattle the brains of your opponents?'' she asked.

''Paramour is a vulgar word, my pet,'' he said. ''I prefer to think of you as my lady fair.''

''A few weeks ago you were calling me your black wench,'' she reminded him wryly, shaking her head in refusal when he offered her his glass. ''You didn't answer my question. What is the difference?''

''It's not really my fault if your dress has a tendency to ride up past your knee. Am I to blame if those lechers can't keep their minds on their cards because they're thinking unclean thoughts? Is it my fault that a glimpse of leg turns the slickest con man into a country jake unable to read his hand?''

''If you're not to blame, I suppose I am,'' she said.

''No, not at all,'' he said, filling the glass and setting the bottle down on a shelf. ''I wouldn't say it was your fault, either. You can't help it if you were born with beautiful legs.''

He pulled the sheer gown up to expose the whole length of her legs. "No, sir, you can't be blamed at all. I guess we'll just have to call it an act of God."

The smile on his face was slowly replaced by another look and he slid downward in the bed to place his lips on the instep of her slender white foot.

"No, you can't be blamed because every poor fool who stares at you wants to see more and twists in his chair like a contortionist trying to find a better angle." He lifted her foot in his hand and ran his lips up the inside of her calf toward the dimpled knee. "It's not your fault that every lecherous idiot wants to see your legs the way I'm seeing them, wants to kiss them the way I'm kissing them."

"They don't want to do that," she protested, the huskiness of her voice surprising her. "They don't want to do that—oh, God!"

His lips had saluted her knee and were eagerly tracing a path of fire up the silken inside of her thigh. "Poor fools, poor damn fools. They'll never know how beautiful you are, never know how soft and fragrant and delectable you are."

Lorinda made a strangled sound like a frightened kitten as she realized what he intended. No—no, he wouldn't do that! Not even Kirk Stryker with his advanced notions about women and love would do that. But he was doing it. He was!

His worshipful mouth crept along the crevice that marked the joining of her thigh to her torso, and then he was searing her, placing the brand of his hot breath and seeking tongue on the very essence of her womanhood.

"Please, please, Kirk. Not like that. It's too—too—"

"Too what, my darling?"

She couldn't find words for it. She had never imagined that a man's loving lips could do the things his were doing, that they could create such exquisite torment and cause such unbelievable pleasure.

"Stop. It's too much. I can't stand it!" she cried, but her thighs tightened against his cheeks and her head rolled from side to side in an agony of wanting.

He wasn't stopping. He would probably never stop, she thought wildly, until he had consumed her body and soul.

She moaned and clutched at his shoulders, her nails almost piercing the skin as something inside her exploded and sent her zooming skyward like a skyrocket to burst into multicolored stars and cascade gently back to earth.

Her legs relaxed as the soft afterglow spread through her, and then she felt him sliding up her body, penetrating her easily and once more starting the escalating rhythm that would carry them both to another pinnacle of joyful release.

The long summer seemed to pass in a dream for Lorinda, a dream filled with cards, roulette wheels and faro games, but also a dream of mornings spent in sweet intimacy during which she changed from a frightened girl into a fully aroused sensual woman who proved as adept at the arts of love as the man who was her tutor.

It was a summer of nights filled with the glamour of elegant salons, of dancing in the arms of her lover and of sipping champagne with handsome young men whose eyes told her clearly of their desire for her while their lips uttered polite small talk. It was a summer, too, of new dresses at every stop they made in St. Louis, Natchez or New Orleans, clothes so expensive that even as Lorinda de Farbin she couldn't have afforded them. Kirk seemed to delight in seeing her gowned more splendidly than the daughters of the rich Creole plantation owners or the wives of the wealthy bankers who traveled the river.

"What would they think if they knew their sons were casting eyes at a slave girl," she asked Kirk one night after they had attended a ball in the main salon of the *Southern Lady*, bound from Memphis to St. Louis.

"They wouldn't be much more shocked than they are to see their daughters making sheep's eyes in the direction of a gambling man, a social pariah like me," he said, kissing the rosy tip of her breast.

There were also lazy days on the hurricane deck when Lorinda would sit in a deck chair and stare at the whitewashed little towns dozing beyond the levees, while the majestic river rolled by, tiny wavelets reflecting the sunlight across its mile-wide breadth.

Other towns were more lively. These were the ones where the packets stopped. Usually a sharp-eyed Negro would be watching from a hillock near town, and as soon as he spotted the rising spiral of smoke that announced a riverboat, he would bellow, "Steamboat a 'comin'!" and the whole town would come to life. People would pour out of warehouses and livery stables along River Street. Men with shaving cream still on their faces would come running from barbershops, and women with flowers in their hands would come from their kitchens.

The wharf would be lined solid as the steamer approached the mooring, people staring delightedly at the long trim craft with its two tall smokestacks, a gilded device swinging between their fancy tops, the pilothouse all glass and gingerbread perched atop the texas deck. The hurricane and texas decks would be lined with passengers, the crew grouped on the forecastle to make ready to tie her up as the pilot steered her into the dock.

Lorinda never tired of those scenes, nor did she tire of listening to the grizzled old pilots and hearing stories about the river, which now was her life.

"Yes, ma'am, Miss Lori, this is a plum remarkable river," one pilot told her, shifting a wad of tobacco from one cheek to the other. " 'Stead of gettin' wider down New Orleans way by its mouth, it gets narrower and deeper. From where the Ohio joins her to a point halfway to the sea, she's a mile wide on the average, but from there on she's little more than half a mile wide and gettin' deeper all the way. At the Ohio she's 'bout eighty-seven feet deep, but before she reaches the Gulf, she's a hundred and twenty-nine feet deep."

"Most rivers get wider toward their mouths, you say?"

"Sure do, but the Mississippi ain't like most rivers. 'Spect she ain't got no reason to be. She's one of a kind, so I guess that lets her set the fashion,'' the old man said. ''I heared tell of some English fella, a book writer, calls himself Captain Marryat, and he named her the Great Sewer. She sure is muddy, for a fact, and they tell me she empties upwards of four hundred and six million tons of mud into the Gulf of Mexico each and every year.''

''That much?'' Lorinda asked in astonishment.

''Yes, ma'am. She built that whole area below Baton Rouge, the scientific fellas say, by pushing mud two hundred miles out beyond where her mouth used to be. Took her a hundred and twenty thousand years to do it, but by cracky, she done it.''

He paused and spat neatly out through the pilothouse door. ''She's got another thing she does that most rivers don't see fit to do—changin' her course by cuttin' through narrow necks of land. Funny things happen when she does that. Sometimes folks livin' in Mississippi when they goes to bed wakes up to find they're livin' in Louisiana 'cause the river has up and changed her course. Heered tell once up in Mississippi there was a fella had a plantation with twenty slaves on it before the river changed course and afterwards that plantation ended up in Illinois and all them slaves was free 'cause they'd been transported from a slave state to a free one.''

That story reminded Lorinda of the times whatever riverboat they were on had stopped at Cairo or some other free-state town and she had stood at the top of the gangplank and known that all she had to do was walk down it to freedom. Given the laxity in the way the fugitive slave laws were enforced in most Northern and Western states, that was all it would have taken. But, of course, she hadn't done it. Becoming free meant leaving Kirk Stryker, and she was bound to him by chains stronger than any slave chains.

As the weeks had passed, she had realized more and more that the big gambler was in her blood. His kisses were like a drug she could not resist. His nearness, the feel of his arms around her, were her real existence.

The pilot, reaching for the chain that blew the ship's whistle, brought her out of her brief reverie. She looked out and saw another riverboat coming around the bend ahead. Both craft were trying to stay as close to mid-channel as possible; the dead trees still standing underwater could tear the bottom out of a steamer.

"The *Memphis Girl*," the pilot was saying. "That'll be Jack Seabrook in her pilothouse. That fella will stick closer to mid-channel than a leech to blood. I'll give him a blast to move over 'cause I sure ain't."

The ship's whistle was answered by one from the *Memphis Girl* and both vessels gave way a little, passing so close that each rocked in the other's wake.

"One of these days, when we're going the same way, I'll show that Seabrook that the *St. Louis Beauty* can outrun anything on the river."

Riverboat racing was one of the banes of the Mississippi traffic. Lorinda had heard of several craft that had blown up when their engineers tried to crowd on more steam than their boilers could stand.

She didn't think she'd care to be aboard when the pilot issued his challenge to Jack Seabrook.

"Funniest thing that I ever heard of about the river changing course, though," the man took up his earlier reminiscences, "was what happened to a little town named Delta. Before the river cut through a neck of land, Delta was two miles below Vicksburg and now it's two miles above."

Lorinda laughed and then wandered off in the direction of Stryker's cabin, thinking about all the things she had seen and heard in the short time she'd been traveling. The river was the whole life of the people who made up the crews of the ships who plied it, a life she had never realized existed before.

Her life and Stryker's, however, revolved around the gambling tables. On board there was every kind of gambling known—blackjack, poker, faro, three-card monte and even the old standby of the carnival sharpies, the shell game. And like many of the professionals, Stryker often played for pleasure when he was ashore. Faro seemed to have a strange fascination for the gamblers. They called it "the tiger" and bucking the tiger on shore cost many a river gambler everything he had won on the long trip up- or downriver.

Canada Bill, one of the more reckless of the riverboat operators, had been stranded one time with a friend in a small river town. He had searched everywhere until he found a faro game and began to play. His friend immediately spotted the fact that the game was rigged and had leaned over to whisper in his ear, "The game's crooked, Bill."

"I know it," Canada said, "but it's the only game in town."

Stryker wasn't as affected by the need to gamble as the others were because of his plan to save until he had enough to buy the thousands of acres of land he wanted in Kansas. He did occasionally visit the gambling dens in New Orleans, Natchez and St. Louis, however, and one night after he had dropped a few thousand on roulette in a Rampart Street dive, when he and Lorinda were in their bunk aboard the *Delta Star* as she churned toward Natchez, he spoke again of his ambition.

"Hundreds of thousands of acres of the best and cheapest land in the world," he said. "That's what I want and intend to have."

"What for?" she asked. "Just so you can have plenty of elbow room?"

"To raise wheat," he said. "That's the best wheat-growing soil in the country, and the world is hungry for wheat. People are starving in Africa, Asia, even Europe, and a man would be doing himself and them a favor if he could raise wheat cheap enough so it could be shipped overseas and sold at a price they could afford to pay."

"Would you be satisfied with that kind of life?" Lorinda asked. "It sounds a lot less exciting than betting your last gold piece on a turn of the cards."

He reached out and tousled her hair. "A man gets enough excitement in life eventually, and he wants to settle down, build himself a house, marry and maybe raise a bunch of kids."

Lorinda almost held her breath. Was he hinting

that he might—that they might—no, that couldn't be. There were laws against interracial marriages.

"When you think about it, this is an artificial life," he said. "Exciting, yes, but without the real satisfactions of normal living. You get fed up with it sooner or later, and when I do, I'm going to have the money to buy my land and do what I want with it."

Lorinda laughed somewhat nervously. "It sounds as though you have everything worked out except who you're going to marry—the woman who's going to have all those babies you want."

He glanced at her in the faint light as the *Delta Star*'s whistle sounded mournfully. "Well, I guess I have some ideas about that, too."

Her heart skipped a beat. Did that mean what it sounded like? Sometimes she'd thought he might actually love her, and it was obvious that he could never get enough of her body. There might be worse reasons for marrying a woman, she thought.

"Is it a girl you met out in Texas?" she asked, unable to stand the suspense.

"No, I didn't meet her in Texas," he said.

"Some rich Creole girl from New Orleans, then?"

"Now, you know those genteel ladies would never marry a gambling man," he said. "They seem to think they were born with silk diapers on instead of naked like the rest of us. Apparently they've forgotten that their ancestors were inmates of La Salpetriere, a home for wayward girls in Paris, before they were shipped out to the colonies to marry the settlers. No, the descendants of the 'correction girls' think themselves too good for a river gambler.''

He yawned and settled back against the pillow, but Lorinda couldn't leave the subject alone.

''I hope you're not thinking of marrying some hussy you met on Rampart Street,'' she said.

''I'm not that kind of fool,'' he said. ''Besides, what would I be doing going to fancy houses to toy with high-priced trollops when I have you?''

''Yes, you have me,'' she said with an uncertain smile, ''but when it comes to marrying . . . ''

''Yes,'' he said sleepily, ''when it comes to marrying . . .''

After a few moments of silence, Lorinda said, ''No white man would marry a black slave, would he?''

''There's a law against it,'' he said and yawned again. ''But I guess some men break the law.''

''Do they?'' Her heart was pounding so hard she was afraid he would hear it. ''You mean some men actually marry slave girls and take them to free states?''

''That's what I've heard, but unless the girl can pass as white they're just making a lot of trouble for themselves.''

''Yes, they would be, but if the girl really looked white, what then?''

''Well, then I imagine it would be all right. No one would ever need to know a thing about what she was.''

Oh, God, is he going to marry me? Am I the girl

he was talking about having a bunch of kids with?
I'd love to have his babies. I'd have a dozen if he
wants them!

"Of course, a fellow would have to be awfully
deep in love to want to marry a black gal. He
wouldn't do it just because he lusted after her body.
Hell, black gals are a dime a dozen. A man can
have as many of them as he wants."

"Yes," she said, and her heart, which had been
swelling like a big, beautiful balloon, began to de-
flate. "Of course he can."

"When a man picks a girl to marry, he usually
picks one he can't get into bed any other way,"
Stryker said. "You know, one of those remote
ladies who keep their knees tight together and never
sweat. Funny, isn't it? You wouldn't think a man
would want that kind of female, so aloof and
ladylike that she would just lie there stiff as a board
when he made love to her."

"No, I wouldn't think any man would want a
wife like that," Lorinda agreed and was surprised
to hear how steady her voice sounded.

"But there's something about a woman like that,
a challenge, I guess. You figure that even if you
have to marry her, even if she's cold and unresponsive at first, someday when she gets used to you
she'll start warming up. And when she does, you'll
know you did it all yourself, that all the heat that
may eventually be generated is only for you."

Lorinda tried not to listen. She was crying deep
inside, but not a sound escaped her lips. How could
he be so cruel?

"I know a woman like that. She's a cool blonde

with blue eyes chilly as a Texas norther and a short upper lip that shows her white teeth when she smiles, which isn't all that often. She wears starched white blouses and walks without any movement of her hips at all. Strange though how it gets me excited just thinking about her.''

Shut up! Dear God, won't you ever shut up! Lorinda screamed silently. *Don't you know what you're doing to me? Don't you care that you're crucifying me with words?*

"It sure is funny that a guy who's known really passionate women would want to possess a snow princess like that, isn't it?'' he said ruefully. "I hate to admit it, but I get horny just thinking about her.''

If I just lie here and will it, I may be able to die. When your whole reason for living is gone, why can't you just die?

"Lori?'' His voice was low and husky now. "Lori, will you do something for me?''

She didn't answer, hoping he'd think she was asleep.

"Do me a favor, honey,'' he said, reaching over to fondle her breast. "You remember those times when I've been nice to you with my mouth? Well, how about you doing that for me? You don't mind taking care of me this time, do you?''

As he spoke, he took hold of her shoulders and pushed her face down across his belly.

I won't do it. I won't! If he had asked me to do it for love or even for passion, I would have been glad to, but to ask me to take care of the swelling he got from thinking of another woman is too much to ask even of a slave!

But even as she rebelled inwardly, her lips were moving toward the strong, pulsing pillar of masculine flesh, and she knew that she would serve him as he wanted this one last time. After tonight there would be no more, even if she had to turn to the river again to end it.

"That's my gal. That's my good little gal," Stryker sighed with pleasure as her lips began to give him the special gratification he wanted.

"I don't know why I want that icy blonde. I've had a lot better women in my time—have a better woman right now. But I can't help thinking about that dry peach fuzz and how it would feel to finally get it damp."

CHAPTER 10

Kirk Stryker was sleeping deeply, completely satiated, with an arm thrown across Lorinda, who hadn't slept at all, when she made up her mind what she was going to do.

Her first thought had been suicide, since her life was no longer worth living, but then she remembered something that changed her mind. With her dead, the Wenzels would be forever secure in their possession of Solitaire and the rest of her father's property. But if she were to go on living, there might be a chance that something could be done to dislodge the vultures.

There should be a clue that would help her in the things Kelandes had said that day in court when he had aided the Wenzels in robbing her of her inheritance. Hadn't he said that her mother had had another daughter? Yes, a daughter fathered by a man from Haiti and that they were both involved in voodoo. What was the girl's name? She knew he had mentioned it. It began with an A—Adona? —Alona?—no. Ajona! That was it! And wasn't she also supposed to be a voodoo priestess in the New Orleans area?

Lorinda gloated over the fact that in using everything he could to cast her in a bad light, Kelandes had given her information she might be able to use to her advantage now. Because wouldn't this half-sister of hers know what had actually happened in regard to their mother's conviction and execution for the murder of her lover? If Felice Provost had indeed killed Caliano Valera, Ajona would know. Yes, the thing to do was to find Ajona and appeal to her for aid against the Wenzels.

She had to go somewhere. She knew she could no longer stay with Kirk, no matter how much she loved him or how wildly her body responded to his lovemaking. Her soul would shrivel up and die if she stayed with him knowing how he felt about another woman.

Having decided to leave, she had to plan how to go about it. She couldn't wait until the riverboat reached Natchez; it would be too hard to get back to the New Orleans area. There were slave patrols, and although no one would suspect she was black, they might stop an unaccompanied young woman and question her.

No, she had to go before dawn, and that meant she would have to swim for it against the strong current of the river. That didn't concern her too much, since she was a good swimmer. There was another point in her favor. There was a narrow channel the riverboats used to avoid a large muddy island that was forming in the middle of the river just a few miles above Baton Rouge. From there it would be an easy swim to shore.

As quietly as possible, she removed Kirk's arm and slipped out from under it and off the bunk. She stood looking down at his relaxed face for a moment, then turned resolutely and tiptoed away. She picked out shoes and underclothing, the plainest, most respectable dress she owned and quickly stowed them in a waterproof canvas bag, along with a small bag of the gold and silver coins Stryker had given her from time to time. Then she pulled on pantalettes and a shift, knowing any more than that would hinder her in the water. Hopefully, at this hour no one would be on deck to see her.

With one more heartbreaking look at the sleeping Stryker, she tiptoed barefooted out of the cabin and up to the hurricane deck. Except for the pilot in the texas and a linesman in the bow, the decks were empty. Clutching the canvas bag, she slipped to the rail, climbed over and dropped into the water, striking out quickly from the ship to avoid the paddle wheel.

It wasn't until she was halfway to shore that it occurred to her that she hadn't left a note for Kirk. He would probably assume she had drowned, by accident or by choice. For one wild moment she thought of turning back, but a glance over her shoulder showed that the lights of the riverboat were already several hundred yards away. Returning would be impossible.

"So let him think that," she said. "Let him think I'm dead. Maybe it will ease his conscience when he goes in search of his ice princess."

A few minutes later her feet touched the muddy bottom and she was wading toward the bank. Using the overhanging branch of a tree, she pulled herself up the bank and stood looking around while she caught her breath. She was in a grove of trees, beyond which she could see a few flickering lights—the outskirts of Baton Rouge.

The first thing to do was get out of her wet clothes and into the dry ones. After daybreak she could walk into town and hire some sort of transportation to take her the forty miles to Lake Pontchartrain. Once there, she would start making inquiries about Ajona. To white people, she would pass as white and would reveal herself as black only to those blacks whose help she would need to locate her half-sister.

Three hours later she was on her way to the lake area. Luck had been with her. When she stopped at a hotel to ask about transportation, a farmer and his wife had just been leaving for Covington and agreed to let her ride with them in their wagon. They had turned down the six bits she had offered in payment.

"Shucks, child," the farmer's wife said, "we wouldn't feel right taking money from a poor orphan girl on her way to her aunt's house."

That was the story she had told in the town, and no one seemed to doubt her. Why should they doubt the word of a well-bred, well-dressed young woman, even one traveling alone without luggage? Who would suspect that a girl with such a pale gold complexion, delicately molded features and softly waving black hair was a runaway slave?

"Is your auntie expecting you, my dear?" Mrs. Caldwell asked.

"Oh, yes," Lorinda said. "I wrote her right after pa died. My cousin Harvey will pick me up in the gig in Covington and drive me out to their place.''

''We could drop you there ourselves, if you like,'' the woman offered.

''Thank you, but I'd better wait for cousin Harvey so as not to get things all mixed up,'' Lorinda said politely.

''Hmmm. You know, I just can't recall a family by the name of Benton in that area.''

''Aunt Ethel and cousin Harvey haven't lived there too long,'' Lorinda hastened to assure her. ''They moved there from Arkansas, and I guess they're not too well known yet.''

''What kind of crops did you say they was raising?'' Caldwell asked.

''I didn't say, but it's mostly rice, I think.''

The farmer nodded. ''Good rice country. Sure is.''

Lorinda breathed a sigh of relief. She hadn't been certain about the choice of crop in that part of Louisiana, but aside from cotton and sugar cane it was the only thing she knew of that was raised in any part of the state.

''My, my, I'll bet all the young fellas over there will be glad to see you arrive,'' Mrs. Caldwell said with a motherly smile. ''You're so pretty I 'spect they'll all be comin' a'courtin' before you're there a week.''

''I hope not,'' Lorinda said absentmindedly and then added hastily, ''not until my trunk arrives with the rest of my clothes.''

''You women and your fancy duds,'' Mr. Caldwell said. ''It ain't the clothes that attracts the young fellas, it's what's in them, and you sure won't have any problem on that account."

"Why, Henry, I didn't know you still had a roving eye at your age," his wife laughed and poked
him in the ribs.

Lorinda relaxed and laughed with them, glad that
the conversation had turned to other things before
they noticed the discrepancies in her story.

Finding Ajona proved much more difficult than
getting a ride from Baton Rouge to the Lake
Pontchartrain area. After parting from the
Caldwells in Covington, Lorinda hired a gentle old
horse and rode on to the little settlement of Mandeville, directly across the lake from New Orleans.
It was a wooded area with small rundown shacks
inhabited by squatters, many of them descendants
of transported Acadians from Nova Scotia. They
were a taciturn group by nature and their mixture of
French and English, called Cajun, was difficult to
understand even for Lorinda, who spoke French
almost as well as she did English.

"But no, mademoiselle, there is no such person
here," a brawny blacksmith told her in a more un-
derstandable version of Cajun. "The voodoos stay
away from here because we are all good Catholics
and Father Girard would run them out."

Others just looked frightened when she asked
about a woman named Ajona without mentioning
voodoo.

One crab fisherman crossed himself and spat into
his hand before answering. "Don't have nothing to
do with no hoodoos. Don't want to even hear about
them."

Supposedly, voodoo ceremonies were held on the banks of Lake Pontchartrain, and Lorinda assumed it would be done on the less-populated north shore. It didn't seem reasonable to hold such rites too close to New Orleans, where the police would be more likely to take notice of them. After talking to the squatters in the Mandeville area, she decided it was worthless to try to get information from whites, no matter what their social or economic level.

"Well, old fellow," she said to the horse, "if we want to find out about a voodoo priestess, we'll just have to ask voodoo worshippers. Everyone else is too ignorant or too afraid to talk."

Plodding south around the lake on a deeply rutted, muddy road, Lorinda passed through Lacombe and continued on to Slidell. Outside the town were a number of cabins where free blacks lived, and although it was almost unheard of for a white woman to enter a black section unescorted, she pressed on, determined to find Ajona.

A plump young black woman answered her knock at the door of a newly painted cabin. "I am looking for a woman named Ajona," Lorinda said. "I have heard that she is known in these parts."

The woman's eyes rolled upward; she clutched the well-scrubbed little girl who was clinging to her skirt and backed into the house. "Don' know nothin'. Don' want to know nothin' about that one," she said and closed the door in Lorinda's face.

With the horse trailing after her, Lorinda picked her way through the mud until she came to another cabin. This one had honeysuckle growing around the door and a bench where an old black man sat, dozing in the sun.

"Uncle!" she called, using the form of address most white people used for elderly black men. "Uncle!"

One eye opened and regarded her with a bright, merry stare. "Iffen I was your uncle, li'l missy, you'd be a lot blacker than you is."

Lorinda laughed. "You have a name then?"

"I do," he said. "My name is Alexander Hamilton Holmes."

"Very well, Alexander Hamilton Holmes, would you be kind enough to give me a little information?"

He opened the other eye and sat up straighter on the bench. "Info'mation is what I have a great deal of since I been pickin' it up for all of my eighty-four years."

"Then perhaps you can tell me where I can find a lady called Ajona."

"I can perhaps, but I ain't gonna. That kind of information is bad for white folks, li'l missy."

"Suppose I was to tell you I'm not really white?"

Alexander Hamilton Holmes regarded her solemnly. "If you tole me that, I'd say your mama should have taught you not to tell lies."

"But I really am a person of mixed blood," Lorinda said, "and I have reason to believe Ajona is my half-sister."

"I'm sorry to hear that, missy, cause you seems like a nice li'l lady."

"I don't understand, Mr. Holmes," Lorinda said.

He shook his head. "For your sake, I'd rather hear you say your grandpappy was de devil than Ajona your sister."

For the first time Lorinda began to doubt the wisdom of her decision to find Ajona. The old man seemed so sharp and intelligent that a warning from him seemed more ominous than the superstitious way the others had acted.

"Are you telling me that Ajona is a dangerous person, Mr. Holmes?"

"I'se tellin' you that her kind is better left alone," he said. "Them that dabbles with voodoo are trouble, and Queen Ajona is dabblin' in more than voodoo."

"Then you won't tell me where I can find her?"

"I'd as soon tell you where you could find Papa La Bas hisself," Holmes said, "but I 'spect somebody will be tellin' you sooner or later."

"Yes, that's right," Lorinda said, leaning forward eagerly, but the old man shook his head.

"No. If someone else tells you, it be on their head. I don' want it on mine."

"Mr. Holmes, it is really most important that I find my sister," Lorinda said earnestly. "It concerns a legacy."

He continued to shake his head. "If Ajona need money, Papa La Bas give it to her. If she need anything, she just dance for Papa La Bas and sacrifice the goat without horns and he give her what she want."

Lorinda looked at him blankly. "Papa La Bas? Goat without horns? I don't understand."

Holmes's bright eyes clouded over. "Better you not understand. Papa La Bas and the goat without horns not something for white folks, even iffen they claims they're not."

"Mr. Holmes, I not only have black blood, I am also an escaped slave," Lorinda said. "It's very important that I find Ajona. I need her help."

"Lots of folks needs her help. Lots of 'em get gris-gris from her and lots of 'em sorry they do."

"Then you don't think she would help me?"

"Oh, she help you awright, but you has to do something for it, even if you is really her half-sister."

Lorinda sighed, trying to think of a way to convince the old man. "Do you know who her mother was?"

"I 'spect it was that snake she keep in her garden and dance with," he said, staring down at his shoes.

"Have you ever heard of Felice Provost?"

The old man looked up, his eyes examining Lorinda's face carefully. "She that quadroon lady who hang back two, three years for murderin' her man, fella name of Valera."

"Felice was my mother," Lorinda said, "although I was raised to believe another woman was, a white woman."

He was still searching her face. Finally he nodded. "Yes, mebbe you could be Madame Provost's daughter, iffen it was by a white man."

"It was, believe me."

"And I recalls hearin' awhile back that some-

times Ajona call herself Mam'selle Provost 'fore
she get to be big juju queen.''

"Then you'll tell me where I can find her?''

Holmes shook his head stubbornly. "If I knowed
how to find Papa La Bas, I sooner send you to
him.''

"Who is this Papa La Bas you keep referring
to?'' Lorinda asked impatiently.

"Missy, you must of been raised as white 'cause
you is plum ignorant. Papa La Bas is the devil, and
he the one Ajona pray to, not the good Lord.''

"Oh.'' Lorinda felt foolish. "I didn't know.''

"Lots of people don't. They think when the voodoos dance the Calinda and Bamboula and sing,
*'Oh, tingouar, ye hen hem,/Oh, tingouar, ye eh eh/
Li appe vini, li Grand Zombi, Li appe vini, pol fe
mouril,'* that they is singin' to the saints, but they
sing to Papa La Bas and it is to him they sacrifice
the goat without horns.''

"And that is?''

"A human being,'' Holmes said heavily. "A
chile perhaps, or even a baby. They say Ajona's
snake is the Grand Zombie, and she would not have
the power she has if she not sacrifice the goat
without horns.''

Lorinda was shocked, but she tried not to let the
old man see it. "She has a great deal of power
then?''

"More power than any other voodooeinne in all
this land. As much as those in Santo Domingo,
where voodoo come from.''

"Surely you don't believe in such things, do you,
Mr. Holmes?'' Lorinda asked.

"Missy, I see things. I seen gris-gris put on folks

by hoodoos one day and dey ups and dies de next. Some was white folks, too, with smart doctors and priests with crucifixes to look out for them, but if they didn't go to Ajona or some other juju woman, they ups and dies jest like black folks done.''

"Well, I'm not sure I believe it," Lorinda said, "but Ajona is my only living relative. I have no choice. She's the only person who can help me. Will you please tell me where I can find her?"

The old man sighed deeply. "I tries, God know I tries to set you right.''

"You did indeed. It will be on my head, not yours.''

"Yes, missy. She have a house on shore of lake near Bayou St. John, a big white house, but they calls it Maison Rouge, mebbe because of all de blood, I don' know. Jest ask for it by name, den folks will know you got a right to find it and will point it out to you.''

"I don't know how to thank you, Mr. Holmes," Lorinda said, offering him her hand.

He took it and squeezed it, but his eyes were no longer bright and he didn't smile. "I ain't doin' you no favor, missy, I sho ain't. I hates to see an innocent chile like you go sashayin' into the Red House, I sho does.''

"Perhaps I'm not as innocent and helpless as I seem, Mr. Holmes," Lorinda said, swinging up onto her rented horse. "After all, Ajona and I had the same mother, you know.''

"Mebbe so, but you didn't have the same papa, and hers might be Papa La Bas hisself.''

The old horse trotted off down the road in the direction Holmes had indicated, and Lorinda mulled over what she had been told. She didn't believe most of what he had said about Ajona's power or her evil. She had known that some of the slaves at Solitaire practiced voodoo and had never seen any startling results from it, or anything very evil, either. To the best of her knowledge, voodoo was simply a mixture of primitive African religion and the Catholicism the slaves had been introduced to in the West Indies and Louisiana. Of course, even before the subject of the rights and wrongs of slave trading and owning had become very important, both the Spanish and French governors of Louisiana had forbidden the importation of slaves from Santo Domingo and Martinique because voodoo was known to be prevalent among the blacks there. The authorities of the time had felt that voodoo was dangerous mainly because some of its priests and priestesses preached rebellion against the white masters.

She also knew that the name voodoo came from the name of an African god, Vodu, which had been corrupted to Voudue, Vaudau, Voudoux, Vaudaux, Hoodoo, Juju and Voodoo. The one word, Voodoo, served as the name of the god, his worshippers and the rites they used.

The ban on importation of slaves from Martinique and Santo Domingo had been lifted early in the American period in Louisiana, and during the French Revolution, when slave rebellions had broken out in the islands, large numbers of planters had fled to America, mostly to New Orleans, bringing their slaves with them. It was during this time that voodoo rose in popularity and had been changed to incorporate some Catholic rites.

In recent years the formerly strict rules against fraternization by slaves had been lifted and the authorities had taken a rather relaxed attitude toward voodoo rites. The dances in Congo Square, attended by hundreds of free blacks and slaves, were a kind of modified voodoo ceremony that drew many white spectators. Other more clandestine and orgiastic rites were held in semisecrecy and included, it was said, white participants as well as black.

While Lorinda had been thinking, the horse had been plodding steadily along. Now they were approaching a thick clump of trees that grew almost down to the sandy beach of the lake. She could see lights winking among the trees and hear a voice singing a strange barbaric melody. The words were in the Creole patois, which she had some difficulty understanding, and the husky voice added to the haunting effect.

"I walk on pins
I walk on needles
I walk on gilded splinters
I want to see what they can do!

They think they have pride
With their big malice
But when they see a coffin
They're as frightened as prairie birds

I'm going to put gris-gris
All over their front steps
And make them shake
Until they stutter!"

The voice and the song wove a strange hypnotic spell, and Lorinda felt herself half swaying to its rhythm as she slid down off her horse and stood listening in the gathering twilight. Moving cautiously forward, she could see a house in the grove of trees, quite a large house and painted white as the old man had said it would be.

"That must be it," Lorinda said under her breath. "That must be the famous, or infamous, Maison Rouge. And that low, husky voice must belong to Ajona herself."

She had intended simply to walk up to the door and knock, but, for some reason she didn't quite understand, she hesitated now, watching and listening in the semidarkness.

There was a white picket fence around the house and smoke rising from a brick chimney. It looked more like an ordinary country place than the den of a voodoo queen. It was only the haunting voice chanting Creole words that gave it an air of mystery, that and the two powerfully built black men standing on either side of the door. There was also an expensive gig hitched to two black horses waiting under a drooping cypress tree a dozen or so feet from the house. A tall, thin black in a top hat and livery stood holding the reins and looking anxiously toward the house.

"It would seem that Ajona has a guest," Lorinda whispered to the horse, which was nuzzling her hand in hopes of some sugar. "A rich and important guest at that."

If Ajona was as beautiful as she had heard, it was possible she was entertaining a white lover; so it

wouldn't do to go barging in and get things off to a
bad start. It would be best to find a comfortable spot
under the trees where no one could see her and wait
until whoever owned the gig took his leave.

She led the horse toward a moss-hung tree, under
which there was a thick bed of leaves and swamp
grass. Testing it with her hand, she found it dry and
warm and decided it would do nicely for as long as
she had to wait.

The horse wasn't so satisfied and whinnied plain-
tively, causing the two horses standing by the carriage to prick up their ears. The coachman looked
around nervously. From deep in the shadow of the
big tree, Lorinda could see the whites of his eyes in
the gathering gloom, but she was sure he couldn't
see her.

*I hope my sister's lover isn't too lusty and con-
tents himself with one round of madness in the voodoo queen's ebony arms,* she thought. There was a
thin mist drifting up off the lake, and it was getting
chilly. She pulled her shawl more closely around
her and watched the house for any sign of sudden
movement.

The smoke was still rising from the chimney, but
the chanting had stopped. The men leaning against
the house had their arms folded and were watching
the coachman, who was obviously getting more
nervous by the minute. He peered at the gathering
shadows as though they were menacing shapes
creeping up from the blackness of the lake.

Lorinda was starting to feel drowsy when there
was a sound she couldn't identify from the house,
followed by another chant.

*"He-ron mande
He-ron mande
Tigui li papa
He-ron mande*

*Tigui li papa
He-ron mande
He-ron mande
Do se dan do-go"*

The white smoke suddenly was replaced by a thick, oily black smoke, and a flicker of flame showed at the mouth of the chimney. The lights in the house went out, and there was a muffled scream.

Wide awake now, Lorinda lurched to her feet and moved a few feet closer to the house, straining to see what was going on. She heard the pounding of running feet, and several black people came out of the woods to the north of the house, where she had seen cabins earlier. The two guards had opened the door and were looking inside. Seconds later, a cloaked figure emerged, head down, a hood covering the face. Lorinda was startled to realize the visitor was a woman.

Lights began to show in the windows again. The black smoke and flame disappeared from the chimney top, and the white column stood once again against the dark sky.

The woman hurried to the carriage. The coachman helped her up into her seat. Then he scrambled up onto the box and shouted at the horses, whipping them out toward the road.

The blacks who had come running from the north stood staring at the house for a few minutes and then slowly drifted back to their cabins. One of the guards made sure they were gone, then muttered something to the other. They both relaxed, dropping to their heels and rocking back and forth.

It was then that Lorinda chose to make her presence known. Leading the horse, she moved out of the shadows and approached the house. She was inside the picket fence before the two men on the porch noticed her. When they did, they were on their feet instantly and moving toward her, not threatening but certainly not friendly.

"Joseph, Louis, it's all right," the husky, melodious voice called from inside the house. "Let her enter."

Startled, Lorinda halted.

"Come ahead, Lorinda," said the woman in the house. "Come on in, little sister, and tell Ajona why you think our mother was murdered."

CHAPTER 11

For a moment Lorinda stood rooted, staring at the Maison Rouge in stunned silence. Then one of the guards swung the door open and motioned her inside.

The interior was lit by a group of candelabra set in the four corners of the room. The carpet upon which she stood was deep and richly ornate, as were the drapes at the windows. The furniture was arranged neatly along the walls. Oddly enough, it reminded Lorinda more of the waiting room of a lawyer or doctor's office than the parlor of a house.

As surprising as the furnishings of the room were, the woman who stood waiting for Lorinda was even more so. She was nearly a foot taller than her white sister, and her skin was like polished ebony. She was dressed in a long flowing white gown, sashed with purple, that did nothing to conceal the Junoesque proportions of her body.

But it was the face that most astonished Lorinda; it was like looking at a black reflection of her own. If she had ever had any lingering hopes that perhaps the story of her black ancestry was untrue, they were dissolved in that moment. Ajona's hair was longer but as gently wavy as her own and the features were just as precisely chiseled, but otherwise there was no evidence she had any white blood at all.

"So we meet at last, little sister," Ajona said, her speech unaccented, the words pronounced clearly. "I have watched over you for some time but have never thought it politic to reveal myself to you."

"You—you have watched over me?"

"But of course. One of my mother's last requests before her unfortunate death was that I care for my younger sister and help her if she ever needed me."

"I—I don't understand. I didn't know you existed until a short time ago but you knew—" Lorinda felt as though her head was reeling, but she didn't know if it was caused by the strangeness of the situation or by the cloying scent of incense in the room.

Ajona noticed her distress and gestured toward a doorway hung with purple draperies. "Come, we will go into the other room. This one is to impress my clients; the other is for sitting."

As she followed her sister across the floor, Lorinda noticed the fire had burned low in the fireplace. A large black kettle bearing strange designs and ornamentation was suspended over the glowing coals. They also passed a small table on which rested a crystal ball.

Ajona smiled when she turned and saw Lorinda looking at the ball. "You, of course, saw Mrs. Van der Kellen leaving. She came to me for a reading. If you heard her scream, it was because the reading was anything but what she was hoping to hear."

"You tell fortunes?"

"A *mamaloi*, a voodoo queen, does many things," Ajona said, pulling aside the hangings and ushering Lorinda into a smaller room decorated and furnished in almost oriental luxury.

"This is my sanctum sanctorum," she said, sinking onto a huge ottoman and waving Lorinda to another. "Every *boumfort* should have one."

"What is a *boumfort?*"

"A mystery house." The woman smiled, showing even white teeth. "Maison Rouge is a *boumfort;* it is here we hold our ceremonies."

Lorinda was more interested in her personal mystery. "How did you know that I was outside and why I had come to you?"

"It is my business to know things," Ajona said and clapped her hands sharply. Instantly a young mulatto girl in a short pink dress came through another door.

"You wish something, *Maitresse?*"

"Yes. My sister is hungry," Ajona said. "Bring food for her and tea for me."

It wasn't until Ajona ordered food that Lorinda remembered she hadn't eaten since the evening before; that was probably the cause of her faintness, she thought. "How did you know that I was hungry?"

Ajona laughed. Lorinda's astonishment at her apparent ability to read minds seemed to please her. "Perhaps the *lois,* the spirits of the gods, whisper in my ear. Or perhaps a girl who looks so pale and trembly could be suffering from lack of food without realizing it."

"And knowing who I was and why I came?"

"Again it could be one of the *mysteres* of my art, or merely that the drums talk from settlement to settlement and I know you have been asking about me."

Lorinda felt a little less awed but also somewhat miffed. If her talented sister had known she was searching for her, why hadn't she made herself easier to find?

Before she could ask, the girl was back with a tray of steaming dishes, making Lorinda wonder if dinner hadn't been already prepared and waiting for her. There was chicken in a delicious savory sauce, a gumbo full of shrimp and crab and crusty bread with butter. There was also strong black coffee without the chicory so many New Orleans families used.

When Lorinda had eaten her fill and the dishes had been removed, Ajona began to question her.

"Why is it you believe our mother was innocent of murder and that the Wenzel family somehow arranged for her to be blamed for the death of Caliano Valera?"

"Because I know the kind of people they are," Lorinda said. "I believe it because they had the most to gain by getting rid of her."

"How? What did they have to gain?"

"Well, I—I just feel that if she had been alive, she would have somehow prevailed on my father to free me. And even though I'm of mixed blood, the will could not have been broken if I had been freed."

Ajona considered that for a moment, then shook her head. "No, I think you are wrong. I was in

Haiti at the time of the murder—I had to go there to study—but I would have heard if anything like you suspect had gone on. My people keep nothing from me.''

''But if you didn't ask, would they have told you? Would they have even known?'' Lorinda said. ''I tell you I know the Wenzels. They are capable of any crime where their greed is concerned.''

Ajona smiled without humor. ''Aren't most of us?''

''Not like them,'' Lorinda said. ''Why are you so sure our mother killed that man?''

''Because he was a person who very badly needed killing. In fact, I had intended to take care of that matter myself when I got back from Haiti.''

Lorinda was shocked. ''Then you would have been hanged instead of Felice Provost.''

''No, I would not have been,'' Ajona said. ''I would not have been so foolish as to stick a knife in his heart right in my own boudoir as our mother did.''

Lorinda felt herself paling. ''She stabbed him in her own boudoir?''

''In her own bed,'' Ajona said. ''A better day's work she never did.''

Lorinda looked so horrified that Ajona's expression softened. In a gentler tone she said, ''Perhaps if I told you more of our background it would be easier for you to accept and understand what she did. Jules de Farbin apparently kept you in ignorance about everything connected with your real mother.''

''Yes, he did,'' Lorinda said.

"Our mother was born on the plantation of a Mr. Riley Rinehard in Warren County, Mississippi, the daughter of a mulatto slave and an unidentified white man. Because of her lightness of color and sunny disposition, she was taken into the big house and more or less made a pet of from the time she was old enough to walk. She ate and played with the white children in the nursery, was taught and spoiled like they were and altogether ruined for the life of a slave.

"So when she was sent back to live in her mother's cabin when she was in her middle teens, she was understandably hurt and resentful. She wouldn't do the work she was assigned, considered herself better than people with darker skin and soon became a real troublemaker. And when a black man from Haiti named Doudou Thiam started visiting the slave quarters at night and talking about voodoo, she became one of his most eager pupils. He was a *Bougan*, a kind of high priest of voodoo, like a bishop perhaps in the Catholic Church. He was a man of much power and whether he won Felice through his own talents or through a love-*ouanga* or—"

"What's that?" Lorinda interrupted.

"A charm. There are birth-*ouangas*, protective-*ouangas*, hate-*ouangas* and murder-*ouangas*. Later I will fashion a protective one for you. When it becomes known that you are my sister, you will need it."

Lorinda was eager to get back to the story. "So you think this man won Felice with a charm?"

Ajona shrugged. "Who knows? He is a tall, strong, handsome man even today."

"You mean he is still alive?"

"Oh, yes. It was he I was studying with in Haiti. He is, of course, my father."

"Oh."

"You see, one can inherit the power," Ajona said. "Usually it is handed down from mother to daughter, but in my case it came from my father, whose power is renowned from one end of Haiti to the other."

"So our mother fell in love with him and married him," Lorinda guessed.

"No," Ajona said, shaking her head vigorously. "Doudou Thiam is not the marrying kind. He takes a woman he wants and leaves her when it pleases him. He is favored of Douballa Oueddo, the most powerful of our gods, and can do whatever he chooses."

"And you were born after your father returned to Haiti?"

"Yes, in grandmother's cabin. And when I was about three months old, Mr. Rinehard decided to sell Felice and leave me with her mother. Your father attended the vendue the day she was put up for sale, bought her and took her home to Solitaire."

"Then it was sometime after that that my father married my mo—the woman I grew up thinking was my mother."

"Yes. Apparently she was unable to bear a child, so your father arranged with Felice to raise you as their daughter. Felice had two reasons for giving you up, one was selfish and the other selfless. Without either of her daughters, she could play the charming belle, playing one swain off against the other and living like white folks. She also wanted you to be raised as white, to pass as white all your life. That appealed to a woman who had always hated the small amount of black blood she had in her veins."

Lorinda heard the note of bitterness in her sister's voice. "She wasn't very nice to you, was she?"

"She cared nothing for me until later," Ajona said. "When things were no longer so gay and easy, she began to think of me."

"I'd say you had little cause to love her."

Ajona shrugged. "I pitied her. I despised her way of life, her toadying to whites, her desire to be as much like them as possible, her wish to be white. Later, as she grew older—she was thirty-eight when she met Valera but still beautiful—I had good reason to pity her."

"Why? What do you mean?"

"Valera was ten years younger than she and handsome in a slick-haired, smooth-talking way. He used her. Accepted her love, spent her money, and then when she was penniless he forced her to earn more money for him."

"How?"

"How do you think? In the beds of other men, of course. He turned her into a high-class prostitute for wealthy Americans. The Creoles had their own mistresses."

"How awful!"

"Yes, how awful. To be forced to bed any man who had the price would be unspeakable. When I love, I rule; I am not ruled."

"And that is why you are so sure Felice killed Valera?"

"Yes. I think she at last recovered enough of her dignity to take revenge on him."

"You saw her before she was hanged, then? Was that when she asked you to look out for me?"

"No, I didn't see her. Another *mamaloi* saw her and she gave me the message about you. As I said, I was in Haiti at the time with my father. I had the power, but I did not know some of the more intricate spells. I particularly wanted the murder-*ouanga* he had used to kill a rival Bougan of great power. It is an *ouanga* that no other *ouanga* can protect against. I intended to use it to kill Valera— he would have died slowly and quite horribly—but when I returned I heard that Felice had taken care of him herself. I was glad for her, even though he would have suffered more at my hands."

Lorinda felt a cold chill travel up her spine at the matter of fact way her sister spoke of murder by magic.

"You don't believe that the Wenzels somehow planned what happened after that?"

"No," Ajona said, "But that doesn't mean that I shall not look into it."

"And if you find they did bring about our mother's death in some way?"

A sweet smile lit up Ajona's face. "Why then I will have use for the Bougan's *ouanga* after all— five of them, in fact. I despise them, anyway, and it would fit in with some of my other plans to kill them after making them suffer.''

Lorinda shivered, almost wishing she had listened to Alexander Hamilton Holmes and never come to Maison Rouge.

''But now we must discuss what we are going to do with you, little sister. You can't stay here, of course. There are things that go on here that would curdle your blood. And besides, I don't care for witnesses who are not of the faith. Do you have any plans?''

''I was hoping I could arrange to go North and—''

''What would you do there, become a seamstress?''

''I—I don't know.''

''Then you would wind up walking the streets.''

''But I'm an escaped slave,'' Lorinda said. ''If I should be picked up by a slave patrol, I—''

''That isn't likely to happen,'' Ajona said. ''That young man who so enjoyed you in bed would never report you to the slave patrol even if he were sure you are still alive.''

Lorinda felt herself blushing. ''So you know about that, too.''

Ajona laughed. ''I wouldn't be much of a *mamaloi* if I didn't know what my sister had been doing, would I?''

''Well, what do you think I should do?'' Lorinda asked. ''I came to you for help against the Wenzels, but—''

''We'll do something about them and your precious Solitaire later,'' Ajona said, ''but first we have to get you settled into a new life. Have you ever heard of the quadroon balls?''

''Of course, everyone in New Orleans knows about them.''

''Well, I know a woman, my grand-mère, in fact, who sponsors girls who are supposedly her daughters or granddaughters at the quadroon balls. I understand this old woman has gathered some of them from Bricktop Jackson's brothel on Dauphine Street. If the pious old bitch I speak of can pass off prostitutes as properly brought up quadroon maidens, she shouldn't have any trouble with you at all.''

''But aren't they supposed to be virgins?'' Lorinda asked.

Ajona laughed heartily. ''Yes, indeed, but there are ways of making up for the lack of a maidenhead. A little chicken blood in a membrane of pig gut will fool the stupid white men who set much store by these things. Inexperience is somehow considered to increase the value of the merchandise—as though one would hire a carpenter because he knew nothing of his craft. But to get back to you—''

''I couldn't do that,'' Lorinda said. ''Those girls are groomed for years for that life. Besides, why should I sell myself to the highest bidder?''

''Because if you don't sell yourself to one man for a high price, you may end up selling yourself to many men for low prices.''

''But I have no mother, no one to groom me for the balls, no one to negotiate for my—my sale.''

''You have *grand-mère*, the woman I was telling

you about. The one who sponsors 'maidens' at the quadroon ball. She lives on Rampart Street and she will be delighted to take you under her wing and negotiate for a white lover for you.''

Lorinda shook her head. ''No, the whole thing would be cheating, would be unfair.''

''Unfair—unfair.'' Ajona repeated the word as though she had never heard it. ''Unfair to whom?''

''Well, for one, to the man who would be my protector.''

''Tell me, little sister, was it fair that you were declared a slave, that your property was taken away from you by a white judge and given to scheming white people? Was it fair that you were threatened with rape and sexual slavery by the Wenzel men?''

''No, it wasn't,'' Lorinda said. ''And it wasn't fair that I was used as the stake in a poker game and had to submit to the sexual abuse of Kirk Stryker.''

''Oh, that,'' Ajona said with an eloquent shrug of her shoulder. ''You loved that, every single moment of it.''

Lorinda was indignant. ''How can you say that? How do you know?''

''By the way you say his name. The words are almost like a caress.''

''Oh. Well, it doesn't matter. He has another woman, a pale, skinny blonde he loves instead of me.''

''Then perhaps you would like one of my papa's death-*ouangas?*''

''No, of course not! She can have him. She's welcome to him, always pawing and nuzzling and kissing a girl in places she might not want to be kissed.''

"Hmmm, you make him sound interesting," Ajona said languidly. "I might find him to my taste.''

"He likes blondes," Lorinda said hurriedly. "I just told you.''

"Oh, I know how to create *ouangas* that would make him forget that. Then again, maybe I wouldn't have to use a charm at all. I've never had trouble bringing men to my feet, white or black.'' She got up and stretched like a sinuous black jungle cat, the white dress pulling taut across her conical breasts, flat belly and full, curving thighs. "No, I've never had trouble getting any man I want.''

"You leave him alone!" Lorinda said in a low, tense whisper.

Ajona laughed mockingly. "You were willing to let him go to his blonde. Why don't you want to share him with your sister? Because she's black?''

"You know damn well I don't want him to go to *anyone* else!" Lorinda said.

"That's what I thought," Ajona said with another throaty laugh. "Come, little sister, we will make you a personal protection *ouanga* and then you shall go see *Grand-mère* Gabriella, who shall make a lady of you and auction you off to a New Orleans fat cat.''

"But I don't want to—"

Ajona leaned down and took Lorinda's chin in her strong black hand. "My dear little sister, you have no choice in the matter. Our mother asked me to look out for you. I intend to do just that, but I also intend to do it in my own way. Now, come along while I make the *ouanga*."

"I don't want any voodoo charm, thank you," Lorinda said, resentful at being told what to do.

Ajona had started to walk away and now she whirled, eyes narrowed and shooting sparks. "Oh, so her ladyship doesn't want any voodoo charm! She's much too good and too proper to have anything to do with her sister's silly superstitions!"

"I didn't say that," Lorinda said stiffly.

"But you were thinking it." Ajona's mouth was a grim red slash in her face. "Well, let me tell you, little sister, you will be hated by many in New Orleans because you are kin to me—other voodoo women who have felt my wrath, the wives of men I have helped, the husbands I have arranged things for. They all hate me and because they do, they will try to strike at me through you. Some of them know voodoo, and the others have access to those who do. Not having a protective *ouanga* in the world you have entered would be like going into a lion's cage without a whip. Do you understand?"

"I don't believe in voodoo."

"And you think that will keep you safe from it? Let me tell you, there is a woman in New Orleans who hates me because I am *la grande mamaloi*. She knows you are my sister and may even now be preparing a little wax doll of you. Soon she will be sticking pins in it and preparing a death-*ouanga*. If you have no protective charm, that could prove fatal to you, foolish one."

A thrill of fear went through Lorinda. She had

seen one of those little dolls of death once. A doll representing a husky young free black man who had supposedly won the favors of a girl desired by a voodoo practitioner. The youth had begun to waste away and in two weeks was dead, looking like a gaunt old man. Neither the minister nor the doctor who had attended him could offer any explanation— until they found the wax doll with scores of pins sticking in it.

Shivering at the memory, Lorinda looked at her sister. "I—I suppose if you think your enemies might become my enemies, it might be better if I had one of your charms."

"Yes, it certainly might," Ajona said, reaching into the neckline of her dress to show a small bag nestled between her magnificent breasts. "Even I wear one and I am known as *la grande maitresse* of the voodoo queens."

Lorinda followed the other woman into a third room. There was little furniture in the room; some shelves containing various types of jars and bowls stood against the wall, and a cabinet with closed doors was in the corner.

Ajona took a key from a pocket in the skirt of her gown and unlocked the cabinet. She took out a large cowhide and spread it on the floor, hairy side up. Next she arranged small candles in a geometric pentagram on the cowhide. Then she removed two machetes from the cabinet and placed them on the doorsill, blades crossed. On the blades were symbols inscribed with white chalk—a swirling serpent, a phallic staff and enmeshed triangles.

"That no uninvited spirit may enter this room

while your protective *ouanga* is being prepared,'' Ajona explained. She took a small square of red cloth from the cabinet and laid it on the cowhide in the center of the pentagram.

"This bright cloth shall be the cover of your *ouanga*, and these,'' she said, laying yellow and red ribbons beside it, "we will use to tie it. All the colors must be happy and friendly to ward off evil.''

Bright feathers were placed on the red square and then various leaves and roots. "Balsam leaves, castor bean leaves, roots of the lime tree,'' Ajona murmured as she placed a saucer of flour, a saucer of ashes, a bottle of red wine, a perfume bottle and a tiny iron crucifix in a row before her.

"Sit across from me, little sister,'' she instructed, "and follow me when I chant.'' She brought forth a brazier and started a small fire in a hollow of the stone floor.

"Papa Legba, ouvri barriere pour la; tout Mystere' gider la,'' she chanted in Creole.

"Legba, open the gate for her and every Mystery protect her,'' Lorinda repeated in English.

Ajona took some of the leaves and crumpled them into the brazier to char over the flame. Then she pounded the ashes with a mortar as she sprayed them with wine from her mouth. "Take the two machetes now, little sister,'' she ordered. "Stick them upright in the cracks between the stones on either side of the *ouanga* to keep out the evil spirits.''

One by one she then took the other ingredients

and pounded them while spraying them with wine and mixing in drops of perfume.

"Now a tuft of your hair," Ajona said, handing Lorinda a scissors to cut off a lock, which she tied to the iron crucifix and laid on top of the mixed ingredients. Next came a paring from Lorinda's right thumbnail and a small square of cloth cut from her chemise.

"It must be cloth that has been worn next to your skin," Ajona explained. "This will protect you against even the most horrible of curses, that in which a corpse is dressed in your stolen clothing and hidden in a wooded area to rot away so that you will do the same."

When everything lay in readiness on the red square, Ajona rose and in a single motion pulled the white gown over her head. She stood there naked, her ebony body gleaming in the candlelight.

Lorinda stared at the splendid jungle creature who was her sister, the outthrust conical breasts with their purplish-red nipples, the smooth flat belly with the thick mat of tightly curling hair covering its base and extending to the upper slopes of the superbly muscled thighs.

Then Ajona began to circle the cowhide and the spot where Lorinda knelt, spellbound. At each move of her lithe body, tiny bells attached to her ankles tinkled and light flickered over the marblelike black flesh. With a graceful swoop she picked up the two machetes, lifted them over Lorinda's head and clashed them together.

"May Papa Legba, Maitresse Ezilee and the Serpent protect you from all evil, natural and unnatural," Ajona chanted.

Dropping to her knees, she gathered the red square around the mixture of ingredients and tied it to form a small bag. She attached a gold chain to it and stood up.

"Bare your upper body, girl," she commanded. Lorinda hesitated.

"Do as I say, you little fool! We need have no false modesty here in the presence of the *lois* and the gods."

Reluctantly Lorinda unhooked her dress and let it fall, undid the chemise and knelt at the feet of the voodoo priestess, bare to the waist.

Ajona leaned over her, fastened the gold chain around her neck and let the red bag fall between the white mounds of the girl's breasts.

"There now, little sister, you are as safe as I can make you for as long as you wear that."

CHAPTER 12

"Allow me, Monsieur Maspero, to present my grandniece, Mademoiselle de Buys." The tiny white-haired wisp of a woman in the black lace gown who was introducing Lorinda to a wealthy young man was Madame Gabriella. She was famous in Creole society for the number and beauty of daughters, granddaughters, nieces and grandnieces she had presented at the *Bals du Cordon Bleu,* where carefully reared and educated quadroon beauties were paraded before the young gentlemen of New Orleans as prospective mistresses.

"Philippa, this is Maurice." Madame completed the introduction in a voice as insubstantial as a mist blowing in off the Gulf. "I hope you will be very kind to my dear Philippa, Monsieur Maspero, because she is a flower of rare fragrance and delicate nature. She was raised on her father's plantation in St. Charles Parish and went to school at the Convent of St. Martin in Paris. I would not have the world come upon her too suddenly."

"Mademoiselle Philippa, I am charmed," said the tall young man in elegant full dress and white gloves as he bent over her hand and kissed her fingertips. "I have been watching you with rising expectations ever since you and your aunt arrived."

The poor fool, Lorinda thought. He doesn't know

that for a fee of two hundred dollars of Ajona's gold, Madame would pass off an alligator from the swamps as a young relative.

Lorinda glanced around her. At the far end of the vast ballroom an orchestra was playing, and hundreds of couples swirled around the dance floor to the gay rhythm of the waltz music. The men wore high-waisted coats and ruffled silk shirts and high, black leather riding boots. The women wore brocaded hoop skirts, and their waists were cinched in tight by whalebone corsets. Black slaves in red livery, carrying trays of rum punch and mint juleps, circulated obsequiously. Along the walls spiraling marble staircases swept upward to great vaulted balconies and ballustrades, from which dignitaries and their ladies sat, sipped drinks and observed the ball.

It had been a busy but productive six weeks at Madame Gabriella's house on Rampart Street. Lorinda had all the required social graces but found it difficult to learn to act with what was considered proper modesty—the downcast eyes and pliant attitude expected of women who were, in effect, about to be sold into a high-class form of slavery.

She had found that the delicate-looking old woman had the nerves of a matador and the heart of a pirate.

"You'll have no problem hooking a fat fish," Madame had said, sitting with her feet up on an ottoman and puffing on a thick, smelly cigar. "I've landed some of the most elusive and lucrative fish with bait not half as appealing as you, some that had already been pretty well chewed up, too."

Seeing the crude little old woman in a dirty dressing gown, smoking a cigar and talking like a fishwife, Lorinda had at first thought it was a mistake to entrust her future to her. It hadn't been long, however, until she began to realize that Gabriella had a cool, calculating mind and was an excellent judge of human character, knowing how to turn the foibles of her betters to her own advantage.

"I've been in this business for almost twenty-five years," the woman told her. "It's not a lot different from what they do in fancy brothels like Madame Delacroix's, or even those on Basin Street, where Bricktop Jackson and Bridget Fury hold forth. No, my business isn't much different from theirs except that mostly I'm selling what they call fresh stock. It's no different, but it's more profitable and, in my opinion, more challenging."

Lorinda remembered when it had been time to get her hair done. She had been seated on a hard, straight-backed chair while a mulatto hairdresser did her hair in various styles. Madame had been watching and commenting on the inadequacies of each. Finally the woman had created a loose, fluffy hairdo in front with a sweep down the back of the head to a cluster of curls at the nape of the neck.

"There, that's it. That's the effect we want," Gabriella said, grinding out her cigar butt in her coffee cup and reaching for another from a silver holder on the lamp table next to her. "That shows innocence, yes, and vulnerability, but it also hints at passionate depths waiting for that one man, he thinks, to awaken."

Lorinda's gowns had been picked with the same kind of care. "We want them to be modest but also to suggest a possibility of abandon."

So she had been dressed in pastels or white with her smoothly curving shoulders and arms bared sufficiently to excite interest but never so much of the rising moons of her breasts to indicate indelicacy. The girlish innocence of the hairdo, the artful display of just enough flesh, even the faint lisp Gabriella suggested, all played their part in making Philippa de Buys a success at her first quadroon ball.

The balls were held several times a week. The most magnificent were inevitably held at the Orleans Ballroom, an annex of the Theatre d'Orleans. For the expenditure of sixty thousand dollars, the proprietor, John Davis, had had constructed the most elaborately decorated and finest ballroom in the United States. The outside of the building had little to recommend it; it was very plain with a low, unadorned facade. The inside, however, was breathtaking, with crystal chandeliers, costly paintings and statuary. Private card and reception rooms took up all of the first floor. The second floor held the ballroom, a long, gaudily ornamented room with high ceilings and balconies overlooking the gardens at the rear of St. Louis Cathedral. Its floor was made of three thicknesses of cypress topped by a layer of quarter-sawed oak. At the rear was a wide stairway leading down into a flagged courtyard, where vines and cordials were served and couples could whisper together as they strolled beneath the swaying cypresses and arbors of bougainvillea and night-blooming jasmine.

Lorinda had never seen so many beautiful women in her life. They were, in truth, the very cream of Louisiana's mixed-blood population. Some were darker than others, although they all tended toward lightness of skin, and all were lovely. They more than lived up to the description of them written by an English traveler who had attended some of the balls while visiting in the area. "They resembled the higher orders of women among the high-class Hindoos; lovely countenances, full, dark, liquid eyes, lips of coral, teeth of pearl, sylphlike figures; their beautifully rounded limbs, exquisite gait, and ease of manner might furnish models for a Venus or Hebe."

Lorinda had been taken aback when she had first entered the ballroom, seeing all the young women, each with a doting mother or grandmother in attendance. "Oh, my," she murmured, "I didn't know there were this many beautiful girls in the world, much less in one city."

"Never you mind, missy," Madame Gabriella, sans cigar and dressed as fashionably as the other chaperones, said. "You stand out even among these yellow roses."

And it seemed that she did, because she had already danced with several very eligible young men in spite of the competition. First there had been Gaston de Pouilly, a tall, broad-shouldered man in his middle twenties with thick blond hair and sideburns. He was independently wealthy and yet a well-known architect in the city.

Joseph Gayarre was saturnine and dark, with a little mustache adorning his upper lip and burning black eyes that seemed to see right through Lorinda's gown. He wasn't considered as eligible as the other young men because he was married. It was considered quite proper, even decent, for a man who had established an octoroon mistress in Rampart Street to continue keeping her after marriage, but it was deemed slightly inelegant for a married man to be out hunting for a new mistress after he had abandoned one.

And now there was Maurice Maspero, the son of a former governor. Rich, elegant and dashing, but to Lorinda's way of thinking just a little too young. No, he wouldn't do at all, she decided, as he chattered merrily at her side. His eyes reminded her of an anxious puppy's, and he was overeager to please. He must be at least two years younger than she, and she had no intention of robbing the cradle for marriage or the more irregular type of relationship that was more often formed at the quadroon balls.

"I believe the orchestra is going to play some Strauss," Maurice said as the music began again. "Yes, 'Roses of the South.' That's most fitting for this affair, don't you think, since the room is filled with true roses of the South."

Lorinda nodded, smiling, and with his arm lightly around her waist, his gloved hand in hers, he led her out onto the floor, where other couples were already circling to the exciting new music.

"Mademoiselle, if you permit, may I call you Philippa?"

"Of course."

"Thank you. I've been coming to these balls for only a week or so, but I'm sure I would have noticed you."

"This is my first, Monsieur Maspero."

"Maurice, please," he insisted, trying to draw her a little closer but not objecting when she kept the respectable distance Gabriella insisted on.

"They won't value you if you are too easy to get," the old woman had said. "No man wants what he believes any man can have or anything that is easy for him to get. He wants to think, if men think at all, that this unique woman was created by God for him alone. They think highly of themselves, these Creole men of New Orleans. They consider themselves very special, and they want their white wives and quadroon mistresses to view them that way, also, especially their mistresses. More men have fought midnight duels over their mistresses than over their Creole wives."

No, young Maurice wouldn't do at all, Lorinda told herself, dancing in his arms and smiling up at him. His lips were a trifle too full and his conversation foolish and dull.

"But he is very, very rich," Gabriella was telling her a few minutes later after Maspero had taken her back to her seat, "and now that his father is dead, it is all his. He has only an uncle who advises him on how to handle his estate. With him you probably would not be living on Rampart like the rest of them but in a big house of your own out in the country."

Lorinda thought about that. It would be nice to live in a house somewhat like the one she had loved at Solitaire, a place where she could have a horse and ride through the early morning sunlight, free and unworried.

No, that could never be. Even with the most indulgent of white lovers, a quadroon girl, no matter how fair-skinned, could never be the fine lady Lorinda de Farbin had once thought herself to be. And if she couldn't have that kind of life, it would be better to settle for a man who would give her one of the quaint little houses that stood row upon row where the old ramparts of the city had once been, a man who would be her lover until he married and who would then pension her off with the deed to the house. Like so many of the others, she could then become a seamstress or a hairdresser and lead a comfortable, if not very exciting, life.

"He's very handsome, isn't he?" a soft voice said.

Lorinda turned to find Adelina, a slender girl in a lavender dress, standing beside her.

"Do you mean Monsieur Maspero?" Lorinda asked, noticing that although Adelina was darker-skinned than she, she had gray-blue eyes.

"Oh, no, not him. The other one you danced with, the man with the darling mustache and startling eyes."

"Oh, you mean Joseph Gayarre. I understand he's married."

The beautiful eyes opened wider. "I didn't know that was permitted."

"The white boss man can do anything he pleases," Lorinda said, "as long as he does it to a black person."

Adelina looked shocked. It wasn't customary among the young ladies of the Orleans Ballroom either to consider themselves blacks or to make disparaging remarks about the men upon whom their livings depended.

"I suppose it is unusual for a man who already

has a wife to be searching openly for a mistress,"
Adelina said, "but he is so divinely handsome that
one might overlook everything else."

As far as Lorinda was concerned, Adelina was
welcome to Joseph Gayarre or Maurice Maspero. In
fact, there wasn't a man present she would care to
attract. There was something about all of them that
she found less than appealing.

The rest of the evening passed in a blur of music,
polite talk and endless dances with a wide assort-
ment of dull young men. Lorinda was weary and
discouraged by the time the hired carriage arrived to
take them back to the house.

"You are still thinking about that riverboat gambler," Madame Gabriella said to her as their carriage bounced through the streets. "You will have
to forget him. He is not for you. He will be happy
with his blonde icicle because he can be sure there
is no taint of black in her as there is in you."

"I don't think that's the reason, *grand-mère*,"
Lorinda said, using the form of address the old lady
insisted on. "I think perhaps he valued me less
because I was too willing. I surrendered myself to
him too easily. That made him want a woman who
held herself aloof."

"Well, now you've gone from one extreme to the
other," Gabriella said. "Tonight you carried my
instruction to be cool to the point of coldness. You
were as stiff in the arms of your partners as your
gambler's blonde must be in his."

"I couldn't help it," Lorinda said. "There
wasn't one of them who was particularly attractive
to me."

"No one particularly attracted you." Madame

Gabriella's voice was scathing. "Well, tell me this, my fine lady, does a life down on Royal Street, where Mary Thompson keeps her brothel behind a cigar store and gets four hundred dollars each for virgins, attract you more? Or would you like to file your fingernails into daggers and carry a knife in your stocking like Gallus Lu?"

"Hardly," Lorinda said. "If I'm to be for sale, I prefer to become a mistress, not a light-o'-love."

"Then you had better not hold yourself quite so dearly," Gabriella said. "This was your first ball, so there was not much harm done, and in spite of your aloofness three of the young men seemed very much interested in you."

"Oh, really?" Lorinda tried to suppress a yawn.

The old lady's eyes glinted angrily. "I am referring, of course, to young Maspero, Joseph Gayarre and that good-looking Gaston de Pouilly. Which of them did you like the best?"

"None of them."

"And what, pray, did you find lacking in three well-bred, wealthy young men?"

"Gayarre is married, de Pouilly is too blond, and Maspero is too young and his lips are too thick."

"Is it his lips or your head that is too thick?" Gabriella demanded, puffing furiously on her cigar. "Who do you think you are, my lady? Do you dare to set yourself up as too good for any man but that riverboat gambler you wallowed in sex with from Cairo to New Orleans?"

"No, it's not that. It's just that . . ." Lorinda couldn't explain what was wrong. Under the pressure of Ajona's powerful personality, she had agreed to this masquerade, had convinced herself it was for the best; but now that she'd seen the men she would be expected to choose from, she just couldn't bring herself to consider any of them.

"I think you have forgotten just who and what you are," the old woman said in a low, vehement voice. "You are no better than the rest of these girls. Just because you were raised as white and look whiter than some of them doesn't make any real difference, you know."

"I haven't said it did, have I?" Lorinda snapped.

"No, but your actions show it. You've taken a superior attitude not only to the men who seek your company but also to the other young ladies, and I find that most provoking."

"Really, *grand-mère*, I have no such feelings," Lorinda protested. "I was polite to everyone, but I can't help it if those men are so dull they stir nothing in me, no excitement, no pleasure."

"So it's excitement and pleasure you want," Madame said grimly. "Well, let me tell you, young woman, those are not commodities we deal in here. We deal in hard business realities, of the monetary value of our young ladies. It is the man who is to be excited and pleased so that he will part with his money. He is the one who is purchasing a sex companion."

Lorinda shrugged. "I'm quite capable as a sex companion. That at least I learned from Kirk Stryker."

"Yes, and that is something the candidates for your favors must be made aware of, but in a subtle way. You are supposed to be a virgin, and your sister will provide proof of that for you to use when the time comes, but until then you must tempt and tease but not give. You must promise a great deal but give nothing. Do you understand?''

Lorinda shrugged again and yawned only to have her head suddenly rocked to the side by a sharp blow on her cheek.

''You foolish little bitch! If you were not Ajona's sister, I would have you whipped! You are no better than the rest of us—not as good! We at least are free. You are a runaway slave. If anyone were to point you out to the patrol, you would be dragged off to the slave jail to await your master's disposition.''

Lorinda's face burned from the sting of the old woman's hand, and her eyes filled with tears from the sting of her words.

''You have made a bargain,'' Madame Gabriella said more quietly. ''Are you one who keeps your word or not?''

''I—I'll keep my word,'' Lorinda said. ''I'll do what you tell me to.''

''Good. Now we understand each other. You are to show interest in the men who approach you, but you will respond with restraint until a bargain is made.''

That night Lorinda lay awake, tossing and turning until almost dawn, thinking of the nights of passion and joy she had spent with Kirk Stryker. She could never go back to that, she knew. Stryker had destroyed her feeling for him forever when he had forced her to appease the lust stirred up by thinking and talking about another woman. That was too much for even a slave girl to tolerate.

"I'll never see him again," she whispered to herself. "I don't care if he does own me legally. I'm a human being and he treated me like a thing, a mere convenience. Being beaten couldn't be as bad as that. The lash would only scar my body, but he has scarred my soul."

That was all very clear. What wasn't clear was why she kept feeling his hands on her body, his lips against hers, the strong thrust of his manhood into the hungry cleft between her thighs.

"Why do I have to remember so clearly?" She pounded her pillow in frustration and shame. "What kind of animal am I that I can't get my mind off the things we did together?"

The way his lips had run down the side of her neck and across the roundness of her shoulder and back to the throbbing pulse in the hollow of her throat. The feel of his kisses burning in the valley between her breasts, of his lips seeking the hardened nipples.

"I've got to forget! Got to wipe it all out of my mind! I'll go mad if I keep remembering and yearning for him."

It was then that she began to wonder if it would be possible to experience that kind of pleasure with another man. Had the ecstasy she had felt when her body responded to Kirk Stryker's caresses been possible only because he was who he was, only because she loved him? Or could she reach those heights with other men as well?

She was slightly appalled at such a daring thought. She had heard enough talk among her contemporaries, as well as her elders, to know that most women did not enjoy sex, or at least did not admit to it. She and her friends had been taught that women "submitted" to the needs of their husbands; they did not share the pleasure. A "decent" woman was expected only to raise her nightdress and allow her husband access to her private parts. Then as he grunted and cursed and sweated, she was expected to lie passively, permitting the act but not cooperating in any way.

To respond the way Lorinda had to Kirk Stryker's vigorous thrustings would have been regarded as scandalous by the average married woman.

"Maybe I'm different. Maybe I'm not a proper woman at all."

Many men turned to what were delicately called fallen women because they found their wives cold and unresponsive. But wasn't it their own fault that their wives were that way? Wouldn't they look down on them if they began crying out with pleasure, rolling their bottoms and grinding up against the surging maleness as it ravished them? Encountering behavior like that, husbands would condemn their wives as loose and promiscuous.

"Blacks aren't the only slaves in this country," Lorinda thought to herself. "Women are, too. Maybe that lady up North, Victoria something or other, is right when she says women ought to be allowed to vote and lead the same kind of sex lives as men. After all, if a person has a passionate nature, why shouldn't she enjoy it?"

She had read somewhere a statement by that Victoria woman, and it had been so startling, so different from her beliefs, that she had remembered it. How did it go? Oh, yes. "I advocate Free Love in its highest, purest sense, as the only cure for the immorality, the deep damnation by which men corrupt and disfigure God's most holy institution of sexual relations."

Lorinda thought about the women who provided men with the pleasure they would have been horrified to receive from their wives. Such females existed on several levels—the slave girls on plantations who were forced into their masters' beds, the bawds and harlots of Basin Street, and the fancier ladies of the evening, who worked out of the plush, discreet brothels that had made New Orleans famous all over the world. And at the very top level of such servitude were the girls of the *Bals du Cordon Bleu*, who were sold to be the sexual servants of their white protectors.

"So I'm really a prostitute of a sort," Lorinda concluded. "I shall simply be asked to satisfy one man rather than countless numbers of them as they do at Pig Trough Carrie's down on Gasquet Street. So if I'm to be a prostitute, why shouldn't I enjoy it?"

Knowing nothing about prostitutes except the fact of their existence and a few of the names of the more flamboyant members of the "frail" sisterhood, Lorinda was unaware that the enjoyment of sex was not an inherent part of the life of the fallen any more than it was of the more fortunate. She had never heard that their reputation for being lusty was derived from careful fakery, calculated movements, moans and cries of pseudo passion. So it was possible for Lorinda to convince herself that prostitutes enjoyed their profession and that, as such, she would be permitted the same freedom.

During the latter part of that long sleepless night, her mind went off on another tangent of her dilemma. No matter what the circumstances, she obviously wouldn't enjoy sex with every man. There were some she found totally repulsive—the Wenzels, father and sons, for example. That meant that she was going to have to be discriminating and develop some means of determining which men stirred and pleased her before she tied herself down to one.

She pictured herself waiting in one of those little white houses on Rampart Street for her protector to call, knowing that when he took her, his caresses would have no meaning, that she would feel nothing in his arms. She imagined living through a charade like that for the rest of her life.

"That would be ghastly. That would be a living hell," she whispered into her pillow. "I've got to know before I accept any offer. I couldn't face a whole lifetime without something at least approaching those months with Kirk."

How could she find out her reaction to a man without actually trying him? After all, the Quadroon Balls were not orgies. The girls were there to be looked at and judged, not handled—at least not beyond a certain point. Madame Gabriella had told her, "You must promise a great deal but give nothing."

Lorinda didn't think that would work. Perhaps

what she should do was promise a great deal but give enough to find out what she had to know, let her prospective buyer touch and kiss her so she could judge her response to him. This was too important to enter into blindly. She had to be sure that even if she didn't care for a man, she could at least enjoy his lovemaking.

Up until now she had just let things happen to her. It was time she took charge of her own life. By using her own methods, she would be doing something to assure at least a small degree of happiness in the future. That was important to her, very important.

CHAPTER 13

"I think that divine Monsieur Gayarre is going to speak to mama tonight about me," said Emeline Lovette, the girl Lorinda liked least among those attending the balls at the Orleans. "I shall like that because he has the most ardent eyes I have seen on a man."

"You should know more about him than that," another girl remarked. "You've spent enough time with him in the darkness of the garden to know all there is to know."

Emeline tossed her dark head disdainfully. "We were only smelling the honeysuckle. A young lady in as much demand as I am does not have to permit undue liberties as some girls do."

Lorinda didn't know who the barb was aimed at, but she gave no indication she had heard. What irritated her most was that there seemed to be no secrets in this place, not on the floor of the ballroom, in the gardens or here in the powder rooms, where the girls chattered like magpies about one another and the men they met. The balls had the reputation of being more strict and straitlaced than their white counterparts but men, being what they were, especially the well-to-do young Creole men, a girl's virtue was bound to be tested and in some cases found wanting. Each incident, real or imagined, was grist for the gossip mill, and Lorinda found the whole thing rather childish and distasteful. So she was polite but kept her own counsel, not caring to become involved in their petty prattle. But she did resent Emeline and her hypocritical morality.

Maybe I ought to teach her a lesson, Lorinda thought to herself. It would be easy to take the hot-eyed Joseph away from her. Except for the last night or two, his torrid glances were mostly for me, and I suspect that with just a little encouragement he would come trotting right back. That would teach Emeline a lesson and give me an opportunity to discover what lies behind Gayarre's burning looks.

It was about time she investigated Gayarre, anyway. This was her fifth ball and since *grand-mère* considered him the third most eligible candidate for her protector, she would have to discover for herself if he came up to her standards as a potential lover. She was sticking to her plan to take charge of her own life and was systematically checking out the way different men affected her. Every evening, after an ice at intermission time, she would walk with a different man in the garden.

Maurice had been first because he was the richest and youngest. She was interested in money not because she was avaricious—those raised in luxury seldom are—but because a great deal of money was the means to the end she had in mind. If she became Maurice's mistress and played her cards right, he would probably be very generous with jewels, if not cash. Jewels could be converted into money and a slave's freedom could be purchased with money. She was almost certain that if she were to plead with Kirk Stryker, he would free her now that she was no longer of any use to him. But she was too proud to do that; she would never grovel to him. But a straightforward business deal was another matter. After she had accumulated several thousand dollars, she would offer to buy her freedom, and once rid of the stigma of slavery she could make her own life. Yes, Maurice was a definite possibility as a source of that money, but first she had to know how he might be as a lover.

"Philippa, you are so beautiful," he had whispered as they sat in the garden, sheltered from view by foliage and hanging moss. "So beautiful that I am almost speechless in your presence."

"There are times when one doesn't need to do a lot of talking," she told him. "Times when the pressure of a hand or some other kind of contact are just as important."

"But I wouldn't dare," the youth said. "You are like a fragile flower that touching might destroy forever."

Lorinda laughed softly. "I'm not all that fragile, Maurice, I assure you."

"B—but," he stuttered, and she grimaced, reminded of Isaac Morgan and his equally hesitant way of approaching her. Apparently she was going to have to help him just as she had Isaac; she hoped it didn't turn out as unsatisfactorily.

She snuggled closer to the boy and whispered, "You may touch me if you like, Maurice."

"I—I m—may? Oh, my. W—Where do I st—start?"

Lorinda sighed. Finding out if Maurice was right for her was going to be more difficult than she had figured and she would have to be more aggressive than a girl attending the *Bals du Cordon Bleu* had any business being. An aggressive octoroon was *contra bonos mores,* against good morals, as the Creoles phrased it. Perhaps she should just forget the whole thing.

Then she was struck by a thought that steeled her determination completely. If her masquerade as Philippa de Buys were discovered, she would be subject to seizure by the slave patrol. At her master's pleasure, she could be lashed or even branded as a runaway.

She reached up and patted her escort's face. "Dear Maurice, what would you say if I told you I've been wanting you to touch me ever since we first met?"

"Why, I—I'd say that was wonderful, b—but—"

"So why don't you start by putting one hand here," she said, pulling his right arm around her waist and placing his left hand on the swell of her breast, "and the other one here."

"Oh, Philippa, I love you so much!" Maurice gasped, and she could feel him shaking.

"Now you should kiss me."

"Y—yes, I want very much to do that," he said and lowered his lips to hers.

The kiss was stiff and awkward, his hands unmoving against the silky fabric of her dress.

Lorinda sighed. This was going to be difficult.

"There now, isn't that nice?" she whispered, turning a little so her breast pushed into the palm of his hand and he could feel the nipple rising in response to his touch.

"Ummm. Nice," he said and then made a half-strangled sound as she ran her tongue teasingly along his closed lips.

She could feel his heart pounding, and he was shaking so badly he could barely keep his teeth from chattering.

The boy has to be a virgin, she decided. She was willing to do a lot of things to gain her freedom, but did she really want to seduce a virgin? It would take a lot of hard work and patience for very little reward, she thought cynically.

"Dear, dear Maurice," she whispered after a few moments longer of futile grappling. "I think we'd better go in. I'm afraid I can't control myself much longer. You are so—so exciting."

She was breathing just fast enough to lend some credence to her lie, and as he followed her back into the ballroom, the youth was preening like a peacock.

There might be something to recommend such tactics, she thought. Maybe if she kept telling Maurice how good he was, he might gain confidence and eventually become the exciting, virile man she wanted and needed.

In the meantime she would check on what Gaston de Pouilly had to offer.

She faced Gaston at the next ball.

Her problem with Gaston was entirely different.

He needed no encouragement and no instructions. The difficulty was to keep the situation in hand, to give something but not everything.

"The moonlight becomes you, little one," he whispered to her on a walk through the ballroom courtyard. "I would love to see you running naked through the grass with the moonlight shimmering on your pale gold flesh," he added lustily while his lips pressed against the side of her neck.

"Oh la, Gaston," she said, tapping him with her fan, "a girl could lose her *Cordon Bleu* for doing just half of that."

"And I would love to pursue you until you fell laughing in the dewy grass and opened the gates of paradise to me."

"You are making me blush," she said, but his kisses only became bolder, brushing across the modest décolletage of her gown to caress the tops of her breasts.

"You have nothing to blush about," he assured her, molding his hand around the firm mound of her left breast and kneading it gently. "You have a body that begs to be worshipped."

"But according to the rules of the *Bals du Cordon Bleu* that worshipping should be done in a more formal, contractual way, in a small white house on Rampart Street."

Gaston smiled at her sadly. "That is all very well when one can afford it, but when one's father has been so unfortunate at cards that one is left dependent on one's earnings as an architect.. Well . . ." His shrug was eloquent.

"Oh, I'm sorry, I didn't know," Lorinda said

and felt a sharp sense of disappointment as she realized he wasn't going to be of much help to her in regaining her freedom. At the moment, however, it wasn't too terribly important, because his fingers had slipped down inside her clothes and were deftly manipulating the aroused nipple while he whispered into her ear.

"I'd like to have you stripped down to your gorgeous hide, naked except for black silk stockings and a ribbon under your breasts. I'd set you on my lap so my hands could roam over you at will. I'd fondle the tender mounds and kiss the sweet cherries on top, slide my hands up and down the curve of your back and over the tempting roundness of your bottom. And when I finally touched that nest of fluffy hair between your thighs . . ."

Remember, you are to promise much but give only a little, Lorinda reminded herself, but the advice was difficult to heed with Gaston's fiery tongue deep in her mouth and his fingers turning her nipple into a point of fire. In just a few minutes he would be asking for a great deal more than she had intended to give, and by the languor in her thighs and the rising heat inside her, she knew it would be almost impossible to deny him.

The only thing fighting that urge to say yes was the fact that a protector without money would be no protector at all—even Gabriella would have to admit that.

"Please, Philippa, my darling, lovely Philippa. Let me. Give me the sweet joy of knowing you tonight."

She wanted to cry, "Yes, yes, and hurry, please hurry!" She knew she could respond to Gaston's lovemaking, that at least one other man than Kirk Stryker could arouse her, and somehow that was a victory over Stryker. Besides, she'd had an active sex life for several months but, after leaving Stryker, had not made love for long, aching weeks. She knew that Gaston would be able to appease the craving of her body, and she wanted desperately to let him take her. But suddenly cold reason stopped her. He had no money and she couldn't buy her freedom without it.

"Philippa, please," he begged.

She tried to say no, but she didn't have the strength. Her limbs felt as unsteady and weak as a rag doll's. He curled her fingers around the hard swelling of his manhood and moved them up and down its length.

"You want it, love, you know you do," he said triumphantly as she tightened her grip. "There is a cozy place over near the fence where the leaves are always dry. You and I could be very happy there."

So this wasn't the first time he had lured a *Cordon Bleu* girl into indiscretion. That knowledge gave her the strength to fight off her languorous desire. There was more than one way to run faster, she thought, and deliberately increased the tempo of her caressing fingers.

"Philippa? Easy. You're going too fast. Don't do that, darling."

She wasn't listening, and in a few more seconds he stiffened and she felt a jerking under her hand

and a warm wetness soaking through the cloth.

"Oh, what happened?" she asked, looking up at him with round, surprised eyes. "I—I guess I got carried away. It was such a strange desire. I just didn't want to stop."

"Yes," he said shakily. "This is most embarrassing, but I'm afraid I'll have to take leave of you at once. My trousers are quite ruined."

"Oh, I'm sorry," she said. "But perhaps it is better this way."

"Better for whom?" he asked.

"For me. I still keep my virtue intact for the man who will be my protector. You said yourself you don't have the money for a Rampart Street house."

"I haven't," he said. "Is that all you think about, money?"

" 'White man run fast, but nigger run faster,' " she said, quoting an old slave song, and he stormed off in a rage of embarrassment and frustration.

That had taken place two nights ago at her fourth ball, and now she was sitting in the powder room at the beginning of her fifth, mulling it over.

"You seem distracted tonight, Philippa," said a soft, familiar voice. "Is something wrong?"

Lorinda glanced around to where Emeline had been sitting, but the girl was gone, as were most of the others. Adelina Valente was now sitting next to her, studying her pretty reflection in the mirror.

"No, nothing's wrong," Lorinda said and smiled at the younger girl. "I was just thinking it might be a good idea to show our friend Emeline that she isn't as irresistible as she seems to think."

Adelina looked alarmed. "You better be careful with that one. They say funny things about her."

"What kind of funny things?"

"That she is mixed up in voodoo," the tiny girl said. "That she has a love-*ouanga* out on Joseph Gayarre and he's about to fall right into her arms."

"We'll see about that," Lorinda said. "We'll see how strong her voodoo charm is when I start batting my eyes in Joseph's direction."

"You could get in trouble, Philippa," Adelina warned. "That girl has a nasty side to her."

"I think she's nasty all the way through. I haven't seen any nice side to her at all."

"You could cause trouble with Maurice Maspero, also," Adelina said. "He thinks you belong to him, and if you start casting eyes at Gayarre, he could get real mad. And Creoles do crazy things when they're jealous and angry."

"I don't know what you're talking about," Lorinda said, her mind already busy with plans to ensnare Joseph Gayarre. He was beginning to look better and better now that Gaston had proven to be practically penniless and Maurice a babe in arms where sex was concerned. With Gayarre she might get the vigorous lovemaking she wanted plus the money she needed to buy her freedom.

"You could even cause a duel," Adelina was saying, "although Maurice would be a fool to provoke one with Joseph, who is deadly with both épée and pistol. But you know how hotheaded and proud the Creoles are, and Maurice might do it if he thought Gayarre was taking you away from him."

"I can handle Maurice," Lorinda said. "I can twist him around my little finger and make him like it."

Adelina regarded her sadly. "I like you, Philippa, but you seem to have grown hard in the last few days. You've changed. You don't seem to care about anyone but yourself."

Lorinda shrugged and got to her feet. "Maybe it's because I heard that song the other night. You know, the one that ends 'White man run fast, but nigger run faster.' From now on, I'm going to run faster."

Adelina looked distressed. "I wish you wouldn't use that awful word."

"What awful word?"

"Nigger. You know we're not that. We're really more white than black."

From someplace in the past, so far back that it hardly seemed to have happened in the same lifetime, Lorinda remembered saying something similar to her maid Sissy. No, that hadn't been her, that had been Lorinda de Farbin, a girl who was dead. She was now Philippa de Buys and she was going to get somewhere no matter how she had to do it.

"I'll see you later, Adelina," she said and started out the door.

"Be careful, Philippa," the girl called after her. "Please be careful. I'm so afraid something awful is going to happen."

Nothing awful is going to happen, Lorinda assured herself as she stepped into the ballroom. Young men came to ask her to dance the moment they caught sight of her, but she turned them all down. Nothing awful can happen if I run so fast that nothing and nobody will ever be able to catch me.

She spotted Joseph Gayarre at the bar just as he was being handed two glasses of champagne. Looking across the room, she saw Emeline sitting primly on a chair between two potted palms, waiting for him.

Gathering up the train of her gown, she swept regally across the floor. Every eye in the room swung to watch her.

Gayarre's eyebrow lifted and his fiery eyes narrowed as she relieved him of one glass of wine without asking permission. The hard line of his mouth twisted into a smile when she said, "Ah, Joseph, how nice of you. You must be a mind reader to realize that I was dying for a sip of champagne."

"Perhaps not so much a mind reader as hoping I might find warmth where I have so far found only chills," he replied.

"Chills, Joseph, are often followed by fever," she said and met his gaze with such utter frankness that no one could have mistaken the invitation in her eyes. "Don't you find it terribly warm in here?"

"Yes, I do," he said, ignoring Emeline and her attempts to signal him from across the room. "Shall we go for a stroll in the garden?"

She nodded and took another sip of champagne, giving Emeline a broad wink over the rim of the glass.

Gayarre took their glasses and set them down,

then turned to take her arm. There was something almost savage about the pressure of his fingers, and for a moment Lorinda doubted her wisdom in renewing the man's interest in her. But remembering her determination to run faster, she shrugged and let him lead her out into the darkness of the garden.

"You have been very cool to me on previous occasions," Gayarre said as he steered her down a path toward the shadowed areas at the rear. "Now you have suddenly become more friendly. Is there a reason?"

"Not really," she said. "Except that I've been hearing so many nice things about you."

"And what would those be?" he asked.

"Oh, the girls talk about how masterful you are and get all excited that you might make an offer for them."

His laugh was short and harsh. "Well, offers may not be precisely what I have in mind. I have a wife, you know."

"So I've heard," she said as they entered an arbor where the honeysuckle hung low. "And it has made me rather hesitant to—"

"The fact that I am married might make it somewhat difficult to set up the kind of formal arrangement that *Cordon Bleu* girls prefer, but there are less formal arrangements that provide their own stimulation and excitement."

His words and voice told Lorinda she had made a mistake. He was not looking for a long-term mistress; he was looking for naive girls to play with, not to protect.

In her desire to get ahead as fast as possible, she had made a bad mistake. She had nothing to gain from this encounter, and it would be best to conclude it quickly before she was in over her head.

"I don't think the organizers of the balls or my *grand-mère* would approve of your 'less formal arrangements,' " she said, turning to leave. "And I don't approve of them myself."

The harsh laugh sounded again as he grabbed her and yanked her roughly into his arms. "You asked for this by luring me out here. It's too late to change your mind."

His mouth was like a cruel brand, his lips crushing the softness of hers and his tongue thrusting brutally past her teeth. She twisted her head and tried to speak, but her words were smothered as he lifted her from her feet and crushed her body against his. She felt his hard masculinity pressing against her, overpowering her with its savage demand.

"No! No! No!" she gasped the moment her lips were free. She struggled to free her arms, butting her head against his chest.

"Shut up, you little fool!" he grated, his voice thick with lust and anger. "You asked for this and you're going to get it!"

"No, no, I didn't! This is not what I wanted!" she said, struggling helplessly as his hand slid down her back to grasp her buttocks, forcing her lower body tighter against his.

"Feel that, bitch?" he snarled and ground viciously into her softness. "You did that to me and you're going to undo it."

"No, no, you can't do this to me!"

"Shut up, bitch! What right do you have to tell a white man what he can or cannot do?"

The words infuriated her. She kicked at his shins with her pointed dancing slippers. He grunted but didn't let go of her.

Her struggles were as furious as they were futile; gradually they weakened as her strength waned. His kisses and the feel of his maleness caused her heart to pound and her blood to race, but it also caused a limpness in her limbs that made fighting even more difficult.

Gayarre dragged her into the deeper darkness at the far end of the bower, backed her up against a post and held her there, his hands like iron claws around her arms.

"Now listen to me, bitch," he growled. "I intend to have you. I have intended to all along and you implied you wanted the same thing when you sailed across the ballroom and practically asked me to bring you out here. If you've changed your mind, that's too bad. I haven't."

He shifted his grip on her, holding both arms behind her with one hand and using the other to pull her skirts up her body.

"Don't. Please don't!" she moaned, hating her weakness and her rising excitement.

Holding her against the post with her skirts hiked up around her waist, Gayarre explored under the petticoats and shift. She felt his fingers roving over her buttocks, across the flatness of her belly and undoing the drawstring of her pantalettes.

"Now, little lady, you're going to be just as the

Lord intended you to be, bareassed and ready for action," he said and yanked the garment down and off.

Lorinda had ceased to struggle. There was no strength left in her. The upsurge of lust his rough caresses had triggered left her helpless in his hands. The months with Stryker had trained her body to respond to a man, and it did so now in spite of all her efforts to deny it.

"That's better," Gayarre said. "I knew you'd like it once we got started. Before I'm through, you'll be begging for more."

He placed her hands on his shoulders, ordering, "Hang on," lifted her legs and placed one on either side of his waist, then began pulling her toward him.

She wanted to cry out, to protest against the way he was treating her, against the humiliation of being taken like some common street girl, but all she could do was cling to his coat and gasp for breath.

His mouth was on her shoulder, teeth biting into the tender flesh even as his fingers dug cruelly into the firm mounds of her bottom. She quivered with fear and something she didn't care to put a name to when she felt the hard roundness of his shaft ramming against the portals of her womanhood.

"This is going to be good," Gayarre panted, bracing his feet and drawing the sheath of her elastic flesh over his.

Lorinda moaned and her buttocks began to roll in Gayarre's hands. It didn't matter who this man was or how she despised him. The only thing her body cared about was the purely animal satisfaction of feeling him deep inside her, of reveling in the contact that sent such messages of pleasure to her brain.

"You're good, you little black witch," he murmured huskily.

"Harder. Harder," she gasped, tightening her legs around his waist and grinding her throbbing inner flesh onto the savage pylon.

"I'll give you harder!" Gayarre snarled, slamming into her in a deliberate effort to bruise her back on the pole supporting the arbor.

Lorinda didn't care. She was beyond feeling pain. If she had to spend the rest of the night picking splinters out of her bottom, so be it. For the moment, she was lost in the savage joy of their coupling. As long as their bodies were joined in a bond of primitive pleasure, there was no room left for other emotions.

Her breath was one continuous sob; she felt the beginnings of her orgasmic spasming just seconds before Gayarre jerked her violently backward and then forward as he reached his own completion.

"You damned hot little witch," he sneered as he let her slide to the ground. "You are good, but you sure as hell were not a virgin."

Lorinda turned her back to him, her intense dislike of the man returning along with her sanity. All she wanted was to be rid of him. She had no desire to talk about what they had done, nor to be reminded of the shameful way her body had responded to his rank maleness.

"I said you were not a virgin," he said, grabbing a handful of her lustrous hair and yanking her around to face him. "So what are you doing at the quadroon balls in the first place?"

"None of your damn business!" she flared, pull-ing free of his grasp and picking up the pantalettes he had stripped off her.

"Well, maybe I'll make it my business," he said. "You're just what I've been looking for, a fancy gal with a passion to match her beauty."

"You can forget that," she said and turned away to draw on silk and lace undergarment, "because you're not going to get it, not ever again."

"The hell I'm not!" he slapped her hard across the bottom as she leaned over to step into her draw-ers. "My carriage will be waiting for you after the next ball. It will bring you to my house and you will spend the night."

Lorinda stared at him open-mouthed. "What about your wife?"

"My wife is very broad-minded, as you'll dis-cover," Gayarre said. "She likes entertainment of an unusual nature and will probably share her bed with us. You may find yourself the filling in a most unorthodox sandwich."

Lorinda felt sick. She had heard rumors of such depraved activities taking place among the more decadent of New Orleans aristocrats, but she had never expected to come face to face with it herself. Revulsion and anger filled her.

"Don't bother to send a carriage," she told him with cold fury, "because I'd die before I got into it. And as for joining a party with you and your wife, no power on earth could make me consider such a thing."

She ran from the arbor and hurried up the path toward the ballroom entrance.

"The carriage will be waiting," he called after

her, ''and you will get into it, or you'll live to regret
the day you were born.''

She didn't deign to answer but she was thinking,
*Not only will I not get into it, I won't even be here.
No, my time at the Orleans Ballroom is over—over
forever!*

CHAPTER 14

Lorinda awakened the next morning feeling depressed and edgy. On returning to the house the night before, she had taken a hot bath in the huge wooden tub Madame Gabriella kept for her girls. She had scrubbed her body thoroughly, soaping and resoaping it in a desperate effort to remove the taint of Joseph Gayarre's lovemaking. Afterward she had scrubbed her teeth and mouth with salt water. Getting out of bed this morning, she repeated the salt-water wash but still felt unclean.

It wasn't that she hadn't been aroused by his assault on her senses or that it hadn't alleviated the sexual tension that had been building up in her. The reason she felt soiled and used had more to do with the fact that Gayarre had known he could take her without going through the formalities that led to the established liaisons the balls were supposed to foster. He had known that she was "easy" and had expected her to be so far gone in sexual degeneracy that she would be willing to join in an arrangement the French called ménage à trois.

Well, he had picked the wrong girl. Emeline might be eager enough for his caresses and dubious protection to agree to such a life, but she wasn't, no matter how much her body yearned for a vigorous, imaginative lover.

But what would come of his implied threat? What if he told the organizers of the balls that he knew Philippa de Buys was not a virgin because he had enjoyed her himself and it had not been the first time for her? It would be a matter of a white man's word against that of an octoroon. There could be no doubt whose word would be accepted.

If that were the case, what could she do? Leave New Orleans as quickly as possible? Run away again? Where would she run to? Back to Maison Rouge, to throw herself on the mercy of her half-sister? Ajona had gone to considerable trouble to set up this arrangement for her and would be quite upset if it turned out badly. Suppose she went someplace else? How could she get along? She knew nothing except the social graces and how to ride a horse. There just didn't seem to be any way out, no way at all.

Lorinda gave up thinking about it and went down to breakfast with Madame Gabriella and Celeste, the newest recruit.

"Is there some problem, my dear?" Gabriella asked. "You look pale and out of sorts."

"No, nothing, *grand-mère*."

"Then it has nothing to do with this?" the old lady asked, reaching into her sewing basket and taking out a doll-like object. "Your glumness has nothing to do with this death-*ouanga* the maid found on the steps this morning?"

Lorinda stared at the floppy arms and legs, the travesty of a human face and the numerous black-headed pins that had been stuck into it. She heard Celeste gasp in horror and glanced from her to Madame Gabriella's grim face.

"Well, it doesn't look much like me, does it?" she said, trying to make light of it.

Madame was not amused. "You know who is responsible for sending this, do you not?"

"Emeline Lovette?" Lorinda guessed.

"Who else?" The older woman's voice was sharp. "You also know what's behind it."

Lorinda shrugged. "I suppose she has a grudge against me."

"A grudge? This means that female hates you enough to claw your eyes out, to knife you in the back, to poison you, if she could."

"But she can't, so—"

"So she resorts to this instead."

"Which can't harm me in the least," Lorinda said.

"Do you really believe that?" Gabriella looked angry and disgusted at Lorinda's careless answer. "Don't you know the power of *ouangas?*"

"I have a protective one of my own," Lorinda said, to placate the woman. "Ajona prepared it for me the first day we met."

"Yes, and you have foolishly left it lying in a drawer in your room among handkerchiefs and sachets. A personal *ouanga* has only the strength its owner attributes to it."

"I'll go get it and put it on," Lorinda said.

"You had better, but I'm not sure that will be enough. This may be a matter for *La Grande Maitresse* herself."

"No, please don't bring Ajona into this," Lorinda said. "The fault is more mine than Emeline's. Perhaps a note of apology from me will satisfy her."

Gabriella snorted. "I've known cold-blooded duelists to accept apologies over some real or fancied slight, but I have never known one beautiful woman to accept the apology of another beautiful woman of whom she is jealous."

"Perhaps if I also offer her something she wants very much, she will accept it," Lorinda said. "I really do not want Ajona to become involved. I'm afraid she might harm Emeline."

Gabriella nodded and her thin old lips tightened. "She would most certainly make the girl regret that she had dared to use voodoo against a relative of *La Grande Maitresse*."

"Yes, and I'd rather she didn't. Of course, if I were really in danger, I would not hesitate to ask Ajona for help, but—"

Madame sighed as though she were dealing with an impossible child. "You *are* in danger, deadly danger. I suggest you get your protective *ouanga*, place it around your neck and never take it off again. I also suggest that you write that letter of apology and I'll have one of the boys deliver it."

Lorinda nodded and sipped at her coffee. "I'll do it as soon as I finish this."

"Do it now!" Madame said in her imperious way. "If you want to be alive by sunset, do it now!"

"Yes, I will," Lorinda said, getting to her feet, finally convinced of the need for haste. "Please excuse me."

"You are excused," Gabriella said formally. "And I'll not call in Ajona unless you sicken and die."

Lorinda smiled, but when she was halfway up the stairs she suddenly felt a frightening shortness of breath. She paused for a minute and shivered. She didn't believe in the *ouangas*, but when a death doll appeared on your doorstep and you experienced a symptom of illness you never had before, you began to question your certainty.

Once in her room, she hurried to the dresser and opened the drawer where she had left her personal *ouanga*. For a heart-stopping moment she couldn't find the small square of red cloth tied into a sachet-like packet. Then, as panic began to grip her with a cold hand, she spotted it under a pile of gloves. Quickly fastening the chain around her neck, she let the charm fall down between her breasts.

"It's silly," she whispered but sighed with relief when her breathing eased.

Crossing to the delicately carved little desk under the bedroom window, she sat down to write to the girl who was trying to kill her.

Dear Emeline–
   This short note is to offer my apology for my rude behavior last evening. I was not truly interested in Joseph Gayarre and I knew you were, but I went out of my way to lure him into the garden with me. I did it to make you jealous and now I am sorry. If you are really interested in Joseph as a protector, allow me to say he is a man of considerable charm and virility and he is looking for a quadroon lady who will appreciate him.
   I wish you best with him and

She stopped and thought. She had been about to write, "with him and his wife," but since she didn't really like Emeline and the girl had never been nice to her and now was using voodoo against her, she certainly didn't owe her a warning about Gayarre's abnormal sexual preferences. Perhaps what she did owe her was a veiled threat to enhance her apology. Yes, that would be repaying her in her own coin. Dipping the pen into the crystal inkwell, she concluded the note.

> *I wish you the best with him and a long life. In fact, I shall ask my sister Ajona, who, as you may be aware, is known as* La Grande Maitresse *of voodoo of New Orleans, to prepare a personal protective* ouanga *such as the one she made for me.*

She signed the note with a flourish, sealed it in an envelope and took it downstairs to give to a young black boy who worked for Madame Gabriella. "Take this to Miss Emeline Lovette at her mother's house at number 110 Rampart Street, please, Nero."

"Yes'm, Miss de Buys," the boy said, smiling broadly at the ten cent piece she gave him. "Does Ah wait for an answer?"

"No," Lorinda said. "I don't believe there will be an answer."

A few days later she heard that Emeline, to her mother's horror and the scandal of the ladies who enforced the stringent moral standards for those attending the balls, had moved into the home of Joseph Gayarre.

Lorinda felt a twinge of pity when she was told the news, but she shrugged it off, thinking that Emeline must have entered into the arrangement with her eyes wide open.

"She's welcome to that life," Lorinda said, "but I'm not sure even she deserves it."

It was almost a week later that Madame Gabriella flung open the door to Lorinda's room, waking her from a nap, to announce excitedly, "We have an offer, my dear, a most exciting offer!"

Lorinda yawned and blinked sleepily. "An offer? From whom?"

"Monsieur Maspero," the woman said, beaming at her.

"Oh, Maurice," Lorinda said, stretching and yawning again. "I've known for weeks he'd make an offer soon, but it's hardly all that exciting."

"Not exciting?" the old lady looked astonished. "Don't you know how rich Maspero is?"

"Yes, you told me he had inherited a great deal of money from his father and has only an uncle to keep an eye on him, but I can't work up much enthusiasm for the poor boy."

"The poor boy?" Madame raised her eyes ceilingward. "A man who is worth over a million you call a poor boy?"

"He's poor because he's so shy and clumsy with women," Lorinda said. "And he's a virgin."

"So are you, my dear," Gabriella reminded her tartly. "You remember that, don't you, *ma petite-fils?*"

"*Oui, grand-mère, oui,*" Lorinda got off the bed and made a little curtsy. "I am virginal to the core, especially the core."

"You may scoff, young lady," Madame said, "but it is the standards that we set on this street and do our best to maintain that guarantee a measure of happiness to many who would otherwise have none.''

Lorinda was immediately contrite. She realized it was her upbringing as a white that made her look down on this half-world of the *gens de couleur libres,* as the law referred to those of mixed race in Louisiana. They existed in a peculiar strata of society, trapped between the black and white segments, and had to make their way the best they could. Many made satisfactory lives for themselves, the men as barbers, clothiers or the owners of small businesses, the women as hairdressers or dressmakers. It was the exquisitely beautiful, well-educated young girls who needed the opportunity afforded them by the *Bals du Cordon Blue,* the opportunity to find security and occasionally a lifelong love with their white protectors.

''I'm sorry, *grand-mère,*'' Lorinda said.. ''I wasn't brought up right for this life.''

Madame Gabriella smiled. ''For one who is not right for it, you have done amazingly well.''

''You mean poor little Maurice?''

''Yes. 'Poor little Maurice,' as you persist in calling him, has offered a settlement of ten thousand dollars for you. In addition, your dowry from him will be five thousand dollars and a house at the end of the street that is newer and larger than this one. You will also be given living expenses of three hundred dollars a month.''

''My, my, he is generous, isn't he?'' Lorinda said. Five thousand dollars would surely be more than enough to buy her freedom from Kirk Stryker. Maurice was a good boy and she'd have to be very nice to him. Ah, but that was the rub. Being nice to the bumbling, backward young man didn't exactly enthrall her.

The old woman noticed the expression on Lorinda's face and frowned. "You are going to accept this offer and you are going to carry out your share of the bargain?"

Lorinda sighed and grimaced. "Yes, dear grandmother by adoption, I intend to accept the offer and carry out my share of the bargain to the very last clause of the agreement. When do we sign the contract?"

"This afternoon," Madame said. "The young man is in something of a hurry it seems."

"I'm sure he is," Lorinda said dryly, sliding a petticoat on over her head and settling it into place. "He knows he has to start early to catch up with his peers."

"Lorinda!"

"Sorry, *grand-mère*. I'll have to learn to control my tongue."

"That would help," the old woman said crisply.

"And after the contract is signed, I presume payment will be made on delivery."

"I beg your pardon?" Madame's voice was icy.

"You know what I mean," Lorinda said, selecting a pale pink organdy dress that was more revealing that those she had worn to the balls. "He pays the money and we deliver the merchandise. Isn't that the way it works?"

"I thought you were going to control your tongue."

"I know, but I've never been bought and paid for before," Lorinda said.

"My dear child," Madame said, drawing herself

up to her full four feet five, "you must not think of this as a business transaction but as an affair of the heart. This young man is desperately in love with you. He has gone far beyond what was necessary to obtain you as his *amie* and you should try to change your attitude toward him and make the relationship as perfect as it can be."

"You are right, as always, *grand-mère*. It will take a great deal of patience, but I think the boy deserves the best I can give him."

"Referring to Monsieur Maspero as a boy is not the kind of attitude I was hoping for," Gabriella said. "You must remember that the Creole men of New Orleans are among the proudest people on earth. They are hotheaded and quick to resent anything that seems like a slight. They carry sword canes to the cafés and to the opera and are known to duel at the drop of a hat. Be sure to show respect for him and never give him any reason to be jealous."

"Since I go to him in all my virginal purity, thanks to sister Ajona, he should have no reason to doubt me."

"I had in mind your actions after your alliance," Madame said.

"Oh, you need have no fear there, *grand-mère*." Lorinda said lightly. "I'm sure Maurice will prove so virile and active a lover that I will have neither the time nor the inclination to look at another man."

"Hmmm," Gabriella said noncommittally, and then, turning away, "I will send Nero to Monsieur Maspero with a note accepting his offer. I believe we can expect the young gentleman to call within the next hour or so."

"Yes, I'm sure he'll be here in less than that," Lorinda said cynically, but Madame had already closed the door and was spared from hearing that final impertinence.

An hour later Lorinda and Madame Gabriella, flanked by Madame's lawyer, were sitting across the table from a grinning, nervous Maurice and his uncle, a dashing old gentleman who sported a pencil-thin mustache and a goatee that bobbed up and down when he talked.

"You dog, sir, you lucky dog!" he had said to his nephew after examining Lorinda from head to foot. "Here I always thought you were the most backward young puppy I'd ever seen, and now I find you are a Lothario, a rake, a seducer of the innocent. You are making off with a rare prize indeed."

"Please, Uncle," Maurice pleaded, acutely embarrassed, but Lorinda rewarded the old gentleman with a kiss on each cheek.

"And now, Mademoiselle de Buys, if you will sign the agreement here," the Masperos' lawyer said dryly after Madame's lawyer had read and approved the document.

As Lorinda complied, she had the oddest sensation that she was signing the papers for the sale of a horse. She had once sold a colt of Firedrake's, and the ceremony had been very similar to this. The only real difference, she reflected, was that it was she who was being purchased and that, unlike the colt, she had to sign the contract herself.

"My dearest, my darling," Maurice murmured, clasping her in his arms as soon as the signing was over. "I am so happy that I can hardly speak."

"You are a lucky young devil," Uncle Raoul said and kissed the "bride" enthusiastically on the lips. "I would give a hundred thousand to be in your shoes."

Then there was champagne all around and everyone toasted the young couple while they toasted each other.

"I know we are going to be very happy," Maurice said as they entwined arms and sipped from each other's glass.

"I'm sure we will be," Lorinda replied, wishing that instead of champagne she could have the raw whiskey Kirk Stryker used to pour into her to warm her up for their sessions of nonstop lovemaking.

Later there was a discreet handing over of a bank draft for ten thousand dollars to Madame and another of five thousand for Lorinda, the latter accompanied by a key to the house at the end of the street. The house would be hers during her arrangement with Maurice and would be deeded to her when he married.

After the lawyers and Uncle Raoul had gone, there was a moment alone with Maurice. He drew her into his arms and bestowed one of his chaste, hesitant kisses on her.

"My *caleche* will call for you and your belongings in the morning, my love," he said. "It will take you to the new house, where the servants are already in residence, and I will join you for dinner."

"Oh, do come sooner," she said demurely. "Come in time for an aperitif first, my dear."

When she was back in her room, she stood staring at the check in her hands. "Five thousand dollars. That is the means to my eventual freedom."

But that was a little more complicated than it seemed. First of all, she had no idea where Kirk Stryker was. She would have to locate him and then somehow convince him to let her buy her papers from him.

"I've got to think. I've got to be clever about this. I've got to find Stryker without his knowing I am looking for him and also without Maurice knowing I am doing it. For that matter, without Maurice ever knowing that I am a slave and not a *gens du couleur libres*."

That, of course, would ruin everything just as thoroughly as it would be ruined if Maurice ever found out that she wasn't a virgin. He might love her enough to buy her from Stryker if he knew she was a slave, but Lorinda was sure Stryker would never sell her to another man.

She sighed. Everything was so complicated. And part of what was making it complicated was her superior attitude to the people she was now living among. She had been brought up to believe she was superior, and even though she recognized that such ideas were part of the whole rotten slave society the whites had set up, it was hard to change. She told herself for the hundredth time that for a person to think they were superior because of the color of their skin was not only ridiculous, it also was evil. And yet she knew that even among the blacks and those of mixed blood, the racial lines were almost as rigid as those of the whites. The *griffe*, offspring of a mulatto and a Negro, looked down on pure-blooded Negroes, a mulatto regarded the *griffe* with scorn and was in turn scorned by the quadroon, while the octoroon considered him or herself above all the others.

I am not white; I am octoroon. But that doesn't make me better than any other racial mixture, nor any worse than white. For the sake of my own future I must not let racial arrogance interfere with what I do. I must be properly grateful to Maurice for all he has done for me and I must do my best to make him happy. Lorinda said to herself.

There was a knock on the door and Madame Gabriella came in. She pressed a tiny canvas bag into Lorinda's hand.

"There, my dear, is your virginity," the old woman said. "Be very careful of it until tomorrow night when you will need it."

CHAPTER 15

Lorinda lay in a large canopied bed, staring unseeingly at the blue-and-silver damask draperies that enclosed it. The three feather mattresses made the bed as soft as a cloud, but it hadn't helped her sleep during the night, and this morning she was restless and fretful. She tried to tell herself that it was the weather that had kept her awake, but she knew that wasn't true.

She had left Madame Gabriella's with a trousseau not unlike a bride's, including a white silk nightgown with a matching negligee. She had found the house every bit as large and splendid as Madame had predicted. A household staff—a cook, a maid and a butler had already been installed. Her luggage had been whisked upstairs, and the maid had unpacked and assisted her in choosing a gown suitable for the first dinner. It was in the mode màde popular in Paris by the beautiful Eugenie, wife of Louis Napoleon, the nephew of the great Bonaparte, who recently had been appointed president of France.

Once dressed, she had stood in front of the mirror studying the way the cream-colored velvet clung to her body, outlining the rise of her breasts and the clean lines of her thighs. One wore only a chemise and a pair of unstiffened petticoats with these dresses and they were considered slightly risqué even in sophisticated New Orleans.

"Do you think he will like me in this, Reba?" she asked.

The girl giggled. "If he don't, you better call the undertaker, Miss Philippa, 'cause he's daid."

Lorinda laughed, but later she couldn't tell whether Maurice had liked the style of the dress or not. They had dined tête-à-tête with candles and wine, the fine damask tablecloth set with gleaming silver and fine china. Maurice had been as gallant as his shyness permitted, admiring her new hairdo with its longer ringlets and the back coiled and pinned up, but not saying a word about the dress.

After dinner was over, they sat in the formal sitting room making small talk until a suitable interval had passed, then Lorinda had excused herself politely and gone upstairs to change into her nightdress and negligee and wait for Maurice to appear at her door in his dressing gown.

Things didn't go at all right. She had left the gas lights on, and Maurice blinked at the brightness of the room.

"Don't you think we could do with a little less light?" he asked with an embarrassed smile.

"I suppose so," Lorinda said, disappointed that he hadn't noticed how enchanting she looked in white against the glow of the light. "Turn the lamp down if you like."

He turned the gas so low that the room became filled with shadows. Then, just as he started toward her, he seemed to think better of it, and she thought he was going to turn it up a little. Instead, he turned it off completely, leaving only the dim light from the windows.

After Maurice had groped his way across the room to where she stood and she had melted against him, raising her lips to his in warm invitation, it became increasingly clear that he had no intention of undressing her. He stood there holding her awkwardly, not seeming to know what to do next. To help him along, she let her negligee drop to the carpet and began to untie the ribbon that served as a sash for the gown.

"What are you doing?" Maurice asked hoarsely.

"Getting undressed for you," she said matter-of-factly. Her months with Kirk Stryker and his reveling in her naked body had left her with assurance of its allure and no sense of shame in exhibiting it to a lover.

"Don't. Please don't," he begged, sounding panicky. "I prefer that you remain partially clothed."

"Yes, Maurice," she said submissively, but she didn't understand. Why wouldn't he want to see her naked, or at least feel her naked against him?

They had fallen back on the bed then and Maurice was kissing her just as he had in the garden that night—hard, closemouthed, little-boy kisses. Should she show him how? she wondered. No, she couldn't let him know she was experienced or even the tiny bladder of blood Ajona had prepared wouldn't convince him he had gotten what he'd paid such a high price for.

Just relax, she admonished herself. Relax and let him find his own way. Every man and boy had to learn how to do it on his own. There had to be a first time for everyone. Of course, she couldn't imagine Kirk Stryker having had to learn how to make love to a woman, Kirk fumbling around under a woman's nightdress but wanting her to stay covered because he was afraid of the touch of her bare flesh against his own.

What was wrong with Maurice? He didn't act like a hot-blooded Latin but more like a cold Yankee. Cold Yankee, ha! No woman who had shared a bed with Kirk would ever again think of Yankees as being cold.

Maurice was searching hesitantly under the skirt of her gown, patting and rubbing wherever he happened to touch. What was he trying to do? Didn't he even know where to find what he wanted? He was paying a fortune for it; he should at least know where to find it.

She made herself lie still under the clumsy caresses, wishing she could take his hand and move it to her warm womanhood and tell him what to do next, but she didn't dare. She could only wait as he pawed at her belly and upper thighs, while his ineffectual kisses failed to thrill her.

"I love you, Philippa," he breathed heavily, his mouth against her shoulder. "You do care for me a little, don't you, my dearest? It isn't just for the money and the house, is it?"

Lorinda's exasperation with him turned to pity. He sounded like a lonely little boy wanting someone to mother him.

"You do love me, don't you, Philippa?" he repeated anxiously.

"I didn't accept your offer only for the money, Maurice," she assured him.

It wasn't exactly a lie and she was glad she'd said it because it seemed to comfort Maurice and make him more sure of what he was doing. Gradually he pushed her gown up until it was about even with her hips and now he rolled on top of her more or less in the proper position. She could feel his reasonably hard maleness pressing onto the triangle of her womanhood. Guiltily she compared it mentally to the larger, ever ready flesh of Kirk Stryker.

As Maurice continued to make love to her in his slow, bumbling way, she felt herself becoming increasingly stirred. When with some low-keyed assistance from her, he finally penetrated her, she began to move a little, but she refrained from her usual uninhibited cooperation.

She closed her eyes and let the sweet madness of sexual pleasure begin to inundate her consciousness. Nowhere near as potent as Kirk, Maurice was still able to stir warmth and a building joy in her loins.

"You are so wonderful," Maurice was whispering huskily. "I was so lucky to have found you."

His movements were mounting in intensity. She slid her arms around him but remembered to keep her hips from rolling or responding too wildly. Her hopes soared along with her passion, but before she could get near her goal, Maurice grunted and after a few spasmodic jerks lay still on top of her.

It was over! Before it had barely begun, the

night's lovemaking was over. Maurice had finished the act as ineptly as he'd begun it and without any thought for her at all. However, she really couldn't blame a shy youth like Maurice for failing in the same way most men of experience failed. Their failure came from not caring; his from inexperience. Inexperience usually cured itself, though, of course, male arrogance never did.

She could wait, Lorinda had told herself then. With patience and practice things would get better. Sooner or later Maurice would learn to satisfy and please her.

That had been well over a year ago, and her hopes of eventual satisfaction in the arms of Maurice Maspero had long since disappeared. His lovemaking of the previous night had been just as dull, short and self-centered as it had been the first time.

Lorinda didn't know how much longer her nerves could stand it. It would have been better to have no sex at all than to be continuously aroused and then left hanging. Despite Madame Gabriella's repeated warnings about the necessity of being faithful to one's protector, Lorinda had been unable to keep her thoughts from other men. More and more often she had drifted off into a troubled sleep and dreamed of the virility of Gaston de Pouilly or awakened to find herself moving sensuously on the bed in the aftermath of an erotic dream involving Kirk Stryker. The only man she did not dream about or fantasize over was Joseph Gayarre, and strangely enough, it was he who had come back into her life.

First she had run into Emeline Lovette one day when she had been strolling past the market.

Emeline had been one of the reigning beauties of the *Bals du Cordon Bleu*, but not she was so pale and thin that Lorinda almost didn't recognize her. When she did, she spoke to her on impulse and then was sorry she had.

"Hello, Emeline," she had said as the other girl emerged from the vegetable section of the market with her basket full. "How are you?"

"I'm fine, Philippa," Emeline said in a voice devoid of the slightest hint of warmth or friendship. "It was a wonderful thing that happened to me when I became Joseph Gayarre's *amie*."

"Oh, then you are still with him and—" She stopped short, knowing Emeline would know what she meant.

"Of course," Emeline said, starting to move around Lorinda. "I'm not the kind of girl men drop quickly, you know."

A glance at the shopping basket loaded with fruits and vegetables made Lorinda almost certain that was exactly what had happened to Emeline. While Lorinda was strolling, Emeline was shopping. She would hardly have been doing the shopping if she were still living with the Gayarres. It seemed likely that, having lost the virginity that was the chief stock in trade of the Orleans Ballroom girls, Gayarre had tired of her and Emeline had been reduced to taking a job as a servant in someone's home.

"I'm glad things have turned out so well for you, Emeline," Lorinda said as the other girl began to move away. "I hope you'll always be as happy as you are today."

A hissing sound that may have been a curse came from Emeline as she disappeared into the crowd.

It had been perhaps a month after that when Lorinda had encountered the Gayarres themselves. Coming out of her dressmaker's shop one day, she heard someone call her name as she was about to get into the small chaise Maurice had bought for her. Turning in surprise, she was startled to see the dark Joseph and his tall, blonde wife sitting in their carriage a few yards away.

Since the beginning of her arrangement with Maurice, Lorinda had been hearing gossip about the Gayarres. He came from an old but impoverished Creole family. His wife was the widow of a wealthy New York businessman and had been a recent arrival in New Orleans at the time of their marriage.

The young Creole gentleman who told Lorinda about it had commented, "Their marriage was not only a business merger of Jessica Quennell's wealth and Joseph's excellent background, it was also a merger of their mutual vices."

"I don't think I understand what you mean," Lorinda had said, pretending for Maurice's sake to know nothing about Gayarre's practices.

"I mean they share a taste for the outré in intimate relationships," the young man had whispered. "More outré than even blasé New Orleans makes allowances for."

And now here was Joseph with his handsome wife beside him, nodding and beckoning to Lorinda.

Only because she didn't want to make a scene, Lorinda walked toward their carriage.

"Ah, the beautiful Philippa," Joseph said, descending to kiss Lorinda's begrudgingly extended hand. "I have told Jessica about you so often that she has been quite mad to meet you."

More reluctantly than before, Lorinda offered her hand. Jessica clasped it in strong fingers and examined the girl with an expression that could only be described as lecherous.

"Now that we have finally met I see that Joseph has not been exaggerating your beauty," Jessica said and to Lorinda's astonishment began to stroke the palm of her hand. "We would like to see more of you."

Extracting her hand from the woman's grip, Lorinda put it behind her to keep from openly wiping it on her skirt.

The woman's pale blue eyes locked with Lorinda's black ones. "You will let us send our carriage for you some afternoon soon, won't you, my dear?"

"I'm afraid not," Lorinda said coolly. "Monsieur Maspero seldom goes out in the afternoon."

Jessica's eyes narrowed. "I don't recall inviting young Maspero. He would be entirely out of place."

"Then I couldn't possibly visit you," Lorinda

said. "Monsieur Maspero is *mon protecteur*, and I do not go out into society without him."

Anger turned Jessica Gayarre's handsome face into an ugly mask. "You listen to me, you dirty little wench! We know about you but have seen fit to keep it to ourselves. However, if you presume to turn your nose up at your betters, we shall be forced to take steps you will find most unpleasant."

Lorinda paled and looked from one to the other. What was it they knew? Was the woman threatening her with the brief but violent encounter with Joseph in the garden of the Orleans Ballroom, or had they discovered her real identity and the fact that she was a slave?

"Now, I'm going to repeat my invitation," Jessica said, "and I expect a more satisfactory answer."

Fortunately for Lorinda there was a timely and welcome interruption. Another carriage was coming down the narrow cobblestoned street. Joseph had stopped out too far and now was forced to order his coachman to move to let the other vehicle through. Lorinda took advantage of the situation to get into her chaise and drive off. For the time being, she had avoided a direct confrontation with Joseph and his sinister wife.

She was glad that Maurice would not be visiting her that evening, especially so when she returned home to find more reports awaiting her from the St. Louis law firm she had engaged to find Kirk Stryker. She had spent over a thousand dollars, but the agents the firm had hired had been a disappointment. They had traced him as far as Cincinnati, where he had resided at a hotel while seeing a great deal of a Miss Alice Randolph, then he had left town abruptly, leaving no forwarding address. Further efforts to trace his movements had so far failed. Lorinda was becoming discouraged, but she couldn't give up. It was important to locate him so she could buy her freedom. At least that was the only reason she admitted to for continuing the fruitless search.

Busy with her day-to-day duties as Maurice's *amie*, she had almost forgotten the threat the Gayarres posed when she heard from them again. A formal note arrived from Jessica:

> *Monsieur and Madame Joseph Gayarre request the pleasure of Mademoiselle Philippa de Buy's company at an afternoon tea on Tuesday next at their home at number 121, St. Charles Street.*
> *We must insist on your attendance.*

Except for the last line, it seemed like an invitation to an ordinary tea, although girls of mixed blood were simply not asked to the homes of well-to-do white ladies. Into the beds of their husbands, yes, but not into their homes. And in this instance everyone concerned knew she was being invited into bed with both husband and wife.

Lorinda stared at the note as though it were a snake she had found under her pillow. She had no intention in taking part in the perverse games the Gayarres played, but her fear of what they might do if she refused them was very real. It gnawed at her for two days after she received the note, which she had burned, unanswered. She became so tense and distracted that even the usually unperceptive Maurice noticed something was wrong.

"What's wrong, Philippa?" he finally asked. "Aren't you feeling well?"

"No, I'm not," she said, knowing full well what would happen if she even hinted at the truth. Maurice was as gentle as he was naive, but he shared the Creole code. If he suspected the Gayarres had been bothering her, he would challenge Joseph out of hand, and Joseph was a deadly shot and almost equally good with the rapier. "Don't worry about it, my dear. It's only a slight indisposition and will pass."

Maurice's face brightened. "You aren't by any chance in the family way, are you, my love?"

For some reason he had decided he wanted to have a child by her, but Lorinda had no intention of bringing an illegitimate child into the world even though she knew it would have the best of everything his money could provide. The measures she used to prevent it went unnoticed. After all, a man who had spent a large sum of money to purchase a supposedly virgin mistress and then was so unaware and shy that he hadn't looked for the proof of her virginity on the bedsheets the night of their first time together would hardly pay any attention to whatever she did on subsequent occasions.

"No, my dear, I'm not pregnant," she told him. "I wish I were because it would please you, but I'm not."

Maurice smiled at her tenderly. "You will be."

She was getting to be an awful liar, Lorinda reflected as she finally dragged herself out of bed that fateful morning, but if it made Maurice happy, so be it. One of them at least should be happy.

All morning she paced restlessly about the house, knowing this was the day the invitation had specified and worrying about the possible consequences of her refusal to acknowledge it. By midafternoon she decided to go shopping to take her mind off her dilemma. She quickly changed from her figured silk morning dress and white lace-trimmed house cap into a more appropriate dark red costume, the skirt banded every eight inches with red velvet and topped by a fitted bodice with a V-shaped velvet collar. A matching poke bonnet lined with white framed her face, and a white shawl was thrown around her shoulders.

By the time she was ready, her driver had brought the chaise around. As she left the house and hurried toward it, a vehicle pulled up behind hers. Joseph Gayarre leaped out of it and intercepted her just as she was about to enter the chaise.

"We will go in my carriage," he said, gripping her arm. "Jessica is waiting impatiently for your arrival."

"I'm not going with you," Lorinda said and glanced at the broad-shouldered black youth who was her driver. "Leon is driving me to the milliner's for a new bonnet."

"Dismiss your driver," Gayarre ordered. "You are accepting our invitation to tea, and I have come to escort you."

"No," she said and tried to pull free of his grasp.

"I want nothing more to do with you, and if you continue to annoy me, I shall complain to Monsieur Maspero."

Gayarre grinned down at her. "You do that, little one. It will give me an excellent opportunity to kill the young fool."

A cold knot of fear formed in the pit of Lorinda's stomach. She didn't love Maurice, and his clumsy lovemaking drove her to distraction, but she was fond of him and didn't want him killed in a duel over her. But neither did she want to become a sex toy for this man and his degenerate wife, so she broke away from him and retreated toward the door of her house.

Gayarre followed her, his glittering black eyes boring into hers as she backed up against the steps. "You had better listen to me, wench. My wife likes a pretty little gal to share our lovemaking. She likes variety, but right now her mind is set on you. Either you go with me and do what we want willingly, or certain facts about your background are going to become public knowledge in New Orleans."

Lorinda had never actually wanted to kill anyone before, not even the Wenzels, but if she had a knife or a pistol at that moment, she would have used it on Gayarre.

"Don't look at me like that," he said. "I have had you, remember? I know what an oversexed little baggage you are. You liked it with me, and you'll like it better with both Jessica and me."

"I did not like it!" she hissed. "You made me feel dirty! And now you and that obscene wife of yours make my skin crawl!"

"Don't you dare speak of my wife that way!" Joseph snarled and slapped her face so hard her head rocked.

"*What do you think you're doing?*" roared an angry voice, and they both turned to see Maurice standing a few feet away. He had ridden up on his horse and dismounted without their noticing.

"Take me inside, please, Maurice," Lorinda said, her heart pounding with fear.

Maurice ignored her, moving steadily toward Joseph. "I believe your name, sir, is Joseph Gayarre."

"You are correct, sir," Gayarre said with a stiff bow.

"Then, Monsieur Gayarre, I will ask you for an explanation of this scene."

Gayarre's lip curled in an arrogant sneer. "Why don't you ask your whore?"

Before Lorinda could say or do anything, Maurice's hand cracked against Gayarre's cheek.

Gayarre smiled frostily and bowed. "Thank you, sir. My seconds will call on you in the morning!"

"I will await them eagerly," Maurice said.

"No, no, Maurice, please!" Lorinda cried. "Please, you musn't! He'll kill you!"

Maurice turned on her angrily. "Go inside, woman, and stay there until I give you permission to leave. This is business between men."

"*White* men," Gayarre said and looked directly at her, smiling maliciously. "First I will deal with this young fool, and then I'll be back to finish with you at my leisure."

"You'll not do anything with me, you—"

Maurice placed a hand on her arm and spoke more kindly. "Go inside, Philippa. You are only making things worse."

Breaking into tears, Lorinda turned and ran up the stairs, slamming the door behind her and standing with her back to it while long wracking sobs of grief and fear shook her.

"I've got to stop it! Somehow, some way, I've got to stop it!"

CHAPTER 16

The next morning Lorinda was up and dressed early. There was only one person she could think of who might be able to prevent the duel between Maurice and Joseph, and that was her half-sister Ajona. Through her control of the blacks by means of voodoo, Ajona was powerful in the black community; she had also attained considerable influence in the white world. She had the ear of one or two city commissioners and a couple of police officials. If she could arrange for the duel to be interrupted by officers of the law, Maurice's life might be saved. The only problem was that she hadn't heard from Ajona in almost a year and didn't know where to find her.

Grand-mère Gabriella will know, she assured herself, as she gave her jehu directions to Madame's home.

Her hopes were high when Madame's servant ushered her into the old lady's sitting room and brought fresh coffee.

"*La Grande Maitresse?*" Gabriella said, puffing on her cigar and shaking her head. "No, I have no way of contacting her at this time."

"But why not?" Lorinda asked. "You are always in touch with her. Surely you know her whereabouts."

241

"I do," Madame admitted, "but she is in Haiti, where, it is said, her father suffered an accident. I cannot reach her because even the Rada drums do not carry so far across the water."

"But I must have help," Lorinda said. "There is going to be a duel and Maurice may be killed."

Madame smiled sadly. "When these Creoles are determined to engage in their chief pleasure of letting each other's blood, there is no one who can help, no one who dares to interfere."

"But it is so foolish for a fine young man like Maurice to risk his life for nothing."

"Perhaps he will only be wounded," Madame suggested.

"No, I know that Gayarre means to kill him."

"Joseph Gayarre? Then you can only ask the priests to pray for Maspero's soul. That man is the devil."

She would have to plead with Maurice himself, Lorinda decided on the way home. If he came by to see her this evening, she would have to convince him of the folly of fighting Gayarre. He had hurried off without coming into the house after the encounter the previous afternoon, so it seemed likely he would call this evening. She bathed, dressed carefully, had a special dinner prepared and sat down to wait, rehearsing her arguments in her mind.

She waited in vain. Maurice didn't come and he sent no message. Frantic with worry but not daring to go out after dark by herself, Lorinda finally went to bed and spent another restless night.

She had never been asked to his rooms at the posh Pontalba Apartments, but feeling that she had to go to any lengths to see him, she set off early the next morning.

Maurice's eyebrows lifted slightly when his butler showed Lorinda into his sitting room in the large, lavishly furnished suite in one of the most expensive living quarters in the city.

"Philippa, my dear, I was not expecting you," he said in mild rebuke. It was not considered proper for an octoroon mistress to visit her *protecteur* in his bachelor domicile.

"I had to see you," Lorinda said. "I have to talk to you before the duel."

"That isn't scheduled until tomorrow morning at eight o'clock. I would have preferred dawn today, but there were so many duels pending that we could not reserve The Oaks before eight tomorrow."

The Oaks was a grove of giant oaks on the plantation of Louis Allard some distance from the city. It had been the most fashionable place for duels since the early thirties, when for some reason *Les Trois Capelines* had gone out of style. Frequently there were half a dozen duels fought there a day, and on one famous Sunday in 1837 there had been ten duels between sunrise and noon, three of which had ended fatally.

"Maurice, you must not go. Please promise me you will not take part in this madness," Lorinda begged.

"There is no other way," Maurice said stiffly. "The code of honor permits of no other solution when a blow has been struck."

"What honor is there in allowing yourself to be killed over such a trifling matter?"

"Trifling?" Maurice drew himself up to his full

height. "The man had accosted you. He laid hands on a woman who is under my protection. I do not consider that a trifling matter."

"But it is not worth getting killed over," Lorinda insisted. "It is not worth giving up all your hopes and dreams for a bullet in your brain."

"It is a question of honor," Maurice repeated, although he looked pale and strained.

Lorinda tried another approach. "If you are killed, what will happen to me?"

"I have provided for you."

"What good will money do me if I lose your protection?" she asked. "You saw the way that man approached me. What's to keep him from forcing me to do anything he wants once you are gone?"

Maurice looked grimmer than ever. "That is all the more reason to kill him—so he never bothers you again."

"My dear Maurice," she said, "the man is an accomplished duelist, a deadly shot."

"I will have right on my side," Maurice said. "That is not a fact to be overlooked."

Lorinda felt as though she were dealing with a child. It wasn't that his belief in the code was so unusual. That was the besetting vice of Creole society. Men had been known to fight at the drop of a hat. Even the best of friends were capable of squaring off against each other with deadly intent. There was one famous case in which six young Creoles were walking home from a ball one night when one of them suddenly exclaimed, "Oh what a beautiful night! What splendid level ground for a joust! Suppose we pair off, draw our swords and make this night memorable by a spontaneous display of bravery and skill!'' The others had agreed enthusiastically and the silly fools had turned to stabbing at one another until two of them lay dead.

No, it wasn't just that he shared the common madness. It was his never failing naiveté, his belief in all the myths and clichés of Southern society, most of which Lorinda had been shaken free of by the knowledge of her birth.

"I'll never forgive myself if anything happens to you,'' she said now and was unable to keep back a sob.

Her obvious concern for him softened Maurice's expression. He took her in his arms. "Nothing is going to happen to me, my darling. I will have the saints to protect me. I am going to confession tonight and will remain in retreat with the holy fathers of the Society of Jesus throughout the night and take communion in the morning.''

That meant that there would be no last time in each other's arms. Once having confessed, Maurice would not wish to commit the sin of fornication before going to communion.

"Then I won't see you again?''

"Of course you will, my dear,'' he said, kissing her with trembling lips, which belied his words. "You will see me at our usual time tomorrow evening.''

Lorinda's eyes were blinded by tears when she left the apartments on St. Ann Street. She was still crying when she got out of the chaise and hurried to her own door. That was why she didn't see the man sitting on the front stoop until she stumbled across his outstretched legs.

She felt herself caught up in strong arms and held against someone who smelled of shaving cream and fresh soap, someone who was laughing and hugging her close.

"Lorinda! Lorinda, at last I've found you!" said a dear, familiar voice. She couldn't believe what her ears were telling her.

"Look up at me, silly little one," Kirk Stryker said. "Look up and let me see that pretty face."

"You!" she said, still blinking away tears as the old familiar excitement flooded through her. "What are you doing here? How did you find me?"

"I found you because you hired such clumsy idiots to try to find me," he said. "I've known for months someone was poking into my business, but it was only two weeks ago in Cairo that I collared one of the dimwits and shook the truth out of him."

"I didn't have them looking for you because I wanted to see you," she said, trying to pull out of his embrace. She couldn't allow herself to be distracted by Kirk Stryker now.

"No?" He was still holding her tight and laughing down at her. "It wasn't because you love me?"

She stopped struggling and looked away. "Put me down, please. What will the neighbors think?"

"I'll put you down once we're inside," he said and reached for her reticule. Opening it, he took out her latch key, opened the door and carried her in under his arm.

"As for the neighbors, they already know you've

been installed here by a white lover, so what difference does anything else make?''

''Because we—we girls are suppose to be inviolate—faithful unto death to one man.'' She was breathless from the way he was handling her. ''Our reputations are all we have to rely on.''

''Ha!'' he snorted, dropping her on the chaise longue near the window and drawing the draperies. ''Inviolate, are you? Faithful unto death. Well, in your own fashion, I suppose.''

''Listen to me!'' she said desperately as he dropped down beside her and put his arms around her again. ''Please listen to me. Even if I had forgiven you for what you did to me that night—and even if I wanted to be with you again—this would not be the time. My protector, Maurice Maspero, has been challenged to a duel, and the man he is to fight is a cold-blooded killer. Maspero will be killed unless I do something to prevent the duel taking place.''

''Once these Creole fools make up their minds to blow each other's silly brains out, it's useless to try to dissuade them,'' he said. ''The best thing you can do is start looking for a new protector, and since I happen to own you, lock, stock and beautiful, lusty body, I nominate myself for the job.''

''And what about your snow princess?'' she demanded angrily. ''Wouldn't she succumb to your masculine charm?''

He grinned. ''You're jealous, so you must love me. As for Alice, I've gotten that nonsense out of my system. It was stupid of me in the first place, but at least I had sense enough to recognize she wasn't for me before I married her. She was ice inside and out, and after you, you little firebox, it was like making love to a marshmallow. It was tamer than playing billiards with someone's great-aunt.''

She was secretly pleased at the comparison, but she didn't dare let him know it or she'd never get away from him. ''Gentlemen used to have a code that prohibited them from talking about the ladies they had made love to. Oh, I forgot, you're not really a gentleman, are you? I suppose you've told a few people about me, too.''

''A few? I've told everyone on the river how good my little slave is in bed!''

''You swine!'' Lorinda aimed a roundhouse blow at his laughing face, but he caught her fist in the palm of his hand, pushed her back and pinned her arms under her.

''Damn you, you sexy little witch,'' he said and kissed her with such passion she couldn't help responding. ''You're so good that you've ruined me for anyone else. Maybe it wasn't Alice's fault at all. Maybe it's yours. Because when you put your mark on a man, he can't get you out of his system.''

Her head was spinning, and she knew that if his caresses went any further she wouldn't be able to resist the temptation to surrender to him totally. And to fall into Kirk's arms and wallow in the lust he could stir in her so easily would be the worst kind of betrayal of Maurice, who was offering his life for wrongs done to her.

"Please, Kirk, let me go. Let me do what I have to do to save Maurice's life."

Reluctantly Stryker released her. "I told you there isn't anything you can do. You can't talk a fool like that out of it if he's decided to get his head blown off over some fancied slight to his high and mighty honor."

"I know. I've already tried with him, but I might be able to persuade someone else and at least prevent his death."

"Who? The authorities always keep their distance when there's an affair of honor in the wind."

"Yes, but there is someone I can appeal to and I have to make the effort."

"Who is it?" he asked again. "No matter what kind of an agreement you have with Maurice I come first because you're still my slave."

"That's the real reason I was trying to get in touch with you," she said. "I have money now and I want to buy my freedom."

He took her by the shoulders and his gray eyes were dark with anger and another emotion she couldn't quite read. "Not for a million dollars! Not for all the money in the National Bank! You're mine and I intend to keep you. I could just pick you up and carry you out of here, you know, and nobody could do a thing about it. Maybe I will."

"If you do, Kirk Stryker, I will hate you for the rest of my life," she said with such deadly seriousness that he had to believe her. "It is my fault that Maurice is involved in this mess, and unless I do everything in my power to save his life I will be as much a murderer as the man who kills him.''

He sighed and let her go. "You're a stubborn little fool, and I can't imagine why I care what happens to you, but I do. All right, go on and do whatever it is you think you have to do. I'll go back to my hotel, but I'll be expecting to hear from you when this is finished.''

"You will," she said and stood on tiptoe to kiss him. "Thank you, Kirk.''

"Don't thank me," he said gruffly, heading for the door. "Just be there.''

Her heart was heavy as she watched him leave. She wanted to run after him, fling herself into his arms and tell him she loved him and never wanted to be separated from him again. But she couldn't do that. She had to save Maurice, and if Kirk knew what she was going to do to accomplish that, he would be appalled. She was appalled herself at the prospect of submitting to the depraved Gayarres but could think of no other way to elicit a promise from Joseph to wound Maurice only slightly.

Knowing that if she thought about it too much she'd never be able to carry out her plan, she rushed upstairs and changed into the sheerest, most clinging dress she owned. Under it she wore only one fine muslin petticoat and lace pantalettes. Looking in the mirror, she was shocked to see the shadowy outline of her breasts showing through the delicate fabric and her stockinged legs clearly visible below. Quickly she donned a voluminous cape to cover her near nakedness and went downstairs to call her driver to take her to the Gayarre home.

Jessica and Joseph were seated in their parlor sipping absinthe frappés when Lorinda was shown in by their smirking black maid. Joseph half rose from his chair and a gurgle of pleased laughter came from Jessica.

"What a delightful surprise," the woman said.

"I thought we might expect a visit from you now that you realize you'll be alone in the world," Joseph sneered.

Lorinda lifted her head proudly. "I came not on my own account but to ask you to spare Maurice's life."

Joseph's brow darkened. "Impossible! The man insulted and struck me in public."

"You wanted something from me," Lorinda said, walking closer to where they sat and letting the cloak drop to the floor. "If you will promise only to draw blood and not kill him, you may have your way with me."

Jessica sucked in her breath at the sight of the lovely body revealed by scandalously sheer clothing. Joseph's burning black eyes roved avidly over the thinly veiled charms, but he shook his head.

"No. Why should I take the risk? I have known men to die themselves in attempting to wound but not kill."

"You will never get what you want from me unless you promise," Lorinda said and then looked directly in Jessica's pale, repellent eyes, "Never!"

"Oh, we'll get you," Joseph said. "It may take a little longer but—"

"Wait, Joseph," Jessica interrupted, her lips parted and her breasts rising and falling rapidly. "Why don't you do it?"

"Why should I? She'll fall into our laps, anyway."

"Do it, Joseph, do it!" Her voice cut like a lash. "I can't wait. I want her now!"

"Very well, my dear," the usually arrogant Gayarre said quickly.

"You promise that you will spare Maurice and only wound him slightly?" Lorinda asked.

"You have my word for it," Gayarre said. "The word of a New Orleans aristocrat."

Jessica got to her feet and set her glass down. "Now that that is settled, let's all go upstairs. Bring absinthe, Joseph, and three glasses."

She moved to Lorinda's side and put an arm around her. As though in a nightmare, the girl felt the woman's fingers touch her breast and caress the nipple showing through the translucent cloth.

"Come, my dear," Jessica said. "We are going to open a whole new world for you, one in which you will learn depths of passion you never dreamed could exist."

Trying to keep her mind blank, Lorinda accompanied the pair up to the bedroom that looked like a room in an oriental seraglio. The floor was covered with a rich deep carpet and on the walls were hangings depicting, in startling vividness, scenes of nymphs and satyrs in the wild abandon of sensual pleasure. Enormous pillows and ottomans were strewn around, and occupying one wall was a bed twice the size of any Lorinda had ever seen.

"Here you are, sweet, hot-lipped Philippa,"
Joseph said, handing her a full wineglass of straight
absinthe. He pulled her roughly against him and
savaged her lips with his mouth and teeth. "Drink
to an experience you will never forget."

To wipe out the full horror of what was about to
happen, Lorinda downed half the bitter-sweet
greenish liqueur in one swallow. Then Jessica's
arms were around her and Jessica's fuller, flabbier
body was molded to hers, while Jessica's lips and
hot tongue took possession of her mouth.

When the woman released her slightly, Lorinda
drained the glass and asked for a refill. Joseph obliged, and then moved up behind his wife to unhook
the back of her dress and help her out of it. When
she was stripped to a tight black corset and long
black stockings, he turned to Lorinda. She felt his
hands fondling her while Jessica watched, her pale
eyes gleaming in the light from a lamp. Then both
of them were quickly and expertly disrobing her.
Two pairs of hands explored her body, touching her
breasts, her belly, her naked thighs and the plush
mound at their apex.

Lorinda gulped the second glass of absinthe, feeling the fiery poison of the stuff numbing her brain
and making it possible for her tolerate what they
were doing, to accept the fact that she was being led
to the bed and stretched out with a lusting male on
one side of her and a lusting female on the other.

It was almost dark when Lorinda staggered down
the front steps of the Gayarre house on St. Charles
Street. She stared around in a daze, unable to pick

out anything in the gathering gloom. Then she recognized her driver and chaise about half a block away, where she had left them. She started in that direction on feet that didn't seem to be her own.

But before she could get far, she became violently ill and had to turn aside to vomit into the gutter. It was partly from the absinthe but mostly from the unspeakably depraved acts she had been forced to take part in during her stay in that incense-filled room on the second floor of the Gayarre house.

Her jehu saw her swaying on the edge of the banquette and came running to help her to the chaise. She leaned on his strong young arm while she tried to blot out the memory of the last few hours. Vile as it had been, she had saved Maurice's life, so the sacrifice was worth it.

She was sick again in the basin in her bedroom while Reba filled the porcelain tub with the hottest water possible. She wanted to wash it all away—the feel of their hands, their lips, their bodies, the smell of sweat and perfume and sexual excretions.

The maid's eyes widened when she saw the bruises, the bite marks and welts just before Lorinda stepped into the tub and began to soap herself. "Why, you pore chile! What did dem people do to you?"

"Don't ask, Reba," Lorinda said almost hysterically. "Don't ever ask."

Her sleep was filled with vile dreams. White bodies, male and female, soft white breasts smothering her face, a red-lipped sensuous mouth on her body, her own lips forced to perform abominations, savage kisses that were not really kisses at all. She woke up sobbing at the memory of the sadistic pleasure on their faces when they had hurt her, hurt her deliberately and with joyful cries of satiation as she had writhed in pain under the combined assault of their evil appetites.

At least Maurice will be safe was the last thought she had after she swallowed a spoonful of laudanum, which at last assuaged her physical and mental distress and allowed her to fall into a deeper sleep.

She awoke with her head pounding like a sledgehammer in the hands of a giant gone mad. She reached for the bell on the nightstand beside her. Weak sunshine was coming in her window, and there was the sound of dripping from the roof. The spring rains had come early, bringing floods and the mosquito season, which meant that malaria and yellow fever wouldn't be far behind.

The dreaded plagues held no terror for Lorinda that morning. She would have welcomed the delirium to wipe away the horror of her recollections, and the fever that might burn her body free of the taint she felt it would carry to the grave.

Reba appeared carrying a tray with a pot of coffee and a cup and saucer. "You be wantin' your breakfast soon, Miss Philippa?"

"No, I don't think I'll ever want to eat again. Just the coffee, please, and draw me another bath."

"You jes had one last night," Reba said.

"I know, Reba, but I feel like I'll never be clean again."

"Well, I 'spects you gotta try," the girl said,

''But there's other ways than jes takin' baths.''

Lorinda was too sunk in misery to pay much attention to the remark, but later she would remember it and wonder at Reba's wisdom.

It was almost seven when a messenger came through the misty streets and rang the bell of Lorinda's house. Reba brought the message up at once. It was written on elegant note paper and the envelope bore a trace of fragrance that set Lorinda's stomach to churning. The note inside read:

Dear darling pleasure girl,

I am taking this means of letting you know how much we enjoyed your obedient serving of our most intimate needs. We are looking forward to even more erotic pleasures in the near future when you move in with us after the sudden demise of your protector on the field of honor this morning. Yes, I'm afraid Joseph isn't as much a man of his word as one might expect from his background. In fact, neither of us was being strictly truthful when we promised to spare the life of that silly little fool you set such store by. You see, that wouldn't be in our interest. With Maurice alive you would have someone other than our loving selves to turn to; with him dead, you will be ours and ours alone. So you see, little pleasure girl, your destiny is decided and the sooner you come to us and submit totally, the easier it will be on you. Let us know when our carriage can call for you.

Love and pain,
Jessica, your mistress

A scream that had been building up in Lorinda all through the reading of the letter finally burst from her lips. She had paid the ultimate price and been robbed of her promised prize. What was worse, she faced a life of perpetual slavery in the obscene embraces of the Gayarres. That she could not face!

In the midst of her horror and despair a tiny wisp of hope raised its head. It was only a little after seven. The duel was not scheduled until eight. If she could reach The Oaks before it happened and somehow prevail on Maurice to listen to her, she could tell about the Gayarres and perhaps convince him that to engage a loathsome beast like Joseph in a duel would sully his honor.

Despite the headache and her mental anguish, she leaped from the bed and started grabbing for clothes, shouting to Reba to order her chaise and to tell Leon to pick the best pair of horses for a fast trip into the country.

CHAPTER 17

Making sure that the small derringer Maurice had given her for self-defense was in her muff, Lorinda hurried downstairs and out to the waiting chaise.

"Do you know the way to the place they call The Oaks?" she asked her driver.

"Yes'm, Ah do, but tain't no place for no lady, Missy Philippa. No place for nobody who got any sense. Dark an' bloody things go on out theah."

"I know what happens at The Oaks, Leon," she said. "That's why I'm going. Can you get me there before eight?"

"Ah spects Ah can iffen Ah stir up the hosses a li'l, ma'am," he said.

"Then please stir them up, Leon. I have to get there to prevent a murder."

Leon rolled his eyes heavenward as he took the reins in his hands and started the horses off at a lively trot.

They were almost to the road that led up to the Allard plantation when Lorinda became aware that they were being followed. Through the misting rain that drifted through the air like thin fog, she caught sight of a solitary horseman trailing them at a distance. A chill went through her at the thought that it might be an agent of the Gayarres, but she resolutely shook off her fear. It was probably some other poor soul on his way to The Oaks for the duel, one of the seconds or a doctor. Chances were it had nothing to do with her at all.

When the grove of tall trees came into sight, it was five minutes to eight according to the little watch that hung from a chain around her neck.

"We're in time! Oh, thank God, we're in time!" she said as the chaise rolled through the evenly mowed grass of the flat field surrounding the grove. The grass was maintained carefully in order to give sure footing to the gentlemen who came here to duel with the favorite weapons of the Creole gentry, the *colchemarde*, the rapier and the broadsword. But today it was to be pistols at thirty paces, and when Lorinda arrived, the seconds were already pacing off the distance and placing markers where the principals were to take their stand.

"Maurice! Maurice, I must speak to you!" Lorinda cried, running across the wet grass to where Maspero was standing, looking pale and ill, in the dim, misty light.

"What in the name of God are you doing here, young lady?" demanded Doctor Sienkiewicz, the Polish physician who took care of all the Masperos and who was now in attendance on Maurice. "This is no place for a lady."

"I quite agree," Joseph Gayarre said from his place a short distance away, "but this is no lady, only a little quadroon whore."

A sound like that of a wounded animal came from Maurice and he started toward Gayarre.

Sienkiewicz intercepted him. "No, none of that, lad. That won't help the situation."

"It is eight o'clock, gentlemen," Gayarre's second said, holding up his watch so all could see. "Shall we begin?"

"I'm ready," Gayarre said. "If someone will kindly clear that whore off the field of honor."

"Miss de Buys, will you come with me, please?" Dr. Sienkiewicz said, reaching for Lorinda's arm.

But she jerked away from him, threw her arms around Maurice and whispered frantically in his ear, telling him about Jessica and Joseph and the things they had forced her to do.

"Oh, my God!" he said in an anguished voice and she realized she had made things worse. A look of horror and disgust crossed Maurice's face such as she had never seen before on another human being. "Why? Oh, God, why?"

"To save you," she said. "I did it to save you. I didn't know he wouldn't keep his word."

"But how could you? I loved you and you—"

"Are you ready, Monsieur Maspero?" Gayarre's second called. Joseph was already standing, stripped to his broadcloth shirt, pistol in hand and a smile of amused contempt on his face.

"Yes. Yes, I'm ready," Maurice said, removing Lorinda's clinging hands. "More ready than ever now."

What have I done? I've destroyed him completely! He doesn't care whether he lives or dies! I've destroyed his faith in me!

As Maurice walked slowly toward the waiting men, Lorinda fumbled in her muff and found the little derringer. There was only one way to stop

Joseph from killing Maurice now, and that was to kill Joseph first. She darted forward, heading for Gayarre.

"Look at me, you pig!" she screamed. "I want to see your face when you die!"

"Look out! She's got a gun!" Sienkiewicz yelled, making a grab for her but missing as she lifted the gun, aimed at a spot between Gayarre's eyes and fired.

Only the quickness of Maurice's second saved Gayarre's life. He reached out and knocked Lorinda's hand upward just as she fired the little pistol.

"Give that to me," the man charged grabbing the gun out of her fingers.

Gayarre's second, a burly man in an overcoat with a quilted lining, hurried over to inspect the pistol. "You should file charges against this creature at once, Joseph," he said, stroking his Imperial and heavy sideburns.

"No, I won't bother," Gayarre said. "The hussy will come to heel. For now, I'll kill her paramour."

"See here, Monsieur Gayarre," said the tall, thin young man who was Maurice's second. "We are on the field of honor and that is no place for further insults."

"Do I offend you, Monsieur Pinero?" Gayarre sneered. "If so, you have recourse, you know."

Young Pinero turned white, but, drawing himself up proudly, he took a step toward Gayarre. He was stopped by Maurice.

"I thought you came here to give me satisfaction, Monsieur Gayarre," Maspero said. "Not to engage in verbal abuse."

"Very well. I shall settle with you first," Gayarre said. "If we can proceed without further interruptions."

"Gentlemen, take your places, please," Gayarre's second said, and when they were standing back to back with pistols raised, he continued, "Do you see this handkerchief, gentlemen?"

Both men nodded. "Very well. You will each take fifteen deliberate paces and turn, holding your weapons at the ready. When I drop this handkerchief, you may take aim and fire."

"You may begin, gentlemen," young Pinero said.

"Maurice, no—no, please!" Lorinda shrieked.

Maspero turned briefly to look at her, his expression devoid of everything but contempt. "Pinero, I will be grateful to you if you would restrain that woman."

Pinero reached out and drew Lorinda into the circle of his long arms. "Be silent, mademoiselle. I pray you," he said.

Lorinda huddled against him, her whole body shaking with the sobs she could no longer control. She could hear someone counting off the paces and was aware of Pinero's labored breathing. From somewhere off in the distance she thought she also heard the galloping hoofs of a horse.

Then there was a sharp, cracking sound and Pinero expelled his breath in a harsh curse and muttered, "Missed! Damn it, missed!"

There was another pause, which seemed to go on endlessly until Maurice cried out, "Damn it, man, shoot! Don't torture me!"

A cruel, self-satisfied laugh that could only have come from Joseph was his answer, followed by another sharp crack.

Lorinda screamed, knowing only too well what the result of that cool, deliberate shot had been.

"Oh, God, that swine!" Pinero gasped, releasing Lorinda and running toward the fallen Maurice.

Maurice was still alive when they reached him, lying on his back with blood running from a hole in his chest, his hand making feeble motions as though trying to pluck out the ball that had felled him. Sienkiewicz came hurrying as fast as his portly form could bring him. Setting his little black bag close at hand, he bent over Maspero. One look was enough to convince him it was hopeless.

"May God have mercy on his soul," he whispered as Lorinda dropped to her knees beside him. Maurice's eyes were open, and she thought she saw recognition in them. He moved his head slightly and opened his mouth, trying to say something. She bent closer to him, listening.

"Forgive—forgive—" was the only word she heard before his eyes closed and his head fell to the side.

"He's gone, my dear," the doctor said, holding Maurice's wrist between his stubby fingers.

Lorinda stumbled to her feet, eyes red from weeping and her lips tight and grim. Joseph was standing a few feet away, a look of such arrogant contempt on his face that she couldn't stand it. Moving with the speed of a tigress, she leaped on Gayarre and raked the nails of both hands down his face.

The man let out a howl like a wounded wolf and lashed out with his fist. "You damn little bitch!" he snarled, sending her sprawling on the wet grass.

There was blood dripping down his face as he bent over her and lifted his foot above her head. "I ought to kill you, whore! I ought to break your damn neck!"

The foot never descended. Strong arms suddenly encircled Gayarre from behind, picking him up bodily and hurling him away from the girl.

"You son of a bitch," Kirk Stryker was saying as he tossed the man to the ground. "You lily-livered son of a bitch! I'll teach you to try to stomp a woman!"

Gayarre lurched to his feet, his face black with rage. "You have insulted me, sir. My seconds will—"

Stryker's fist jammed the rest of the words down his throat and staggered him backward. Leaping after him, Stryker grabbed the front of Gayarre's shirt and dragged him forward, stopping him with another blow in the pit of his stomach. Gayarre doubled up. Before he could fall, Kirk struck his chin with such force that the man's knees folded under him. Lorinda watched fascinated as Gayarre seemed to just sit down and topple slowly over backward.

The other men came rushing toward them as Kirk leaned over to help her to her feet. Her lip was cut and there would be a bruise on the side of her face, but otherwise she was unhurt. Kirk's arm went around her, and for the first time since this whole nasty affair had begun she felt safe and secure

"What is the meaning of this?" Gayarre's second demanded as the physician worked over Joseph. "Sir, how dare you intrude on an affair of honor and turn it into a vulgar brawl?"

"An affair of honor, is it? Kirk drawled in his best Western style. "Do you honorable gentlemen usually jest stand 'round and talk while a bully beats on a lady?"

The doctor was kneeling beside Gayarre, helping him to sit up; it was he who answered. "I assure you, sir, we were about to make a protest."

"A lady? Did you say a lady?" Gayarre was still sneering, despite the blood on his face. "This is a slave wench named Lorinda de Farbin, who has been posing as a free person and calling herself Philippa de Buys. Anyone has a right to beat a runaway slave."

"Maybe so." Stryker's voice was even but steely. "But nobody has a right to beat a slave in her master's presence, and this woman just happens to belong to me."

Gayarre got to his feet and stood looking at Kirk, his face distorted by hate. "As for you, sir, you struck me."

"I sure did, just as hard as I could," Kirk smiled easily, "and I'd of hit you a couple more times if you hadn't fallen down so easy."

"Ordinarily," Gayarre said, having trouble forming the words because his lip was starting to swell, "ordinarily in New Orleans a gentleman who engages in fisticuffs places himself outside the code."

"Well, since I'm not a gentleman but just a

riverboat gambler,'' Stryker drawled, ''I never was really within the code.''

''Nevertheless,'' Gayarre said, ''I have an extreme urge to kill you, so I am going to put all considerations of honor aside.''

''Why now, Mr. Gayarre, I suspect that's something you been adoin' for a long time.''

Gayarre lunged forward, grabbing the empty pistol from the ground and brandished it over his head as though he intended to beat Kirk to death with it. The big Texan laughed and stepped aside, Lorinda still in the curve of his arm, and let the man go slithering past in the slippery grass.

''I'll kill you! Damn you, you scum, I'll kill you!'' Joseph was shouting as he turned to face Stryker again.

''Why, I'd be happy to give you a chance to do that,'' Kirk said. ''Any time you think you're able to stand up.''

A man of Gayarre's character, adept at sneering and mockery, couldn't tolerate having it turned against him. He screamed in impotent rage and tried to grab the sword cane his second was carrying.

''You better hang on to that little pig-sticker of yours, mister,'' Kirk said to the second. '' 'Cause if fancy britches gets holt of it and tries to use it on me, I might just take it away from him and jam it up his ass.''

''This is intolerable,'' Gayarre's second broke in. ''The man is a barbarian. You must ignore him, Joseph.''

''No—no, I'm going to kill him!'' Gayarre

yelled. He was still having trouble keeping his balance, but his black rage frightened Lorinda. "You're my second, Paul. Arrange it at once!"

The man moved toward Kirk warily, as though he expected the gambler to pounce on him. "May I have a word with you, sir?"

"You sure can, friend," Kirk said.

"My principal desires to call you out," the man said with a formal little bow.

"Yeah, I heard what he said."

"Kirk, please don't," Lorinda pleaded, but Stryker paid no heed.

"Will you accept the challenge?" the burly man asked, pulling nervously at his Imperial.

"Sure will," Kirk drawled, "and since I'm the challenged party, I reckon I'll just pick the weapons, too."

"Yes, that is your privilege," the second acknowledged with an uneasy glance at Gayarre.

"Hmmm, let's see." Kirk pretended to think. "I shore do have to admit your man is a dead cool shot 'cause I seen him stand there and kill that young fella in cold blood after makin' him squirm for a while.. So I guess we won't use pistols. And it seems like I've heard tell that he's pretty good with the rapier and probably the épée."

"He's a master of the saber, also," Lorinda whispered anxiously. "Don't do it, Kirk, for God's sake!"

"You shush, girl," Stryker said quietly. "I know what I'm doing."

"So, no pistols, no rapier, no épée and no

saber,'' the burly second said, venturing a slight smile. ''That does not leave much in the choice of weapons, does it, *sir?*''

''Oh, seems like I've heard of some others,'' Stryker said, his voice taking on an edge of insolence. ''There was a couple of fellows awhile back who fought with double-barreled shotguns, I hear tell. Another fellow—he was a blacksmith, and he was challenged by a bigshot duelist—got his choice of weapons and picked sledgehammers. He also got to pick the place to fight and chose Lake Pontchartrain in six feet of water.''

Stryker paused, letting a grin cross his face as both Gayarre and his second stared in outraged dignity and awaited the end of the ridiculous tale.

''Well, sir, that sledgehammer and that six feet of water presented kind of a problem to that fancy-assed duelist 'cause he was only five foot eight and could hardly lift a sledgehammer. So he just had to come down off his high horse and apologize to that there blacksmith.''

The second looked bewildered. ''Am I to understand that you propose to fight with sledgehammers in six feet of water?''

''Shucks, no,'' Stryker said. ''I wouldn't know where to find two sledgehammers and getting to the lake would take too long. I'd kinda like to get this over with and take the *lady* out of this damp.''

''Then what is your choice of weapons?''

''Why, I reckon I hanker after Bowie knives at one pace with him and me having one hand tied behind us and our knives in the other,'' Kirk said, all pretense of politeness leaving his voice. ''That's the way I like to kill a man who really needs killing 'cause it takes longer for him to die.''

The second took a hasty step backward, and Gayarre's doctor came toward them. ''I really must protest. This is most irregular. It is downright barbaric.''

''Might seem so to you, mister, but that's the way we do it down in Texas.''

Having recovered his wits if not his courage, the second shrugged slightly. ''You spoke of not being able to find two sledgehammers. I am equally at a loss as to where to locate two Bowie knives.''

''That's no problem,'' Kirk said, moving toward his horse, ''I always carry a couple in my saddle bag.''

In a moment he was back with a wooden case, which he opened to reveal two of the heavy, curved knives. ''These little tokens was given to me by Colonel James Bowie when I was just a shaver. He's the fellow who invented 'em, you know, afore he got himself kilt at the Alamo.''

He took one of the wicked-looking weapons out of the case and tested it with a finger. ''Probably needs a bit of sharpening, but that don't rightly matter since they're already sharp enough to cut a man's head right off his body with one swipe.''

Gayarre, his second and his doctor were gaping at the savage blade. To Lorinda, Joseph looked as though he had suddenly developed the ague. His friends had paled visibly.

''Now this here blade is only about ten inches long and it's kind of thick for a good thrusting weapon,'' Kirk said, ''but when it comes to hack-ing and slicing off hands and ears and noses and the like, there ain't no equal.''

"This is barbaric,'' the doctor repeated.

"Sure is,'' Stryker agreed. "Why, they tell me that when they found the Colonel's body at the Alamo there was almost a dozen Mexicans stretched out around him. Some of 'em was dead and some alive, but there wasn't a one still had a nose.''

Suddenly realizing Stryker's game, Lorinda smothered a giggle as she saw the vain Gayarre raise a hand to touch his nose.

"Some had both ears missing, too,'' Stryker said, tossing a knive into the air and catching it with his other hand behind him.

"Joseph, you do not have to fight this man,'' the second said. "He has no standing under the code of honor. In fact, you could have him horsewhipped and driven out of town, and—''

The Bowie knife, which had been in the air a second before, was suddenly quive ing in the ground beside the burly man's boot. Astonished, Lorinda could see that the leather down one side of the boot was split wide open clear to the sole where the knife had passed without leaving even a scratch on the leg within.

"What was you saying about horsewhipping, mister?'' Kirk asked. "There's not a fella in New Orleans, nor several fellas even, who could horse-whip Kirk Stryker without getting their hands sliced off in the process.''

He was balancing the other knife in his hand and had opened his coat to reveal the Colt revolver nestled against his bright checked vest. "Now I figure I been challenged and we ought to get on with the fight just as soon as your man there can stop his knees from knocking together."

Gayarre blanched.

"That is," Stryker amended, "unless your man is ready to apologize."

"You don't have to apologize to this savage, Joseph," the doctor said. "You can just walk away from here and no one will think any the less of you."

Joseph Gayarre's eyes went from the doctor to his second, who nodded encouragingly, then to Pinero, who merely shrugged, and finally to Dr. Sienkiewicz, who scowled at him.

"Yes," Gayerre said as though trying to convince himself. "There would be no honor gained from engaging in the sort of bloodletting this—this person proposes. I will not sully myself."

Lorinda's laugh rang out, as bitter and angry as a curse.

Gayarre turned scarlet and flashed the girl a look of such venomous hate that she almost wished Stryker was serious in his proposal to carve the man up with his dreadful knife.

"Come, Joseph, let us go," the second said, taking Joseph by the arm. "This is all so vulgar."

"Yes, Monsieur Gayarre," the doctor said. "The only part a gentleman can rightly play in an affair of this nature is to turn and walk away, putting it all behind him."

It was Sienkiewicz's turn to laugh, but Gayarre chose to ignore it.

"I don't think you gents had better leave just yet." Stryker said, the drawl more exaggerated than before. "You see, I got a feeling that the only way this can be properly settled, outside of some pig-sticking, is with an apology."

"You expect me to apologize to you?" Gayarre asked. "It was you who struck me."

"Shucks, no, I don't need no apology," Stryker grinned. "I got my satisfaction when I split your lip and gave you a bellyache."

"Then what are you talking about?"

"I'm talking about you apologizing to this little lady," Stryker said, pushing Lorinda forward with his big hand.

"Me apologize to that slave?" Gayarre's color was more normal and the sneer was back in his voice.

"That's right. You apologize to this girl for the way you were knocking her about when I came riding up or—" Kirk tossed one of the knives into the air and the second one after it. He caught both of them with one hand, then balanced one on the end of his thumb while he grinned menacingly at Gayarre.

Lorinda's eye fell on Maurice's body, and the full horror of the day's events swept over her. Trembling, she turned to Stryker. "Let him go, please. I'd just like to get away from this place."

Stryker ignored her. "I'm going to give you five tosses of the knife into the air, Gayarre," he said, and all trace of the back country drawl was gone. "If you don't apologize by then, I'm going to throw one of these knives at your feet. When I do, you'd better grab it up quick because I'm going to be coming after you with the other.''

Faced with a pistol or a sword, Gayarre was sure of his superior ability and passed for a brave man; but with the threat of the savage-looking knives staring him in the face, he was more cowardly than Lorinda would have believed possible. His ague came back and his face turned deathly pale. ''I'm not well,'' he whined. ''The blows have weakened me. You wouldn't take advantage of that, would you?''

''I wouldn't if I hadn't seen you stand there with a loaded pistol and torture that boy before you killed him,'' Stryker said. ''You knew he was frightened, but he didn't shake and he didn't try to worm out of it after he missed you. Now, are you going to apologize, or do I cut off your nose and ears before I carve a hole in your belly and let your guts come tumbling out?''

''I—'' Gayarre looked at the doctor and his second. ''You gentlemen have sword canes. Help me!''

''I wouldn't do that if I were you, gentlemen,'' Stryker said, balancing one knife in his right hand and holding the other in his left, ''because before either of you got three feet toward me with those pretty toy swords, you'd each have a Bowie sticking in your throat up to the hilt. Then I'd be put to the trouble of pulling one out so I could carve up your cowardly friend.''

''For God's sake, apologize, Gayarre, and let's get out of here,'' the doctor said. ''Do it before this savage kills us all!''

Gayarre looked as though he were being forced to swallow poison. "I—I regret that I struck you," he said icily to Lorinda.

"Hold on now," Stryker said as the man started to turn away. "I don't rightly consider that a proper apology."

"Let him go, Kirk, please," Lorinda said. "I can't bear to look at him any longer."

"All right, honey," Stryker said and waved the knife at Gayarre. "Get your ass out of here before I change my mind and shock this *lady* by splattering blood all over this place!"

CHAPTER 18

"You were magnificent," Lorinda said, snuggling naked under a sheet in Kirk Stryker's bed in his palatial suite at the St. Charles Hotel, the newest and finest in New Orleans.

"I was rather good, wasn't I?" he said. "Especially when I lifted you right up off the mattress without using my hands."

"Idiot!" she said, slapping his bare bottom lightly. "I meant at The Oaks, when you turned those arrogant Creole tigers into mewing kittens. Although I thought the frontier accent and the description of all those noseless Mexicans at the Alamo was a little farfetched."

"Nope, I counted them myself," he said, stretching in a way that made his powerful back muscles ripple, filling her with delight. "I checked each one to make sure he didn't have a nose."

"Ha! You weren't old enough to have been at the Alamo, and if you had been, you'd have been killed with all the rest of the gringos."

"Some women are just too smart for their britches," he said, rolling toward her to kiss the tip of her nose.

"I don't have any britches," she said. "And you haven't even let me put my pantalettes on for three days."

"Always said you looked better without clothes than with them," he teased.

"Around you I'll never get a chance to find out how I look dressed," she countered.

"Oh, you can get dressed," he said. "We might quit having all our meals in bed now that the edge is off my appetite."

"Some appetite! I was beginning to think I was going to get calluses on my bottom."

He laughed and kissed the pink tip of each breast, the deep eye of her navel and each dimpled knee. "I'll pass up my favorite place for now, or we'll never get out of bed."

"Yes, please do, because we have to think of something else, and when you start doing that, I can't think at all."

"What's to think about?" he said, sitting up and stretching again, causing his deep chest to expand and making her want to kiss him as he had kissed her.

They hadn't talked about what had happened at The Oaks since the first night, when she had fallen apart and sobbed for hours. He had held her and soothed her until she was calm enough to tell him the whole sorry story of the events that had precipitated the tragic duel. In fact, they had talked very little about anything in the last three days because they had discovered how desperately their bodies needed to be together. Lorinda still didn't want to discuss Maurice's death, but now at least she felt able to deal with Kirk's part in the affair.

"I'm glad you didn't kill Joseph," she said. "He deserved it, but I'm glad you didn't do it."

"If I had known about that business between you and him and that obscene female of his, he wouldn't have gotten off so easy," Stryker said grimly as he reached for his pants and pulled them on.

"What you made him do was more humiliating," she said.

"Yeah, I guess it was. Taking away a man's self-esteem in front of his friends might be worse than killing him."

"And you don't have his blood on your hands."

He looked at her with raised eyebrows as he put on his boots. "And what were you trying to do when you fired that derringer at him?"

"Kill him," she admitted, "but I would have regretted it later."

"That's odd," Stryker said with a dry laugh. "I could have put a bullet or a knife in him and never given it a second thought."

"I don't believe you," she said. "You're much more sensitive than you pretend to be."

"Yeah? Don't be too sure. The way I look at it is, if I had killed him I'd never have to worry about him again. Now I'm going to be walking around with my shoulder blades twitching. He hasn't got the guts to face me again, but he has the money to hire someone to bushwhack me on a dark street."

She smiled up at him as he got to his feet and put his shirt on. "You've got me to guard your back."

"That's not exactly the job I had in mind for you," he said, "and if you don't get out of that bed and put some clothes on, I'll get back in and show you what your real job is."

"I don't have any decent clothes," she said.

"You ripped them all off me a couple of days ago."

He laughed. "Guess I was kind of in a hurry, but I'd been without for a long time."

"Without? I don't believe it! As long as there's a woman left in the world, Kirk Stryker will never be without."

"Well, let's say I'd been without the special kind of lovin' I get from you."

"Flatterer!" she said, sitting up and letting the sheet fall.

His gray eyes widened and grew dark with desire. "Damn if you aren't the most perfectly put together piece of woman flesh I ever saw!"

"Thank you, but I still don't have any clothes."

"Sure you do," he said. "That first night after you went to sleep I sent for your things from that house on Rampart Street. They're in trunks down in the storage room. All you got to do is pull the bellrope and have someone bring them up for you."

"You did that without a word to me?"

"Well, I figured you wouldn't want to be going back there for a while at least."

"See, you are more sensitive than you admit."

"Hardly think so," he said. "I was probably just jealous because you belonged to that young fellow longer than you've belonged to me."

"But you don't need to be jealous of poor Maurice," she said. "You know how I feel about you."

He smiled as he tied his cravat. "Yes, you do seem to indicate some slight interest."

"What are we going to do, Kirk?" she asked. "Where are we going?"

"Kansas," he said promptly. "Told you that a long time ago."

"But Kansas is still closed to settlers, isn't it?"

"It is right now, but by the time we get up to St. Louis, they'll be seriously considering opening Kansas and Nebraska to settlers. Us smart fellows will get in on the ground floor and get all the land we want."

"I don't understand this craze of yours for land," she said.

"If you'd been raised on a tiny five-acre farm in Maine, where it's difficult to raise anything but an amazing variety of rocks, you'd understand. Owning a lot of rich, fertile land has always been my ambition. I told you before I want to raise wheat. Most of it is being grown in Illinois, Indiana and Wisconsin, but in my opinion, the best wheat-growing land of all is in Kansas, and I intend to have my share."

"And I suppose you'll be taking slaves there to work your overgrown farm," she said, hoping he'd deny it. No matter what she had believed in the past, she knew now that slavery was wrong. It was wrong in the states where it existed, and it would be doubly wrong in any new states that were to be created.

"I sure am," he said, and her heart sank. "I'm taking my whole crew of slaves and I'm going to hook her up to a plow and make her push it."

She laughed in excited relief. "She'll do it, too, if she can have a jackass named Stryker to pull the plow while she pushed."

He reached for her and pulled her down into his

lap. "The trouble with some slaves is that they get too high and mighty and have to be taken down a peg or two."

He tilted her head back and kissed her deeply and thoroughly, calling a halt only when they both began to breathe hard. "Whoa there, missy. A few more minutes of that and we'll be right back where we started from. And before we put in another three days, I'd like to go out and have a steak about a foot thick, some oysters, some bouillabaisse and a little champagne. So you ring that bellrope and have your duds brought up pronto."

An hour later they were in the plush velvet and damask interior of Antoine's, enjoying the kind of superb meal that only that elegant restaurant could produce. At first, Lorinda had been hesitant about going there because Antoine had known her father. She was afraid that if he had heard of the change in her fortunes he might refuse to serve her.

Luckily there was no problem. Whether he knew of Lorinda's new status or not, he was his usual urbane self, suggesting dishes he was particularly proud of and the wines that would go best with them.

Kirk loved the gumbo and found the lobster exquisite, but he cringed when he discovered what the escargot Lorinda had ordered really were.

"You're going to eat snails?" he demanded, his Anglo-Saxon squeamishness coming to the fore.

"But of course. They are delicious fixed this way."

He pretended to shudder. "Just think, I've been

in bed with a snail-eating Frenchie and didn't know it.''

"Snails are a far better aphrodisiac than oysters," she told him.

"Really? Can't say as I've ever seen snails making love," he said, breaking and buttering crusty bread. "In fact, I would say a snail is a creature even another snail couldn't love.''

Lorinda was laughing but stopped abruptly when she saw a tall, hard-faced man standing in the doorway. He was dressed in black except for a gray vest and had two gold teeth that gleamed in the subdued light of the restaurant. He was talking to another man who wore a heavy black mustache.

"What's the matter?" Kirk asked, looking up from his lobster. "See someone you know?''

"No, I don't know them, but they seem to know us," she said. "Those two in the entryway are watching us.''

Turning casually, as though she had called his attention to the gown of one of the elegantly dressed women who were just entering with their escorts, Kirk inspected the two men.

"Do you know them?" she asked.

"Can't say that I do, but maybe they know me. Could be they're a couple of country jakes looking for a game.''

"They don't look like country jakes to me," she said, "and they certainly are not typical New Orleans gentlemen. They make me nervous, staring at me that way.''

"Eat your snails before they crawl off your

plate,'' Kirk advised. ''Those fellows are probably just thinking what a lucky gent I am to have such a raving beauty at my table. They'd be even more jealous if they knew I also had you in my bed.''

The two men had moved through the entryway and were now out of sight. Feeling less uneasy, Lorinda returned to her food.

She didn't think of the pair again until she and Kirk were on their way back to the St. Charles in the *caleche* Stryker had rented. They had just turned into Common Street and were approaching St. Charles Avenue when she noticed that a closed brougham had also made the turn. The face staring out the window of the brougham was that of the man with the ferocious-looking mustache.

''Kirk, I think those men are following us,'' she whispered.

Stryker had eaten well and drunk more than he'd eaten, so he wasn't at his most alert. He was slumped down in the seat, long legs stretched out and his Stetson tipped over his eyes. ''Huh? What men?'' he asked sleepily.

''Those two who were in Antoine's. Why would they be following us?''

''They got their eyes on you. Maybe they think I'll throw you away after I've used you a few more times.''

''Don't talk like a damn fool!'' she hissed. ''This is serious. They could have been hired by Joseph Gayarre. You said yourself he might hire someone to shoot you in the back.''

''Doubt it,'' Kirk mumbled. ''Good shooters

don't make themselves so obvious before they pull the trigger.''

"Well, they're up to something. They haven't taken their eyes off of us.''

"Forget them,'' he said, putting a hand on her knee. ''We're almost back to the hotel and I got more important things on my mind.''

"I've never seen you when you didn't have that on your mind,'' she said, ''but you've had too much to drink to do much of anything. I told you not to have that third brandy.''

"Now you're starting to sound like a wife,'' he said with a yawn. ''I don't like wives unless they belong to someone else and are looking for a playmate.''

"You couldn't play with anybody in the state you're in.''

"Want to bet?'' he asked.

"Bet,'' she said.

Ten minutes later they were in their room and Stryker was sprawled across the bed with his clothes still on. She was staring down at him, hands on her hips and a look of exasperation on her face.

"Look at you! You get me all in a dither with your kisses and fumblings in the carriage and then you collapse when we get here.''

His answer was a half snore.

"Well, I'll have to get your clothes off. You can't sleep in those.''

She started with his boots, pulling them off after quite a struggle. Tossing his feet up onto the bed, she undressed herself until she was down to only her shift. Then, kneeling beside him on the bed, she began to work on him.

When she finally had him undressed, she turned down the gas, yanked her shift off over her head, and snuggled down beside him. She pulled the blankets up over them and stretched out full length along his side, feeling her breasts flatten against his arm, her thighs rub the sides of his.

"Kirk," she whispered in his ear, "you didn't do what you said you were going to, what you bet you could."

He muttered something unintelligible. She slid her hand across his belly and began to caress him with light, daring fingers.

Somewhere outside the hotel a banjo was strumming and a voice was singing.

> *"We loved each other then, Lorena,*
> *More than we e'er dared to tell."*

"What is it?" Kirk murmured. "What's going on?"

"I'm trying to seduce you," she whispered.

The tender and melancholy music was still drifting in the window, making her feel both sad and amorous.

> *"It matters little now, Lorena,*
> *The past is the eternal past,*
> *Our heads will soon lie low, Lorena—"*

"What's going on?" Stryker was definitely awake now and apparently feeling as romantic as she was.

"I'm trying to love you now," she said, rolling over on top of him and wriggling around until every nerve ending in her slender, high-breasted body was in contact with his flesh.

His hands caressed her satin-skinned back as he responded to her movements and surged deep inside her.

"More, darling, more!" she urged with her lips molded to his while her hips moved in anguished circles to take in all of him.

They seemed to melt and blend together, the fine instruments of their physical beings leading them to a sense of oneness while still retaining their unique individuality.

It may have happened to every pair of lovers since the world began, but Lorinda didn't believe it. This was their own private rapture, and it ended only when something wild and wonderful exploded inside of them, sending fingers of multicolored fire to spin around in her brain. It reminded her of a swamp fire she had seen once in Mississippi. She screamed as the flames consumed her; then, with a sob of pure joy, she relaxed in the warm afterglow, knowing that Kirk had experienced the same fantastic sensation.

Later she slipped off him and slept in the crook of his arm, a sleep so deep and contented that not even the savage thunderstorm that shook the city during the night awakened her.

What did awaken her was Stryker gently removing his arm and getting out of bed. Through her long lashes she watched the play of watery sunshine across his arms and shoulders.

"Do you have to get up so early?" she asked.

He grinned down at her. "I think it's time I went

down and booked passage for us on a steamer for St. Louis.''

''Why are you in such a hurry? This is an awfully nice bed.''

''They have nice beds on steamers, too,'' he said. ''I've been thinking about those two men you saw giving us the eye last night. I don't like it.''

''You didn't seem bothered about it last night,'' she said.

''I know, but last night I was in what the Greeks used to call a euphoric state and it didn't seem to matter.''

''You mean you were drunk.''

''Pleasantly liquored up,'' he corrected. ''But this morning I got to thinking about it and decided it's time for us to leave.''

Lorinda was out of bed, reaching for her clothes. ''I'll go with you to the booking office. I don't want to stay here by myself. There's something about that pair that makes me nervous.''

They were both nearly dressed when a stealthy sound outside the door caused Stryker to turn quickly and reach for the holstered Colt hanging from the bedpost. Before he could get a hand on it, the door was suddenly thrown open and half a dozen men poured into the room.

''There she is, boys. There's the runaway!'' said the fleshy man dressed in black. ''I have a warrant for the apprehension of a runaway wench belonging to August Wenzel of Claiborne County, Mississippi. Take her!

''Take her, hell!'' Stryker growled and grabbed the arm of a bullet-headed bruiser in striped shirt and duck pants who was reaching for Lorinda. The waterfront bully snarled and swung a fist gleaming with brass knuckles at Stryker.

Kirk blocked the blow with a raised arm, but Lorinda saw him wince. She made a dash for the derringer she had left on the nightstand. The man with the two gold teeth intercepted her. She turned, screaming and kicking at him as he twisted her arm behind her and tried to force her toward the door.

Stryker had pulled the bullet-headed man to him by the arm, now he brought his knee up to catch him in the groin. The plug-ugly doubled up, groaning. But he recovered quickly, straightened up and locked both hands above his head, aiming a double-fisted blow at the back of Stryker's neck. Stryker ducked his head and rammed it into the man's belly, sending him sprawling.

"Use your saps!" the man in black was yelling. "Don't worry about smashing his skull; he's a slave stealer!"

Two other men had closed in around Stryker. Cautiously, they circled him, each carrying a blackjack, looking for an opening. Alert, hands up like those of a wrestler, Stryker feinted and parried, keeping them off balance.

Lorinda had managed to break free from her gold-toothed attacker and now was desperately trying to open the case in which Stryker carried his Bowie knives. If she could toss one of them to him, she knew he would be more than a match for the six intruders.

But it wasn't to be. Before she could get the case open, the gang leader and a man in a red stocking cap grabbed her, one by the waist, the other by the feet. As she was carried kicking and screaming from the room, she saw Stryker stunned by a blow from a blackjack. The bullet-headed thug he had butted to the floor rolled over and grabbed him by the legs, and a second man sapped him again. Stryker crumpled to the floor.

Outside in the hall, Lorinda screamed and struggled. The man holding her about the waist shifted his grip upward to pinion her flailing arms, and she sank her teeth into his wrist. He swore and released her, but before she could move, he clipped her across the chin, stunning her. He seized her wrists and twisted both arms up behind her back.

"She's a hellcat! Watch her!" yelled the man in the red stocking cap, getting an arm around her neck.

"Finish him off and come on!" the gang leader shouted to the four still in the room with Stryker.

And as they carried Lorinda downstairs, she heard the sound of fists, booted feet and blackjacks thudding into Stryker's unconscious body. Seconds later, the men came clattering down the stairs, savage grins on their faces, blood splattered on clothes and weapons. "He's finished," the bullet-headed man said. "Let's get the hell out of here!" "Gag that slave!" the leader bellowed.

Lorinda tried to scream again, but a dirty handkerchief was jammed into her mouth, almost choking her. Then she was carried down a long hallway to the rear of the hotel.

Outside, another man was waiting. Through a

haze of anger and grief, Lorinda recognized him—
Joseph Gayarre!

"My thanks to you, Mr. Gayarre," the gang boss
said. "The tip you sent us in Vicksburg is what put
us on the trail of this here runaway."

"And thank you, Ankins," Gayarre said, "for
finishing off that bastard of a gambler for me and
taking this wench back to her master. My only regret is that I won't be on hand at the plantation
when they whip this bitch. Tell 'em to lay it onto
her, teach her not to run away again."

Too heartsick to care what was going to happen
to her, Lorinda was screaming inside her head.
*They've killed Kirk! I'll never see him again! Never
love him again . . . never feel the strength and
warmth of his body against mine . . . never feel his
lips on mine! Oh, God, I can't stand it! Let me die,
too!*

CHAPTER 19

"Yes, that's good, that's the way I want her, Turk," Jacob Wenzel said, surveying the way his two black slave drivers had bound Lorinda's arms to the whipping post in the basement of Solitaire. "You boys are beginning to show some understanding of my methods."

"Yes, suh, Masta Jacob suh." Turk was a huge scarred black who had been one of the few troublemakers on Solitaire in Lorinda's father's time. A bullying savage, he had made the lives of other slaves miserable. Now he seemed to be Wenzel's favorite. "Yo' wan' Ah should whop her, Masta Jacob suh? Kinda give me pleasure, it would, to slice that pretty white skin."

"No, Turk," Jacob said. He was older and more fleshy than Gideon, but he had the same fuzzy blond hair, the same pinkish complexion. His mouth showed the same weakness, but in some way it was more sensual and more cruel. "I wouldn't allow anyone else to share this pleasure, and besides, I don't want her cut or marked up."

"Yes, suh, Masta Jacob, suh," Turk said, looking disappointed. He had an old score to settle with her, Lorinda knew. He had been nursing a deep resentment against her ever since she had discovered him brutalizing young Sammy, a crippled teenage slave she had made a pet of. She had seen to it that Turk had been confined with only bread and water for a week. Turk had never forgotten that.

"See this whip, Turk?" Jacob held up a whip made of a stout, flexible stalk covered with a tapering leather plait, which formed the lash. To the end of the lash was attached a soft, dry, buckskin cracker approximately ten to twelve inches long. The cracker was the only part allowed to touch the bare flesh of the person being beaten. An experienced hand could make it sting and burn the flesh without actually cutting it. "This is a marvelous creation for inflicting pain without marring that smooth, delicate white flesh."

"That ain' the kind o' whip Ah'd use on her," Turk said. "That'll nevah teach her nuthin', Masta Jacob, suh."

"Yes, Turk, I know what you'd do. You'd cut her up just to see the blood spurt and she wouldn't be worth a damn for the rest of her life."

"Wouldn't care iffen she warn't," the big black said, with a venomous look at Lorinda. "She jes' a black slave wench under that white skin, an' she so uppity when Masta Jules alive that she look right at you and not see you."

"Nevertheless, that white-skinned body is a valuable piece of property, Turk," Jacob said, flexing the whip. "Unscarred, it will bring a great deal of money. Cut to pieces, it wouldn't be worth any more than any flea-bitten field hand."

"Yes, suh, Masta Jacob, suh," Turk said. "You wants Turk to he'p you whop her with that fly-swatter?"

"No, I think not," Jacob said. "Now that you've got her all trussed up and ready, you and Jeremiah can go. This is very personal between me and this little beauty. I have my own memories of this one. You're right about her being so uppity she looked right through folks without seeing them. She did it to me, too, but now she's going to learn to see me. In fact, she's going to learn to get down on her knees and beg for my loving. Yes, you boys go now and leave me to my pleasure."

Lorinda heard the two slaves thumping up the stairs. She saw Jacob moving closer to her. He picked up the lantern that had been sitting on the floor and hung it on a rafter so that she was standing in the center of a circle of light.

"And now, my dear, we are alone," Jacob said, his voice low and caressing. "Alone and ready to enjoy each other's company."

Lorinda said nothing. At first she hadn't cared what happened to her. With Kirk dead, nothing else had seemed to matter. But now that she had arrived at Solitaire and seen how things were going for the folks she and her father had taken such good care of, she had a reason to go on living. Revenge for herself was one thing, but when she thought of what had been done to Kirk Stryker and the people at Solitaire, she knew she would never rest until Joseph Gayarre and the Wenzels had paid for their crimes.

After that miserable ride from New Orleans she

had been dragged off the wagon and dropped unceremoniously on the ground, only to find the familiar face of Sissy bending over her.

"Oh, Miss Lori . . . Miss Lori darlin' . . . they catched you." Lorinda felt a rush of tenderness as she gazed into Sissy's haggard face. There was a scar on the girl's left cheek and a purple discoloration around one eye. Instead of the clean, neat clothes she had worn when she had accompanied Lorinda to New Orleans, Sissy was clad in a ragged, dirty dress.

"Hello, Sissy," Lorinda croaked, her throat so dry she could barely speak. Her mind was reeling with shock and dismay.

"Kin Ah git yo' anything, Miss Lori?" Sissy whispered, looking around fearfully to where Ankins and his partner were talking to August and Jacob Wenzel.

"Water, please, Sissy. I'm so thirsty."

The girl scurried away and soon came creeping back with a tin cup of cool spring water. Lorinda sipped at it eagerly.

"I'se so glad to see you, Miss Lori," the girl said. "Them Wenzels is the awfulest thing that evah happen to us."

"What do you mean? Have they sold some of our people?"

"No'm, but most of 'em wish they had. I sho' wish they sold me. They a 'turnin' Solitaire into a slave-breedin' farm. They settin' up our cabins like they was brothels so's they kin breed us an' sell us for profit."

Lorinda remembered now that Gideon had told

her his father intended to do that. She had heard of slave-breeding plantations where the only crop was black flesh but had never known one to actually exist. It was one of those things the slave-owner class considered immoral. It was all right to buy and sell slaves, but to breed them was thought to be un-Christian, and if a member of the planter class had dared set up such a place, he would have brought down on his head the condemnation of the whole neighborhood. But the Wenzels were not members of the planter class and had none of the paternalistic noblesse oblige attitude of most plantation owners. As for the good opinion of their neighbors, it meant nothing to them.

"That's terrible, Sissy. I wish there was something I could do."

"So do I, Miss Lori," the girl said, close to tears. "That ole Gideon, after he pestered me hisself, he give me to Turk, and that Turk's the baddest nigger you evah did see. He so plum mean he cain' pester a gal 'thout knockin' her around. Jes gotta be somethin' you can do."

Lorinda shook her head. "No, I'm afraid not, Sissy. I'm in the same boat as all of you. I'm a slave, too."

"But you cain' be. You white, and white folks ain' slaves."

"I'm only white on the outside," Lorinda told her. "Inside I'm the same as you and the others."

"Hey, you! What you doin' there, gal?" Ankins yelled and came toward the two girls. "What you think you're doin'?"

"Jes' givin' her some water, thass all, jes' some water," Sissy said.

"Well, you've given it to her. Now get the hell back where you belong, or I'll give you a few lashes 'crost your black butt."

"Ah'll try to talk to you later," Sissy whispered. "Ah tell Chatti you heah."

After Ankins had collected his reward money and driven off, August and Jacob had come to stand over Lorinda, who was still bound hand and foot. August had hooked the toe of his boot under her bedraggled skirts and flipped them up to expose her legs up past her knees.

"Pretty as ever, ain't she?" he said. "Been busted long since but don't look any the worse for it."

"They say she's a regular hellcat though," Jacob said. "She clawed up two of the bully boys Ankins hired to get her away from that slave-stealing gambler."

"So I heard. Well, I'll be depending on you to break her, my boy. You're good at destroying the spirit of horses and women. What happened to the gambler?"

"He cashed in his chips," Jacob chortled in a high-pitched, almost falsetto, voice.

"Good! Then there won't be any trouble about that bill of sale your stupid brother gave him."

"No," Jacob agreed. "He sure won't be around waving it in front of any judge."

"You planning on working on her tonight?" August asked, pushing the toe of his boot into the small of Lorinda's back. "I'd like to have her ready for breeding as soon as possible."

"You just leave her to me, pa. I'll spend the whole night working on her if necessary."

It was then Jacob had called Turk and Jeremiah and had Lorinda carried into the basement and lashed to the whipping post with chains replacing the rope around her wrists and ankles.

"How do you feel, my dear?" Jacob was asking now. He came up so close behind her that she could feel his breath on the back of her neck.

"I feel like I'd like to kill you!" she spat.

"Naughty, naughty," he said. "That's very un-ladylike. When you thought you were a hoity-toity white heiress, I remember you were always a per-fect lady."

Jacob's fingers were caressing the back of her neck. "Such a pretty thing, but always so inacces-sible in the past. Now you are nothing if not acces-sible, aren't you, my dear?"

"Go to hell, you mincing swine!" She turned her head quickly and sank her teeth into the pudgy white hand.

"You damn little vixen!" he snarled. But he re-gained control of himself almost instantly. "No, no, I must not lose my temper. This must all be done calmly and without anger so that I may savor every subtle nuance of it."

He came around in front of her, and she saw the sadistic smile on his face and the gleam of anticipa-tion in his pale blue eyes. She raised her chin proud-ly, glaring at him, not wanting him to know how she was trembling inside.

"I think we'll begin by taking a more intimate look at that extraordinary body of yours. You don't mind if I, ahem, undress you, do you?"

He reached into a pocket and drew out a folding

knife. Flicking it open, he drew the sharp blade slowly down the front of her dress. In spite of her resolution not to appear afraid, Lorinda sucked in her breath as the razor-sharp edge cut through the layers of cloth. She stood motionless while he slit open the shoulder seams and let all her garments fall in a heap around her feet.

"Ah yes, exquisite," he said, standing back to admire her nudity. "I do think, my dear, that you are the most beautiful female I have ever seen. You have to be whipped, but I must be careful not to mar you in any way. Your value lies in the perfection of your form."

Her back stiffened as his fingers trailed down her spine, stroked across the roundness of her buttocks to her thighs and then touched the soft intimate center of her being. She couldn't control the tremor of revulsion that passed through her. Jacob laughed his shrill, womanish laugh and withdrew his hand.

"Yes, yes, this is going to be fun," he said, backing away and raising the whip. "There is no pleasure if the woman is willing."

Lorinda braced herself for the first stroke. It came in a hot, stinging slash across her shoulder blades. In spite of her resolution not to cry out, she heard herself scream.

"Oh, that's nice. That makes me feel ever so lusty and virile," Jacob said, and the whip moved down her spine to sear the soft globes of her buttocks.

Later, she never knew how much later, there was a red haze of fire consuming every part of her. The pain extended the entire length of her back and on

down over her buttocks to the backs of her thighs.
Slowly, she became aware that Jacob was unlock-
ing the chains that held her to the post. Once released, she slumped to the floor. He picked her up
under the arms and half-dragged, half-carried her
into a smaller room beyond the main chamber of the
basement.

"Now you've had a good lesson," Jacob was
saying. "It is necessary to break in a slave with a
good lashing. If the slave is humble and appears
duly sensitive of the impropriety of his or her conduct, only a moderate chastisement will be adminis-
tered. If, however, the slave is stubborn, a slight
punishment will only make bad worse. She must
then be thrashed very soundly and have salt rubbed
into her wounds. Are you going to be sensitive to
the impropriety of your conduct, little Lori, or will I
have to use the lash on you next time?"

The pain was so bad she could hardly think, but
the words he was mouthing sounded familiar. Slave
owners often wrote long letters to the local newspa-
per expressing their philosophy on the disciplining
of slaves. Jacob apparently had read them and was
acting on their principles.

He had let her sit down on a low cot under a
barred window and was standing over her now.
Eyes dulled by the pain, she stared up at him. Some
time during the beating he had stripped. Now his
plump body, as grayish white as a dead fish,
loomed monstrously before her. He was in a state of
sexual arousal. Her insides convulsed with horror as
she realized how completely she was at his mercy.

"I asked you a question," he said, leaning forward to take her chin in his fingers, "and I expect an answer."

She wasn't sure what the question was, but she opened her mouth and tried to speak. Her voice was only a husky croak again, this time from screaming. The flaming torture of her back and thighs made her want to scream anew.

"Don't be stubborn, Lorinda," Jacob warned; he still held the whip in his hand. "Good slaves answer when their master asks a question."

"I—can't—throat—" she managed with great effort.

"Your throat is sore, is it? Well, whose fault is that? Certainly not mine. I didn't tell you to do all that screaming. Now answer my question, dear, or I'll have to punish you some more."

No, no, she couldn't stand that! Anything was better than more of this terrible, all-consuming pain.

"Wh—what did you ask?"

"Ah-ha, you weren't listening. Not listening is a very bad habit, Lorinda. A good slave should listen carefully when her master speaks."

"I hurt."

"And you'll hurt more unless you've learned your lesson. The question I asked was whether you were humble and duly sensitive of the impropriety of your actions up to now?"

"Yes. Yes, I am," she said.

"Very well. Then I shall let you off with only the slight punishment you have already had," he said, smiling as he laid the whip aside. "And you shall be rewarded by the loving of your white master."

She closed her eyes as she felt his hands on her thighs, forcing them apart, spreading her for penetration. Then she felt his soft belly against hers, the weight of his bulk forcing her down. Nausea rose inside her at the touch of his wet lips and the feel of his fat tongue in her mouth.

Agony from her back hit her in an overwhelming wave as the man's weight fully rested on her. The pain was no longer endurable, and she knew she was losing consciousness. She welcomed the warm velvety blackness. It blotted out not only the pain but also the sound of Jacob's heavy breathing, the disgusting taste of his tongue, and his degrading violation of her body.

When she awakened, it was to the knowledge that the pain was still with her. But there was also a gentle touch as something soothing was applied to her back and thighs.

"There, there, honey chile. You jes' lie still and let ole Chatti he'p y' feel better."

She was lying face down and the gentle hands were smoothing a pungently smelling but marvelously cooling balm onto the areas that hurt the most. She opened her eyes and . . .

"Dis make it feel bettah, honey," Chatti was saying. "Dat voodoo woman over to Yokama way mixed it up special for me. We been havin' to use lots of it since them Wenzels come, but Ah nevah 'spected to use it on my baby."

"Oh, Chatti, Chatti." Lorinda reached for one gnarled black hand and kissed it. "I missed you so much—so much."

"Don' take on so, honey. Yo' ole mammy heah now and she make it all right."

"That horrible Jacob, that evil, vicious animal!" Lorinda sobbed. "To have him touch me, to have him take me was almost worse than the beating."

"Yes, he a bad one," Chatti agreed and helped the girl to sit up.

"He's a monster!" Lorinda said. "All the Wenzels are monsters! I'm beginning to think all whites are—that even my father was."

"No call to talk thet way 'bout Masta Jules," Chatti said reprovingly. "He a good man. Always do the best he could for us people. We a lot happier when he alive than now."

"But you weren't any more free," Lorinda said.

"No, no more free," Chatti admitted, "but backs surely hurt a lot less."

She took the cover off a steaming bowl and offered it to the girl. "Here, you drink this, honey. It make you feel bettah. It turtle soup. Ah cotched me a big one down to the bayou the othah day and made soup for the folks 'thout 'em Wenzels knowin' 'bout hit. They so mean that jes' knowin' we was gettin' 'nuff to eat onct in a while would make 'em froth at de mouf."

Lorinda sipped at the hot soup and found it delicious. Chatti had always been a good cook. She could take table scraps that someone else would have thrown away and transform them into palatable food.

When the soup was almost gone and the warmth in her stomach and the soothing ointment on her back was starting to make her feel human again,

Lorinda twisted her head and tried to see her back. "Is it terribly scarred, Chatti?"

"Not scarred at all, honey," Chatti said. "They a lot of red welts, but they be gone in a few days. Thet no good white trash Jacob know how to use a whip 'thout markin'. He practice with all de whip masters on othah plantations afore his pappy stole all you money an' land."

"Did they steal it, Chatti, or does it belong to them legally?"

"Don' know nuthin' 'bout legal, but it should be yo'ahs jes' like you papa wanted it should be."

"I'm not sure I care about the property and money," Lorinda said. "What I care about is not being free."

"It happen someday, honey. Someday we all a'goin' to be free. Till then, day come, day go, Lord send Sunday, as they say."

"I hope so, Chatti," Lorinda sighed. "You know, I almost wish he had cut me and marked me, even my face."

"Lordy, chile, don' say things like thet!"

"But if you only knew the things that have happened to me because of the way I look, because of the way men feel about the way I look."

" 'Cause yo' beautiful, you mean?"

"Yes, I suppose that's what I mean," Lorinda said. "If I were ugly or all scarred up, they'd leave me alone."

"They leave you alone thet way but make yo' life miserable in othah ways," Chatti said. "Look out de winda and see what dem wenches got to do."

Kneeling on the cot, Lorinda could see out

toward the quarters, where the morning sun was just starting to appear over the tall sycamores. A long straggling line of women was moving down the path toward the cotton fields. Dressed in ragged dresses of cheap, rough osnaburg, the women looked cold and unhappy in the last of the early dawn mist. They all carried hoes and were preceded and followed by slave drivers carrying whips. Bringing up the rear was an overseer on horseback.

"Dem wenches not out theah 'cause o' they beauty," Chatti said, "an' dem whips the kind thet cut. Scars all ovah dem pore gals, jes' lak near ever'body at Solitaire 'cepten the pretty gals saved for breedin'."

"But, Chatti, those women are doing men's work, hard, back-breaking labor. They never had to do that in papa's time."

" 'Course not! Not de lil chilluns, either, but now ever'body work 'cepten the light skins used to get suckers to sell."

"My God!" Lorinda said, watching out the window as the slave driver cracked his whip, urging the women on faster toward the fields. "They've turned Solitaire into a hell, haven't they?"

"Hell not this bad 'cause de Lord created it," Chatti said. "Dem Wenzels worsen de devil evah could be."

Tears in her eyes, Lorinda turned to the old black woman. "Oh, Chatti, what's going to happen to all of us?"

Chatti sighed heavily. "Don' know, Miss Lori, but for right now, they makin' you downstairs maid. Tole me to bring you dis dress and start teachin' you how to wait table an' sech thing.''

Lorinda looked at the outfit Chatti had unfolded and laid out for her. It was a black dress with a crisp white apron, like those worn by maids in the more fashionable mansions in New Orleans. ''They certainly are getting up in the world. When they first came South, they were considered the poorest of poor white trash. Now they fancy themselves entitled to luxuries like maids and butlers.''

''They still looked on as pore white trash,'' Chatti said. ''Not a single family around who invite them or come heah.''

Lorinda was inspecting the underclothing that came with the dress. It was expensive and scanty and included black silk stockings and slippers with high French heels.

''Wants you to look like one o' dem fancy French whores,'' Chatti said. ''Them Wenzel men not only mean but raunchy mean.''

Lorinda shrugged. ''Well, at least being a maid is better than some things I can think of, like what happened last night.''

Chatti looked unhappy. ''Honey, Ah hates to tell you, but they keep you heah in de big house so they can do whatevah they wants to you. All three o' them de'gen'rats all het up ovah you an' you gonna be pestered moah than a gal ought to be all o' her life.''

''Oh, dear God!'' Lorinda sobbed. ''What am I going to do? What am I going to do?''

''You gonna do the best you can till Ah figures out a way to get you outa heah,'' the older woman said, ''finds some way to let you escape.''

CHAPTER 20

The humiliation of waiting on the Wenzel women hand and foot was almost as bad as the sexual abuse Lorinda suffered from the men of the family. The sour, pinch-faced Charlotte nagged at her constantly and occasionally struck her in a fit of rage. Pudgy, simpering Elsie seemingly spent half her time thinking up unpleasant, abasing tasks to be performed.

"I left my drawers at the foot of my bed, Lori," she would say. "Wash them out for me yourself."

Since Elsie hadn't the slightest conception of personal cleanliness and sometimes wore her undergarments for a week at a time, it was a repulsive job to wash them by hand.

"Comb my hair, Lori," she would order, "but don't you dare hurt me like you did the last time."

The hair would be so tangled from lack of care that it was impossible to comb it without pulling, and this always brought furious retaliation from Elsie.

"Damn you, you hurt me, you black bitch!" she would yell and pick up the big wooden paddle used to punish slave children when they misbehaved. "Now you lift your skirts and pull down your drawers! I'm gonna sting your butt and sting it good!"

The paddling wasn't nearly so hard to bear as the

305

fact that this pig of a girl had the right to inflict it on her any time she wanted to, with or without reason.

Jacob and Gideon inflicted another kind of degradation on her. Seemingly insatiable where Lorinda was concerned, they would summon her one night to Jacob's bed and the next to Gideon's. Jacob was savage and cruel in his lovemaking. Gideon was less vicious but no more palatable to Lorinda. She submitted to them because she knew that if she didn't she would be returned to the basement room where she had first been beaten and from where she now often heard the screams of other slave girls who had displeased their vindictive masters.

And while she submitted, hatred grew in her like a cancer. She loathed them all: the mealymouthed, hypocritically pious Charlotte; nasty, petty Elsie; gawky, dirty-minded Gideon; the sadistic Jacob and lecherous old August. The latter never quite got around to actually bedding her, but it was obvious he was much tempted. He fondled her every chance he got out of sight of his viperish wife, whom he seemed to fear. He would reach to squeeze her breast as she leaned over to serve him breakfast, lift her skirt to fumble under her pantalettes when she passed him in the hall, and corner her on the landing of the main stairway in order to force his vile kisses on her. And she could refuse none of it, any more than she could refuse the more intimate advances of the two younger men.

Not being able to refuse was the worst part. A prostitute on the streets of New Orleans had more choice. Her body was not her own; it belonged to men who enraged and disgusted her. And so night after night she lay passive and unresponsive as they thrust into her, schooling herself not to resist but utterly unable to make even a pretense of responding to them.

Oddly enough, neither Jacob nor Gideon gave any indication that they cared whether or not she did. As long as they could dominate her, could command her to strip and service them, they gave no further thought to her.

But she thought about them almost constantly. Every time she saw a sharp kitchen knife or an ax left lying around, she imagined what it would be like to use the knife on Jacob. To make him incapable of inflicting his vile caresses on her or any other woman. To use the ax to split open Gideon's thick skull and spill out the sawdust that she was sure served him for brains.

"I despise them, Chatti," she told her former nurse. "I loathe them so much something dies inside me every time they touch me."

"We gets you out o' heah, honey," Chatti said, patting her with a callused hand. "We gets you out away one day an' you go up North and jes' fade into all them other white people."

News of the outside world reached Solitaire only through an occasional slave trader making up a caravan of blacks to sell in Natchez or New Orleans. Outcasts among the planter aristocracy, such men had no objection to breaking bread with people like the Wenzels, who were regarded as beyond the pale by their neighbors.

It was through the slave trader who came most

often to visit the Wenzels that Lorinda's status at Solitaire finally changed. His name was Tudd Garrison, and he seemed to like the Wenzels, possibly because he was very much like them. He had come to Solitaire several times, but he first seemed to notice Lorinda during a visit in June. He was sharing dinner with the Wenzels, discussing the opening of the Nebraska and Kansas territories to settlers, and Lorinda was serving. Near the end of the discussion, August grunted, and Lorinda hurried around the table to serve him more black-eyed peas and biscuits.

"Say," Garrison grinned, showing the gaps in his front teeth, "that's a right pretty li'l wench you got there. Nobody'd ever know but what she's white. If you ever figure on sellin' her, let me know first. She'd fetch a damn good price after I'd got me a piece or two of her ass."

"We're not thinking of selling her," Jacob said.

His father, however, said nothing. August needed the goodwill of men like Garrison, or his plan to turn Solitaire into the largest slave breeding plantation in the South would never come true.

"That right, Mr. Wenzel?" Garrison asked, picking at what teeth he had with a gold-plated pick he wore on a chain attached to his belt. "You don't mean to ever sell this wench?"

"That's true, Mr. Garrison," Wenzel said and then looked up at Lorinda. "Bring me some hot gravy, gal. This stuff in the bowl is cold."

When Lorinda returned with the hot gravy, which Wenzel slopped over everything on his plate, Garrison had a pleased look on his face and Jacob looked angry. She didn't know what it meant, but it made her feel very uneasy.

She found out what it meant that night. Deep in sleep, she was suddenly aroused by a knock on her door. "Damn them," she thought, staggering to answer what she assumed was a summons to the bed of one or the other of the Wenzel boys.

But on opening the door she was surprised to find August standing there. Her stomach was suddenly queasy. Had he finally gotten up the nerve to defy his wife? The thought of adding him to her bed chores was revolting. She wanted to cry out, to scream, to run. She had spent half the evening washing Elsie's dirty stockings, and the smell of unwashed feet still lingered in her nostrils. On top of that, did she now have to endure sharing August's bed?

He surprised her, but not pleasantly.

"Look here, gal, I want you should go up and start getting Mr. Garrison's bed warm for him. We're closing a big deal for fifty slaves, and I promised him a little something extra. Don't want to sell you, but it won't hurt to let him enjoy you every once in a while. Can't see no good reason why not."

The scream Lorinda had been suppressing refused to be held in any longer. "*You* can't see any reason!" she screeched, and with all her pent-up hate and fury slapped him across the face. "Well, *I* can! Garrison is a filthy, greasy pig, and I wouldn't touch him with a ten-foot pole, much less with my body! There's your reason and it's the same reason none of you are ever going to—"

Wenzel's fist exploded in her face like a thunder-bolt. An expanding universe of red stars burst before her eyes. She went flying backward into the room to land sprawling on the floor. As she attempted to get to her feet, his boot crashed into her stomach. She fell back, retching.

"You ungrateful little bitch! I was giving you a chance to sleep with a gentleman, and you think you're too good for him!"

His foot struck out again, rolling her over and sending streaks of pain all through her body.

"Well, that's the end of your being treated good, bitch! You been privileged, living in the big house, eating white folks' food and sleeping with my sons. There won't be any more of that! First thing in the morning, you're going where you belong, out to the quarters with your own kind! I got just the man for you, one who'll break you proper and give you plenty of kids to keep you out of trouble. I'm going to give you to Zack the blacksmith. That'll teach you where your place is in this world!"

He left her there doubled up on the floor, slamming the door on his way out. For a while she lay there sobbing. Then she began thinking about what August had said. He intended to punish her in the most terrible way he could think of, by turning her over to a black man to use until she became pregnant. He was also removing her from the vicinity of his degenerate sons. She would no longer have to submit to the vile caresses of Jacob and Gideon. That was her punishment for refusing to warm the bed of a third obnoxious white man.

"Oh, that's funny, that's really funny," she

whispered, sitting up and laughing through her tears. "Well, you listen to me, August Wenzel! I'd rather be in the bed of a black man in the dingiest cabin in Mississippi than be the mistress of the richest white man in all the South. I'd rather be with one of my own than be loved by the handsomest white man in the country!"

She could say things like that with Kirk Stryker dead. She could say them and mean them, because with him gone it didn't matter who she bedded as long as it wasn't any of the Wenzels or their friends.

In the morning two black slave drivers came for her. She was told to strip off the fancy maid's outfit and was given a frayed calico dress. She had to put it on with nothing underneath, like the rest of the slaves. Then she was marched out of the house and down toward the slave cabins. Along the way she was aware of the other slaves watching her as she was led down the dusty little street between the rows of tiny houses.

A quadroon girl with taffy-colored hair and eyes that were almost blue was to be installed in the big house as the new maid and bed companion of the Wenzel men. Lorinda didn't envy the girl, although she looked happy enough when they passed halfway between the two worlds. As for herself, Lorinda would rather have worked in the fields with the feel of the whip across her back than go on the way she had been. No matter what the truth was about Zack, he couldn't possibly be as mean and hateful as Jacob and his brother.

"My, my, you sho has come down in the world, gal," Suzy called as she was led past.

From the corner of her eye, Lorinda saw Suzy leaning in the door of the cabin she shared with a tall, slender griffe. Lorinda said, "On the contrary, I think I've come up in the world. I was in the middle circle of hell, and now I'm merely in one of the outer circles and as far away as I can get from those white devils."

"You hush up, gal, or Ah'll cut you wiff dis whip," one of the drivers said.

"No, you won't," she told him, "because if you do, I'll set Zack on you."

"Jes' hush up talkin' 'bout white folks," he ordered, but he didn't threaten her again.

The blacksmith's shop was at the end of the row of cabins. In Jules de Farbin's day the cabins had been neat and clean and those who lived in them had been decently clothed and fed. As she walked along, Lorinda saw the deterioration in their condition, saw the dirty threadbare clothes and the peaked look on the children's faces.

Smoke from the forge was coming out of the smithy; they could hear the clang of the hammer on metal as they approached.

"Zack! Zack, you come on out heah!" one driver called.

The clanging of the hammer went on. The driver pounded on the door with the butt of his whip. "Zack, you come out! Masta Wenzel done sent you a new woman!"

"Ah got a woman," a deep, resonant voice said above the noise of the hammer.

"Masta Wenzel he say you got to change, wants you should cover dis wench."

"Don' care what he say. Ah got a woman Ah satisfied with."

"You wants Ah should go tell Masta what you say? You better come out heah, now!"

"Come on out, Zack," the second driver coaxed. "You surely wants to see dis gal. She somethin' special."

The hammering stopped and footsteps came toward the door. "You bettah be talkin' true, boy," the man said as he loomed in the doorway, well over six feet tall and muscled like an ebony Hercules.

"Heah she be," the second driver said, shoving Lorinda forward. "See fo' yo'self."

"You is foolin' me, boy," the blacksmith said, wiping his hands on his apron, "an' Ah'm a bad man fo' even a whopper to do dat to."

"Ain' foolin' you a'tall. She de gal Masta wants you to have."

Zack shook his head. "She white. Ole man Wenzel nevah sent me no white woman."

"She ain' white," the first driver said, "jes' look white. Masta wants some big good-lookin' quadroon children outen her."

Zack grinned, showing white even teeth between his thick lips. "Ah got lots of sap, Ah does, and iffen it's children he a'wantin', Ah kin git her cotched quicker'n a wink."

"Better git to hit then," the whopper said, pushing Lorinda toward the big man.

Lorinda shrank back a little, but a huge black hand closed around her arm and pulled her into the warmth of the smithy.

"Come on in, li'l gal, an' let me have a look at you," Zack said mildly. "What yo' name?"

"I—I'm Lorinda," she faltered.

"Too long. Ah calls you Lori." He led her over near the anvil and forge, looking her over in the light of the glowing coals. "You sho a pretty wench."

"Thank you," she said, thinking that the strong fingers that held her arm could break it as easily as they would a stick. She had told herself that this was better by a thousand times than being bed wench to the Wenzels, but now that she was faced with it she was frightened.

"You wants Ah should pester you now?" he asked.

"I—I don't know. Couldn't we wait a little while and maybe get to know each other better?"

He looked puzzled, scratching his head and pursing his lips. "Ah don' unnerstan' what you mean, gal. All Ah esked was do you want Ah should pester you now or wait till I damps down the forge?"

"Please. Yes, please wait at least that long," she said.

He grinned. "Sho, Ah can' wait thet long." His hand moved from her arm to her breasts, squeezing the firm mounds through the cotton dress. "You sho titted out nice. Ah likes gals who titted out nice."

"I'm glad," Lorinda said, her heart pounding with fear at the enormous strength of the man.

She tried to calm herself as she watched him go about the task of shutting down the smithy. It didn't take nearly as long as she had hoped it would. His powerful shoulder muscles glistened in the red glow of the fire as he moved about the dimly lit smithy. He reached to lower a damping device from the ceiling to cut off the air that kept the coals glowing. Then he dipped the hot metal he had been pounding into a bucket of water, sending up a cloud of hissing steam. When he had put his tools away, he barred the door and turned, a slow smile crossing his face. "Thet keep anyone from buttin' in on us."

"You—could we—just talk for a while?" Lorinda asked nervously.

"What you wanna talk 'bout, gal?" he said, looking puzzled again.

"I—I—oh, Lord, I don't know."

"Ah 'spects you better jes' shuck down, gal, so's Ah kin see what you got."

For a few seconds, Lorinda considered resisting. But she realized it was hopeless. A struggle against the powerful man who frightened even the slave drivers was pointless and could possibly end in her being injured. No one would bother to come if she screamed, and trying to run away would be futile.

"Shuck down, gal," Zack repeated firmly. "You mah woman, and Ah wants to see what you got."

Resignedly Lorinda reached for the hem of the dress and skinned it off over her head. She let it fall and stood naked before the huge black man. It seemed like everyone had a right to her body but herself.

Zack's eyes widened until they seemed to be nothing but whites. He gazed at her outthrust breasts, the smooth flat belly and the delicately curved thighs.

"You de best-lookin' wench Ah evah seen," he

said, reaching to run his hands up and down her flanks.

Lorinda tried not to let him see she was afraid as he took her hand and placed it on his body. "You feel what Ah got. Maybe it make you git all het up like Ah is."

She began to shake at the size and strength of him.

"Don' you be scared, gal," he rumbled hoarsely and picked her up in his arms. "Don' be scared 'cause Ah ain' gonna hurt you any moah than Ah can he'p. Ain' gonna hurt you a 'tall iffen Ah can he'p it."

CHAPTER 21

Lorinda thought she had never known such contentment. She sat in the glow of the fire in Zack's forge, watching the play of muscles across his back and nursing her baby.

It had been over a year since August Wenzel had decreed she become the woman of Zack the blacksmith, and during that time she had come to respect, if not love, the big black man. She would never forget or cease to mourn Kirk Stryker, but now she could accept his death. And that made it possible for her to appreciate what she now had, even though she was still a slave and subject to the will of people she hated.

Truthfully, she had seen little of her blond tormentors since she'd been with Zack. The three Wenzel men were engaged in business dealings to the exclusion of almost everything else. Business often kept them away from the plantation for weeks at a time. And when they were gone, Nicholson, the overseer, relaxed the back-breaking routine. It wasn't that Nicholson was any more merciful than August or Jacob; it was simply that he was a naturally lazy man who preferred to spend his afternoons sipping mint juleps with Elsie on the gallery of Solitaire or slipping with her down behind the spring house.

So while Nicholson neglected his duties, his assistant, Seth Parker, did the same, spending most of his time in his cabin with a bottle. In turn, the Negro drivers also took their ease and the slaves did only enough work to keep the vegetable patches weeded, the hogs swilled and the corn tended. Men with no stake in the products of their labor could hardly be faulted for neglecting that labor. Only the food crops that kept the blacks fed were willingly cared for.

"Why they want to fool wit cotton, anyhow?" Tom, the mason, would ask Zack. "Dis place ain' in business of raisin' cotton no moah like it was when Miss Lori's father ran it. Dem Wenzels done turned Solitaire into a nigger farm, an' all da people wants to do is pester."

Tom had been at Solitaire when the de Farbins owned it; now he had become Zack's best friend, but he still insisted on calling Lorinda Miss Lori, as he always had.

"It don' make no difference whether anyone work or not long as dey pester and git de wenches cotched. Long as dey produce chillun, no call to produce cotton no moah."

Zack swung his hammer in an arc above his head. "Don' make me no nevermind iffen anybody work or pester foah the Wenzels."

"Den why you work so hard, man?" Tom asked.

"Ah workin' foah myself now, foah myself, my woman and my chile."

It was because of Lorinda's shrewdness that much of the work Zack was turning out in his endless hours at the forge benefited them both. The big man was able and willing to work extremely hard, and when she had shown him how that work might be turned to their advantage instead of that of their masters, he had been eager to join in her plan. In addition to mending the wagons, shoeing the horses and fixing the hinges of Solitaire, Zack was now making shovel and ax heads, hinges and metal ornaments for sale. The idea had occurred to Lorinda the first time she had seen Simon Klein come rolling up the drive in his little one-horse cart. Klein was a Jewish peddler who regularly made the rounds of southern Mississippi plantations.

She had known Simon in the old days and found him honest and reliable. There was a certain amount of danger in what she proposed, but she felt she could trust Simon with her own and Zack's safety. Only the most kindly of masters ever permitted slaves to do outside work; indeed the black codes of most states either prohibited it or so restricted it as to make it almost impossible. But if one were willing to take the risk, it was possible to make some money.

The money Lorinda had received from Maurice Maspero had been stolen by the Wenzels on the pretense that, since she was their slave, the money belonged to them. To have contested that claim would have required the services of a white person to act in her behalf since slaves were forbidden to hire lawyers on their own. With Maurice and Kirk Stryker both dead, Lorinda had no such person to help her and could not hope to gain her freedom that way. The only other way she knew was to run away and reach a free state. To do that she needed money.

She had broached her idea to Zack one night after

the baby had been put to bed and they lay on their sleeping mat together.

"Wouldn't you like to be free, Zack?"

"Sho'," he said with his slow smile. "Sho', jes' like Ah'd like to fly."

"Men have flown, Zack."

"Yeah, honey, Ah knows from them books you been teachin' me to read, but Ah nevah hear tell o' no black man a'goin' up in one of them balloon things."

"No, but being free is possible."

"Sho', an' next time Masta Wenzel come by, Ah ast him to turn me loose," Zack said sleepily.

"No, not like that," Lorinda said. "I wouldn't have my freedom as a gift from them! No one has a right to hold another person as a slave."

"Law say they does."

"It's an evil law," she said, positive about her feelings now, rid of the ambiguity she had expressed to Kirk. "It's an evil law that conflicts with the Constitution and the Bill of Rights and with moral law as well."

" 'Spects that Con-sti-tu-tion of yourn ain' got much say in Mississippi," Zack observed.

"It would have if there was any justice," Lorinda said, "but since there isn't, we have got to free ourselves."

"That's nice talk, honey, but talkin' don' make nothin' so."

"No, but *doing* does," she said.

"Doin' what?"

"Making plans to run away," she said.

"Runnin' gits you whopped or worse," Zack

said. "No point in runnin' lessen you got some-place to run to."

Lorinda rolled over on her side, supporting her-self on one arm so her face was in the light from the coals. "Look at me, Zack."

"Sho', honey, sho'. That no hard thing to do."

"Look at me and tell me if you think anyone who didn't know me would believe I'm not one hundred percent white."

"No doubt 'bout that. Ah know you better'n anyone and sometimes Ah cain' believe you not white. Why you bring that up?"

"Because outside of Claiborne County, where everybody has heard about me and many know me by sight, I can go into any hotel, ride any riverboat, take any train and pass anywhere as a white per-son."

"Yeah, you could," he agreed. "Iffen you got a good start on the slave patrol, you could be long gone and no one evah cotch you."

"That's right," she said, "but I'm not going without you and the baby, Zack."

"That make it harder," he said. "A lot harder."

"Maybe while we were in the South," she said, "but once we reached the North we could be to-gether, even marry, if you wanted to."

"You knows Ah wants to be wiff you, gal, but Ah don' see how—"

"Suppose I was to go aboard a riverboat at, say, Memphis, where no one knows me, accompanied by my manservant, who just happened to have his baby with him. Do you think that would arouse any suspicion?"

Zack thought it over for a few minutes. "Ah reckon you an' a manservant could do it 'thout anyone bein' 'spicious. But a baby, 'specially a mulatto baby, might cause some talk."

Lorinda had to admit he was right. Miscegenation always seemed to be uppermost on the collective mind of the South, and any hint that a white Southern lady might be traveling North with her half-caste infant would almost certainly cause trouble.

"Yes, I see what you mean," she said. "Maybe we should take someone with us, another woman—Sissy, maybe."

"What 'bout Chatti? You gonna leave yo' ole mammy behind?"

"Of course I wouldn't if I could persuade her to go, but she's told me several times that this is her home. She won't leave even if it has been taken over by thieves."

Zack nodded. "Lots o' folks feel that way. All the people they know is on the plantation. Solitaire or any othah place. They been raised in slave quarters; it the only life they know. 'Spect that why so many runaways go back to the ole place no mattah how bad they treated. Be a lot moah runaways iffen it wan't foah the 'tachments they has to each othah."

"Is that the way you feel, Zack?"

"Some, but mostly you and li'l Zack where my 'tachment is. Ah could leave iffen Ah thought there any sense to it."

"There would be if we had money," she said.

"Money to buy white-lady clothes for me and luggage to carry it in, money for our fares and hotels, money to take care of us when we get North, money to last until you could get a job."

He laughed. "Then it be jes' as hard as flyin', ain' hit? Where at we gets any money?"

"You're going to get it by working for it," she said and then told him about her idea of his making tools and things and having Simon sell them. The peddler would deposit most of the money in a Memphis bank under the name Lorinda would use when she withdrew it. A small part, in gold coins, would be handed over to them to make their escape easier.

"What do you think, Zack?" she asked after she had outlined the plan to him.

"Ah think Simon a white man, an' Ah cain' trust no white man."

"He's a different kind of white man, Zack. He knows what prejudice and oppression is, just like us. I've talked to him and he's willing to help us."

"But we be a'trustin' ever'thing to him," Zack said. "The stuff Ah make, the money he sell it foah, puttin' money in bank, not tellin' on us— ever'thing."

"And that bothers you?"

"Bothers me some. Seems Ah heah Jewish fellas pretty sly an' a'lookin' out foah themselves in all their dealin's."

Lorinda was surprised at such a bigoted statement. "Where did you hear a thing like that, Zack?"

He frowned and thought about it. "Reckon maybe Ah heared Masta Gideon a'tellin' it to Mista Nicholson one time."

"I see," Lorinda said. "Do you mean to tell me you believe anything a Wenzel would say?"

He looked sheepish. "No, Ah guess not. Jes' said it 'cause Ah didn't know what else to say."

"Then you do like the plan?"

"Likes it iffen it keeps you an' me togethah," he said, reaching to place a large black hand on her white thigh. "Thass all Ah cares about, you and li'l Zack."

"Oh, Zack, I want to stay with you, too," she said, blending her body against the strength of his.

And soon he was surging into her, so large he would have hurt her if he hadn't been so gentle. But there was no pain, only intense pleasure.

That had been several months ago. Now as she sat here watching her man work, she thought of the progress they had made.

"Simon says we have almost three hundred dollars in the bank," she told Zack as he bent to examine the ax blade he was honing. "Don't you think that's almost enough?"

"Maybe," he said, "maybe not."

"What do you mean?" she asked, putting the baby over her shoulder and patting his back so he would burp.

"Ah don think goin' North is goin solve nothin' for us."

"Oh, Zack, we can't stay slaves all of our lives!" Lorinda cried.

"Not a'sayin' we should. Jes' think if we

a'goin', we oughta keep right on goin' up to that Canada place, where no one can bring us back.''

"Of course, of course!" she said eagerly. Why hadn't she thought of that? Maybe because she had been so sure she could pass in the North and no one would bother her because of her white skin. But she should have thought of Zack and the baby.

"But it's very cold up there, Zack."

"Don' care," he said. "Rather be a'shiverin' from cold than from fear the rest of my life."

She got up and went to him, slipping her arm around his sweaty waist. "I've never seen you shiver in fear before any man, white or black."

He grinned and leaned down to kiss her. "An' Ah hopes you nevah do."

A few days later they were awakened by an excited pounding at the door, and Zack lifted the bar to reveal a wild-eyed Sissy standing outside.

"Miss Lori, oh, Miss Lori, honey, somethin' awful gonna happen!" the girl said hysterically.

"What's the matter?" Lorinda asked, drawing her into the warmth of the smithy. "Are the Wenzels threatening to take you away from that Jason boy you like so much?"

"Oh, it worse than that, Miss Lori, lots worse than that. We is all gonna be taken away and sold!"

"What do you mean by 'all'?" Lorinda asked. "All who?"

"All us folks at Solitaire," the girl said. "Ah heard Miz Wenzel tellin' Miz Elsie that Masta August had business losses an' they got to get up a big caravan of slaves to pledge to dealers to keep from losin' their business."

Lorinda looked at Zack. "Ain' heared nothin'," he said. "Most times men passes on news when they come in to get a hoe fixed or an ax, but Ah ain' heared nothin' like that."

"This jes' happen," Sissy said. "Miz Wenzel got one o' them telegrams from N'Orleans, fella rode all the way out from Vicksburg to deliver it. It says Masta August and them boys be heah in a coupla days, and then they start—what'd he call it?—combin' out the most valuable slaves for the caravan. An' all three o' us be valuable and fust to go."

"What do you think, Zack?" Lorinda asked.

"Ah think iffen they lookin' for slaves they kin git the most money foah, you be the fust one sold," he said.

"So would you an' me," Sissy said, her voice rising with her fear. "Ah jes' know where Ah'd end up—in one o' them cribs down to Natchez with every white man who come along pesterin' me, all the river rats an' po' white trash, and Ah'd nevah see Jase again!"

"Hush, Sissy, and let me think," Lorinda said. What Zack had said was true, and what Sissy was saying might be. A powerful, skilled man like Zack would go for a good price, and all the attractive girls would be among the first to go. Yes, all three of them would be sold to different masters and in all probability would never see one another again. And what would happen to little Zack? The Wenzels were only letting him stay with her now because she was nursing him, but if they sold her, they'd just take him away and give him to a wet nurse until he was weaned, and she'd never see him again, either.

"Ah jes' don' know what Ah'm gonna do," Sissy moaned, wringing her hands. "Ah jes' don' know!"

Zack and Lorinda looked at each other. They had agreed that when the time came, they would take Sissy with them but would keep their plans to themselves until it was almost time to go. Sissy was not a person who could keep a secret. But with the present situation, they might have to leave within the next twenty-four hours; so Sissy would have to be told. Zack inclined his head slightly in answer to the question in Lorinda's eyes, and she drew the other girl to a seat at the tiny table.

"Sissy," she began cautiously, "have you ever thought about running away?"

Sissy's pretty brown eyes widened. "Run away? Yes, Ah 'spects Ah has, but where would Ah run to?"

"Suppose you knew of a place you had a good chance of getting to that would be safe?"

"Well—" Sissy wiped away a tear with her snowy white apron. "Well, Ah guess Ah'd go but sho' wouldn't want to leave Jase behind. That boy sure do pleasure me."

Lorinda grimaced. The expedition in search of freedom was beginning to become complicated. She looked at Zack for advice and knew from the frown on his face that he was thinking the same thing. They had only so much cash, and the more people they took along the less chance their plan had of succeeding.

"You wouldn't go without Jase? Is that what you're saying?"

"Reckon what Ah'm sayin' is that Ah'd sho'

rather take him with me than leave him—'' Sissy paused suddenly and looked from Lorinda to Zack. ''You serious 'bout runnin', ain' you?''

''We didn't say that, Sissy,'' Lorinda said.

''Don' you go jumpin' in the wrong direction, gal,'' Zack warned. ''We jes' givin' you a fo'instance.''

''You got a way!'' Sissy's eyes were bright with excitement. ''You know how to git away!''

''Sissy, we've been thinking about it, but we really haven't come to a firm decision,'' Lorinda said, already sorry she had mentioned the matter. She should have waited until the very last minute and then sprung it on her so she didn't have time to spread the word.

''Sissy, you listen to me,'' Zack said. ''You not to go tellin' nobody 'bout this. You unnerstan', gal?''

''Sho', sho','' she said. ''When is you goin'?''

''We didn't say we were going, Sissy,'' Lorinda said in exasperation. ''We just wanted to know how you felt about it.''

''Ah is ready any time,'' she said. ''Don' want to git sold to no Natchez-under-the-hill crib, don' wanta be pestered by all them riverboat men an' all.''

''Well, just remember not to mention this to anyone,'' Lorinda said.

''Cross my heart,'' Sissy said. ''Nobody gonna know 'bout hit from Sissy.''

As soon as the girl was gone, Lorinda moved close to Zack and whispered, ''I think we had better go tonight before the Wenzel men get back and before Sissy can talk too much.''

"She say she keep her mouf shut," Zack said. "What she got to gain by ruinin' it fo' us?"

"Nothing, but Sissy is a natural-born gossip," Lorinda said. "She can't keep her mouth shut. It just seems to open of its own accord and the words pour out."

"But we only got three hundred dollahs in the Memphis bank," Zack objected. "We say we wait till we have six hundred."

"I have another fifty silver dollars hidden under the floorboard over there," Lorinda said. "It will have to do. If we wait, we could both be sold and never see each other again." Her voice broke on the last few words.

Zack gathered her close. "Sho', honey, sho'," he said soothingly, "we go tonight. We go, no matter what."

"I'm glad," Lorinda said, clinging to him. She had lost Kirk Stryker forever. She couldn't bear to lose Zack, too.

CHAPTER 22

But Kirk Stryker wasn't dead. He was sitting in a cell in a New Orleans jail, charged with murder. And while he sat there his mind kept reviewing the events of the past year and a half since Lorinda had been dragged kicking and screaming from his room and he had been left for dead by her abductors.

After the savage beating and stomping, he had tried to get to his feet and go after the screaming girl and the slave catchers but had been overtaken by a deep darkness, which hadn't receded even when he heard the voices of two men at the open door.

"Some sort of struggle seems to have taken place in here," one voice said. "Did you hear a woman scream, Major White?"

"Yes, I did. I had just sat down to buck the tiger in the game room when I heard it. I came as quickly as I could. I say, there's a man in there on the floor, Mr. Powell. He seems to have been attacked. Let's have a look."

Through the haze of pain that threatened to drive him back down into total darkness, Stryker heard the footsteps of the two men as they came across the room. Then he sensed one of them kneeling beside him.

"Good God, Powell, it's Stryker!"

"A colleague beaten?" the other man exclaimed.

"How terrible! We must do something for him, Major."

"Yes, indeed," the other man agreed. "I'll get the desk clerk and the manager up here at once! I'll want an explanation of this and a carriage to take Mr. Stryker to a physician."

The names Powell and White were familiar to Kirk, but he hurt too badly to concentrate on remembering just who they were. He drifted off into unconsciousness again until the indignant voice of Major White roused him slightly.

"Do you mean to tell me that you, an assistant manager of this fine hotel, permitted one of your guests to be attacked by a gang of thugs and did nothing to help him, didn't even summon the police?"

"But Major White, they said they were slave catchers and that there was a slave wench in this room with Mr. Stryker."

"And did you see a black woman in this room, sir?" Powell was as indignant as his friend.

"No, sir, but there was a woman here."

"What was her color?" White demanded. "Was she partly black, perhaps a mulatto?"

"No, she seemed to be white, Major," the manager said.

The clerk quickly agreed. "She was white, I'd swear to it."

"And yet you two incompetent fools let those thugs come up here, beat a man nearly to death and carry off the young woman who was his companion! Never mind. Get a chair, and you two help lift this gentleman into it. And carry him down those stairs very slowly and carefully.''

There was an agony of pain as they started to move him and under its impact Stryker sank like a stone into a pool of black water.

When he next opened his eyes, he was lying in a hospital bed with a nun bending over him.

"Ah, Monsieur Stryker, you feel better, no?"

"I feel awful, yes," Stryker said, raising a hand to touch his face. Except for his eyes, it was covered with bandages. His entire body ached. There was a tight bandage around his ribs and another around one arm.

"I will get Dr. Carnot at once," the nun said and disappeared through the door of the whitewashed room.

In a few minutes, a dapper little man in a white coat with a pince-nez perched on the bridge of his nose hurried to the bedside.

"Ah, so you are alive, Mr. Stryker."

"You couldn't prove it by me," Stryker said and discovered two loose teeth in his mouth.

"Two weeks ago you could not prove it, as you say, by me, either," the doctor said. "It was impossible to assure your friends that you were going to live. In fact, if I had been a betting man, which I understand they are, I would have wagered the cemetery had a good chance of being your future residence."

"You show great confidence in your skill, Doctor," Stryker said dryly.

The doctor looked insulted and drew himself up to his full five feet five. "It is not my skill I doubted, Monsieur, but the ability of you or any other man to recover from such a beating.''

"*Am* I recovered?" Stryker asked.

"You are well on the way to it, sir. I am amazed at your recuperative powers.''

"It comes from leading a good clean life of gambling, drinking and chasing women,'' Stryker said and then drew in his breath sharply as though in pain.

The doctor looked concerned. "Did you feel a stab of pain, perhaps in the area of the ribs?"

"No, no,'' Stryker said. "I just remembered something, and it hurts.'' He closed his eyes and could see Lorinda being dragged out of the hotel room; he could hear her screams. *Lori! Oh, God, Lori! What have they done with her?* From behind clenched teeth, he managed to ask, "How long has it been? How long have I been here?"

"A month,'' Dr. Carnot said. "The first two weeks I considered it a waste of my time and your colleagues' money. The second two, I still expected you to die, but you did not. You are, as we mentioned earlier, recovering.''

A month! Lori had been in the hands of those ruffians all this time! He had to find her! He had to get out of this place and find her at once! He couldn't lose her again!

"Help me up,'' he said to the doctor. "I've got to get out of here.''

"Don't be ridiculous!'' the doctor snapped. "The day before yesterday you had both feet in the grave, and today you want to get up and go carousing with your friends.''

"See here, Doctor, this is most important. I—''

Kirk's voice faded. He sank back onto the pillow, realizing that he wasn't going to be able to get up, much less leave the hospital. Just trying to sit up started his head to whirling and turned his arms and legs to water.

"Ah-ha, so he is not so strong after all," the doctor said, pulling at his beard as though pleased with himself. "Is it not so?"

"I need food," Kirk said. "What have you been feeding me?"

"Gruel."

"And what am I going to get now?"

"Gruel," the doctor said. "It's all your poor stomach can tolerate."

"My stomach is the only thing there isn't something wrong with, as near as I can figure," Kirk said. "But it is strangely empty. I'd like a steak and fried potatoes, a bowl of gumbo and—"

"Gruel," the doctor said and left the room.

The next day Kirk had visitors.

"Kirk, my boy, how are you?" Major White greeted him warmly. He was a portly, dignified man with a white goatee, wearing darkly conservative clothes. He had a reputation on the river as one of the squarest gamblers in the business and was said to have won and lost a dozen fortunes since beginning his career in 1825.

Following him into the room was John Powell, a native Missourian who lived in New Orleans when ashore and was known as the *beau ideal* of the river gamblers. Tall, handsome and distinguished, he was well educated and always richly dressed, without the vulgar flashiness of many of his colleagues.

"I am most grateful to you gentlemen," Kirk said when the greetings were over.

"Nonsense," Powell said. "Only the crudest sort of clods would have left a colleague in distress."

"Nevertheless, I am deeply in your debt," Kirk insisted.

"Not at all, sir," Major White said. "It is we who are in your debt."

"I don't understand," Kirk said. "You owe me nothing beyond the courtesies one professional extends to another."

"On the contrary. It has long been said that there are only four square gamblers on the river, and we have to admit, Powell and I, that this has been so. Recently, however, we have observed your operation and have come to the conclusion that we have a fifth honest gambler afloat. We can ill afford to lose him."

"My thanks, just the same," Kirk said, shaking hands with both of them. "I wonder if I may presume a bit more on your kindness by asking that you obtain some information for me?"

"We would be delighted to assist you, sir," Powell said. "What is it you wish to know?"

"Well, you see, there was a young lady with me when I was attacked. She was carried away while I was being beaten. The lady's welfare is most important to me and . . ."

White and Powell exchanged glances, and the

Major spoke up. "It so happens that we have already made inquiries concerning your attackers and the young person who was with you. We have learned that the assailants claimed to be slave catchers and stated they were seizing a runaway slave named Lorinda de Farbin."

"Slave catchers, hell! They were all common ruffians!"

"Ahem! They said the young woman was a slave, in spite of her fair complexion."

Kirk looked from one of the gamblers to the other. "All right, gentlemen, I'll lay my cards on the table. Yes, the girl has a trace of Negro blood, and yes, she is a slave. She is a slave because her mother, the mistress of Jules de Farbin, was a slave and de Farbin neglected to free her before his untimely death. She is not, however, a runaway since she was in the company of her rightful owner. She is mine; I have the papers to prove it. I won her in a poker game from a young swine named Gideon Wenzel aboard the *Mississippi Belle*. She traveled the river with me for months. You remember her, Powell. You left a game once because you found her too distracting."

"Ah, yes, the lovely child you had perched on your chair arm," Powell said. "You said she was your luck."

"And she was," Stryker said, his eyes darkening with emotion as he remembered those idyllic days. "So you see, gentlemen, those men who took her were slave stealers. And I'll have her back if I have to hunt them down one by one and wring their filthy necks!"

"Ahem." Major White took out a big, square monogrammed silk handkerchief and mopped his brow. "We came across another piece of information, which might alter your plans for retaliation."

"What is that?"

"The men who broke into your hotel room were not members of one of the usual groups who trace and return runaway slaves. They were free-lancers hired by a certain gentleman of this city."

Kirk swore under his breath. "By any chance is his name Joseph Gayarre?"

"The very same," White said. "A gentleman of some notoriety as a duelist—and other things as well."

"Yes, I know Gayarre's reputation and I know for what purpose he wanted Lorinda." Kirk was cursing himself for an utter fool. He should have taken Lorinda out of the South as quickly as possible. Once in the North he could have freed her and married her. Now it was too late. If she was back in the hands of the Gayarres, it would probably take violent action to free her. "I must confess, gentlemen, that I was terribly negligent in regard to Gayarre."

"In what way, sir?" Powell asked.

"I had a chance to kill him and contented myself with humiliating him," Kirk said. "That is about as dangerous as letting a copperhead loose in one's bedroom. I must remedy that neglect as quickly as possible."

"Would you like me to call on him and ask that he send his seconds as soon as you are well enough?" Powell asked.

"No," Kirk said. "I'm not sure he deserves to be killed on the field of honor. I'll call on him in person as soon as I get out of this place."

Actually it took much longer for him to make that call. When he left the sanitarium, he was still far too weak to think of confronting Gayarre. He hired agents to make discreet inquiries in the city while he convalesced for several weeks in the sun and sea air of Biloxi, on the Gulf coast.

Tanned and fit, he was back in New Orleans in early autumn of 1857. Now he was ready to confront Gayarre and demand the return of Lorinda. After that, he would meet Gayarre at The Oaks or *Les Trois Capelines*.

Kirk called in person at the Gayarre mansion one brilliant fall morning. As he rang the bell he remembered the humiliation and sexual abuse Lorinda had suffered in this place. He didn't think the Gayarres would have dared bring her here knowing that he would be looking for her, but he was sure she was being held prisoner some place in the city. And he trusted in his ability to wring information out of Gayarre by one means or another.

A tall, dignified black butler, dressed in the latest English style, answered the door. He did his best to look down his nose at Kirk, but it was somewhat difficult, since the Westerner was nearly a head taller. "An' whom may Ah say is callin'?" he asked.

"You may tell Monsieur Gayarre that the owner of a pair of matched Bowie knives is here to see him."

"An' what, if Ah may ask, do it concern?"

"It concerns a gang of thieves who claimed to be slave catchers."

"Yes, suh, but Ah don' believe you sent round yo' card fust, suh," the butler said, taking refuge in the customs of the city.

"No, I don't believe I did," Kirk said.

"Then Ah'm afraid, suh, that neither Monsieur nor Madame Gayarre are in. But if you would care to leave yo' card now."

"Of course," Kirk said, handing the man a card on which he had already written a message.

"Ah don't believe Ah understands," the butler said after a glance at it.

"Monsieur will," Kirk assured him and turned to leave.

He had written: "I took the liberty of stopping by unannounced to return the visit you and your friends paid me at the St. Charles hotel. I know you will forgive the informality of my call since you stood on no ceremony when you called on me. I will return the day after tomorrow and will expect to find you at home and ready to continue the discussion we had concerning Bowie knives at The Oaks some time ago."

True to his threat, Stryker was back at the Gayarres' door two days later. This time the bell was answered by an attractive mulatto maid in a costume cut low in front to expose the upper slopes of superbly shaped breasts.

"*Oui,* monsieur, you may come in," the girl said with a curtsy. "Monsieur Gayarre is not at home, but madame said to announce you as soon as you arrived.''

What the devil was the man up to, Kirk wondered. He had no business with Madame Gayarre no matter what part she had played in Lorinda's mistreatment. He didn't make war on women.

He watched the provocative swing of the maid's derriere as she left the entry hall. Was Gayarre so frightened of him that he would hide behind his wife's skirts? Well, it wouldn't do him any good. If necessary, Kirk would publish the man's name and brand him a coward for hiding. In Creole society that would be unbearable for a man of Gayarre's nature.

''Madame will see you in the morning room,'' the maid said when she returned, curtsying prettily.

Kirk glanced at her deep cleavage, noticing a livid bruise across one tempting breast. So the Gayarres were practicing their usual brutalities on her. Well, he would free her of one of her tormentors; as soon as he had wrung from Gayarre the truth about Lorinda, he would kill the man.

The girl led him down a hallway to a large sitting room. The sun was pouring in through several high windows. Madame Gayarre, dressed in a diaphanous gown of pale green silk, was stretched out languidly on a chaise longue.

Despite what he knew of the woman's perverted tastes and cruelty, Kirk had to admit she was stunning. Her blonde hair gleamed like gold in the sun, and her voluptuous body was obviously naked under the fragile dressing gown.

''What a pleasure to meet you at last, Mr.

Stryker," she said, offering a slender white hand. "I have heard so much about you."

She obviously expected Kirk to kiss her hand, but he merely bowed over it.

Her china blue eyes widened a little. She showed her teeth in a provocative smile. "I had imagined that a professional gambler would be a trifle more bold." She moved her legs, and one bare calf and knee peeked out from under the gown. "Sit here, Mr. Stryker," she said, patting the chaise. "Sit here beside me."

Kirk looked around. There was no place else to sit. He perched on the edge of the seat and tried to ignore the pressure of her thigh against his.

"What would you like to drink, Mr. Stryker? Or may I call you Kirk and you call me Jessica?"

Before he could reply, she picked up a silver bell and rang it. "I'll have an absinthe frappé, Matteil," she said when the maid reappeared. "What would you like, Kirk?"

She said his name with a special emphasis, like a caress with a velvet glove, and it set him on guard at once.

"I'll have bourbon and branch water," he said, wishing he could edge his way farther down the chaise and escape the musky scent of her perfume.

When the maid had brought the drinks, Jessica touched her glass to Kirk's, her eyes wide and inviting.

"Madame Gayarre," he said, clearing his throat after the first taste of almost straight bourbon, "I have business with your husband."

"Yes, I know," she said, "and I'm glad because

it gave me a chance to meet you. Would you care to discuss the matter with me?''

"Madame, this is not the kind of business one can discuss with a man's wife.''

"Why?'' she asked bluntly. "Is it embarrassing for you to tell me you intend to kill Joseph?''

Kirk's eyes narrowed to slits. "You know?''

"But of course,'' she said, and her lip curled. "Why else would Joseph be hiding out? He's a coward, and I despise cowards.''

"He's hiding out? Where?''

"I don't know and I don't care,'' she said, letting her fingers trail lightly up his wrist under his sleeve. "I hate cowards, but I adore strong, brave men.''

This one had to be watched, Kirk thought as he took another sip of his drink. She was alluring and she was clever and whatever she had on her mind she obviously didn't mind using sex to attain her goal.

"You must be very good with those knives of yours to have terrified Joseph,'' she purred. "It makes me wonder if perhaps you are not also good at other things.''

Having a woman make a play for him was no novelty to Kirk Stryker, but he had been forewarned about this one. It occurred to him that he might learn more by pretending to go along with her; she probably knew where Lorinda had been taken. A woman scorned was deadly, but a woman in the throes of passion might let any secret slip. His only moral qualm about using her came from what he knew of her foulness. Certainly he wouldn't hesitate out of concern for Joseph Gayarre's honor—or the woman's either. Neither of them possessed any such virtue.

"Have you ever killed a man with those Bowie knives of yours?" she asked.

"Yes."

"How many?"

"Several."

"Is it a fast death, or does it take a long time? Does it involve a lot of painful cuts?"

"It depends," he said.

"But you could do it very slowly if you wanted to?" she asked eagerly, leaning forward; she seemed not to notice when the dressing gown fell away to reveal firm round breasts tipped with surprisingly red nipples.

"I could if I wanted to," he said and looked down at his drink. He had finished the first drink more quickly than he intended and had barely noticed when she signaled for another.

"Have you ever used a knife on a woman?" She was smiling with some secret pleasure of her own.

"Of course not."

"Have you thought of using a knife on me?" she asked, blue eyes fixed on his and nostrils flaring with excitement.

"No, why should I?" he said.

"Revenge," she said and laughed. "Revenge for what I did to that pretty little wench you set such store by. Oh my, but I did have fun with her."

Rage almost choked him. He wanted to lash out with his fist, smash that mocking face with its sensuous, sneering lips. "Where is Lorinda?" he demanded. "The girl is legally mine. I demand to see her."

"Oh, she isn't here," Jessica said, obviously pleased at having provoked such an angry reaction from him. "If she were, I'd have her brought in and let you watch us together. Would that excite you, Kirk, to see me and that pretty little black girl in each other's arms?

He wanted to kill her, but he fought against the urge. He had to control himself for Lorinda's sake. The woman was slightly insane, and she was also as lustful as a waterfront whore. Playing on that lust would get him what he wanted quicker than violence.

"Wouldn't you like to watch while I whipped her?" she said. "After all, she is a slave. She's your slave. You must have whipped her. Don't you think the two of us could do some very exciting things to her?"

"No," he forced himself to say softly. He let his eyes travel down the length of her wantonly displayed body. "Why bring in a third person? Aren't two enough? Aren't a man and a woman enough?"

Her laugh had a mocking tinkle to it, but her hand moved without hesitation to his thigh and then to the more intimate area between. "That depends on how much man there is here."

In spite of his feelings of disgust and hatred for her, his body reacted automatically to the caressing fingers.

She laughed again as she felt the size and strength

of his arousal. "Oh, yes, that's a lot of man," she said, lying back on the chaise and allowing the translucent material of the gown to fall open. "Perhaps even man enough for Jessica."

Stryker had never felt less inclined to dally with a woman, but her fingers were working on him expertly.

Coaxing and teasing, she drew him to her. Without quite knowing how or when he had succumbed, he found himself pressing down on her, the fullness of her breasts against his chest. Her thighs opened and her fingers guided him to her. She whimpered and whispered obscene incitement in his ear as he thrust and thrust into her. Her thighs came up to lock around him. She was a raging fury beneath him, rolling and bucking upward to meet him, her nails raking down his back as he pounded savagely at her.

He didn't try to temper his merciless pounding. He didn't care if he broke the bitch's back. All he wanted was to keep smashing into her with murderous rage until . . . no, no, he had to stop . . . calm down . . . get hold of himself. He had to remember his purpose.

It took a supreme effort of will, but he slowed his attack until he was barely moving.

"What's the matter?" Jessica wailed. "Don't stop. Don't stop! You're torturing me!"

He gritted his teeth to keep from responding to the writhing of her body, using iron control to hold the act suspended while she strove frantically to complete it.

"I want some information," he said.

"Information?" she screeched, mad with lust and frustration. "What the hell are you talking about? Information be damned!"

"Where's the girl?" he demanded, gripping her hips to keep her from moving. "Tell me where she is and I'll give you what you want."

"You damn cold bastard! I'm going crazy!" She fought to escape his grasp.

"Tell me where you're holding Lorinda de Farbin," he said, "Or I'll leave you right now." He made a slight movement of withdrawal.

She shrieked in rage and frustration. "You can't do this to me!"

"Tell me," he said. "Where are you keeping her?"

"All right, damn you! I'll tell you for all the good it'll do you! We haven't got her, you idiot! We sent her back to her owners! We sold her up the river to the Wenzels for two thousand dollars! Now quick, do it. Finish before it's too late!"

Triumphant at having tricked her into revealing Lorinda's whereabouts, Kirk didn't stop to think what the rest of her words meant. He released his rigid control and began to respond to her wild gyrations. Jessica sobbed and gasped out exhortations that would have scorched the ears of the lowest gutter whore in the city. He rode her with all the relentless ferocity he was capable of. She met him on his own ground, writhing in a frenzy of excitement. The fact that he had made her wait had seemingly increased the depth of carnal passion in both of them.

Finally he felt her spasming in a last wild surge of lust, and he exploded in the rage of his own completion.

She pulled away from him almost at once, pulling her gown back around her. In a hurry to seek out Lorinda, he rose at once, adjusted his trousers, and reached for his coat. He had just slipped his arms into it when she suddenly let out a piercing scream.

"No! No!" she screeched, ripping at her gown so that it hung from one shoulder. "Let me alone! Rape! Rape!"

Stryker stared at her in open-mouthed surprise.

"Help! Help! Please, someone, help! I'm being raped!"

It took Kirk a few moments to understand what was going on and those few moments almost proved fatal. But when he heard feet pounding down the hallway and Joseph Gayarre's voice answering his wife's phony cries for help, he knew instantly what was happening. He reached for the gun in the pocket of his coat.

"It isn't there," Jessica said, laughing at him. "I have it."

He darted toward her and grabbed her by the arms just as the door was flung open and Joseph walked in, gun in hand.

"Well, Mr. Stryker, what is the meaning of this?" he asked with a thin-lipped smile.

"So it was a setup all along," Stryker said, trying to estimate his chances against the cocked revolver in Gayarre's hand.

"Yes, except for the lengths to which my dear

wife went to sample her erotic pleasure.''

"Kill him; don't talk to him!" Jessica hissed.

"Kill him! I've had what I wanted."

Kirk surreptitiously reached toward the knife in its sheath along his left leg. Jessica grabbed him.

The woman was amazingly strong and managed to swing his arm behind him.

Gayarre was enjoying the situation. Kirk could see his finger tightening and then relaxing on the trigger. "It's all so simple, really," he said. "A man who has publicly expressed a dislike for me is found assaulting my wife. I kill him. New Orleans society will approve and the law will look the other way."

"Kill him, Joseph! Don't play with him!" Jessica ordered, still clinging with all her strength to Kirk's arm. "He's dangerous!"

"Yes, my dear, as you say," Joseph said and the finger curled around the trigger again.

At that moment Stryker moved. With a quick yank he freed his hand from Jessica's grasp and moved it upward to the back of his neck.

Gayarre hesitated one second too long. The moment that Gayarre froze was all the time Stryker needed. The second knife was out of its sheath between his shoulder blades and turning over in the air. There was a sickening thud as it embedded itself in the throat of the startled Creole.

Then a breathless silence, while the man stood swaying, finger still on the trigger of the pistol. Slowly, his hand relaxed, and the gun fell to the floor. Gayarre's knees buckled, and he collapsed on top of it.

Jessica's screams were still echoing in Stryker's ears as several neighbors who had overheard the scene burst into the room.

"My husband!" Jessica sobbed hysterically. "This man raped me and killed my husband!"

Stryker was grabbed by half a dozen hands, hustled out of the mansion and loaded into a carriage.

"Take this ruffian to the sheriff's" he heard several men shout. And before he knew it, he was sitting in a tiny cell in the jail on Jackson Street, staring at the ceiling and thinking about Lorinda. Now he knew where she was but could do nothing to help her. In fact, there was nothing he could do to help himself. His whole future rested on an appeal that Major White and John Powell had carried to the governor in Baton Rouge. If it was refused, there would be only the hangman's noose.

CHAPTER 23

The dogs were not far behind when Lorinda and Zack reached the little stream that ran into the Yazoo River north of Vicksburg. It was midday and the hot Mississippi sun glared down on them unmercifully. In three days and nights of running, broken only by a few hours sleep and a stop for food once a day, they had put sixty miles between them and Solitaire. But now the pursuers were drawing closer.

Specially trained to track runaway slaves, the dogs could pick up a scent as much as thirty-six hours after a fugitive had passed. They seldom failed to find their prey. The men with them were professional slave catchers, a profitable profession since a runaway was redeemed at a percentage of his worth. Lorinda and Zack were valuable property and the Wenzels, she knew, would spare no expense to get them back.

"Into the water," Zack said, wading into the stream. He held the baby in one arm and his sledgehammer in the other. "We heads upstream fur as we can to throw off the dogs."

Lorinda nodded wearily and followed him as best she could, carrying their canvas bag of food and a few extra articles of clothing for little Zack. Lacking Zack's physical stamina, she had discovered that she was more of a hindrance to the blacksmith than she was a help. Not only could she not keep up with him but her presence made it extremely difficult to get help from local blacks. Free blacks were almost always willing to aid their runaway brothers—which was one reason planters disliked having them live nearby—and other slaves aided their fellows as far as they were able, but Lorinda and Zack were offered no such help. Her white face brought only suspicious looks from free blacks once they were beyond the immediate area around Solitaire, and it was useless to approach slaves on other plantations.

"I can't go much farther," she told Zack as they splashed through the chilly knee-deep water. "I'm exhausted."

"Got to keep goin', honey," Zack said, shifting the baby up onto his shoulder so he could put a supportive arm around Lorinda. "Can't let them dogs git us and li'l Zack."

"No, no," she agreed. The dogs often mauled runaways when they caught them. They were not pointers or tracking dogs; they were dogs that relished the taste of the flesh they hunted and were frequently permitted to sample it.

The muddy water pulled around Lorinda's legs, slowing her to a snail's pace. Now that she had left it behind, she recalled the cozy safety of the smithy with longing. With the prospect of freedom rapidly fading, the simple creature comforts took on more importance.

No, she mustn't allow herself to think that way. Zack hadn't given way to despair and she shouldn't, either. The big man had been a pillar of strength during their frantic flight. He had kept up his spirits and had never once blamed her for the way their plans had gone wrong. The trouble, she saw now, was that she had planned mostly for what they would do once they reached Memphis and began their masquerade as a white woman traveling with her slaves. She hadn't given a great deal of thought to the fact that they had to travel over two hundred miles on foot before they reached the city. They had prepared only a small store of silver dollars, corn pone and bacon for this part of the journey.

The rocks in the stream were slippery, and Lorinda would have fallen several times without the support of Zack's arm. The baby was awake and fretful, and Lorinda was worried about the cough he had developed.

"Dogs ain' so close now," Zack said after nearly an hour of struggling upstream.

"How—how can—you tell?" Each breath was an effort.

"They ain' yelpin' lak they do when they think they 'bout to git a nip o' black meat," Zack said. "They is kind o' howlin' angry and circlin' roun' lookin' fo' the scent."

"It would be easier if we could travel on dry land," she gasped. "Do we still have to stay in the water?"

"Farther we can go, better chance we got," Zack said and splashed along determinedly.

The baby coughed again. Lorinda put a hand to his forehead. It was hot. His tiny hands were tight fists, his face screwed into an unhappy frown.

"I've got to stop and feed him," Lorinda said. "And we should eat ourselves."

"Better iffen we eat on the run," Zack said. "Dogs start upstream pretty soon. Slave cotchers know the way we got to go."

They stumbled on for another hour or so, but finally Lorinda staggered to the bank and sank down onto the grass. "I—I—can't go—any farther. Let me nurse the baby, then you take him and go on. Find some slave woman to nurse him later."

Zack stood looking down at her. He cocked his head to the side and listened for the baying of the dogs. They were no closer, but in spite of the desperate pace he had set, they were no farther away, either.

"Feed li'l Zack," he said, placing the infant in her arms. "Then you eat and rest fo a while 'fore we goes on."

"I *can't* go on, don't you understand? I can't go on. Leave me and save yourself and little Zack."

He shook his head stubbornly. "No. Ah won' leave you. We stay together."

Tears were running down her cheeks. "Please, Zack! Please go! If we're caught, they might kill you."

"They have to, 'cause Ah ain' goin' back. No mo' slavery fo' me, no matter what."

"Then go! Run!" she urged. "You're strong and can get away without me holding you back. Leave the boy with me, and I'll stay here until they come. They won't harm him and they won't hurt me, either; I'm too valuable a piece of merchandise."

"What do freedom mean to me 'thout you an'

mah son?'' Zack said with simple dignity. ''No. We rest an' then we go on.''

Lorinda fed the baby and ate some of the cold pone and was feeling somewhat better by the time Zack said they had to be on their way again. ''Dogs a'gettin' closer.''

She didn't have to be told that. The yelping sounded only a few hundred yards away. She made one more appeal. ''Leave me, please, Zack. There's still a chance for you.''

''We go together, or we stay here,'' Zack said with a calm certainty. She sighed and braced herself to step into the water again.

''No, not that way,'' Zack said, taking her hand. ''You cain' go on that way. We tries it ovahland but walks fast as we can.''

Grateful not to have to reenter the stream, she let him lead her through groves of live oak toward the open, hilly country that lay ahead.

''Maybe we find us a place to hide,'' he said as she limped along beside him. ''A cave maybe. Worst come to worst, I beats 'em off wiff this.'' He swung the hammer as easily with one hand as most strong men could have with two.

''They'll have guns and whips,'' she said, breathing hard again.

''They have to use guns,'' he said grimly. ''Ah don' go back. Ah nevah go back.''

''Oh, God, Zack, I'm sorry I ever got you into this,'' she moaned.

''Yo' listen to me, gal,'' he said, pausing to pull her against him. ''You git me into nuthin'. Ah was dumb an' happy like a dog be happy, fat with food an' content with wenches they give me. Yo' teached me love an' freedom. No matter what happen now, Ah don' go back to that.''

Lorinda was touched and had to blink back tears. She had given this man a vision of freedom and that vision was about to be torn from his grasp. He didn't blame her for that, but how could she not blame herself?

The going was getting more difficult, the grass giving way to rocks and thick brush. They were going uphill. The sound of the dogs was getting closer. Once, looking back over her shoulder, Lorinda saw them—six or seven ugly-looking brutes urged on by two men with whips, followed by others carrying rifles and shotguns.

"Come on, honey, we got to find us a place where they cain' come at us 'cept one at a time,'' Zack said, pulling at her arm.

Now they could hear not only the yelps of the dogs but also the shouts of men. Zack's powerful thigh muscles rippled under his pants as he struggled up the rocky slope. He was carrying the child and dragging Lorinda after him.

"Stop there, one of the men shouted above the howling of the dogs. "Stop or we'll shoot!''

"Shoot, an' to hell with yo', white devil!'' Zack yelled back over his shoulder. They were in a ravine filled with thick brush, and he had to let go of Lorinda to beat a way through for them with his hammer. She staggered after him, hardly noticing the scratches she was getting or the brambles that caught at her hair and clothes.

"Up ahaid. Ovahhangin' rocks an' a narrow

path,'' Zack said. "We take shelter and hold 'em off.''

"Can we, Zack, can we?''

A shot had rung out just before they plunged into the ravine, but it had been wide, and although they could hear the dogs and the men, it was almost possible to believe that here in this rugged ravine they might find at least temporary shelter.

Zack had scrambled up over some rocks and was standing on a huge boulder. "Up heah, honey,'' he said. He reached down and half-lifted Lorinda up beside him. Behind the boulder was a level area about twenty feet wide. Through it ran a tiny rill of sparkling water. There was white sand on either side that looked warm and dry, and beyond the rill were more rocks and then a precipitous drop down into a tree-covered valley below.

"They gotta come at us the same way we come,'' Zack said and scooped a hollow in the sand into which he placed the sleeping baby. Then he examined the rocks and boulders with which the area was strewn. "An' we got a lot of rocks to throw at 'em when they try to git us.''

Too exhausted to speak, Lorinda sank down onto the warm sand beside little Zack. She stared down the slope up which their pursuers must come. If they had a gun, almost any kind of gun, they could probably have held out here as long as their food lasted, she thought. But even in such a protected place, resisting with their bare hands seemed hopeless.

"You rest,'' Zack said. "Ah'll keep watch.'' Lorinda closed her eyes in exhaustion, grateful for even a few moments of respite.

Suddenly a bullet ricocheted off the huge boulder in front. Opening her eyes with a start, she could hear the dogs and men shouting very close by. She looked around for Zack and didn't see him. Had he left her after all and somehow managed to scramble down the sheer cliff at their backs? Frightened, but also rejoicing that the big blacksmith might have escaped, she reached for the baby and cradled him in her arms. She could hear men scrambling up through the brush, but she was so numb with exhaustion that she hardly cared.

"Hey, you up there, give yourselves up and we go easy on you!" one of the men bellowed. "You is valuable slaves, so we'll keep the dogs offen you and take you back safe and sound to your master."

Lorinda put little faith in that promise, but it was possible she and the child wouldn't be physically harmed, at least not until they were back at Solitaire. Slave hunters were mainly interested in the rewards they received for bringing in runaways, and very few planters were willing to pay for a dead carcass or a damaged slave.

"We're comin' after you," another voice shouted. "Better come peaceful like."

Lorinda could see them now, sweating white men in rough clothes and boots. The bearded man in the lead with the rifle must be the professional hunter, and the others his hirelings. The two dog handlers were back farther, restraining the yelping hounds on heavy leashes.

They were so close now that she could hear their labored breathing as they came up the steep path

Zack had beaten through the brush. Clutching her son to her breast, she rose to her knees, ready to surrender.

But before she could speak, she heard a grunt behind her. Turning, she saw Zack rising up against the sky, an enormous rock balanced over his head.

"Look out, Mr. Drum!" one of the dog handlers shouted. "Look out, that one's got a rock!"

"Duck! Get the hell out of here!" The men in the lead suddenly started to scramble back down the steep slope.

It was too late. Zack heaved and let fly. The huge boulder traveled several feet into the air and then went rolling and bouncing down the ravine. It struck the boss of the gang a glancing blow that knocked him to the side. The man beyond him, however, was hit square and tumbled down the slope. The boulder bowled over two more men before crashing out of sight through the underbrush.

A rifle and a shotgun were fired in Zack's direction, but he was already down out of sight behind a pile of rocks.

"Damn you! Damn your black hide to hell!" the leader yelled, holding one arm with the other hand. "Ah'm gonna burn you, slave! Ah don' care how much you're worth! Ah'll tie you to a tree and turn you slow tili the flesh melts off yo' bones!"

The threat terrified Lorinda. She knew only too well that when faced with defiance or menace from their slaves, white masters were perfectly capable of forgetting monetary values and doing incredibly savage things.

But it didn't seem to faze Zack at all. He looked

toward where she crouched with the baby in her arms, a light in his eyes she had never seen before. He was enjoying doing battle with his oppressors. He had said he would die rather than go back, and now it was obvious he would kill to avoid being taken. Of the four men who had been bowled over by the boulder, one lay dead at the foot of the slope, and another was writhing on the ground.

The white men had withdrawn down the hill and were clustered around the injured man. Finally one of them took off at a run in the direction of the river. Zack crawled over to Lorinda and put his arm around her.

"What will they do now?" she asked. "Just stay down there and starve us out?"

"Naw, they too mad fo' that. They so mad they kin hardly think. You kill a white man, an' all the othahs starts figurin' out how to kill you no matter what the cost."

"Oh, Zack, I'm so sorry about all of this."

"Don' be, gal," he said calmly. "Ah'm glad. Iffen we hadn' run, Ah'd nevah of got a chance to kill me a white man. It feel good. It sho do feel good. Maybe Ah gits to kill 'nuther fore this is ovah."

"But we can't hold out very long. That young fellow who ran off, he must have gone for help. What can we do?"

At first she had been the one with the ideas, the one who had suggested the path they should follow; but now that the time for action had come, Zack was the leader.

"What can we do?" he repeated. "Well, yo' kin

take care of li'l Zack whilst Ah builds us a kind of fort. They won't do nuthin for a while, seein' as there's only one healthy one left. Then we eats, and this time we kin cook the bacon 'cause dey ain' no doubt in nobody's mind where we is at.''

While she nursed and changed the baby, Lorinda watched the seemingly tireless Zack pile up rocks and boulders to form a barricade across the path to their eyrie. Even he was breathing hard by the time he had completed the task. At one end he left an open spot where the slope fell off into a deep ravine that was almost as precipitous as the one behind them.

''Why did you do that?'' she asked, looking up from the fire where she was cooking bacon on the end of a pointed stick.

''So's Ah has a place to roll the biggest rocks down on 'em.''

She had thought she was very hungry, but once the bacon was ready and the stale pone warmed, she barely touched it.

''What's going to happen to us, Zack?'' she asked, watching him wolf his food with the appetite of a man who had put in a hard day's work.

''Don' rightly know,'' he said, licking bacon grease off his fingers and reaching for another piece of corn pone. ''Do know Ah ain' goin' back and they ain' gonna burn me; won' give 'em the pleasure of burnin' me.''

''Will they come after us tonight?'' she asked. It was almost dusk now and she could see torches down below and hear shouts of greeting as more men arrived to help the original crew.

" 'Spect not," he said. "They have to use torches to come up, an' lights would make it easy fo' me to hit 'em as they come."

"Then why don't you get some sleep and I'll keep watch," she said. "You haven't slept in twenty-four hours."

Zack yawned. "Yeah, sho could use some shut-eye." He stretched out on the white sand with his son snuggled against him, and Lorinda took up a place near the barricade where she could watch and listen for anyone approaching.

At first she was very alert, sitting wrapped in her heavy shawl, but gradually the toil and sleeplessness of the preceding four days and nights began to catch up with her. Twice she caught herself nodding and jerked awake. A third time she actually dozed off for a few minutes and woke to the sound of something crashing through the underbrush down below. She was about to scream for Zack when a deer bounded out of a clump of trees and raced off down the ravine, a sure sign that no one was coming up the path.

Through most of the long night she could hear a great deal of talking, shouting and occasional cursing from down below. The voices seemed unnecessarily loud, and she decided the men must be drinking. Maybe they were doing it to keep away the night chill, but it frightened her. A group of men like this were dangerous in any case; drunk they were even more so. She began to doubt that even she and the baby would survive the night. Mobs of drink-crazed white men had burned women and slaughtered children in the past in the South, and there was no reason to think they would hesitate to do it again.

The moon rose about two hours before dawn, and the slope of the hill was suddenly almost as bright as it had been when they scrambled up it the afternoon before.

Getting to her feet and stretching stiffening muscles, Lorinda peered over the barricade toward the campfires, examining each spot where the shadows were deep. She couldn't see anything, but she had the feeling something down there was moving. As she watched, quiet fell on the camp below and the fires began to die out.

Zack was still asleep. She hesitated to wake him on mere suspicion, but he had told her to wake him at moonrise and it was already at least a half hour after that.

Was that a footfall down there where the boulder had struck the first of their attackers? Was that shadow moving, or was it only her imagination?

"Zack, Zack," she whispered, reaching to touch his arm. "Zack, I think they're coming."

The big man was awake instantly, picking up his hammer and getting to his feet. "Git yo'self some rocks, gal, and be ready to throw 'em."

He listened intently in the silence for a few minutes, looking down the slope. "Yeah, they a'comin' all right, a whole bunch of 'em. Got to git another boulder, a nice big 'un an' play ninepins with them white devils."

He laid his hammer down, picked up a boulder even bigger than the first one and staggered over to the opening in the barricade.

There was a sudden shout from below and a flash of fire.

"Zack, look out!" Lorinda screamed just as a blast of buckshot hit him in the chest and arms. He had allowed himself to be silhouetted for a moment against the lightening sky, and someone had taken aim and got off a shot.

Lorinda crawled toward him on hands and knees, watching in horror the blood running from his body even as he stood erect refusing to be bowed by his wounds. A look of pure defiance and triumph spread over his face, and with a superhuman effort, he hurled the boulder down the hill. There was a yell of pain and curses from several of the men. At least one of their attackers had been hit, but the rest were still scrambling up the path, shouting threats and swearing vengeance.

Zack looked at Lorinda, his eyes filling with tenderness. "Ah loves yo', gal. Ah loves you but they ain' goin' burn me or take me alive." He was losing blood from a dozen wounds but refused to fall.

White men were scrambling through the breach in the wall. The leader came right at Zack, one arm in a sling and a pistol in the other hand. Zack picked up a rock and started toward him. Lorinda saw the slave hunter's eyes flash white. He raised the horse pistol, took aim at Zack's legs and fired twice. Zack dropped to his knees, hit in both legs.

Obviously the man intended to keep his promise to burn Zack, otherwise he would have killed him rather than just crippled him with the big pistol. Now he stood looking down at the huge black, a smile of incredible cruelty on his face.

"Grab him, boys, and drag him down the hill. We got the stake and wood all ready for this one."

Two of the men leaned their guns against a rock and approached Zack. But before they could touch him, in one last superhuman effort he lunged suddenly upward, throwing his arms around the slave hunter in a bear-like hug. And somehow managing to propel himself to the edge of the precipice with the white man struggling in his arms, he uttered a shout of triumph and toppled them both over into the darkness below.

Ah loves you, gal, but they ain' gonna burn me or take me alive, Zack had said. In the momentary stunned silence that followed, Lorinda knew it would be best if she followed his example. She had started toward the cliff when she remembered her child. She couldn't leave a defenseless baby in the hands of these monsters. Turning, she darted back to snatch up her son.

"Stop her! Don't let the bitch get to that cliff. That black bastard robbed us of a burning, but she won't!"

"Get her! Get the wench! We'll burn her in the bastard's place!"

Hands reached for her, and men closed in around her. Little Zack was torn from her grasp, and she was knocked to the ground. Savagely kicked and beaten, she was dragged from behind the barricade and down the hill.

"Get the fire started down there," one youth yelled. "We got us a black bitch for a slow fire. We is gonna make her scream all day long."

"Burn her! Burn her!" others were yelling excitedly. "Burn her and throw the pickaninny into the fire with her!"

Lorinda wanted to faint but couldn't. Her screams went unheeded, as did her struggles. Her nails, raking out, connected with a face, and that brought a fist smashing into one breast like a sledgehammer.

"Burn her! Burn her! Get the fire good and hot!" The shouts filled her ears as her pain-wracked body was dragged down through the brush by the heels.

CHAPTER 24

"What the devil is going on here?" a man on horseback was shouting above the roar of Lorinda's tormentors.

Nobody paid any attention. All eyes were fixed on the struggling girl who was being tied to a small tree while dry leaves and kindling were piled up around her knee high.

"Burn her! Burn the bitch! She helped kill Drum and the other two!"

"Get out of my way!" the man on horseback roared, trying to force his way through the crowd. "I am Sheriff Lister! Clear the way for me and my men!"

"To hell with him. Burn the bitch!"

A teenage boy approached with the torch to set the tinder on fire, leering at the breast that had been bared when Lorinda's dress was torn in the struggle.

A shot rang out, followed by two more. The boy turned, the torch held high, a look of astonishment on his face.

"You, boy, drop that torch, or the next shot won't be into the air, it will be through your hand," the mounted man said into the startled silence. His revolver was aimed at the boy. The three men behind him carried rifles and wore deputy sheriff badges.

"What the hell's the meaning of this, Sheriff?" demanded a fat man in a checked shirt. The deputies were using their horses to force the crowd of men away from the terrified girl. "We're just administerin' the law accordin' to Judge Lynch. Since when has that been illegal in Mississippi?"

"Yeah," someone else demanded. "When'd it get to be against the law to burn a nigger for killin' a white man?"

"It's illegal as long as I'm sheriff of Warren County," Lister said. "I have a court order here to detain a runaway slave name of Lorinda de Farbin, and this girl fits the description."

"Aw, hell, he jes' wants the reward!" the round-faced boy said. "He's not interested in justice!"

The sheriff leaned over in the saddle to address Lorinda. "Are you Lorinda de Farbin the runaway slave belonging to August Wenzel?"

She was too frightened to split hairs, so she just nodded and said, "Yes, I'm the one you are looking for."

"Cut her loose, Jake," Lister ordered one of the deputies, "and mount her up behind you."

Then he turned to the would-be lynchers, taking out his watch. "I'm gonna give you boys about five minutes to get your asses out of here. If you're all gone by then, I'll just forget I ever saw any of you. If not . . ."

With the sheriff's eyes roving from face to face,

the men began to slowly drift away from him.

One of the other deputies found the baby lying on the ground, crying and hungry but unhurt. He handed it up to Lorinda. At a signal from the sheriff, the small procession headed off toward the Vicksburg road.

Zack, Zack, my poor darling Zack, she was thinking as she wrapped the heavy shawl around herself and her fatherless child. *Kirk's dead and now Zack. It seems like everything I touch I destroy.* She would never forget the look on Zack's face when, knowing that he was going to die, he had told her he loved her.

A week later Lorinda was back at Solitaire and found a different kind of terror. On her arrival she was hauled into the downstairs room that had previously been her father's study and was now used by August Wenzel as his office.

"So you are back," August said. He was seated at a desk, with Jacob standing beside him.

Lorinda said nothing, just stood holding her baby and looking back at them.

"Twice you have run away from us," August said. "Twice we have had to pay out good money to redeem our property."

It was pointless to deny that she had run away the first time. The Wenzels simply chose to ignore the fact that Gideon had lost her in a card game and turned her papers over to Kirk Stryker.

"Do you have anything to say for yourself?" August asked. "An excuse for your behavior?"

"I need no excuse for trying to win my freedom," she said defiantly.

"So you need no excuse!" August's hand slammed down on the desk. "I suppose that means you'll run again if you get the chance."

Again Lorinda said nothing.

"You are impossible!" August said. "An ungrateful troublemaker of the worst kind. Despite the kindly treatment you have received from us, you have returned evil for the good we have done you."

Lorinda wondered briefly if in his heavy German way he was attempting irony, but she saw he was perfectly serious. He really believed he had treated her well.

"We also went to the trouble of giving you a good man. A man whose skills were worth a great deal to us. And how did you repay us? Tell me, wench, what did you do?"

Lorinda saw no point in trying to defend herself.

"I'll tell you what you did! You talked Zack into running away with you! Running away, killing two white men and killing himself. That was all your fault and that cost us money!"

The guilt she felt over Zack's death would be with her forever, Lorinda knew, but costing the Wenzels money didn't trouble her in the least.

"How do you think you can make amends for what you've cost us?" August asked. "Perhaps you have some ideas."

"I think we ought to take it out of her hide, pa," Jacob said. "I have a new rawhide whip that would do a proper job. It would take off her hide in thin little strips."

The father looked at the son, then took off his spectacles and wiped them with his handkerchief.

"And how much do you think that would increase this wench's value, Jacob?"

Jacob shrugged. "Not much, but it would keep her from running off again and costing us more money."

"That is a shortsighted view, my boy. I understand your justifiable rage, but one must not seek justice at the cost of material gain."

"She deserves anything she gets, pa," Jacob said.

"And we deserve anything we can get *for* her," August said. "There is only one sensible way to deal with a troublemaking slave and that is to get rid of it." A smug, self-satisfied smile crossed his pudgy face. "I have an idea that will get us the highest possible sum for her and will at the same time punish her more severely than your whip."

Jacob's pale blue eyes lit up. "What is the idea, pa? How can we make money and punish her at the same time?"

"I propose to hold an auction," August said. "Not one of your usual auctions, not a vendue, but a private sale right here at Solitaire. There will be only one chattel offered for bidding—this beautiful young female."

Jacob looked puzzled. "I can see how that might bring a good price, but how is that going to punish her?"

"That will happen because of the nature of the business of those I have invited to attend our private vendue," August said, enjoying his little game.

"Yes, pa, yes," Jacob said excitedly. "What is their business?"

"They are brothel keepers," August said. "All the most famous ones from New Orleans and Natchez will be here the day after tomorrow to bid on what I assured them was the most beautiful and talented whore they could obtain anywhere."

"You amaze me sometimes, pa," Jacob said. "Depend on you to get the most out of any situation. Profit and justice at the same time."

Both men turned to look at Lorinda. She kept her face carefully blank. She would not give them the satisfaction of seeing her react in any way to the sadistic proposal.

August frowned as his icy eyes surveyed her critically. "I told these people she was the most beautiful wench money could buy, but look at her! She's filthy dirty, her hair is a mass of tangles and her clothes are in tatters. We won't get much for her in that condition. Something will have to be done about it. Get that light-skinned black gal. What's her name? Sissy? She used to be this one's maid, didn't she?"

Jacob nodded.

"Have Sissy bathe her and fix her hair. Get her some decent clothes, the most provocative ones you can find. Oh, and take that damn brat away from her and give it to one of the slave women to raise. Beautiful whores are not supposed to have mewling brats with them."

"No, no, damn you!" Lorinda spat, holding little Zack close. "You can't take my baby! Do anything you want to me, but leave my child alone!"

Jacob laughed, strode around the desk and twisted one of her arms up behind her back. She screamed as he pulled the baby out of her grasp and dangled it at arm's length. The frightened child began to cry. She tried to reach for him, but Jacob held her off and lifted him higher, holding onto only one small ankle.

"Please, you're hurting him!" Lorinda cried. "He's only a baby, Jacob! He's never done you any harm."

Jacob let go of her arm and backhanded her across the mouth. "Master Jacob, sir, to you, wench! Now ask me politely, and maybe I won't drop him on his head."

"Mr. Wenzel, please," she begged, extending a pleading hand to August, but he just leaned back in his chair with his thumbs hooked into his vest pockets and watched with a glint of amusement in his faded eyes.

"You know, I could do worse than drop him," Jacob said, starting to swing the suspended child back and forth; its cries had turned into terrified wails. "I might throw him against the wall and bash his brains out. Or I might toss him headfirst into the fireplace. Would you like that?"

"No, no! Oh, God, no!"

"That's one way I could punish you without diminishing your value one bit," Jacob said. "Spattering this brat's brains all over that white marble his grandpappy was so proud of wouldn't make you worth one cent less."

"Please, please, just tell me what you want me to do," she said, beside herself with fear for her son. "I'll do whatever you say, just tell me."

"First, get down on your knees and ask me real

nice not to kill this pickaninny. He's not worth much, you know, so we wouldn't be losing any real money, and it sure would make me feel good to stop this kid's howling once and for all.''

Lorinda dropped to her knees in front of him. ''Please, Master Jacob, sir, please spare my child.''

''Tell me you'd rather have me take him away and give him to some black mammy to raise, or I'll put him out of his misery right now.''

The glint of madness in Jacob's eyes told her what she must do. ''Please, Master Jacob, sir, I would rather you gave him to another woman to raise. I don't want him killed.''

''That's more like it,'' Jacob said, still holding the child suspended but no longer swinging him back and forth. ''But it's not quite enough. Tell me what else you'll do if I let your child live a while longer.''

''Anything you want,'' she said abjectly. ''I'll debase or degrade myself in any way you want and as often as you ask me to.''

He laughed derisively. ''You forget, I've already had you in every way I wanted you. You've nothing new to offer there. But I'll tell you what I will do. I'll let this brat live if you put yourself out to bring the highest price possible from those who attend our auction the day after tomorrow. You have to promise to do everything they ask and, once bought, make the best damn whore there ever was, on the river or off it.''

''I promise,'' she said. ''I'll do anything you say if you spare my son's life.''

''Good. Now kiss my feet like the good little

black whore you are and get the hell out of here before I change my mind!''

Unhesitatingly Lorinda kissed his boots. ''Thank you, Master Jacob, sir, thank you very much.''

Later she sat soaking in a tub of hot water while Sissy washed her hair.

''Ah swears, Miss Lori, you must o' cotched every jigger and sticker in Mississippi in yo' hair,'' the girl complained.

''I know, Sissy, but that's not important. Poor Zack is dead, they took my baby away from me, and you think I'm going to worry about my hair?''

''Ah's sorry, Miss Lori, but you an' Zack shouldn't have runned.''

''And what about you, Sissy? You were ready enough to listen to our plans when you thought you might be sent off to be sold in New Orleans or Natchez.''

''Yes'm, Ah knows, but Ah was scairt, and half of the hundred and fifty black folks on Solitaire was sold, you know, so's I had reason to be. Hear tell they gonna sell mo' of us, too.''

''Well, I know of at least one who's going to be,'' Lorinda said dejectedly.

''Who dat?'' Sissy asked in alarm. ''Who gonna go?''

''Not you,'' Lorinda said. ''Me. They're going to auction me off to a bunch of brothel keepers.''

Sissy's eyes became larger and rounder than ever. ''They ain'! Oh, Miss Lori, you gonna let 'em do that to you?''

''I haven't any choice, Sissy,'' Lorinda said bitterly. ''They have my baby and Jacob will kill him if I don't cooperate.''

"Masta Jacob one mean man," Sissy said. "All de Wenzels is mean, but Jacob gits mo' pure pleasure out o' hit than all the rest."

"He's a devil," Lorinda agreed. "I'd kill him with my own hands if I had the strength."

There was an air of expectancy about Solitaire on the eve of the private auction. The blacks were all excited about something, and the Wenzels were looking forward to the affair eagerly. Lorinda was confined in the basement room again. When Chatti brought her a tray of supper, she told Lorinda the two Wenzel women were to be left out of the festivities the next day because August had decided the auction might be too explicit for their respectable eyes.

"He jes' don' want that ugly dumplin' of a daughter to see what a beautiful gal look like," Chatti said.

"She's lucky she looks like a dumpling," Lorinda said. "She'll never face being sold as the star attraction in a whorehouse."

"No, she have to buy her way in," Chatti said. "Eat some mo', honey chile. You must eat to keep up yo' strength."

"What for?" Lorinda asked, pushing the tray away. "That doesn't take strength. You just lie on your back and let them do it to you."

"Didn' mean that," Chatti said. "Mean somethin' else. You nevah know wot might happen."

Lorinda looked at her sharply. "That's a strange thing to say, Chatti. What do you think might happen?"

The older woman shrugged. "Don' know, but a lot o' talk goin' on 'roun here. All de folks hates them Wenzels, an' voodoos been stirrin' things up lately.''

"Voodoos?" Lorinda said. "I didn't know there were any in this area."

"Didn' use to be, but they is now," Chatti said. "Don' you heah the drums a'goin' at night? Drums say things that would scare the Wenzels iffen they could unnerstan' dem.''

"Is there a woman priestess leading the voodoos?"

Chatti shrugged. " 'Spects so. Most always is."

"But do you know the name of this particular one?''

"No, Missy, Ah sho' don'," Chatti said with a vigorous shake of her head. "Ah has as li'l to do with voodoos as Ah can."

"But you did say that the voodoos being here means harm may come to the Wenzels," Lorinda said. "How do you know that?"

" 'Cause de drums keep sayin' hit," Chatti said.

"And you can read the drums?"

"No, Miss Lori, Ah cain', but them as do sez that's what they a'sayin', and Ah seen the *gris-gris* myself.''

"What *gris-gris?*" Lorinda asked, her heart beating fast.

"De one nailed to the front door the othah day."

"Tell me what it looked like, Chatti."

When the old woman had described the object found pinned to the front door, Lorinda nodded. "I think you're right, Chatti. That was a death-*ouanga*.''

Lorinda was more cheerful when Chatti left than

she had been for days. Just knowing there were voodoos nearby and that her sister might be among them gave her hope. She had been very impressed with Ajona's ability to get things done, with or without her alleged magical powers. If Ajona had decided to cause trouble for the Wenzels, it was fairly certain they would live to regret having earned her enmity.

"Even if I'm not here to see it, I'll know they aren't getting away with all their crimes," she whispered to herself before she fell into a troubled sleep.

The private vendue the next day was much worse than Lorinda had imagined it could be. In the barn, a temporary auction block had been set up by stretching heavy boards across two sawhorses. Jacob had talked his father into letting him handle the actual sale. He lifted Lorinda up onto the platform and vaulted up beside her while Gideon and August ushered in the prospective buyers. Lorinda, looking beautiful in a tight black lace gown with a plunging neck, eyed the crowd fearfully.

The brothel owners were mostly a crude-looking lot, big hard-faced men in checkered vests, trousers stuffed into boots and derbies tilted back on their heads, but two of them were atypical. One was a tall, statuesque woman addressed with grudging respect by the others as Bricktop. From her hennaed hair to her red boots, she was a tough-talking harridan whose voice had a rasp to it that would take the paint off walls. The other unusual member of the group was a tiny, effete man dressed in a silk shirt and black morning coat worn with light gray trousers. He was the last to arrive and as he approached the others he not so much walked as pranced.

Bricktop walked over closer to the platform and squinted up at Lorinda, who stared down at her in hostile defiance, her breasts heaving with emotion.

"Is this the troublemaking slave you want to get rid of?"

"This, Miss Bricktop, is the lovely little lady who will light up the premises of your establishment," Jacob said.

"Don't know about that," Bricktop said, shifting the cigar she was smoking to the other side of her mouth. "The scum that come to my place like some heft to a woman. She's a skinny little thing. Don't seem like she'd have much stamina."

"Oh, but she's stronger than she looks," Jacob said. "She has some black blood and you know how passionate those black wenches can be."

"Hmmm. How many times can you do it in one day, honey?" Bricktop asked.

Lorinda turned scarlet. "I beg your pardon?"

"I want to know how many men you can take on in a day," the redheaded woman said. "My gals have got to be able to handle a couple of dozen a day. When you're getting a dollar a roll, you got to do a lot of rolls."

"But my dear Miss Bricktop," August spoke up. "You should raise your prices. With a female like this as your lead item, you ought to be able to get four or five times the usual price."

"Don't know about that," Bricktop said, blowing out a cloud of smoke. "Them roustabouts and riverboat men are animals. If you don't have big, tough girls, they tear them to pieces in a few days. Whoring at the Lighthouse is hard labor.''

Lorinda felt sick to her stomach. She wanted to vomit but forced herself instead to swallow the bitter bile that rose in her throat.

''Ah, but she would be perfect for my clientele,'' lisped the dapper little man, who had identified himself as Vasco Nunez. ''The ladies who patronize my Whisper Club prefer girls who are delicate as well as beautiful. I shall bid high for this lovely trifle.''

''Yeah, but remember she has black blood,'' Bricktop said, ''and even those roughnecks who come to my place like their poontang to be all white.''

August cleared his throat and announced pompously, ''You have my personal assurance as a man of integrity that this gal is ninety percent white.''

''Look at her yourself, Miss Bricktop,'' Gideon threw in. ''Nobody would know if you didn't tell them that she ain't a hundred percent white.''

''I got my ethics,'' Bricktop rasped. ''I don't pass nothing off as white 'cepting it is.''

''Yes, but who would care with such rare beauty,'' Nunez said. ''My customers have husbands who spend all their time with quadroon mistresses. They would see only her delicate beauty and never question her race.''

''Maybe so,'' Bricktop said, ''but remember that even if they are the cream of Creole society, they have what are called unnatural desires, and there ain't too many places that cater to them."

"So do not bid, my dear Bricktop," Nunez said. "It will be the better for me, no?"

"I didn't say I wasn't gonna bid. She sure as hell would add some class to my joint, even if I only used her in exhibitions in the main parlor with a couple of studs I sometimes hire."

"Then shall we get on to the bidding?" Jacob said. "Will someone open with three thousand dollars?"

"Now, hold on here just a minute," one of the other men said. "It's all very well for Bricktop and Senor Nunez to be willing to buy the gal sight unseen. They got special needs and lots of eagles to spend. What Ah'm looking for is a good-looking, hardworking whore and, folks, a whore's assets ain't in her pretty face, it's in her body. Ah wants to see the flesh."

"But of course, Mr. Pickens," Jacob said. "We had no intention of auctioning off this superlative merchandise without giving you buyers the fullest opportunity to examine it as carefully as you care to. Any other policy would not be in keeping with the reputation for integrity that is the hallmark of August Wenzel and sons."

He turned to Lorinda and gave the order she had been dreading. "Shuck off that dress, gal, and let them see what you got."

Lorinda looked at the hard-eyed crew that was closing in on the auction block. An involuntary shudder ran through her and she hesitated. Jacob's thin lips twitched. "You are going to be cooperative, aren't you, gal?"

"Yes, Yes, of course," Lorinda said hastily and began undoing the buttons of her gown. When the top was loosened, she let it slide off her shoulders to expose the white globes of her breasts, then downward leaving her standing naked and vulnerable before the crowd.

"Well, she's titted out nice," Bricktop said. "That's in her favor."

"Got a pair on her. Yes sir, she sure has," Pickens said.

"A flat belly, good thighs" —Bricktop took inventory— "and even naked there is an air of innocence about her. Let's get her down here where we can get our hands on that flesh."

Strong arms lifted Lorinda off the auction block placing her in the center of the gaping crowd. Then they all began to handle her. Lorinda gritted her teeth, knowing she had to tolerate the indignity of being fingered and felt as though she were a piece of cotton goods or a blooded mare.

She shut her eyes and stood absolutely still, wanting to die with the shame of their probing hands. In a way this was worse than the things the Gayarres had forced her to do. To stand here naked while they poked and patted was exquisite torture for her. Jacob knew it and deliberately was prolonging the ordeal, she suspected, for his own vicious reasons.

The bidding finally began with Nunez, Pickens and Bricktop leading and the others gradually dropping out as the bidding passed five thousand dollars.

Lorinda listened in sick fascination as the bid mounted. It made little difference to her who won, since the choice between putting on sexual exhibitions in a waterfront brothel or being a perfumed toy for bored, neglected wives of the well-to-do amounted to no choice at all.

When the bidding passed six thousand, Pickens cursed and turned away. "Damn it, that's too rich for my blood. I'd like to have her, but that's too much money."

Bricktop laughed. "Come by the Lighthouse and see her in action, my friend. As a professional courtesy I'll give you a special rate for a night with her."

Pickens grinned and said with a lewd wink, "I just might take you up on that."

"Don't go offering favors until you've won the prize," Nunez advised.

"Don't suppose you'd make me the same offer, would you, Nunez?" Pickens joked.

"But no, my friend," the Spaniard said. "We do not entertain gentlemen at my establishment."

The bidding was head-on then between Bricktop and Nunez, and when it reached seventy-five hundred, even Bricktop seemed nonplussed.

"That's a lot of money for a gal who's used to buying flesh by the pound," she said. "A lot of money."

"You could buy a dozen of the type of women you usually feature at the Lighthouse, my dear," Nunez said.

"What do you see in her?" Bricktop asked. "Seems to me you'd want something riper and more decadent."

"Ah no, not at all," Nunez said. "It is the innocence of this one that makes her worth so much to me. Look at her. See the shame and fear in her eyes. The seduction of the innocent, my dear Bricktop, is one of the most deliciously evil pleasures in the world. Each of my valued customers will feel that she is the first to introduce this girl to her kind of lovemaking.''

''Yeah, I get your meaning,'' Bricktop said. ''The seduction of the innocent. That gives me an idea. I know where I can get this trained donkey. I think that will be part of the act, this little gal and that donkey. That'll really get the boys excited, won't it? Yes, sir! Mr. Wenzel, I bid eight thousand!''

Lorinda's knees started to buckle as she realized just what it was Bricktop had in mind for her. For one of the few times in her life, she fainted.

CHAPTER 25

"Wake up, Miss Lori, wake up!" The voice seemed to come from far away. It sounded like Chatti's, but that couldn't be. Lorinda had been dreaming she was in a place of horror called the Lighthouse, that she was the chief spectacle in an exhibition of such vile bestiality that it soiled her very being. No, Chatti couldn't be in that place. Chatti couldn't be there watching the vile things her child had been forced to do.

But the voice kept on. "Miss Lori, you gots to wake up!"

Someone was shaking her. Was it that vile woman, that Bricktop? No, she was still at Solitaire. She had fainted before the auction was over, and she didn't know who had bought her or in what filthy way she would be used.

Lorinda opened her eyes and saw Chatti bending over her.

"Thass right, chile, wake up! We gots to git you away afore they comes fo' you in the mornin'."

"Who's coming for me?" she asked, fear jolting the last remnants of sleep from her mind.

"Dat Bricktop woman's bullies. She say to keep you fo' the night 'cause she don' want to take a chance on losin' you by travelin' at night."

"Oh, God, Chatti, not that! Oh, Chatti, you

don't know what she intends to do to me, to make me do!''

"She ain' makin' you do nuthin' 'cause Ah'm a'gettin' you out of here.''

Lorinda was once more in the little room in the basement of Solitaire where Jacob had locked her before, but this time when she tried to sit up she discovered her wrists and ankles were chained to the steel cot.

"How can you get me out?'' she asked in despair. "You can't break these chains.''

"Don' have to break 'em,'' Chatti said, "Ah got the key. That Sissy took it from the overseer afta he passed out when he got through pesterin' her.''

"Sissy did that for me?'' Lorinda asked.

"Sho' did. Sissy loves you, honey. We all loves you, and we cain' jes let them cart you off.''

Lorinda was touched, but she had no real hope of escaping.

"Even if I get away, I'll be brought back,'' she said as Chatti unlocked the chains from her wrists. "You saw what happened when I tried to run. Besides, I don't want any of you hurt or killed for trying to help me like poor Zack was.''

"Don' you worry 'bout that, honey. Nobody bring you back this time. Somethin' gonna happen 'round here and maybe we all gits free o' them Wenzels.''

"What is it, Chatti? What's going to happen?''

"Don' have nuthin' to do with you an' don' want you to pay no 'tenshun. You jes hide out till it all ovah, den Ah come gits you.''

The chains were off Lorinda's ankles now, and

Chatti was helping her to her feet. "Does whatever is going to happen have anything to do with voodoo?"

"Don' ask, honey. Ah ain' gonna ask, Sissy ain' gonna ask. No black folks at Solitaire know anything 'bout it. When it come, it come like a bolt out of the sky."

"Why are you being so mysterious? Why won't you tell me what's going on?" Lorinda asked.

Chatti opened the door and looked out cautiously. " 'Cause Ah don' know, honey. Ah don' know 'cause Ah don' want to know. Iffen Ah don' know, Ah cain' tell nobody nuthin'."

She beckoned the girl to follow her, and they crossed the big room where the whipping post was. Remembering her own beating by Jacob after her first return to Solitaire, Lorinda wasn't surprised to see bloodstains on the floor around the post.

"Been using that all the time," Chatti said. "Using it so much all the whoppers git sore arms. They kilt pore ole Juda a week ago by whippin', and Tully a'fore him. 'Spects iffen somethin' happen to them Wenzels, even God is gonna look the othah way."

"Chatti, is there a woman named Ajona with the local voodoos?" Lorinda asked.

"Tole you, don' know and don' wants to know," Chatti said, leading her charge up the stairs to an outside cellar door. She lifted the wooden covering carefully to look around before venturing out. "You go down by the bayou and you finds a li'l abandoned cabin back in a grove o' willow trees.

You hide theah, chile, and Ah brings you food soons Ah can.''

"But Chatti, that's so close to the house. They'll find me sure when they search the area."

"Not gonna have time for searchin' a'fore somethin' happens."

"Chatti, for a person who doesn't know anything and doesn't want to know anything, it seems to me you know a lot."

The old woman shook her head stubbornly. "Don't know nuthin'."

The moon had risen. They were passing through the grove of willow trees, the dark shadow of the cabin looming up ahead.

"Couple o' blankets in there, and soons Ah bring you some food, you eats and goes to sleep, you hear? That way you ain' see what goes on."

That Chatti knew a great deal about what was going on was obvious, but Lorinda had given up trying to get her to talk. But what was it that was going to happen? Was Ajona out there in the darkness working her voodoo? Was she casting spells that were supposed to harm the Wenzels, spells their slaves didn't want to know about, or at least wanted to pretend they didn't? Or was it something else? Voodoo practitioners were often accused of arson. Could it be that Ajona, if it was indeed Ajona, planned on burning the big house at Solitaire, hoping perhaps to incinerate the Wenzels along with it? Whatever was planned, it was clear the local blacks didn't want to be involved.

It was damp and chilly in the cabin. Lorinda

wrapped the two thin blankets around her and sat down near the empty fireplace. It must have been almost an hour before Chatti came back, bringing a slice of fried ham, corn bread and, most welcome of all, a pot of coffee.

"Eat hearty, chile," Chatti urged. "It might be a long time a'fore you gits mo'."

"That sounds like another dark hint," Lorinda said and sipped at the steaming coffee.

"No," Chatti said in a troubled voice, "but Ah gots to tell you 'bout something else. Seems like a man was heah last night askin' 'bout you. He come to the big house, but Ah didn' heah 'bout it till Ah talk to Page the butler afta Ah brung you out to the cabin."

"A man looking for me?" Lorinda paused with a piece of corn bread halfway to her mouth. "Who was he?"

"Don' know, but Page say he been heah a'fore, long time ago when yo' papa still alive."

Lorinda was aware of a sudden wild pounding of her heart. "What did he say about me?"

"Wanted to know where you was an' when Jacob say you not at Solitaire, he grab him by the shirt front, lifts him up an' starts to shake him."

"Oh, God, can it be, can it really be?" Lorinda didn't know whether to laugh or cry. "It sounds like him, but how can it be? They said he was dead."

"Page say he went away afta that, but he tole Jacob he be back with a warrant to recover his property an' iffen they didn't hand you ovah, he'd horsewhip the lot of 'em."

"It's Kirk! It has to be Kirk!" Lorinda said, hugging her old nurse. "He's alive, Chatti, he's alive!"

"Don' know as Page say his name, but he got the Wenzels pretty scared. That's why they hid you and chain you up. They a'hopin' that redheaded woman come git you and pays fo' you a'fore that fella come back with his warrant and horsewhip."

"Oh, Chatti, he's alive and he loves me! He's coming to take me away!"

"Sho' hope he don' come today," Chatti said.

"Oh, Chatti, don't say things like that! The sooner I see him the better. Don't you understand? I thought he was dead! I thought he had been killed by those ruffians who took me away from him and brought me back here to the Wenzels. I can't wait to see him!"

"He bettah not come today," Chatti said glumly, and suddenly it occurred to Lorinda how odd it was for the old woman not to be happy for her, to almost be warning her against a reunion with the man she loved.

She took the woman's hands in hers and looked into her unhappy eyes. "Chatti, I think you'd better tell me what's going on. You know you can trust me. This has to do with voodoo and the drums, doesn't it?"

Chatti shook her head. "Ah cain' tell you, honey. You could git in trouble jes knowin' 'bout it."

"I've *got* to know, Chatti. If there's going to be any danger, I've got to warn Kirk Stryker to stay away."

The old woman rocked back and forth, face puckered up in an agony of indecision. "Ah jes don' know what to say, chile. You my baby. I don' want you to git hurt an'—"

"Chatti, I love him!" Lorinda broke in. "I thought he was dead, but he's alive and I have to see that he stays alive. I appreciate your concern for me, but this is more important. Please, please tell me what's got you so frightened."

Chatti took a deep breath and nodded. "Shouldn' oughta tell you but sees Ah got to. Them voodoos got a couple hundred slaves back in the boonies that is goin' burn Solitaire to the groun' and kill the Wenzels. They also is gonna kill any othah white folks they gits their hands on. That woman you talk 'bout, that Ajona, she say the time is come to wipe out the white devils. She say onct the blacks all ovah the South see what they do heah in Claiborne County they all rise up and kill the oppressors."

Lorinda was stunned by the implications of what Chatti was telling her. If what she said was true, this would be the largest slave rebellion since that of Nat Turner, probably even larger. But how could it possibly succeed? Turner's uprising hadn't helped the slaves. In a way, it had made matters worse for them. The immediate retaliation of the whites had been savage, far more so than the rebellion itself, and over the long run it had led to a hardening of the lot of the blacks all over the South. But if men didn't strike out for freedom, how would they ever win it?

She shook her head. Those were philosophical matters, and right now she was mainly interested in the safety of the man she loved. "I've got to warn Kirk, Chatti. You'll have to help me get to him."

"Don' know wheah he at, Miss Lori."

"But you know where the voodoos are, don't you?"

Chatti looked terrified and clutched at Lorinda's hands. "You cain' go near them, chile! You may be black inside, but you face is white and they is powerful mad at white faces."

"They won't bother me, Chatti," Lorinda said gently. "Ajona is my half-sister. She is the daughter of Felice Provost by a man who knew her before my father. He was a voodoo priest from Haiti."

Surprise and a sudden understanding showed on Chatti's round face. "Then that why she send word for you to be got out of the way. Ah was a 'goin' to do it anyway so's the Wenzels couldn' sell you, an' it puzzled me why she care 'bout you. Ah din' know yo' mama birthed anothah chile."

"Not many people did, I guess," Lorinda said. "If I can get to Ajona, she will see that no harm comes to Kirk."

Chatti looked skeptical. "You really think she spare some white folks?"

"Chatti, I'm afraid that if Ajona and her followers kill the Wenzels and others, they will be hunted down themselves. Soldiers will come, the militia, and all the whites have guns. It could be a terrible thing for the slaves. They could be slaughtered. That's why I'm glad you and the rest of Solitaire's people are not involved."

Chatti sighed. "Yes'm. You goin' try to talk Ajona out of what she meanin' to do?"

Lorinda thought about that while she took a sip of coffee. "No. No, I don't think I have any right to tell people they shouldn't try to break their chains, that they shouldn't attempt to win their freedom even at the cost of violence."

"They gonna be plenty of that," Chatti said. "Plenty vi'lence and plenty killin'. Ajona say git the Wenzels fust 'cause they kill someone she love."

"She means our mother, Chatti. I thought from almost the beginning they had something to do with her being hanged for murder, but Ajona said I was wrong then. I guess she's changed her mind."

Chatti shrugged. "Don' know, but she say they go fust."

That bothered Lorinda. As much as she hated and feared them, she wondered if it wasn't her simple human duty to warn them. But there was one over-riding reason why she couldn't. Knowing them as she did, she realized that if she warned them, the Wenzels would set up a trap and the blacks would be systematically slaughtered. She couldn't be responsible for that. No, all she could do was see that Kirk was safe. She wouldn't interfere in any other way. If that was wrong, then she would have to live with it.

"Will you help me find Ajona, Chatti?"

"Don' see why Ah should. You is the one Ah'm worried 'bout. Don' care 'bout de rest."

"But, Chatti, if Kirk gets hurt, that will hurt me. Don't you see?" She put her arm around the woman and kissed her wrinkled cheek. "I love you just like you love me, but I love Kirk, too, and he's the one in danger.''

"Theah you go," Chatti smiled. "You always could git 'round me, honey, you and you sweet talk.''

"Then you will help me find the voodoos?''

Chatti nodded and sighed again. "Shouldn', but Ah will. You know the old Marsten plantation? The house that burned back in forty-five?''

"Yes.''

"Ajona an' her people stayin' theah. Ah 'spects they be a'comin' down the old log road jes a'fore dawn to git the Wenzels. Iffen you dead set on goin', you has to hurry.''

"Yes. I need a horse.''

"Lotsa horses down to the back pasture, chile, but no one Ah kin trust to catch an' saddle one fo' you.''

"If Firedrake's there, one of these blankets will do for a saddle," Lorinda said. In the threadbare calico dress Chatti had brought she wasn't exactly dressed for riding, but it would have to do. She could fold the other blanket diagonally and use it for a shawl.

"Thank you, Chatti," she said, putting her arms around her old mammy. "Now you go hide with the rest of the people and don't worry about me.''

Half an hour later Lorinda was mounted on the back of the horse she loved best of all. He was older now and less frisky but still strong and willing. It seemed almost impossible, but Firedrake remembered her and came to her at once when she whistled for him. "Good boy, good boy," she said, pleased at his recognition and taking it as a good omen of what lay ahead.

Then she was galloping along a well-remembered trail that intercepted the log road Chatti had mentioned. The moon shone bright and full, lighting her way and casting a silver glow to the trees along the path. If Ajona and her rebels were heading for Solitaire, she should meet them on the way.

She heard the marchers before she saw them. A few moments later she saw their torches and finally the group of perhaps seventy or eighty men and women came into sight. Some were carrying axes, others pitchforks or machetes. Perhaps a dozen or so in the van had shotguns, fowling pieces or ancient muskets. A few carried pikes. At their head was a tall figure wrapped in a cloak and mounted on a mule.

"Ajona!" Lorinda called as they came within hailing distance. "Ajona, I must speak with you! It is I, your sister!"

The marching column came to a halt, those behind surging toward the front. Three men with muskets ran forward to surround Lorinda.

"It's a white woman!" one of them yelled, snatching the reins out of Lorinda's hand.

An ominous muttering went up from the blacks. At least one musket was aimed at her from the crowd. A man with a gun in his hand and a knife in his teeth advanced toward her threateningly.

"Ajona! I am your sister! Surely you recognize me!" Lorinda shouted. Then, before she could say more, she was dragged down off her horse.

"She's a spy! Kill her!" the cry went up as she was hustled through the hostile crowd.

"Hold! Hold!" It was Ajona's voice, powerful and commanding. The crowd parted to let her through. "Is that you, Lorinda? What the devil are you doing here? I sent orders you were to be taken to a safe place until this was over."

"I was, but something has come up that I must discuss with you before—" she looked around at the angry slaves on every side— "before things start to happen."

Ajona's lip curled. "If you've come here to try to talk me out of leading this uprising, you're wasting your time."

"No, no, it's not that," Lorinda said. "I just want to ask you to see that no harm comes to the man I love."

"I assume from that that he's white," Ajona sneered.

"Yes, he is, but he's not like the others, Ajona."

The handsome black woman laughed. "None of them are to hear them tell it. We will kill them all, and let the gods decide who is good and who is bad."

Lorinda hadn't intended to make any attempt to change her sister's mind, but as she looked at the group around them, she knew she had to speak out. "Ajona, this is madness. You have less than a hundred people here. You can't defy the whole system with such a small force."

"There will be thousands once the bloodletting begins," Ajona said.

"And every white man in Mississippi will come down on you," Lorinda said. "The army will be sure to intervene."

"In Haiti there were thousands of armed white men," Ajona said. "The French sent an army, but my people won! They can win here in America, too!"

"Not this way," Lorinda said. "I know how you feel, sister. God knows I've had my nose rubbed in the cruelty and vileness of the system, and if I thought there was any chance of success, I'd join you."

"You with your white face," Ajona sneered, "how could you possibly know what my people have suffered?"

"You forget, I've lived the life of a slave. I've felt the whip across my back, I've been forced to let white men I despised use my body, and I've been humiliated and degraded by whites who think I'm not even human."

"A very eloquent speech," Ajona said, "but if you've suffered all of that you should be delighted to join us."

"I told you, I would be if I thought you had a chance."

"We do have. There are thousands of blacks in this state alone waiting to rise up when the first blow is struck. Once they have guns in their hands, they will be unstoppable. Driven by the righteousness of their cause, they will sweep away the evil of slavery forever."

"Where are they going to get arms?"

Ajona's eyes glittered in the light from the

torches. "They will take them from their white masters! They will kill the white snakes as my forefathers did in Haiti and take their fangs to kill other white snakes!"

It was useless to argue, but Lorinda kept on. "Ajona, what you want to do is just, but—"

"Do you wish to save the fat German pig Wenzel and his brood of vipers?" Ajona demanded. "It was you who first suspected they had been responsible for our mother's death. It was you who persuaded me to find out what really happened. Well, I did. My mother's lover did not die at her hand. He was killed by a hireling of August Wenzel. He died in her arms and she was falsely accused by the lawyer Kelandes, who now sits in Washington as a congressman. She was hanged on perjured testimony, and I know that for a fact because I've talked to two of the men who gave it. They told a great deal when they were staked out naked in a forest glade and a box filled with fer-de-lances placed on their chests."

"Then the Wenzels and Kelandes could be brought to justice," Lorinda said, "if those two men would testify in court."

Ajona laughed. "They might have trouble doing that without their heads."

Lorinda stared at her. "You—you killed them?"

"Of course I killed them!" Ajona spat. "You little fool, if it hadn't been for them and others like them, you would still be mistress of Solitaire instead of a runaway slave! Now say no more. Take your horse and mount up. Ride out of Claiborne County, out of Mississippi, out of the South! Take your man with you if you would save his life.''

"No, Ajona, no!" said a huge, ebony-skinned man with a shaved head. "She cannot leave! Your sister or not, *maitresse,* she could betray us. She will have to go with us. You can free her later if you wish, *maitresse,* but for now she is too dangerous."

A loud chorus of agreement came from Ajona's followers. She looked around at them searchingly then nodded. "You are right, Raoul." She turned back to Lorinda. "I'm sorry, little sister, but you have interfered in a matter you shouldn't have and must bear the consequences. I'll see that you get to safety after the killing, but for now you must not be out of my sight."

It was almost daylight when the march began again, Lorinda on Firedrake riding beside Ajona on the mule. Lorinda was tempted to make a break for it, knowing that her fleet-footed stallion could out-run the mule or any of the men on foot. The reason she didn't was because she didn't know where to find Kirk. If he showed up at Solitaire this morning, he would be in deadly danger, but perhaps she could save him if she was with the rebels.

The scouts Ajona had sent ahead came back to report that Solitaire was directly ahead and that there was no sign that the Wenzels had been warned.

Ajona stood up in her stirrups and pointed with the whip she carried. "They are there in that house, the white devils who have oppressed and enslaved you! There are the beasts who have killed your brothers and raped your sisters! Go and take your revenge! Kill! Kill! Kill!''

CHAPTER 26

It was a scene of utter havoc and madness. Exhorted by voodoo chants and a waving of *gris-gris* by their *maitresse,* Ajona's people struck out in the dawn mist and hurled themselves at Solitaire. Nicholson the overseer and his assistant were killed as they rushed from their cabins, pistols in hand. Lorinda watched in horror as Nicholson was felled by a blast of buckshot in the face and then hacked to pieces with machetes. Seth Parker shot down two of the attackers but was then pinned to the wooden door of the cabin by several pitchforks. He hung there screaming and turning slowly from side to side until Ajona calmly put a bullet through his head.

The big house came next. The front doors were battered in by a dozen husky blacks and, screaming in fury, the mob streamed inside. Gideon Wenzel, looking tousled and half drunk, came staggering down the center staircase, trying to pull on his pants and fasten his belt. Raoul, who seemed to be the combat leader of the rebels, bore him to the floor, with the help of two other blacks.

Standing beside Ajona, Lorinda watched him being dragged from the house.

"What are you going to do with him?" she asked.

"Burn him," the voodoo priestess said. "Burn him alive like they do blacks!"

"Oh, my God!" Lorinda gasped. Much as she despised Gideon Wenzel, she couldn't help feeling a twinge of pity at the fate he was about to meet. Having so recently faced the same hideous death herself, she knew what he would be going through.

Jacob and August Wenzel appeared at the top of the staircase. Jacob was armed with a revolver and whip, his father with a shotgun. The forty or so blacks who had surged into the parlor and dining room roared with fury when they saw the two men.

"What do you people think you're doing?" August roared. "Leave at once or I'll—"

"You'll do what, old man?" Ajona shouted. "Order that young swine to use his whip on us?"

"You're through with whipping!" Raoul yelled.

"Get out! All of you, get out of here!" August ordered.

"Look, there's Lorinda with them!" Elsie said, standing behind her brother in nightdress and kerchief, her mother cowering beside her. "She's behind this!"

"Yes, I see her," Jacob said, lifting his gun. "I'll finish her once and for all."

Lorinda found herself staring into the muzzle of the pistol. A shot rang out; she winced, expecting to feel the impact of the bullet. Instead, Jacob crumpled, clutching at the spreading redness on the white of his nightshirt, and Ajona lowered the smoking pistol she had used on him.

The gunfire seemed to break the momentary spell that had held both sides in check. With a screech of murderous rage, the blacks charged up the stairs toward the petrified whites. Lying on his side and holding his chest wound, Jacob fired rapidly, sending two of the attackers tumbling over backward. August got off one blast from his shotgun before he was buried beneath cursing, bloodthirsty blacks.

"Kill them! Kill them!" A man was standing on top of Jacob, jumping up and down on him with heavy shoes. A large brawny woman was smashing at Jacob's head with a hatchet. Lorinda was backed up against the wall of what had once been her home, watching, heartsick and horrified, while her enemies were being destroyed one by one.

Four men grabbed August Wenzel and began dragging him down the stairs by his feet, letting his head bump on each step. Elsie's nightgown had been stripped off her body and she, too, was carried downstairs above the heads of five black men, their hands a startling contrast against the whiteness of her flesh. Mrs. Wenzel, screaming endlessly, lay on the floor not far from Jacob's body. Someone had pinned both her hands to the floor with knives.

Those carrying Elsie tossed her roughly in the middle of the parlor rug. Now two women were holding her legs and two others held her arms. A line of slaves waited with their pants down. As soon as one man finished with her, another dropped down and thrust into her brutally, performing a ritual act of hate, not lust.

Elsie's screams and those of her mother echoed through the whole house. Lorinda tried to shut out the terrible sound by covering her ears with her hands.

"What's the matter, little sister?" Ajona jeered. "Does your soft heart bleed for those who tormented you? You're a fool! They'd laugh to see you in the blonde girl's place."

Lorinda knew that was probably true, but she couldn't help but pity Elsie as she watched her futile struggles and heard her screams fade away into pitiful whimpers.

Just outside the parlor door, August Wenzel was slowly being beaten and torn apart by a screeching band of rebels. The fat man's terrified shrieks almost shattered Lorinda's eardrums as he was pushed back and forth within a circle of taunting, shouting blacks. Each one struck out with fist or weapon every time the man staggered within striking distance. Lorinda caught a glimpse of the battered thing that had been August's round, self-satisfied face. It was now a bloody pulp with one eye hanging halfway down his cheek, the other obliterated. She hoped he would die soon, praying that the last life in his broken body would flicker out quickly.

The rebels were through with Elsie. All those who cared to had relieved themselves on the girl's battered body. Now she was lying still and quiet, either dead or mercifully unconscious from the brutality. Her rapists had turned to looting the wine cellar thirstily drinking whatever they found there.

Ajona was angry. "Stop it! Stop it, you fools! Our work is only beginning! If you drink yourselves sodden, you'll never be able to carry out the rest of it!"

Most of them ignored her, smashing the tops off

LOVE'S WICKED WAYS   403

bottles and collapsing into corners to drink. Ajona moved from group to group, trying to drive them to their feet, but with the blood lust temporarily slaked and the excitement of the march on Solitaire fading, most of them wanted now to eat and drink.

Food was brought from the kitchen; hams, butter and other perishables were carried up from the spring house. The rebels were laughing and singing. Lorinda made her way through the downstairs rooms, looking sadly at the remnants of what had once been its elegance. Memories of her happy childhood here mingled with bitter memories of later years. She couldn't bear to go near the bodies of the Wenzels, but she steeled herself to go to Elsie, who still lay naked on the floor.

Raoul was now in charge inside the house, Ajona having gathered a small band of dedicated rebels and sending them out to nearby plantations to spread word of the rebellion and recruit more slaves. They had found none of Solitaire's people on the grounds. Lorinda knew Chatti and the others must have hurried off into the woods to hide until they knew which way things were going to go.

Lorinda bent over Elsie Wenzel. The girl's blackened eyes opened and stared at her in terror.

"Let me help you, Elsie," Lorinda said.

"You! You did—this to us!" the blonde sobbed and glared hatred at her.

"I'll get some water and wash you off."

"Stay away from me, you black bitch!" Elsie hissed. "You stink like all the others! Oh, God, the things those beasts did to me, the awful loathsome things."

Lorinda went to the kitchen, poured warm water from the teakettle into a bowl and went back to sponge Elsie's face and hands, closing her ears to the girl's curses and muttered threats. When she finished washing off the rest of the bruised body, Lorinda covered the girl with a shawl and managed to get a few sips of brandy into her.

Raoul strolled over and looked down at the battered woman. "Why do you want to do things for her? Was she good to you?"

"No, I can't say that she was."

"You believe that Christian stuff about returning good for evil?" Raoul seemed to be better educated than the average slave or free black.

"I don't know whether I do or not," Lorinda told him. "I was raised a Christian, but now I know it's the white man's religion and I don't feel the same about it."

"No point in makin' her feel better anyhow," Raoul said. "We're going to burn her at the stake along with her brother just as soon as *la maitresse* comes back."

"Oh, Raoul, must there be more bloodshed?"

"The bloodshed has only begun," Raoul said and ordered two of the rebel women to tie Elsie hand and foot. "This county will be runnin' in blood before this is over."

If Lorinda had ever thirsted for revenge, she had had enough of it. She had no desire to see Elsie and Gideon perish horribly, no matter what they had done to her. She would have to watch for a chance to free them before Ajona returned.

She waited quietly while the rebels, glutted with

food and drink, wandered off to the bedrooms upstairs to sleep it off. Finally only a few of the really
heavy drinkers remained in the parlor, lolling
around on the floor.

Lorinda waited until they passed out. One man
was snoring with his head on the dining room table,
a spilled bottle of wine beside him. There was a
long-bladed knife in his belt. Approaching him silently, Lorinda managed to slip it out without waking him.

Holding it in a fold of her skirt, she returned to
Elsie's side. The girl was in a daze but roused
enough to glare her hatred at Lorinda.

"I'm going to cut you loose," Lorinda whispered, pretending to adjust the shawl. "You've got
to run from this place as quickly as possible."

"Why? I want to be here when the soldiers come
and you and your black friends get strung up and
flayed to death," she spat.

"You fool!" Lorinda whispered through tight
lips. "Didn't you hear what that man said? They
intend to kill you and Gideon! You've taught them
to be as savage as you are, and they're going to burn
you at the stake like the whites have burned so
many of them."

Frightened but showing no lessening of the hate
that burned inside her, Elsie let Lorinda cut her
bonds and took the knife that was forced into her
hands. "Your brother is tied to a tree outside. Most
of the rebels are drunk or asleep. If you want to save
your life and his, go cut him loose and then both of
you get away as fast as you can."

"All right, but we'll be back," Elsie said.

"We'll be back to see you flayed alive over an open fire for what you did to all of us."

"I'm glad you're so grateful," Lorinda said, draping the shawl around the girl's body and tying the ends to hold it in place.

She watched while Elsie slipped out a side door. Then she went to sit on the floor with her back against a wall, wondering as she dozed off what Ajona and the others would do to her if they discovered she had freed Elsie and Gideon.

It must have been several hours later when she was roused by shouting and angry voices. While her sluggish brain tried to sort out the words and their meaning, she noticed that the sun was now almost directly overhead.

"White man! White man a'comin'!" a voice was yelling. "Le's go git him!"

Fear closed like cold fingers around Lorinda's heart. She hurried to a window and looked out. A wagon and team were approaching the house along the tree-lined drive from the main road. The tall, lean figure on the driver's seat could belong to only one man. Kirk Stryker was coming to find her and had no way of knowing the house was occupied by black insurgents.

She had to warn him, had to save him. She opened the window and dropped onto the lawn below. A shot rang out from the house, and then another. She crouched beneath the window so that those inside the house couldn't see her. She saw Kirk stand up in the wagon and draw a pistol. A fusillade of shots followed, and one of the horses reared. She saw Kirk stagger in the wagon reaching for the seat back as the frightened horse lunged and kicked. Then the team bolted, throwing him from the wagon.

Lorinda's first impulse was to dash toward Kirk. He was lying on the graveled drive, apparently injured. He still had the pistol. But she realized it would be useless when she saw men pouring out the front door. They advanced on Stryker angrily, waving machetes and other weapons. Several carried guns.

Desperately, Lorinda looked around for some way to get to Kirk before the angry mob did. Then out of the corner of her eye she saw Firedrake contentedly grazing in a nearby field. She whistled for him softly, and the big stallion picked up his head and cantered in her direction.

There was shouting from inside the house. A shot whizzed past her head just as the animal reached her and she vaulted onto his back. Riding low, she kicked the horse into action, heading him toward the downed Stryker.

The blacks dashing from the house had almost reached the graveled drive. When they were only a few dozen yards away, Kirk raised up suddenly on one elbow, and aimed his revolver at point-blank range.

"Stop where you are!" he yelled. "Get back! I don't want to shoot you!"

Angry shouts answered him. The rebels came on, brandishing machetes. Lorinda saw Kirk rest the pistol coolly across one free arm and fire two quick shots. The rebels scattered, two of them going down with leg wounds. The momentum of the charge was broken. The remaining blacks quickly sought cover behind tree trunks and fences. That gave Lorinda the advantage she needed. Whispering in Firedrake's ear, she dashed through the middle of the rebels. Kirk saw her coming, his face lighting up.

"Lorinda! Lorinda, my darling!"

Her heart sang as she heard his voice and Firedrake responded to her urging, practically leaping through the air toward Kirk.

Shouts and curses sounded behind her and shots whistled by on either side. Suddenly she was beside him, reaching out to help him scramble up behind her. Slowed only slightly by the extra weight, the big horse galloped off down the drive.

"What's happening?" Kirk asked when they were out of danger. "What were those blacks doing with arms?"

"A slave uprising," Lorinda told him. "Three of the Wenzels are dead. Elsie and Gideon may have escaped."

"My God!" he said. "It's a miracle you weren't killed too. I couldn't bear to have lost you that way," he cried, his arms tightening around her waist.

"Nor I, you," she smiled tremulously.

"Lorinda darling, I've looked everywhere for you. When I first recovered from that beating Gayarre's hoodlums gave me, I became convinced he and his wife had you. I confronted them on it and had to kill Joseph."

"You killed Joseph?"

"It was my knife against his pistol. The knife

won and I was detained by the state on a murder charge.''

"Murder? Then how did you get here, Kirk? Did you escape?''

"No. Gayarre's wife was the only witness, and she claimed I killed him in cold blood. Some friends of mine investigated her background and discovered so much incriminating evidence about her first husband's death that she changed her story, admitting I'd killed Gayarre in self-defense. As soon as I was released, I came looking for you. I have your papers and a judge's order for you to be turned over to me. I was on my way to present it to the Wenzels.''

"I know," Lorinda said. "Chatti told me last night. That's why I was there waiting for you. Thank God we're both safe.''

"But are we?" Kirk asked. "What's all this about a slave rebellion?''

"Oh, Kirk, let's just ride away from it! Let's ride out of Mississippi and the South forever! Let's keep on going until we reach your Kansas!''

"But, darling, we can't just go riding off and leave people to be murdered by rioting rebels," Kirk protested.

"Is it murder to kill those who have enslaved and mistreated you, or is it justice?''

Kirk looked at her for a long minute before replying. "Do you really think that's justice? You saw the Wenzels killed. Was that justice?''

"Yes—no—oh, God, I don't know! They were fiends but—''

"What about the other white people who live

around here? The folks who used to be your friends and neighbors? Don't you think they should be warned?''

''If they are, the whites will retaliate and the slaves will be slaughtered. My people will be massacred.''

''Aren't they both your people?'' Kirk asked quietly.

''You don't understand,'' she said. ''No one can unless they've been a slave. When I see what the whites have done to the blacks, I despise my white blood and my white skin.''

''Isn't there anyone in this area that you feel you owe anything to?''

''No! What did they do for me when they found out I was a slave? They turned their backs on me and pretended I didn't exist!'' But she knew even as she said the words that she couldn't let her former friends be slain by the rampaging blacks. She had been unable to stand by and see Gideon and Elsie meet such a fate, so how could she do less for the people among whom she had been raised?

''The Rutledge place is a mile up that road,'' she said, pointing. ''We'll go warn them and they can pass the word to others.''

Kirk smiled and kissed her. ''That's the girl I knew you were.''

''I feel like a traitor,'' she said.

''Warning the innocent is not a traitorous act,'' he said. ''A rebellion like this is hopeless from the beginning. A few hundred slaves can't take on a whole society, you know. The militia will be alerted, vigilante groups formed and—''

"I know, I know," Lorinda said. "I tried to warn her of that."

"Her? Who do you mean?"

"The woman, the leader of slaves, a voodoo priestess," Lorinda said, not sure that she wanted to admit even to Kirk that it was her sister Ajona.

They were approaching the Rutledge house. Kirk's shouts brought people running out onto the veranda. Lorinda recognized John Rutledge and his son Roger. Behind them she could see Mrs. Rutledge peering out the door.

"What do you want?" Rutledge demanded, eyeing Lorinda coldly and omitting her name. When she was small, he had delighted in balancing her on his knee. Now he looked at her as though she didn't exist.

"There's been a slave rebellion," she told them. "The rebels have taken over Solitaire. August Wenzel and his older son are dead and so is Mrs. Wenzel. The slaves may be heading for other plantations."

Rutledge turned to his son without a word of acknowledgment or thanks. "Roger, get your gun and take the women out to the stone cabin in back. Get Johnson and the other overseer. I'll ride to Port Gibson."

"May we water the horse?" Lorinda asked.

Rutledge looked at the horse as though estimating how much it might contaminate his trough.

"Yes, go ahead," he said grudgingly. "Take what you need for yourselves and your beast."

Back out on the road, they headed north toward the county line to the home of a widow named Anna

Fairfax. They were riding at a slower pace now, to rest Firedrake, and that saved them from disaster. When they came to a crossroads and were about to turn, they heard a babble of voices from around the corner. Lorinda quickly urged Firedrake off into a thicket.

A few seconds later about a hundred blacks hurried by, armed mostly with farm implements. Most of them carried bottles of whiskey and other loot. It was not the same group that had been with Ajona, but there was no doubt they had been on the same mission. Horror and revulsion overtook Lorinda as she noticed the grisly trophy carried by a tall bearded man in the lead. It was the head of a white man impaled on a pruning hook.

"The other slaves are rising just like the priestess claimed they would," Lorinda whispered.

"This is going to be a bloody business before it's over," Kirk said when the last of the straggling blacks had passed. "The whites' revenge will be more terrible than the original uprising."

"Isn't it always?" Lorinda said bitterly.

They found the Widow Fairfax sitting in a rocking chair on the gallery of her magnificent porticoed house. An aging black woman quietly polished the brass knocker of the big front door.

"Mrs. Fairfax!" Lorinda called as they rode up. "Mrs. Fairfax, we've come to warn you."

The woman peered over the railing at them. "Why, it's Lorinda de Farbin. Land sakes, child, I ain't seen you in a coon's age. Light and have some lemonade."

"No, thank you, but we can't, Mrs. Fairfax,"

Lorinda said, surprised that the woman hadn't heard of her fall from grace.

"What's the matter, honey? Has your papa took sick?"

"No, Mrs. Fairfax," Lorinda said, knowing it would be useless to try to explain about her father or anything else. "You'd best have one of the boys hitch up the wagon and take you into Port Gibson."

"Land sakes, what for?" the old woman asked.

"There's been a slave rebellion, ma'am," Kirk said, "and all whites are in danger, especially on an outlying plantation like this."

The widow looked concerned but not frightened. "Well, I'll just stay on here, I reckon, where all my folks is buried. Always been good to my people, I have, and they'll take care of me."

It was no use arguing with the poor thing, Lorinda decided. She didn't realize it wasn't her own slaves who might harm her but outsiders who had already tasted blood and were convinced they had justice on their side.

Mrs. Fairfax refused to leave her home, but she insisted on helping those who had come to warn her. She had a saddled horse brought from the barn for Kirk and had the groom find an extra saddle for Lorinda. And she stuffed both saddlebags with food before letting them leave.

"I hope that sweet old soul will be safe," Kirk said as they forded a stream, heading south toward Abingdon.

"Look over there. Something's burning," Lorinda said, pointing off to the left. "It must be the Grierson plantation. Kirk, this thing is spreading faster than we thought. Maybe we had better separate so we can spread the word more quickly.''

Kirk slipped an arm around her and kissed her. ''If we separate, where can we meet? I don't know this country as well as you do.''

''Let's make it somewhere we can get a riverboat heading north,'' she said. ''How about Vicksburg?''

''Is there a hotel there?''

Lorinda mentioned the name of the only respectable one she knew of in Vicksburg. ''If you ride south along the bayou road from here, you'll be able to alert the plantations that line it. I'll head for Port Gibson and warn those between here and there.''

At the next crossroad they kissed again and parted. Pushing Firedrake to an extra effort, Lorinda managed to give warning to three more plantations before dark. She was riding toward Port Gibson when she passed a troop of mounted men in militia uniform.

''Better get into town, ma'am,'' the young sergeant in command said. ''The slaves have burned four plantations and killed at least a dozen people.''

''That's where I'm heading now,'' Lorinda told him. ''Do you think there will be much fighting?''

''Yes, ma'am. The militia is mustering at Tillman, then we're gonna go get 'em.''

Lorinda rode on, slumping wearily in the saddle. She had done everything she could to save lives— white lives—but had she also contributed to the destruction of those who were trying to seize their freedom by force? Would she ever be able to rationalize her heritage? Despite the fact that she was almost all white, she somehow felt that she owed her chief loyalty to the blacks. Except for her love for Kirk, she felt she had no ties to the white race.

She was about a mile outside Port Gibson when she heard a large body of horsemen coming toward her. Assuming it was more militia heading toward the rendezvous at Tillman, she rode forward to meet them. Instead of militia, it was a band of mounted civilians, all armed to the teeth. Vigilantes on their way to help put down the rebellion. The official reaction to the uprising would be harsh enough— the militia, the magistrates and elected officeholders would not be easy on captured rebels—but the vigilantes would retaliate savagely. It occurred to Lorinda that she might be able to divert these men and leave the problem of dealing with the rebellion to organized law forces.

"Gentlemen," she called, riding up to the group, "you're heading in the wrong direction."

"What do you mean, ma'am?" asked the man in the lead.

"I saw militia in pursuit of the main body of slaves," she said. "I was riding to warn the riverfront plantations when two hundred mounted militia passed me with the slaves being driven ahead of them."

The blond mustache twitched over the man's harsh, down-curving mouth. "That so? We heard they was over 'round the Solitaire place. How come you a'tellin' us they going in the other direction?"

"She's telling you that because she's one of them!"

The loud familiar voice made Lorinda weak with fear. It belonged to Gideon Wenzel.

He was pushing his horse to the front of the vigilantes. "I was at Solitaire when she came with the rebels," Gideon said. "She's one of our slaves, and she stood there and watched while my father, my mother and my brother were murdered. I tell you she's one of them."

"That isn't true," Lorinda said. "I was a prisoner just as you were. If you don't believe me, ask your sister. Ask Elsie who freed her and gave her a knife to cut you loose."

Gideon was smiling in triumph. "By claiming to have helped us escape, you are admitting you were with the rebels. You were there when my sister was repeatedly raped. Elsie told me how you stood by and watched while those savage beasts sullied her forever. You are one of them!"

"That's a lie," Lorinda said. "I was not one of the rebels and I've spent most of this day riding from plantation to plantation warning people."

Gideon turned to the thickset leader of the vigilantes. "Are you going to take this wench's word or mine?"

"Yours, of course," the man said. "A couple of you boys tie this gal up and we'll take her into Port Gibson. I'd hang her right now, but I 'spect she knows things we oughta know. A taste of the bullwhip and the feel of a hot iron on the soles of her feet will loosen her tongue. She'll talk then. Talk so much we'll have to gag her to shut her up."

CHAPTER 27

The rebellion ended as Lorinda had feared it would—in bloody reprisal by frightened whites. Sitting in a jail cell in Port Gibson, she saw the militia bring in over a hundred blacks chained together, many with untended wounds. She heard the beating of the drums and the muffled thump, followed by the cheers of onlookers, as one in every five of the rebels was hanged. She heard the whistle of the whips that cut bloody slashes on the backs of the remainder before they were deported for sale in the West Indies. That in itself was a death sentence to blacks raised in continental America, because they lacked the immunity of island-raised Negroes to the tropical diseases of that region.

She didn't personally witness the torturing of the leaders of the rebellion but she was kept cheerfully informed of the grisly details by her jailer, Jake Mabry. He seemed to take special pleasure in the suffering of Stang, Raoul and Ajona herself.

"That big black bitch sho' is a tough one," the paunchy, tobacco-chewing man would tell her. "They done everything but pull her to pieces in lil bloody chunks, but she ain't talkin'. She jus' keeps her eyes closed and goes on mumblin' that hoodoo shit when they put the hot iron to her."

Poor Ajona! Oh, my poor sister! Lorinda wept

inwardly but kept a wooden face turned toward the jailer. If only there were something she could do, but she was helpless. She couldn't even pray for Ajona, because after sitting day after day in his prison listening to the screams of those who were receiving his ''justice,'' she had rejected the white man's religion along with all the rest of his ways.

''Them others ain't half as tough as the voodoo queen,'' Jake told her another time. He spat a wad of tobacco into a corner of her cell, ''That Raoul is talkin' so much he'll have half the blacks in Mississippi in jail 'fore he's through. Talkin' 'bout you, too, sugar. Guess they'll git around to usin' that hot iron on you pretty soon. Kind of a shame though, 'cause you're right pretty for a black wench. Wouldn't mind tearin' off a piece of your tail myself. Would if my old woman wasn't always hangin' 'round keepin' an eye on me.''

Lorinda endured this in stony silence, but it was hard to see how even so insensitive a swine as the jailer could find her attractive. She had been in this cell for three weeks with no water to wash in, no change of clothes and no comb. She hated her own smell as much as she hated the smell of the jail itself.

That she was still alive and relatively unharmed was something of a miracle, because the vigilantes, egged on by Gideon, had intended to torture her and burn her at the stake. This had been prevented by the proclamation of martial law in the area and the arrival of grim-faced, laconic circuit judge Marcus Aurelius Appleton to preside over the special court set up to try the captured slaves. The judge was extremely harsh in his sentences but absolutely forbade any free-lance reprisals, using the militia to enforce his rule.

"Old M. A. Appleton just don't want nobody to have no fun but him," the jailer said. "Every slave that gets stretched or has the meat cooked off him has gotta be his personal victim."

Conditions being what they were, Lorinda was willing to believe him.

Less than a dozen whites had been killed in the rebellion. Property damage had been limited to five looted and burned plantations, one of which, it gave Lorinda grim pleasure to learn, belonged to lawyer-turned-congressman Kelandes. The psychological effect of the uprising on the whites, however, was inestimable. Coming on top of news that a fanatical abolitionist named John Brown had murdered five proslavery men in an area now being called Bloody Kansas, and combined with the constant attacks on slavery by men like Gerrit Smith, the South was thrown into a state of hair-trigger emotion.

Lorinda's jailer had grinned from ear to ear when he showed her a front page editorial of a local paper that proclaimed the author to be ready for "the fagot and the flame," ready to let "every tree in the country bend with Negro meat."

Along with the guilty, several hundred perfectly innocent blacks had been arrested and subjected to severe questioning and whipping. Also arrested were five white men and one white woman suspected of being abolitionists come South to urge bloody rebellion on the slaves.

"When they start askin' you about them abolitionist devils and how much they had to do with starting the bloodletting, you better tell 'em quick," Jake Mabry advised Lorinda. "The sooner you tell, the sooner they'll string you up and put you out of your misery."

"Suppose for the sake of argument that I don't know anything about abolitionists stirring up the slaves," Lorinda said.

"You better tell 'em anyhow," he said, handing her the slop that passed for the black prisoners' food. "Everybody knows they was in on it, so it won't do no harm to say they was."

Most of the innocent blacks were released after a few days' detention, usually on demand of their masters. These men argued that they were being denied their property rights because their slaves were being held against their—the master's—will. It was the only argument that had any force.

As innocent as any of those released, Lorinda had no master make an appearance to demand her return. In fact, Kirk Stryker seemed to have vanished from the face of the earth. Had he been killed by rebels? Had he perhaps been one of the strangers in the area lynched by vigilantes before Judge Appleton and the militia intervened?

Day after day and week after week, the trials, the torturing, the hanging went on, and Lorinda lay huddled under her ragged, vermin-ridden blanket and listened numbly to the sounds of the mob milling around the jail. The mob had been there ever since the first black prisoners had been brought in. There was murder in its heart, Lorinda knew, restrained only by the stern reputation of the judge and the bayonets of the militia.

She didn't fear for her own life. If Kirk was dead or had deserted her to save his own skin, she hadn't much interest in living. There was her son, of course, but Chatti had seen that he was in a safe place with people who would raise him as their own. He probably would be better off without her, but she did wish Chatti would bring her news of him. She couldn't understand why her old nurse hadn't made any attempt to communicate with her. The Solitaire slaves, because of their foresight in hiding out in the woods during the rebellion, had not been arrested or harassed, and for this she was glad. Chatti, of course, could not have come to Port Gibson and requested permission to see her, but the slaves had their own ways of communicating and some kind of whispered message could have been passed to her through the blacks who did the menial work around the jail. Just the briefest word concerning little Zack would have helped keep up her spirits.

"Hey, sugar," the jailer said to her one morning, "that big black hoodoo finally died. Guess even that rawhide body of hers couldn't stand the things they was doin' to make her talk. But that Raoul and Stang made up for her thickheaded stubbornness. They give all the evidence needed to tar and feather them abolitionists and ride them out of town on a rail. All that's needed to git you, too."

Lost in her private grief over Ajona, Lorinda barely heard the last sentence, but Jake wasn't one to be discouraged easily.

''Told the whole thing 'bout you and that Ajona bein' sisters and plannin' the uprising with the help of the abolitionists and their money.''

Stung into reacting, Lorinda said, ''Ajona and I were half-sisters, yes, but the rest of it isn't true and those men know it. Why would they say things like that?''

Jake laughed, showing his few remaining rotting teeth. ''I reckon anybody tortured like they was is gonna say anything they is asked to say.''

Sickened, Lorinda turned away.

''Reckon your trial be held in a coupla days,'' he said. ''Won't be much of a trial since they got all the evidence they need to hang you already. Too bad they outlawed burnin' awhile back. Bet that would be quite a sight. Been wantin' to see you naked. Would if my old lady wasn't always around. Even she wouldn'ta been able to object to my watchin' the edifyin' sight of a murderin' slave wench bein' burned at the stake. The clothes always burn off first, you know, so you'd be bareassed by the time you started a'wrigglin' and a'writhin'.''

Lorinda picked up the swill he had brought for her to eat and threw it into his face. ''You sadistic monster! Get away from me and stay away!''

''Damn you, bitch!'' he snarled, wiping the dripping mess off his face. ''I oughta come in there and rape your ass off!''

''Jake, what you doin' in there gassin' with that wench?'' Mrs. Mabry's querulous voice was as musical as a rasp being drawn across wood, but it was a welcome sound to Lorinda. Jake had to hurry away with only a murderous glance back over his shoulder at her.

Even if she had to suffer for it later, Lorinda was glad she had thrown the swill at him. It was a small act of defiance, but it gave her a slight glow of satisfaction to know she had done it.

Two days later her trial began and ended. She was taken in chains to the courtroom of Judge Marcus Aurelius Appleton. Facing the flint-faced man on the bench and seeing the total absence of humanity or mercy in the set of his mouth, Lorinda couldn't help comparing him with the Roman emperor after whom he had been named. In a supposedly less civilized time, the emperor had been noted for his justice and mercy as well as for his philosophy; his namesake was ideally suited for savagely enforcing savage laws.

The trial began with the prosecuting attorney reading into the record the "confessions" of the executed slaves, Raoul and Stang. Then Gideon took the stand and, without having to take an oath since he was testifying against a slave, calmly lied away Lorinda's life. He was followed by Elsie, dressed entirely in black, her face pale behind a mourning veil. She avoided Lorinda's eyes as she more or less confirmed her brother's story of Lorinda's complicity with the rebels.

The seedy, sallow-complexioned lawyer who had consented reluctantly to serve as Lorinda's representative in court rose to ask a question. "With the greatest respect for you in your bereavement and the suffering you underwent at the hands of those barbarous blacks, I would like to ask if there is any truth to the defendant's claim that she cut your bonds and gave you a knife to free your brother."

Fleetingly Elsie's pale blue eyes flickered toward

Lorinda; there seemed to be a momentary wavering in her expression.

Gideon was instantly on his feet. "Your Honor, must my sister be put through this sort of harassment after what they did to her?"

The judge's flinty eyes zeroed in on Gideon. "Sit down, young man, or you'll be in contempt. I'm running this court. Answer the question, Miss Wenzel."

"I—no, there isn't any truth in it. That wasn't the way it happened," Elsie said. Lorinda started to protest, but her lawyer ignored her.

"If there are no further questions or testimony, I am ready to impose sentence," the judge said.

"Impose sentence? Why, he hasn't pronounced a verdict yet," Lorinda whispered to her lawyer.

The man flicked a piece of tobacco off his puffy lower lip. "Guess he thinks that's obvious."

"Having convicted Lorinda, the slave of Gideon and Elsie Wenzel, of armed rebellion and murder, I pronounce the sentence of death," Appleton intoned. "The sentence is to be carried out on Friday next at eight o'clock in the morning. The method of execution will be hanging by the neck until she is dead. This court further orders that in addition to those white folk who will be eager to see justice triumphant, all free blacks in the area under my jurisdiction and all slaves from surrounding plantations be brought into Port Gibson to witness the execution. The court feels that this will have an exemplary affect on these people and will help them resist in the future the blandishment of outsiders who would destroy our social order. The prisoner will be permitted the consolation of a clergyman of her choice before she is executed.''

Cold fear struck at Lorinda's heart, but she was determined not to show it to the gaping crowds that thronged the courtroom, the corridors and the lawn outside. With head held high, she was escorted to a special cell where the condemned were held under close observation lest they kill themselves and rob the law and the mob of the pleasure of seeing their torment.

A matron with the face of a harpy shoved her inside, clanged the door shut and sat down in a rocking chair facing the cell. With one eye on her charge and one on her knitting, she began to rock.

The next day Lorinda was visited by a thin, pinched-face minister with tightly pursed lips.

"Perhaps I can offer you some comfort," he said, looking as though he had about as much interest in her comfort as he had interest in Euclidian mathematics.

"How?" she demanded. "What kind of comfort can you give an innocent person about to be murdered by a system that is a stench in the nostrils of all decent men?"

"I'm afraid I don't know what you're talking about, young woman. What system do you mean?"

"My God, are you blind? I'm speaking of slavery!"

The man looked pained. "Then you have been misinformed. Slavery as an institution has the full blessing of God."

"It has *what?*"

"Anyone who is at all versed in the Scriptures

can tell you that in Genesis IX:25, God decreed slavery with the words, 'Cursed be Cain; a servant of servants shall he be unto his brethren.' You blacks, of course, are the descendants of Cain. The patriarchs from Abraham to Moses counted their slaves among their goods just as they did their oxen.''

''I don't think I've ever heard such hypocritical tripe,'' Lorinda said. ''Using the Bible to justify the unjustifiable!''

The clergyman drew himself up to his full string-bean height and pointed a finger at her. ''Already condemned by man's law, you would set yourself against the law of God as well. In Leviticus XXV:44-46, God's word on slavery is even more explicit: 'Both thy bondmen, and thy bondmaids, which thou shalt have, shall be of the heathen that are round about you; of them ye shall buy bondmen and bondmaids.' '' He recited the passages like one long used to employing them in argument. ''It is clear that you people are the heathen and we, the children of God, have not only a right but also a duty to enslave you and hold you as bondsmen and bondsmaids subject to our will.

'' 'Moreover, of the children of the strangers that do sojourn among you, of them shall ye buy, and of their families that are with you, which they began in your land; and they shall be your possession.' Were not your ancestors strangers in this our land and were you not born in it, young woman, to be the slave of the chosen people?''

Lorinda stared at the man for a few moments, unable to speak. Then she screamed, ''Get out of here! You're a disgrace to your religion!''

"Now see here, young woman, Judge Appleton was good enough to order that you be permitted the consolation of religion during your last days and—"

"Well, I don't consider anything you have to say at all consoling," she interrupted. "The judge also said I could choose my religious counselor, and you're not it! No white minister is! Get out of here and send me a voodoo priest!"

The words were spoken in anger and hurt. She didn't really desire to see a voodoo priest and didn't think one would be permitted to visit her in any case. She was surprised a few hours later when the jailer brought in a furtive looking little black man with white hair and a whispering voice.

"You ask for juju man, white lady? I'se Docta Tully. What you want? A *gris-gris* on de judge? Don' do *gris-gris* on no judges."

"No, that's not what I want," Lorinda said. Until that moment she hadn't had the slightest idea what a voodoo man could do for her. Then she remembered a story Ajona had told her about New Orleans' greatest voodoo priestess, the first Marie Laveau. It was Marie's custom to visit prisoners in jail who were about to be executed, and on at least one occasion Marie had seen to it that the prisoner died before the appointed hour, thereby cheating the hangman.

"Do you know of Marie Laveau?" Lorinda asked Doctor Tully.

"Ever'body know 'bout Marie Laveau. She consorted with crocodiles and talked with Lucifer."

"She also made wonderful gumbo, they tell me."

The old man looked frightened but said nothing.

"They say she made some for Antoine Cambre the night before he was to hang," Lorinda said. "It was very good gumbo. Because of it Cambre was never hanged."

"Yes'm, I heared of that," Dr. Tully said in his whispery voice, looking nervously over his shoulder as he spoke.

"I think I would like some good gumbo before I die," Lorinda said. "Do you make gumbo, Dr. Tully?"

"No, ma'am. No, I no good cook," he said, his eyeballs showing white. "I don' know how to make gumbo."

"I'm going to be hanged by the neck until I'm dead, Doctor Tully. It's a terrible way to die."

"I know, very bad, very bad."

The old man was upset and sympathetic, Lorinda saw, so she pushed a little harder. "Dr. Tully, will you please make me some gumbo and bring it to me tomorrow night?"

His watery eyes looked into hers; finally he nodded. "Maybe I know a woman who make gumbo. Maybe I bring it to you."

"Thank you," she said. "You are a good man, Doctor Tully."

The old man bobbed his head and scurried out, looking more harried than when he had entered.

For the first night since she had been captured, Lorinda slept peacefully.

Having faced the fact that she was going to die, she was composed and quiet. She spent the next day on her cot, sorting out her memories, good and bad, and trying to make some sense of her life. What was it Dr. Johnson had said about the prospect of hanging concentrating one's mind? She couldn't recall the exact wording, but that was the gist of it. She had never understood what it meant before, but now as she reviewed her emotions and marshaled her thoughts, it seemed as though the meaning was becoming clear.

Her throat ached with unshed tears as she remembered her happy childhood, her father's love and care of her. She could forgive him now for raising her as white, because he had done it with what he considered her best interests at heart. It wasn't really his fault that such terrible things had happened to her, even though it was a result of his putting off setting her free. That was the one point that still puzzled her. She had heard him order Kelandes to prepare the papers. *Why* hadn't he carried out his plan? It just wasn't like him not to follow through once he had made up his mind.

She was still grieved at events in the more recent past, the deaths of Zack and Ajona in particular. But she had to temper her anger at the way they had perished, had to admit that each of them had chosen to die for freedom and would do it over again if given the same choice. Maybe the same strong desire would live again in the heart of little Zack. Perhaps by the time he grew up, there would be a chance of making his father's and aunt's dreams come true.

The only things she couldn't quite reconcile herself to was Kirk's unexplained disappearance and Chatti's apparent desertion. Her mind kept coming back to them no matter where it started out.

"Hey, gal, that hoodoo spook is here to see you again," the jailer said, poking at her through the bars with a stick. "Don't know why you want to sleep your last day away nohow. You gonna swing come seven o'clock tomorry mornin', wench. You oughta be praying or something. Ain't you blacks got no respect for God?"

Lorinda looked at him silently.

"Well, anyhow, that hoodoo man is back," Jake said, shifting from foot to foot. "He brung you something to eat. Gumbo I think. It shore smells good. Think maybe you could save me some?"

Thinking about what was in the gumbo, Lorinda really did want to share it with him. But she shook her head. "This is my last meal. I will eat it all."

A few minutes later Dr. Tully came in carrying a covered pot. "I brung you what you ast, miss. I sho hope it warm and comfort you."

"I am most grateful," Lorinda said as the little old man set the pot on the upturned barrel that served as a table. "I wish there was some way I could repay your kindness."

"No payment necessary," Dr. Tully said. "My only son was burned to death by vigilantes five years ago. I don' forgets that."

"No, I'm sure you haven't," she said and leaned forward to touch his hand. "Please accept my sincere thanks then, and could you tell me how soon—"

She paused at the look of warning he gave her and leaned closer to hear his whisper. "That which you seek is not in the food. It inside a hard wax ball at the bottom of the pot. You eat tonight but keep the ball for mornin'. When they come to git you, put the ball in yo' mouth. It small and no one notice. Den, jes' a'fore they drop the trap door, bite down on the wax. That which is inside acts fast. You will be beyond their power to hurt you in moments."

"But why delay until the last minute?" Lorinda asked.

Dr. Tully took both her hands in his. "The gods move in strange ways. Papa Legba, Ogoun Badagris and Ayida Oueddo sometimes act at the very last to save us. One should not deny them that opportunity."

He left then, and Lorinda dipped her wooden spoon into the pot to find the wax ball. It was her pass out of this world without having to suffer. She did not intend to wait as Dr. Tully had suggested; waiting left too many chances for things to go wrong. Suppose the wax ball should be discovered on her person before she could use it.

No, she mustn't wait. She must act tonight to cheat the hangman. She located the ball and lifted it carefully out of the gumbo. It was as small as the old man had described it and, she hoped, as deadly.

She started to lift the ball to her mouth.

"Hey, gal, you eat all that gumbo yet?" Jake called as he came toward the cell. "It shore do smell good."

Quickly she palmed the ball and looked at the pot of gumbo. She had what she wanted from it. "Take it all," she said, "I'm not hungry."

"Reckon you ain't.' the jailer said. "Reckon I

wouldn't be either in your place. Decent of you to give it to me, seein' as how we ain't exactly been friends.''

He took the pot and started out the door, then turned back. ''You been so decent 'bout this that I gotta tell you something.''

''What's that?'' Lorinda asked, wishing he would just go.

''Well, t'other day a black gal come here and wanted to see you. Couldn't let the old woman in, o' course, without the judge's say-so, so I sent her away.''

A faint hope sprang to life in Lorinda. ''What was her name?''

''Din' give no name but say to tell you some fella tryin' to do something to help you. Wasn't gonna tell you 'cause there ain't nothin' nobody can do for you now. Wasn't gonna tell, but this gumbo shore make good eatin', an' my old lady the worst cook in the whole county.''

After he was gone, Lorinda sat staring at the tiny wax ball in her hand. Had it been Chatti who had tried to see her? Was a man—Kirk perhaps— actually trying to help her? Why now after all this time? How could anyone possibly save her at this late date?

She almost wished the jailer hadn't told her. She had resigned herself to death—as long as it was not death by hanging. Should she wait until the last minute? Should she chance things going wrong just on the strength of a few words from a suddenly grateful jailer?

Even if Kirk were alive and hadn't deserted her,

what could he do? She was legally condemned to hang, and in a matter of hours that sentence was to be carried out. There would be no last minute reprieve from the governor; he was calling for more and more hangings and wasn't likely to intervene in one at the importuning of a riverboat gambler.

Dr. Tully had said the gods occasionally saved the life of a believer when all hope seemed lost, but she didn't believe in voodoo gods any more than she did in the Christian God.

She lifted the wax ball to her mouth and was about to slip it between her lips when another thought stopped her. If it had been Chatti who came to the jail and left that message, then Kirk must know what she faced. And even if he couldn't help her, wouldn't he at least try to see her?

To see Kirk one more time, to gaze on his dear face, perhaps to touch his hand. If there was the remotest possibility of that happening, did she want to take the poison now?

She knew the answer before she asked herself the question. With a sigh that was partly relief and partly annoyance at herself for being so foolish, she tucked the wax ball into the hem of her ragged dress and waited for dawn.

"It's time to go, gal," the jailer said. He and two other men stood in the open door of her cell. He held a lantern up high so the deputy sheriff could read the copy of the death sentence he held in his hand.

Lorinda had sat up all night, hoping against hope that Kirk would come to her. On toward dawn she had fallen into a fitful, dream-haunted sleep, and now she had been awakened to face her final hour.

"Are you ready, gal?" the deputy asked. "We got to get this over with."

This was the worst thing that could have happened. She had intended to take the poison at dawn but had drifted off to sleep, and with these men standing here watching her, she didn't have a chance. She had to think of something, some way of gaining a few seconds to get the ball out of her hem and into her mouth.

"Are you ready?" the deputy asked again, his voice impatient.

"I—would you please—could you gentlemen step outside for a minute? I was asleep when you came in and—and I have to relieve myself."

The deputy guffawed. "Shure, gal. Cain't have you ruinin' the solemnity of the occasion by pissing your pants when we string you up."

He herded the other two out into the corridor, where the three of them turned their backs and began talking loudly. Working quickly, Lorinda retrieved the pellet from her hem and put it in her mouth, pushing it out of the way with her tongue so she could talk without losing it or biting down on it until she was ready.

"We can go now," she told them in a steady voice, determined not to falter, not to let them see she was frightened.

The deputy tied her hands behind her and then led the procession down the hall.

Strangely, there was still a flicker of hope somewhere in Lorinda's heart. Perhaps Kirk was outside already. Perhaps he and Chatti had conceived a brilliant plan to rescue her. She kept the wax ball with its deadly contents in the hollow of her cheek, remembering what Dr. Tully had said about the ways of the gods. She would give them a chance. She would give Kirk a chance.

A huge crowd was gathered outside the courthouse. An animallike growl went up from the people when Lorinda came into sight. She was led toward the gallows, which occupied the center of the grassy square. Standing beside the scaffold was a hulking, stoop-shouldered man. With a catch of her breath, Lorinda recognized the substitute hangman. In her agitation and anxiety she had forgotten until now what Jake Mabry had told her about him.

"There's been so many hangin's lately that Busch, the regular hangman, collapsed of overwork. Got a substitute name of Hairslip doin' it now, and he don' know his job for beans, that fella don't. Can't tie a proper hangman's knot and when he drops 'em through the trap, they jes' hang there and strangle. Takes about fifteen or twenty minutes and makes quite a show when them black gals choke to death. They kick around so much they show off everything they got, I can tell you. Lookin' forward to seein' all you got, gal, even if it won't do me any good."

Lorinda shivered but kept her head high. She was marched between a line of militia with their rifles and bayonets and led to the foot of the gallows. The roar of the mob grew when she refused a blindfold. Anger and defiance replaced her fear. "No, I don't want your blindfold," she said so the crowd could hear. "I want to watch their faces. I want to see that mob of slack-jawed, illiterate degenerates you call the flower of Southern manhood right up until the end. I want to see them revealed for what they really are."

A gasp of astonishment came from those near her. The crowd surged forward with a howl of fury, pushing against the soldiers. The officers ordered the troops to about-face and level their bayonets.

"Let's get on with this," the court official said hastily. "Let's get it over before a legal hanging turns into a lynching."

"Is there a difference?" Lorinda asked. "I see little to chose between the proceedings of Judge Appleton and those of Judge Lynch."

There was no reason now not to say the things she had been thinking about Mississippi justice and its whole social system. She wished she had said them earlier.

"I think you had better shut up," the court official said.

"What are you going to do if I don't?" Lorinda demanded. "Send me to jail?"

"Hurry along, hurry along," the deputy said and gave her a shove toward the ladder up to the scaffold.

Moments later she was standing beside the bumbling substitute hangman. He grinned at her and shifted his wad of tobacco to the other side. "Hi there, honey. You a mighty purty li'l gal. Too bad you an' me couldn' have us some fun a'fore I got to stretch your neck."

"You filthy, swinish imbecile!" Lorinda said, her eyes shooting sparks at him. "I wouldn't spend five seconds with you if you were the last man on earth!"

"Li'l spitfire, ain't she?" the hangman said. "Can see why we gonna string her up."

Lorinda spat full in his face, bringing a snarl of rage from him and a blow across her face that brought blood from her upper lip. But she refused to cringe or back away.

"Get on with it before something else unseemly happens!" the court official ordered.

"Aren't you going to ask me if I have a few last words to say before I die?" Lorinda taunted.

"No, you've said enough!" the man said and turned to read aloud the death sentence. The mob screeched and howled its approval at every word.

Now was the time. If she waited any longer, it would be too late. But still she hesitated, and looking out over the sea of faces, she spotted a familiar one. The dark face of the voodoo man was strained and frightened, but he smiled as though to reassure her that the poison would work.

The noose was being placed around her neck. As she felt the harsh rope against her throat, she bit down on the tiny ball of wax and tasted something bitter seep out of it.

Thank God, she thought and swallowed the poison. Almost at once everything began to blur.

Through the haze she heard the minister who had visited her in her cell intoning, "May God have mercy on your soul."

"Iffen she's got one any more'n a baboon has

one,'' the hangman said and with his ax cut the rope that held the trapdoor.

Lorinda was vaguely concious of falling. Then the darkness closed over her. There was no pain, just the darkness.

At that moment, the crowd surrounding the scaffold was startled by the cracking of a whip and the wild whinnies of horses. Those at the rear turned to see a team of stallions, pulling a crazily lurching wagon, charging into their midst. In the driver's seat, his whip licking out to drive the mob aside, a revolver and the reins in the other hand, stood Kirk Stryker. On the seat beside him was Chatti.

"Oh, God!" cried the old black woman. "They done it, Mista Stryker. They done hanged my baby!"

Stryker dropped the whip and reached to the back of his neck. When his hand came out of his collar, it held a Bowie knife, and before anyone could stop him the knife was arcing through the morning sunlight. With a flash of razor-sharp steel, it severed the rope from which Lorinda dangled.

"Come on, Chatti, follow me!" Stryker said. He grabbed up the whip and leaped from the wagon, the pistol in his other hand.

The crowd surged around him but quickly gave ground when he came close as the fury in his eyes was intimidating.

A man in a frock coat and broad-brimmed hat had stood up in the bed of the wagon and was waving a paper over his head. "That girl is innocent!" he bellowed at the top of his lungs. "This is a pardon from the governor! Let her go free! I am Governor Turner's secretary!"

"The hell with the governor!" someone in the mob yelled. "Don't let her go! Lynch her! Let's get her and burn her this time!"

Kirk knew such things had happened before in the South. Prisoners freed by a court or the governor had been dragged away and lynched. Fighting his way through the angry mob, Kirk cracked his whip across the face of a screeching man in sagging pants and torn shirt. His pistol whipped the side of the head of another coming at him from the other side. Both hands working, he fought his way toward the scaffold.

But it was someone else who got to Lorinda. Dr. Tully lifted her up and looked down at her. He shook his white kinky head sadly. "Don't make no never mind if she guilty or innocent," he said. "She daid. Her neck is done broke."

"Shee-it!" the jailer said. "That stupid imbecile must have finally learned how to tie a hangman's knot, and at the wrong time, too."

His words were loud enough to carry to those at the head of the mob. The information was passed from person to person, and the fury died away.

The officers commanding the militia had regained their wits, and the troops began moving the crowd out of the square. Kirk and the sobbing Chatti reached Tully's side. Looking down at Lorinda's body, Kirk slammed his fist into the palm of the other hand.

"Damn it! Goddamn it to hell! Too late. Oh, God, too late! If only I could have broken down that lying swine of a Gideon Wenzel a little sooner."

"T'warn't yo' fault, Mista Kirk suh," Chatti said, tears streaming down her face. "T'warn't nobody's fault but them hateful Wenzels.''

Kirk leaned over to pat her shoulder. Suddenly he saw Dr. Tully raising a small vial to Lorinda's lips. ''What are you doing?'' he asked in alarm.

The black man looked up at the white man and slowly winked. ''Jes' a li'l voodoo *gris-gris* juice,'' he said, ''to see that soul of girl go to good place 'stead of bad.''

Kirk sucked in his breath, suddenly realizing that only the old voodoo man had actually examined Lorinda to make sure she was dead. He turned and stepped over to the deputy sheriff, who was talking to the governor's secretary.

''Isn't there somewhere we can take the body?'' he asked the deputy.

''Well, I reckon the black undertaker down in the hollow would take her. Reckon she can be buried in a regular slave cemetery, seein' as how she's supposed to be innocent.''

''She was innocent,'' Kirk said, eyeing the man coldly, ''and she wasn't a slave.''

He walked back to where Chatti and Dr. Tully were still crouched over Lorinda. Chatti was no longer crying.

When she looked up at him, he knew she had conferred with the voodoo man. She was almost smiling. ''Best we gits the pore chile's body out of the sun,'' she said. ''People down the street a ways, pore free coloreds, an' Tully say they lets us lay her out theah.''

''I'll carry her,'' Kirk said. He stooped to lift the girl's limp form in his arms. A surge of joy rushed through him as he felt the slight rise and fall of her breast against his arm.

The remnants of the crowd stood back sullenly and let them pass on down the street, the tall white man carrying the supposedly dead girl, the old black man and woman walking on either side of him.

"Why is she unconscious?" Kirk asked when they were far enough away not to be overheard.

" 'Cause I gave her a powerful poison at her request to spare her the hanging," Tully said. "But since the gods sometimes sees fit to intervene, I waits nearby with the antidote."

"Did you get it to her in time?"

"She alive," Tully said, "so it must be in time."

Two weeks later a wagon loaded with supplies, furniture and a few antiques rescued from the shambles of Solitaire rolled north along a dusty road. Driving the double team of horses was a happy, whistling Kirk Stryker. Beside him on the seat was a pale but smiling Lorinda. Next to her sat Chatti, holding a tan-skinned baby who almost never cried, and observed the world with big, solemn brown eyes that reminded Lorinda of his father's.

Another wagon followed along behind them, driven by Jase, with Sissy up beside him. In it were piled the clothes, all their personal belongings, and whatever else Lorinda had considered worth taking from Solitaire.

Lorinda moved closer to Kirk. "Tell me again how you discovered I wasn't a slave."

Kirk laughed and slid an arm around her. "After you left me on the day of the rebellion, I warned two more plantation owners, but when I got to the third one I saw the slaves had beat me to it. The house was afire and a man was lying on the drive, felled by a rebel bullet. He said he was a law clerk and begged me to take some important documents to Jackson and give them to his employer. I didn't know it was Kelandes's plantation, but after the man died, I took his documents along with me to Vicksburg. While I waited for you, I looked through the papers to find the owner's name, noticed the name de Farbin on one of the files and read it through. In it were the manumission papers Jules had signed and filed to free you. Kelandes apparently found it in your father's desk after his death and conspired with the Wenzels to keep it secret. He didn't destroy it because he needed it and the threat of exposure to hold over old August's head from time to time.''

''But why didn't you bring it to the jail and make them turn me loose?''

''Because, my dear wife, I didn't know you were in jail. Martial law was slapped on the whole area, travel was restricted, and I couldn't discover what had happened to you. When I could I rode back out to Solitaire, thinking you might have returned there, and it took Chatti more time to locate you through the slave grapevine. Then we had to find out what the charges were and who was going to testify against you. I immediately left for the state capital to intercede with Governor Turner. He wouldn't see me for days and then insisted on having all the records checked by his personal staff, and after Elsie and Gideon testified against you, he refused to act unless they confessed they had lied. Elsie was easy, what little conscience she has had been bothering her, but Gideon needed a little demonstration with the Bowie knife first. Chatti had gone to Port Gibson to tell you to hold on, but they wouldn't let her in. Anyway, my darling, by the time I rushed to the capital again and back to Port Gibson, it was almost too late.''

Lorinda sighed happily. "Yes, but it wasn't, thanks to you and Dr. Tully. Now tell me about Kansas and what it will be like there.''

"It will be what we make of it,'' Kirk said.

"Do you think it will be all right for little Zack?''

"It had better be, or someone will answer to me.''

She hesitated before she asked her next question; finally she blurted it out, knowing she'd have no rest until she asked it. "Kirk, you're not sorry about us, are you? You looked so gloomy when you came out of that hotel back in Memphis that I thought maybe you were regretting the bad bargain you made—I mean in marrying me.''

"Bad? That's the best bargain I ever made in my life,'' the ex-gambler said. "No, I was regretting the bad bargain the Democratic party made. They've sold the country down the river to Dixie with that damn Buchanan. He's not worth a tinker's damn. They could have had Douglas or even Sam Houston. They went looking for another Jackson, so why the hell didn't they take the man Jackson thought of as the son he never had. Why didn't they take Sam Houston?''

"A Southerner?''

"A Texan. A Union man before he's anything

else. He could have held the Union together the same way Andy Jackson did, by threatening to hang any governor who tried to take a state out of it.''

"But what about the slaves? Would he have freed them?''

"The slaves are going to be freed," Kirk said. "There just isn't any other way to it. They will be freed.''

"How do you know? Did you turn in your deck of cards for a crystal ball?''

He grinned down at her. "No, they're going to be free because it's in the wind. There's a wind blowing out of the West, and there won't be any stopping it. Why hell, gal, I may even free you someday.''

"You'd better not!" she hissed, slipping the Bowie knife out of his belt scabbard and jabbing it lightly against his ribs. "You better not ever even think of that!''

"Oh boy, did I ever catch me a wildcat," he said, pulling her tight against him, "and do I ever love it.''

"You had better. By God and Andy Jackson, you had better!" she said, surrendering her lips and her life to him.

HISTORICAL ROMANCES
FROM
PLAYBOY PRESS

WILD IS THE HEART $1.95
DIANA SUMMERS

Born into wealth and privilege, Aurelia was sheltered from the gathering storm of revolution. But with the fall of the Bastille, her golden world was shattered forever. Swept into the dark currents of political intrigue, she must use her dazzling beauty to survive as she becomes wife, mistress and courtesan to the most powerful men in France.

LOVE'S GENTLE FUGITIVE $1.95
ANDREA LAYTON

A runaway to the New World, ravishingly beautiful Elizabeth Bartlett tries to escape her secret past—only to learn that shame and degradation are the price for her freedom. Frightened and vulnerable, she is rescued from brutal slavery by the one man who could return her to England and disaster.

MOMENT OF DESIRE $1.95
RACHEL COSGROVE PAYES

In London's seamy underside, where the teeming masses knew only of deprivation and hunger, Mellie's survival depended on her expertise at an exclusive brothel. In all the nights of love, only one man kindled a fire in her: a mysterious nobleman whose mission was shrouded in secrecy. Their one night of passion ignited a raging fire of forbidden love, hate and revenge.

DANCE OF DESIRE $1.95
BARBARA BONHAM

In a country seething with the terror of the Inquisition, young Micaela rose from poverty to become one of the most famous flamenco dancers Spain has ever known. Devastatingly beautiful, she was sought after by men of power, wealth and position. But her heart belonged to the one man she could not have—the dashing Javier, escort to the powerful Duchess de Vallabriga.

PASSION'S PRICE $1.95
BARBARA BONHAM

In a heart-rending story set against the harshness and isolation of the vast prairies of 19th Century America, a lovely young widow and a lusty family man struggle in vain against a forbidden but powerful attraction for each other.

PROUD PASSION $1.95
BARBARA BONHAM

In a breathtaking tale that captures the turbulence of an era and the stormy emotions of its characters, lovely Odette Morel flees the brutal excesses of the French Revolution, endures the hardships of an ocean voyage to America and faces unthinkable dangers in the frontier wilderness.

SO WILD A RAPTURE $1.95
ANDREA LAYTON

Enticed against her will by a passionate liaison with a wealthy French baron, young, innocent Juliette is wrenched from the arms of her first lover and swept to the heights of ecstasy and the depths of shame. But, always, from the virgin pastures of the countryside to the sensuous intrigues of a king's decadent court, her heart remembers the one man whose tender caresses had scorched her soul for eternity.

BLAZE OF PASSION $1.95
STEPHANIE BLAKE

As wild as the 19th Century Australian outback where the novel begins, this larger-than-life story weaves a passionate tale of three towering Australian families. Their struggle for control of a new nation would sweep them from the sweltering penal colonies of the Australian jungle to England to the throes of the industrial revolution; from glittering Parisian salons to the lawless frenzy of the California gold rush.

THIS RAVAGED HEART $1.95
BARBARA RIEFE

A powerful story of one woman's tender love and another's overwhelming jealousies. Their struggle for the same man sweeps across continents and across time—from the 19th Century world of aristocratic splendors to plague-ridden London; from the heights of passion to the darkest pits of hell.